Rural Bliss

Also by Lou Wakefield

Tuscan Soup

LOU WAKEFIELD

Rural Bliss

Hodder & Stoughton

copyright © 2002 by Lou Wakefield

First published in Great Britain in 2002 by Hodder and Stoughton
A division of Hodder Headline

A CIP catalogue record for this title is available from the British Library

ISBN 0 340 73381 0

Typeset in Plantin Light by Phoenix Typesetting, Burley-in-Wharfedale, West Yorkshire

Printed and bound in Great Britain by
Mackays of Chatham plc, Chatham, Kent

Hodder and Stoughton
A division of Hodder Headline
338 Euston Road
London NW1 3BH

To Avril

To find out more information about Lou Wakefield, visit her website on www.louwakefield.co.uk

ACKNOWLEDGMENTS

My huge indebtedness to the extraordinary talents of Clare Alexander goes without saying – at least, that is the only reason I can think of to explain how I came to omit this declaration in the acknowledgements for *Tuscan Soup*. Without her wisdom and her friendship, my books would be the poorer, and so would I.

While I'm on the subject of unsung heroes, I'd also like to thank Rochelle Stevens for her unflagging support, continued encouragement, and loyal friendship over the many years we've been together.

My thanks to Daryl Fielding of *Ogilvy*, and to James Simpson, for their generous help in answering all my dumb questions about the advertising business; and to Gilbert Bankual for correcting my French.

One

It was when the third badly constructed paper plane hit her (this time between the eyes), that Fran Holdaway seriously wondered if she were not now too old and too female, for this job. Screwing the offending projectile into a ball and returning it with force from whence it came, ('Ooh! Got your period?' was Silly Willy's inane response, which had Zack, Steve, Mark and Robbo giggling like the teenaged idiots they had so recently been), she looked around the open plan office and thanked God it was Friday.

When she had first arrived here fourteen years ago, a fresh-faced graduate (good grief – was it fourteen years?! It was – Jesus! Her life was slipping away unlived!), she had barely been able to believe her luck: a plum job in the plummiest agency of the day. Now things were different, of course, but at the time Q & A was at the cutting edge of advertising: a small but perfectly formed new company that had eager clients flocking to its doors in droves to engage the talents of its happening young team. And she had been part of its birth. Had seen it expand to take over most of the building. Had worked through nights, weekends – who needed sleep when there was the world to conquer? Young, then, she'd been, and keen as mustard. She had gone in as gofer, and within minutes – or so it had seemed – had risen to copywriter, where she had stayed. And stayed. And stayed. Other colleagues (male, natch) had gone on to become Creative Directors either here or with larger corporations, while Fran had continued to chip away at the coalface, in the company of ever younger co-workers. Perhaps she hadn't taken herself seriously enough; hadn't pushed and bullied – and quite frankly, cheated and stolen – enough, as her erstwhile peers had done, and as her current peers continued to do.

But then, staying in advertising had never been part of her plan. It was to have been the 'day job' which paid her way while she wrote her first novel, and after that – success! The Booker! The Whitbread! A three-book deal! It had worked for Fay Weldon and Salman Rushdie before her, to name but two, so why not for Frances G. Holdaway? Why not indeed? But in fact, two and a half chapters of what she later judged to be cringe-making juvenilia had been the grindingly slow result of that great pipe dream. That, and being the oldest and longest-serving copywriter in a medium-sized ad agency whose name was no longer the first on people's lips, nor even the twenty-first. Was it time for a change? Well, yes. But to what? To go (or try to go – she was thirty-five, after all – no spring chicken) to another firm where there was more going on? To stay put and simply *demand* the job of Creative Director this time around, when Ben inevitably moved on? To go back to her novel (untouched for a decade) and revamp it? To start work on another? For surely there must be more to life than trying to write scintillating copy about financial products for direct mail, with a boysy partner whose IQ was less than half her age? Where was the glamour in that, where the fulfilment?

The boys had now started to pack their bags and drift towards the door. There were no brownie points to be earned in staying late when there really wasn't much work to do, and what there was could certainly wait until Monday. Her partner, Willie (Wills to his friends: Dickhead to Fran in the privacy of her mind), called to her out of politeness to join them in the usual bar next door, knowing she wouldn't come, and she demurred just as politely. She had nothing in common with these barely twenty-something lads, and anyway, home was where her heart was these days. She threw down her pen and scrabbled around under her desk for her shopping bags. Like most women, Fran had been a practised multi-tasker for years before the phrase had been invented. Today she had used her lunch hour to whizz up to John Lewis to buy the living-room wallpaper she'd been agonising over for a fortnight, and this weekend, while Paul was still away, she'd finish off the decorating if it killed her.

Hampered by her shopping, she went outside to the corridor to wait for the lift, where a couple of the account executive babes were muttering to each other about the possibility of lay-offs in the near future, and already planning for their next move. They knew the drill, or assumed it. Last in, first out would be the order of the day, and both of them had joined the company in the last twelve months. They smiled at Fran ruefully. She would be quite safe from the firing line, years further up the track of seniority than them. But what if the unthinkable were to happen, she mused, and she was asked to leave? In her present state of mind it could only be a blessing – she'd be forced to change her life. Maybe even write that accursed novel. It wasn't as if they were exactly desperate for her salary now that Paul's business was taking off so well . . .

Her musings ceased as the lift arrived and the doors opened to reveal her old friend Allie, an account handler who worked on the top floor. She was older than Fran by several years, but would have killed rather than admit it.

'Hi there! Paul back yet?'

'No. Another week, I think.'

'Where is it this time – Rome?'

'A whistlestop tour of the whole of Europe more like. I've been trying to get hold of him, actually – can't find his itinerary that he left me – but his mobile's always either engaged or switched off. I'm pretty sure it's Paris today.'

'So how are you going to fill your lonely weekend?' Allie asked her, as the lift disgorged them on the ground floor.

Fran held up the carrier bags of wallpaper for her inspection. 'Why? Do you want to help?' she asked in jest. Elegant, sexy, sophisticated Allie in a pair of old joggers and sweatshirt with a paste brush in her manicured hand?

'I take it that's a rhetorical question?' her friend batted back firmly. 'What are you doing for fun?'

'I'm seeing Sam.'

'And you a married woman! Tell me more.'

'*She* is the estate agent who sold us the house. I've told you about her – she lives in the village and we've become friends.'

'The one with the married lover?'

'Yeah. There's a fair on in the next village this weekend, so we're going to go.'

'Oh, you rural folk – what you get up to! Such larks!' Allie said drily as they pushed their way through the revolving doors and out into the crowded London streets.

'And you're doing something wildly sophisticated I daresay?'

'Hm. Does waxing my legs count, I wonder? Could a town girl come and play?'

Fran was delighted. 'God, yes. It's about time you saw the house! About six, tomorrow evening?' They had come to Leicester Square tube station where Fran would start the first part of her long journey home.

'I think you're crazy to have moved so far out,' Allie, whose Bloomsbury flat was a mere stroll away, admonished her. 'Ten minutes and I'll be sipping my first gin and tonic. And you . . . ?'

'A couple of hours, *if* you'll let me go and catch my train.' They hugged goodbye. 'See you tomorrow then.'

'Will I need a visa?'

'Ha ha.'

Walking down the escalator to the tube, Fran's progress was impeded by the usual tourists who didn't know the London rule of standing on the right so that serious commuters like herself could speed past them on the left, and she looked anxiously at her watch. If the northbound Piccadilly line train came within the next couple of minutes, then she might just make the 1802 from St Pancras mainline station and be home by half past seven.

The god of public transport, though not beaming beneficently at her (a Scandinavian with a backpack kept swinging around and hitting her in the chest), was at least not bent on mischief, and allowed her to cram herself like the proverbial canned fish into an overcrowded carriage full of irritable fellow passengers, and to arrive, breathless, on the platform at St Pancras with ten seconds to throw herself on to her departing train, where she was obliged to stand for the first fifty miles of the homeward journey while others sat comfortably, avoiding her eye. But, as always, the crowds thinned out as they left London further behind them, and within forty minutes Fran enjoyed the luxury of having two seats all to herself to spread out her shopping, and to watch with contentment as the urban sprawl gave way to open fields, meandering rivers, and graceful copses, all glowing gold in the light of the evening sun.

Allie was right: it was undeniably a hassle living so far out of town. But arriving at Little Langton station, with its white-washed tubs of flowers and trailing hanging baskets, was never anything less than a joy, and walking home through leafy village streets breathing clean air again at last, Fran always felt that however agonising the journey, it was worth it. She and Paul had taken the big decision to move out of London eighteen months ago (at the same time as they had taken their big decision to get married), and with every passing month she felt more and more a part of this small community and less and less a stranger, so that on this particular evening on her way back home, she was obliged to stop and chat, to pat a dog, to look up and return a cheery wave across the street, to compliment the clement weather half a dozen times before she had arrived back at her own garden gates. It felt good. It felt real. It felt like – coming home. Of course she had now almost forgotten that, for most of that eighteen months, she had been coming home to a building site.

It had been a huge enterprise to rescue this house from neglect and decay, to replace rotten timber, to patch up crumbling brickwork, to haul it, groaning and protesting, into the twenty-first century. Thank God for Archie, the local builder who had retired the week before they'd bought it, and, at a loss to know what to do with himself in those few short days, had joyfully escaped from his retirement as soon as village gossip had alerted him to their project. Juggling her shopping bags, Fran let herself in through the front door and saw his customary note on the table. This time it read, 'Nearly there! Back to finish upstairs cupboards a.m.' She smiled. He'd become less of a builder to Fran over the months they'd worked together, particularly since Paul had been at home less and less, and more of a favourite uncle.

Thinking of Paul, she dodged between the ladders and trestles and went over to the answering machine to see if he'd called her, but the red light of the digital display was registering a disappointing double zero. There had been a time in her life, especially during her first marriage, when alarm bells would have started to ring shrilly in her mind at this point (and with good cause, as far as her first husband had been concerned), but with Paul, thank God, things were different. There was something to be said for growing older, which was just as well. There had to be some compensation for the lines around the eyes, the less supple skin, the thickening of the waist, didn't there? Thirty-five! Who would have thought it possible? She'd always been convinced as a teenager that she would die young, completely incapable as she had been, like most kids, of ever imagining a grown-up version of herself. But here she was, edging ever closer to middle age, and happy to be so. It was nothing short of a miracle, really. And it had only been made possible because of the security she felt in her relationship with Paul. They had both been married before, and both of them had learnt from their mistakes. Now they were more easy-going, less intolerant, gave each other space. In a previous life, not having heard from him in two days would have had her dialling and redialling his mobile again and again, working herself up into a fever of nightmare scenarios, but these days – she felt a warm glow as she thought this – she could just safely assume that he was working hard, getting on with his life, as she was getting on with hers. What was the rush, where was the panic? She'd see him soon enough, and she would try to call him later. But for now, a cup of tea, a bite to eat, and back into those decorating clothes. The challenge of papering the living-room ceiling awaited her.

There is an art to pasting paper to a horizontal plane above one's head, an art which is possible only by refuting the laws of science. Art demands that the paper must go up, while science decrees that, having done so, it must come down on one's head. What had been a blow for enlightenment and the founding of the principles of gravity for Isaac Newton in his orchard four centuries earlier was the source of endless, intense irritation (not to mention weeping near-hysteria) to Frances Holdaway in her living room this evening. Just as Canute had howled at the tide to no effect, so Fran exhorted, cajoled, made bargains with the wallpaper from John Lewis. But unlike the old king, Fran was no quitter. Three hours, two wasted rolls of paper, a screaming fit, a hot bath, a butching-up talk, and a large gin later, she had succeeded where the conqueror of Denmark, Norway and England had failed. After that, the walls were a breeze, and at two a.m. she recharged her glass and lifted it in weary celebration. 'To you,' she announced to the room, but after a moment's reflection she cancelled that. 'No – sod it – to me,' she corrected, eyeing the fruits of her labour malevolently, and chugged down half her gin.

Bone-tired, she ascended the staircase (whose carved oak

banisters she had lovingly restored over last month's evenings in), and decided that she would reward herself for her hard labour by going straight to bed without first showering, sticky with wallpaper paste as she was. Her original promised reward for finishing the living room was to have been to try to call Paul again in Paris, but now, what with the time difference, it was far too late for that. Entering her bedroom she peeled off her work clothes with her last ounce of strength, and flopped gratefully into bed, snuggling up to Paul's empty pillow and inhaling the lingering vestige of his aftershave. Not as good as having him there in person to cuddle up to, but a comfort nonetheless. And thus, exhausted, she drifted easily and swiftly into the deep, satisfying sleep of the virtuous and the productive.

Outside, in the English countryside, all was dark save for the waxing moon. An owl hooted. A susurrant breeze gently bent the treetops and, penetrating Fran's bedroom, billowed the net curtains. A vixen screamed.

Two

⌐⌐

Archie was as good as his word, and by the time Fran woke he was hard at work sawing wood for the new cupboards in the upstairs study – the sound of which Fran's inventive unconscious mind, unwilling to let any stimulus pass by unused, had incorporated into a dream where she was being sawn in half by a man with curling moustaches and lilac eyes. Strange.

However, after checking her midriff and a brief period of mental confusion, she was fully awake and, shrugging off the images of her recent evisceration, she shuffled down the hall in slippers and dressing gown to see Archie.

'Ah,' he greeted her, unsurprised at this stage in their relationship to see her in her nightclothes. 'Busy night, then.'

'You're not kidding,' she rejoined. 'But I finished the blasted thing. Was the ceiling paper still up when you passed through?'

'It certainly was. You done a good job and all. Have you working for me next.'

High praise indeed. Fran grinned with pleasure. 'Tea?'

'Ar,' Archie agreed phlegmatically. 'Ay,' he added, calling after her as she was leaving, 'Big day for you today.'

'Is it?' asked Fran, pausing in the doorway. 'Why's that?'

'Be rid of me indoors.'

Fran was astonished. 'You've finished in the attic?'

Archie nodded, pleased with himself. 'Just got to do these cupboards here today, and that's me done. You and hubby done your sums yet? Know if you want me to do the paving in the garden?'

'I don't know,' Fran said apologetically, 'I couldn't get hold of him. I'll try again this morning.'

'Been a long trip this time, ent it?'

'A fortnight so far,' she agreed. 'Back at the end of this coming week, apparently. Or that was the plan last time we spoke. Shall we have our tea outside, Archie, and talk through the possibilities again?'

'Ar,' he said accommodatingly, economic as always with his words.

Fran returned to her bedroom to pull on some clothes and, having done so, checked Paul's itinerary on the bedside table. 'Saturday the fifteenth, Hôtel Royal, Paris,' she muttered to herself, and dialled the number. The phone was answered before she was fully ready to try out her schoolgirl French.

'Ah, hello . . . er, allo,' she corrected herself. 'Monsieur Paul Holdaway – est-il . . . arrived . . . avec vous maintenant? C'est—' What was the word for wife? If only she'd been more attentive in class. 'C'est Madame Holdaway ici.'

'Oldaway, Paul . . . Un petit instant, s'il vous plaît, Madame . . . Ah oui, il est arrivé hier soir. Voulez-vous lui parler?'

There was a slight delay on the line, due not to the distance their voices had to travel through coils of cables beneath the soil of two different countries and the cold grey waters of the English Channel but to Fran having to dig deep into the recesses of her memory to understand a language she had never excelled at, and which she hadn't spoken for a decade and a half. 'He had arrived on a winter's evening' had her completely stumped, until she suddenly remembered that winter was 'hiver', and that 'hier' meant yesterday. 'Did she want to speak to him?' was easy. The answer was most assurément, oui.

'Je vous le passe,' was the next knotty little translation problem on offer, which Fran deduced must mean something like 'Trying to connect you,' since, after a brief pause, the receptionist followed it up with, 'Ça ne répond pas, Madame. Est-ce que vous voulez lui laisser un message?'

Did she want to leave him a message? 'Er . . . oui, s'il vous plaît,' Fran faltered. But what message was it possible for her to leave? The pen of my mother is on the chair of my aunt? The naughty brown dog is chasing the ball? Why didn't school French lessons prepare a woman for a moment such as this? 'Lui dire que sa—' what was the wretched word for wife? 'Lui dire que Madame Holdaway a téléphoné pour lui parler, et peut-il – er – téléphone moi, s'il vous plaît?'

'Que sa femme a téléphoné—' Femme, of course, it was the same word for wife as for woman! Your *woman* has called. No wonder she hadn't been able to remember the word. It sounded so prehistoric in English – or so sixties, at the very least. She saw herself for a moment, leaning in a doorway, lit by the guttering flame of a gaslight, wearing fishnet tights and fuck-me pumps, her hand on her hip, a black beret worn at a jaunty tilt, a Gauloise dangling louchely from the corner of her painted, pouting, hot red mouth, 'Tell him his woman called.' *So* much sexier than 'wife'; she could almost hear Jane Birkin sing it, complete with groans and sighs.

'Répondez, s'il vous plaît. C'est tout?'

'Oui. Merci.'

'De rien, Madame Oldaway. Au revoir.'

Phew. Exhausting. Time for tea with Archie.

As hard as Fran had worked inside the house since she had become its co-owner, she had matched it with her industry in the large garden. What had been a mass of thicket and brambles when they had first moved in had succumbed gradually, and by dint of dogged determination, to her pruning and hacking, slashing and burning, humping and clearing, until, stripped of its overgrowth, one could now see the remains of the careful planting somebody had done at some stage in the past, which had matured into well-established (and with Fran's nursing) burgeoning shrubs and trees. So it was with a sense of some satisfaction that she now sat with Archie on an old bench near the house in the early summer sunshine, surveying her garden with a critical eye, and preparing, like an indulgent parent, to hang the expense and spend spend spend. For there was no getting round it. The concrete path which bisected the lawn and cut through the flower beds with such merciless angularity simply had to go.

'If you want it paved with York stone flags I'll do it,' Archie conceded, sipping his freshly brewed lapsang souchong tea with his customary distaste (for no matter how many times he had told her, she still couldn't seem to grasp the fact that he actually preferred 'bog standard British Rail', as he called it, 'with the bag left in till you can stand your spoon up in it'). 'But it'll cost you an arm and a leg.'

'I know, that's the trouble,' agreed Fran, 'but still . . .'

'Whereas,' said Archie, accepting a cigarette from her rather than rolling his own, 'we could do it in herringbone for cheap. Jack Blackmore's fetching down his old outhouse – lovely old brick it is – he'd give us 'em for nowt just to get shot of 'em.'

'Herringbone,' Fran mused, half closing her eyes the better to envisage a terracotta brick road winding through her garden. It *would* look rather fabulous. 'But the work, Archie, like a jigsaw puzzle – it'd take for ever and a year.'

'Wouldn't tek me that long. And if it did, it'd be on my head. Do it cheap for the love. Beautiful craft that.'

'You couldn't do that!'

'I'm semi-retired, I can do what I want. Got a nice pension, don't need the money. And I ent done herringbone in years. 'Sides, the wife'd tell you, keeps me out the house. Complained I got under her feet before you come along.' Pathologically incapable of sitting for longer than two minutes, he stood up now and walked down the concrete path, gesturing, still talking, so that Fran was forced to follow him as he traced out his plans. 'Bring it round here, then split it in two – main path carries on down through the rhodies, small path takes you over here, winds round in a circle, making a new bed, bingo – you've got your herb garden. Teks off again, round the back of your fruit trees, ends up behind the currant canes, Bob's your uncle, you're in your vegetable patch. Neat. Tidy. Out of sight from the house. Everything in its place, and a nice stroll to get here.'

From eighteen months' experience, Fran knew when she'd been talked round to Archie's point of view. 'You're absolutely right, of course,' she conceded, 'it would look lovely. But we'd pay you the going rate, Archie, no arguments about that!'

Archie grinned. 'We'll see if you're still saying that when I'm here five years on,' he teased, but seeing the alarm pass over her face, he recanted. 'Doon't worry, me duck, it woon't tek more'n a couple of weeks. Now then, what you going to do with your field?'

'The field?' echoed Fran. She hadn't thought about that in ages. Abutting the rear garden fence, a small parcel of land of some two or three acres came with the deeds of the house. Giddy at the prospect of becoming landowners after the small confines of their London flat, she and Paul had talked of getting horses once they'd finished the house and settled down, but now that time was almost here – shouldn't they at least learn to ride first?

''Cos you could have it harvested this year, for hay – good grass that, shame if it goes to waste. I could get Geoff Bradshaw down, back end of summer, mow it, bale it, sell it to the riding school or summat. Money in your pocket.'

'Yes, why not?' agreed Fran, relieved not to have to take any more big decisions. And what a laugh, to become the producer of hay. If the boys in her office could hear her now!

'Right then,' announced Archie, chucking his tea leaves (and half his unwanted tea) into the shrubs. 'Back to them cupboards.'

'Okay, see you later,' Fran replied, distracted, to his retreating back. For her gardener's eye had spotted evidence of a snail fest in the new plantings which needed her attention, and that led on to weeding, which in turn led to raking, taking her inevitably to the compost which was in urgent need of turning, which led to sorting dead branches which were soon enough for a bonfire, and before she knew it Archie was calling his goodbyes and there was just time for a quick shower and a change of clothes before her friends Sam and Allie would arrive for their girls' night out, country-style.

Three

Sam was as punctual as ever and, typically, Allie was late. While she'd been showering Fran had started to question the wisdom of introducing these particular friends of hers to each other. Just because she liked them and they liked her, it didn't necessarily follow that they would like each other, and Sam and Allie could not have been more different kettles of fish. So when Fran answered the doorbell, rung promptly at six o'clock, and saw that Sam had decided to wear her Laura Ashley this evening, she started to get more than a little nervous about Allie's imminent arrival and the clashing of her worlds.

'Oh, Fran! You've done wonders!' Sam exclaimed, peering over her shoulder through the front door and seeing the recently decorated living room beyond. She was thirty-four, a country girl, and still as coltish and fresh-faced as she must have been at seventeen. She didn't so much *enter* a room as enthusiastically *explode* into it, which was what she did now; Fran followed good-naturedly in her wake, righting a toppling vase and steadying the umbrella stand.

'Utterly lovely!' she proclaimed, examining the new wall-paper. 'You were so right about the colour. And look! You've even got the seams straight and stuck down properly and not overlapping – I can never do that. I only tried it once, and I made such a mess!'

Fran could well believe it, which was why, ever since she had moved in here, as kind as Sam's continued offers of help had been, she had always, always demurred.

'Glass of wine?' she suggested, walking through to the kitchen.

'Oh yes, please! Lovely!'

No matter if, between now and her deathbed, Sam were to be offered fifteen thousand, three hundred and seventy-six glasses of wine, thought Fran affectionately, her response would always be as if she had never *heard* of such a delightful treat *ever* before in her *entire life*!

'Actually, you know, do you think I could possibly have a *spritzer*?' she asked, as Fran splashed chilled wine into their glasses. She could even make white wine and fizzy water sound more exciting than vintage champagne.

'Sure,' said Fran. 'By the way, Sam, I invited my friend Allie from work to join us this evening. I hope you don't mind?'

'No, of course not. Super,' Sam replied, with a sudden and distinct lack of exclamation marks in her voice. Of course, thought Fran, surprised at first at her lack of enthusiasm, she'll have been looking forward to a girlie one-to-one, raking over the glowing embers of the latest conflagration in the ongoing Nigel saga. As fond as she was of Sam, she now became even fonder of Allie. There was only so much sympathy a wife could summon up for the mistress of a married man, and Fran had so far listened uncomplainingly to this sad and sorry tale for more than a year.

To forestall any attempt on Sam's part now to try to cram the latest episode of her own soap opera into the next few minutes before Allie would arrive (please God!), and feeling only slightly disloyal, Fran suggested they take their wine for a walk round the garden so that she could outline, for Sam's benefit, Archie's plans for the new paths and beds. Generous and biddable as ever, Sam soon recovered from her disappointment at not being presented with an opportunity to talk about what ailed her, and instead added her own enthusiasm to Fran's personal ongoing saga, My House and My Garden.

'What are you going to do with the front?' she asked, after an animated discussion about the successful cultivation of basil, and how to banish greenfly without endangering the ecosystem.

'The front?' Fran queried, worried now. The field, the front – what was wrong with these people? Couldn't they just let her rest on her laurels for a moment? She'd just finished the house, for God's sake! 'Nothing. I hadn't . . . I'd thought it looked okay as it is?'

'Oh it does,' Sam rushed to comfort her. 'It looks lovely. I was just thinking, if Archie's going to do herringbone brick in the back garden, he could do the same between the gate and the front door instead of that old concrete, and reroute the path to meander round your shrubs and trees, like he's going to do here. Make coming on the house from the street more exciting, more of a surprise!'

This had to be seriously considered *in situ*, and so the two of them wandered round to the front garden and were surveying trees, sipping their wine, pacing out putative paths, deep in discussion of the comparative merits of a woodland theme, which would be at its best in the spring, or herbaceous planting, which would be a blaze of colour in the summer, when, with a squeal of brakes, a slewing of wheels, and a volley of expletives never before heard in Little Langton, Allie made her entrance.

'Allie, meet Sam. Sam,' said Fran, noting that Sam's jaw had dropped to the hem of her floral frock, 'this is Allie. Don't take it personally. She's always like this.'

Always like *this*, thought Sam, skintight leather trousers and breasts barely contained by décolletage? She struggled to recover her voice and her social skills. 'Hello, Allie, how are you?'

'Exhausted and pissed off. Hi,' said Allie, batting back her salutation with barely a glance in her direction, still intent on blaming Fran. Sam's eyes widened in surprise. Generally speaking, the usual response to this enquiry in Little Langton and environs was, 'Fine thanks very much, and how are you?'

'How can you do this every day?' Allie continued to Fran. 'I got in the damned car two and a half hours ago. I've clocked up a hundred a twenty miles.'

'Then you definitely came the long way round,' Fran told her firmly, taking her by the arm. 'Come on, let's get you a glass of wine.'

'Are you sure?' Allie asked her, unwilling to let it go. 'Shouldn't I be setting off for home now, before the night is over?'

'Only if you're frightened you'll turn into a pumpkin,' Fran teased her. 'Come on, Sam,' she called behind her, 'she won't hurt you. Her bark is worse than her bite.'

'You haven't heard the office gossip about my rabies then?' quipped Allie. At least, Sam assumed it *must* be a quip, surely – or wouldn't she be in quarantine? She braced herself for the evening to come and followed in their wake, feeling very unsophisticated indeed. If *only* she'd thought to wear slacks!

'Fran put this paper up herself,' she offered enthusiastically to Allie as they walked through the living room to the kitchen. 'Isn't she clever?'

'Oh very,' Allie responded, with what Sam hoped was irony, and not undisguised, contemptuous sarcasm. 'I always say nuclear physicists are overrated in the cleverness stakes. For me, it's wallpaper hangers every time.'

'Nicely,' warned Fran, handing her the *very* large glass of wine she'd ordered. 'Come on, like it or not, you're getting the tour.'

'Okay,' said Allie, after emptying half her glass and with a quick glance round the room. 'Kitchen. Very domestic goddess, very Nigella. Next?'

'On second thoughts,' sighed Fran, giving her an old-fashioned look as she refilled her glass, 'forget it. Come on, let's take our drinks into the garden. Sam, can you bring the olives and the dips?'

Allie clapped her hands in mock delight. 'Ooh goody, a

country picnic outdoors – how spiffing! What shall I bring? The home-made pickles, or the handmade bread?'

'Don't trouble yourself with anything,' Fran batted back with no less irony. 'You've got enough to carry with your hugely hilarious and sophisticated sense of humour. Come on, you unreconstructed metropolitan, you!'

'All of which is very true, but I think I might just manage to carry the wine,' said Allie, eyes twinkling, much to Sam's relief. She hadn't been sure whether this interchange had been badinage or a declaration of war.

Outside in the garden, they ensconced themselves in a clematis-covered trellised enclave on rustic wooden seats at an old stone table, where Fran wisely decided to spare Allie the details of Archie's exciting new plans for the herringbone paths. She only hoped that Allie would likewise spare her the details of her impressions of this chocolate-box setting, of which Fran was so proud and so fond.

'Air not too fresh for you, I hope?' she asked mischievously, handing out plates. 'We do keep an emergency cylinder of Low Oxygen/High Sulphur Dioxide Polluted for our visiting city friends if our native mix is too rich.'

Allie smiled at Sam, nodding towards Fran. 'So clever *and* so witty. A paper-hanging prodigy. Isn't she a marvel?'

Sam chanced a laugh, getting into the swing of this barbed banter now. 'Oh she is, she is,' she agreed.

'Eat, just eat,' Fran chided them both. 'I'm not having you ganging up on me already – you've only just met!'

'Did you manage to track down the gorgeous Paul on the phone last night?' asked Allie, consenting to take only a single olive at Fran's prompting, and waving away bread and cheese with, 'No really, I need to feel more of the effects of the wine after my travels, before I send in the troops to start mopping it up.'

Fran gave up on her munificent hostess routine and helped herself to the food instead. 'I was too busy being a decorating genius last night. But at least I managed to find his hotel this morning. Left a message in French. I was rather proud of myself, actually. I bet you *anything* he'll call me while we're out at the fair. Sod's Law. Still, as long as he's out bringing home the bacon . . .'

Reminded of errant partners and the vagaries of telephonic communication, Sam riffled through her handbag surreptitiously under the table to find her mobile and check that it was on. She, too, had left a message for her man on his voicemail, and she was expecting a response. Or *dreading* his response might perhaps have been more accurate under the circumstances.

'Sorry?' she asked now, confused, as she lifted her eyes from her lap and saw that both Allie and Fran were looking at her expectantly. 'What did you say?'

'Nothing of any importance,' Allie admitted. 'I said, "So, you're an estate agent?" Don't worry,' she added, lifting her glass to empty it once again, 'I'm not one of those who think that's synonymous with "scum of the earth". After all, I am in advertising myself – not one of the most popular professions at parties, I find.'

Sam's large, liquid eyes widened, and she faltered in her response. 'I – yes, I am. Estate agent, I mean. But out here in the country we aren't exactly . . . We're not as . . .'

'Mendacious? Avaricious? Cutthroat?' supplied Allie with a disingenuous smile.

'High-pressured,' asserted Sam stiffly, struggling to regain her equilibrium. '*You'll* probably find this funny, but actually I care about the houses I sell just as much as I care about the buyers and vendors – especially a house as wonderful as this. I like to think that I match the right client to the right property. For instance, when I first met Fran, I was as happy for this house as I was for her. I knew that at last I'd found it the right person who'd love it as much as I did, and who'd be prepared to put in the work.'

'Heavens,' said Allie, lifting an eyebrow. 'A veritable matchmaker. Tell me, do you turn this gift of yours to matching men to women, too? *I'm* in the market to buy.'

'You're always in the market,' agreed Fran. 'But not to buy, surely? You hyperventilate at the thought of a six-month lease.'

'Six months!' exclaimed Allie, her hand clutching her throat in mock hyperventilation. 'Quick! Get me that cylinder of thin city air *now*! I can't breathe, I tell you! I'm suffocating at the very idea!'

'Have you never wanted to be married then, Allie?' asked Sam, glad to have the focus of attention taken from herself.

'Been there. Done that,' said Allie succinctly. 'Pass me the wine.'

'She has, I was there,' Fran confirmed, topping up her glass. 'In fact, we were both young marrieds together when I was on my first time around, weren't we, old friend?'

'We were indeed. Oh, the bliss of the terminally innocent! God, were we ever that young?'

'Were we ever that innocent?' Fran riposted, and they cackled together like crones.

'What went wrong?' Sam pursued. 'How long did it last?'

'Minutes,' was Allie's reply. 'Fran stuck it out much longer than me. I'd sussed my – shall I be polite? Shall I say "incompatibility"? Yes, that's a nice word for this tranquil rural setting. I'd sussed my incompatibility with that slimy, creepy, two-timing toad after less than a year. But then, of course, he did bring his shit into the family home. Into the family bed, actually.'

'Quite a learning opportunity that one, wasn't it?' said Fran, remembering the tears and the screams and the suitcases flung from top floor windows.

'Oh, I learnt all right,' agreed Allie. ' "Love 'em and leave 'em" is now my refrain. Enjoy the jollies, then pack them off home. I mean, who wants the extra laundry?'

'Me,' admitted Sam guiltily, eyes cast down again. 'Actually, it's something I long for.'

Oh well, thought Fran wearily, Sam's silence on the Nigel saga couldn't have lasted for ever. Now for the latest blow-by-blow account.

'Nonsense. Why?' Allie challenged her. 'Surely you've got the best of all possible worlds. Didn't Fran tell me that your lover's married?'

Sam bit her lip and nodded, full of shame.

'So,' continued Allie, 'his wife does all the tedious maintenance, while you get all the fun of the sex and romance.'

'But I don't like it,' Sam insisted. 'I'm really not comfortable about being in the wrong. I mean, look what women like me have done to wives like you and Fran.'

Allie raised her glass to her in a toast. 'For this, we salute you. Anyway, Fran's right, it was a learning experience. You get wiser. You change – for the better. My life now is one hundred per cent improved. I'd never have been able to devote as much of my time and energy to my job if I'd stayed married and had kids. And I love it. I'm fulfilled. It just meant a rather large investment of pain for a rather long period of time. But it dulls, it dulls. And now I know me, and I'm happy. Me, I can rely on. Here's to me!'

'And all who sail in you,' Fran reminded her.

'Well, heavens, I'm not saying that I don't simply *adore* men when they're doing what they're best at,' Allie informed them both airily. 'It's just talking to them before and afterwards that I always find a chore.'

But Sam was unwilling to be so disillusioned about the merits of marriage. 'You're happy now with Paul, though, aren't you, Fran? You like being married?' she insisted.

'Well, yes,' agreed Fran. 'But then, we're both on our second time around, and I think we learnt a lot from our first mistakes. And of course we're more grown-up this time, less wide-eyed – we have more realistic expectations of partnership, I hope. We talk things over a lot – something neither of us did with our exes.

We negotiate, try to be flexible, observe our differences, give each other space.'

'That sound romantic to you?' Allie challenged Sam rhetorically. 'No. You see, it's as I said. Oil and water. They don't mix.'

'What – me and Paul?!' Fran protested, choking on her wine.

'Romance and reality. You have to choose which one you want.'

Sam was thoughtful for a moment, and then conceded, 'I suppose that is what Nigel's been trying to do – have both. His wife's his reality, and I'm the romance. Or have been,' she added darkly. 'Things have got a bit blurred of late.'

'Have you been with him long?' asked Allie.

'Seven years.'

Fran was astonished. 'Good grief, Sam – I'd no idea!'

Sam shook her head in long-suffering despair. 'I know. And he won't leave her, for the sake of the children. Sometimes I feel like the invisible woman,' she complained.

'Strange,' said Allie. 'That's how *I* felt when I was married.'

The sun was now setting behind the tops of the trees, and it was getting chilly in more ways than one, thought Fran. Enough of chewing over old bones. She drained her glass and stood up, motioning them to follow suit.

'Come on, help me in with these dishes,' she instructed her two best friends. 'It's time for the fun of the fair.'

Four

Sam was elected to drive them in her car since she had barely touched her spritzer, whereas, between them, Fran and Allie had put paid to a bottle of wine. As far as Allie was concerned, sitting in the back seat, watching the countryside race past them in a giddy whirl of dark hedges and dangerous blind bends, the thrills and spills of the fair rides started right here.

'You drive like an absolute maniac,' she said admiringly, her knuckles white from holding on, her opinion of Sam having risen in bounds.

Sam took her foot off the accelerator immediately, reducing her speed. 'I'm sorry, it's habit – I'm always dashing about between properties, always late. Is this better?'

'Absolutely not,' Allie chided her. 'Put your foot down, girl! Do you think that a townie like me is a wuss? I *live* for the thrill of danger and speed.'

'Now that's one thing about living in the country that you *would* like,' Fran said, turning round to grin at her. 'No crawling along at walking pace in traffic-choked streets, so you can give it lots of wellie.' But as soon as the words were spoken, Sam hit the brakes.

'Well, that put the kiss of death on it,' Allie announced, looking past Fran through the windscreen. 'Haven't I told you about touching wood?'

Turning back to face the front, Fran saw the tail lights of a queue of cars ahead of them, all waiting impatiently to turn into the field which had been designated for the nonce as the fair-ground car park. Legions of traffic cones defended both sides of the road, preventing the expediency of dumping the car where it stood.

'This'll take hours,' Sam said decisively, wrenching the car round in a three-point turn. 'We'll park at the Wheatsheaf and walk back.'

'*Walk?*' Allie protested. 'In *these* heels?' But when Sam had driven them only a couple of hundred yards down a small twisting lane which branched off almost invisibly from the road they were on, and Allie discovered that their destination was in fact the car park of a public house, her complaints turned to compliments forthwith.

'Oh, clever girl,' she proclaimed, as Sam squeezed the car into a tight spot beside the pub. 'What a very good idea!' And before either Fran or Sam had so much as unfastened their seat belts, she had disappeared from their view through a door labelled 'Off Sales'.

'What a – fun person,' said Sam stoically, but without conviction, as they stood by the roadside and awaited Allie's return. 'So vibrant.'

Fran's smile muscles twitched. 'That's one way of putting it,' she said, watching Allie re-emerge from the lighted doorway bearing several cans of lager, laughing over her shoulder at some bon mot left behind. 'Scored already?' she called, at her friend's tottering approach.

'Hardly, love – he was old enough to be my father. But sweet, nonetheless,' Allie conceded, linking her arm through Fran's for support as they walked back down the lane. 'And one has to keep one's hand in. Now, lead me to the frolics!'

The town girl's enthusiasm for excitement was infectious, and the three of them giggled their way to the gates of the fairground, swigging lager out of their cans.

'Long Throssle?' declared Allie incredulously, as they passed by the village sign. 'Is that the name of this place, or the usual male boast?'

Checking on Sam with a quick sideways glance, Fran was pleased to see that even she had now started to relax into the spirit of the evening, spraying lager from her mouth as she burst into laughter, mopping her face on her sleeve.

'Is that a long throssle in your pocket, or are you just pleased to see me?' Allie continued irrepressibly under her breath, as, nearing their destination, they walked past a bemused young police constable on traffic duty, leaving him wondering in their wake what it was that made him quite so amusing.

'I shall never be able to say the name again without thinking rude thoughts!' Sam protested through an explosion of chortles. 'And I've got two properties on the market out here!'

'Could be worse,' Allie told her. 'Imagine trying to flog anything in a place called Short Throssle. It'd be a ghost town, I tell you. Men would leave it in droves!' Her mood, undoubtedly buoyed up by the wine and the lager, was also enhanced by the heady atmosphere of this village event. Fran was right: the country air was invigoratingly different from its stale, pale imitator in town, and as they walked along the rutted farm track and through the gates, the mouth-watering savoury scents from the hot dog stall and the sweet-smelling fragrance of the candyfloss machine jostled sharply and distinctly with the exciting mechanical smells of the thrumming fairground generators. Even the lights of the fairly tame-looking rides glowed more luminescent against the surrounding rural darkness than could ever be matched in London's over-bright, halogen-lit streets. Allie could not remember a time when all her senses felt so alive and so energised. At least, not without the help of recreational drugs.

'Will you *look* at the Waltzer!' she exclaimed, wending her way between the darts stall and rifle range, making a beeline straight for the ride, and pulling the others behind her.

'I'm not ever so good with things that whirl round fast,' Sam admitted, now dragging her heels. 'But you two go on it.'

'It's not the thing that's whirling round, but the hunk that's whirling round on it!' Allie informed her, with true reverence in her voice, eyeing the glistening muscles of the tattooed youth who was showing off at the centre of the ride, spinning the carriages till girls screamed. In one movement, it seemed, she had liberated Fran's lager and dumped it with Sam to look after, with the admonition of 'Party pooper', and in a manner which brooked no disagreement grabbed Fran's hand and marched her to an empty carriage as it slowed to a stop.

'That is the kind of boy I have secret, dirty fantasies about,' she confided, her eyes never leaving him as he wove between the new passengers, collecting their fares.

Fran looked at him doubtfully. 'Well, I suppose you wouldn't have the chore of talking to him, either before or afterwards,' she said. 'He looks as if he could barely string two words together.'

'As long as he understands "Don't stop!"' whispered Allie, still holding him in her gaze as he approached them. 'Two, please,' she said, smiling at him and batting her eyelashes as she handed over their fares, and she wriggled down in her seat in an unequivocal display of body language which needed no translation, even for the cranially challenged. She licked her lips, slowly and provocatively. 'We like to go *very* fast,' she instructed him, 'so don't forget to keep coming back to give us a twirl.'

The boy grunted by way of an answer, and swaggered to the centre to start up the ride.

'Actually,' said Fran in a small, faint voice as the world started to spin around her and, worse, began to pick up speed, '*I* don't like to go very fast at all.'

The boy was now moving swiftly between the whirling carriages, pushing them off with a macho flick of his wrist to spin them round. Fran gasped involuntarily and gripped onto the sides of the carriage as, with a sickening lurch of her stomach and brain, she felt the giddying effect of him obeying Allie's instruction to the letter. The whirl of the fairground lights reeling around her was making things worse, and she squeezed her eyes tight shut, hours seeming to pass by with no respite. Through the blare of the rock music, as the boy spun them again, ever faster, she could hear Allie's delighted laughter, and a woman's terrified scream. It wasn't until the ride was finally, mercifully, slowing to a stop that Fran realised she *was* that woman.

Allie turned to her, exhilarated. 'Again?'

'You've *got* to be kidding,' said Fran in a firm voice which belied her physical condition, and getting out of the carriage on trembling legs, she wove her way unsteadily back to terra firma.

'That looked like fun,' said Sam mendaciously. 'Here's your lager.'

'Thanks,' said Allie, grabbing hers and downing it in a trice.

'You have mine,' Fran instructed Sam, waving away the can. 'We'll all of us regret it if I try to drink that now.'

'Cheers,' said Allie, availing herself of it, and dispatched it immediately to join its twin. Eyes bright, she looked around her voraciously. 'So what's next? The "Flying Torpedo"?'

Fran followed her gaze and saw, to her horror, two large spinning capsules at either end of a rapidly rotating metal arm, disappearing and reappearing over the heads of the crowds, being flung at great speed through the night sky. 'You know what?' she said. 'I think I'll sit this one out. But be my guest.'

Allie frowned, and pouted a protest. At that moment, she had only to stamp her feet and threaten to be sick, to be a dead ringer for Violet Elizabeth Bott. 'Don't tell me I've come to Thrill City with two cissies!' she complained.

'No, you've come to Long Throssle with a couple of women of delicate constitution,' Fran said. 'But if you think we deserve to die for it, there's a rifle range right here. I'd sooner you shot me than made me go on that thing.'

Allie's mood lightened immediately. 'Guns! How fabulous!'

she exclaimed, and strode off to the stall to arm herself to the teeth.

'You okay?' Fran asked of Sam, as they followed behind at a more leisurely pace. 'You seem a bit preoccupied.'

'Sorry,' Sam apologised. 'Is it so obvious? I've been trying to make an effort not to think about it, but obviously I've not been doing too well.'

'Not think about what?'

Sam bit her lip in an attempt to look more guilty than pleased. 'I think I might be pregnant.'

'Oh – my – God,' said Fran, drawing out each syllable as she computed this information. 'Have you told Nigel?'

Sam nodded unhappily. 'He's furious. Well – very upset. He's been calling me ever since to check if my period's come. I'm expecting him to ring again any time now. I had hoped that maybe he'd be . . .' Tears escaped from her large brown eyes, choking off what Nigel's hoped-for reaction might have been, and Fran fumbled for a tissue in her jacket.

'Here,' she said, handing her a crumpled wad. 'It's not as pre-used as it looks – it's just been in my pocket a while.'

'Thanks,' said Sam through her sniffles.

'Oh really! What *is* she like!' Fran demanded, her attention caught momentarily by Allie, who was flirting outrageously with the man at the rifle range, holding her gun awkwardly and pretending to be dumb. Unable to resist such a lure, the man came out of his stall to stand behind her, folding her in his arms as, together, they pointed the gun at the pitted metal targets. With a plink, a duck bit the dust. Allie turned in his embrace to laugh at something he said, caught Fran's eye, and winked.

'Sorry,' said Fran, shaking her head in disbelief, her attention now back with Sam. 'You were saying . . . Are you sure?'

'Not a hundred per cent, but – I sort of *feel* pregnant, if you know what I mean?'

'But why not go to the doctor, find out one way or the other?

You might be worrying unnecessarily. Or at least get a predictor kit from the chemist.'

'I've got one, I just can't bring myself to use it,' Sam admitted, shame-faced. 'To be honest, I don't know which outcome I dread more. I mean, it's not as if I *meant* to get pregnant, but ever since it's been a possibility, I've felt . . . Oh, Fran! The fact is, I'd love nothing more than to have Nigel's baby—'

'But he'd want you to have an abortion?' supplied Fran, taking a less than wild guess.

'Yes,' agreed Sam, her voice now a grief-stricken whisper.

Fran took her in her arms to comfort her, and Sam wept on her shoulder. 'Well, Sam, honey, look – I know it's tough, but as a married man, with kids already, you can see his point.'

'I know,' began Sam, but stopped abruptly, lifting her head to confirm the muffled ringing in her bag. 'It's him!' she said, scrabbling frantically through its contents for her mobile. 'And he's going to be so disappointed!' From what Fran had heard about Nigel, that was putting it on the mild side. Finally finding her phone, Sam clamped it to her ear and moved a few feet away, but not before Fran heard her adopt a mollifying tone with, 'Hello, Angel . . .'

'She can't be selling houses at this time, surely?' said an incredulous voice at her side, and turning, Fran discovered that, while she had been otherwise engaged giving pregnancy counselling, Allie had won herself a cuddly toy and a hat which said 'Kiss Me Slow'.

'No,' said Fran, not deigning to comment on her ill-gotten gains. 'It's Nigel.'

'Ah yes, of course,' said Allie. 'The modern mistress's tool, the cell phone. You are never allowed to phone him, but he can get hold of you whenever he wants.'

'She thinks she's pregnant.'

'Oh dear. So the excrement has hit the air conditioning, as it were.'

'You have such a delicate turn of phrase. Such a lady.'

'Kind of you to say so, but really, I'm more of a tramp,' Allie grinned at her. 'What's next?'

'I was rather hoping you'd tell me. You seem to be making so many friends with the natives.'

'Can I help my natural charm? Don't answer that,' she cut in swiftly, as Fran, eyebrows raised, opened her mouth to reply. Allie surveyed the stalls around them. 'Hm. Well, I could throw three ping-pong balls into a glass jar, but then I'd win a goldfish, and I've never been big on pets. Except the two-legged kind, of course.'

'Naturally.'

'So, throwing hoops over bottles of Scotch it is,' said Allie, making off in that direction. 'Bring Sam along when she's finished speaking to the proud father-to-be,' she tossed back over her shoulder. 'And buy some candyfloss on your way!'

'Yazzum, Missie Scarlett,' Fran called after her, dipping a mock curtsey, but Allie, oblivious, was already eagerly swapping a handful of change for an armful of hoops and closing one eye to take aim.

The phone call with Nigel had been as bad as Sam had feared, and in an ideal world she would have gone home now, put herself to bed, and cried herself to sleep. Instead she found herself being told to 'hang on to these' (a tin of tomato soup, a cuddly toy, and a bottle of cider – the Scotch having proved somewhat elusive) while she watched Allie hurl wooden balls at coconuts.

'More balls,' Allie demanded of the stallholder, as her last projectile failed to dislodge the prize. 'And less glue.'

'They're just sitting on sawdust,' he replied with a grin, taking her money and providing her with more ammo. 'You need to chuck 'em harder.'

'Or buy a coconut from Sainsbury's,' said Fran drily. 'At less than half the price.'

By way of an answer, Allie took off her coat and tossed it to Fran, rolling up her sleeves and glaring at the coconuts with grim determination. She was not a woman who admitted defeat. 'I'll pretend it's Nigel, shall I?' she offered, winking at Sam.

'Oh no, don't be horrible,' Sam protested, struggling for magnanimity. 'It isn't his fault. I can see why he's upset.'

'What on earth were you doing, anyway, not using protection?' asked Fran, who had been puzzling over this for some time.

'We did. It burst.'

'Use two,' said Allie, drawing back her arm and taking aim. 'I do.' One eye half-closed, she unleashed the first of her wooden artillery with more strength in her arm than Fran would have credited. 'Shit. You are making me really cross now,' she warned the implacable coconut. 'It's only a question of time.' Grabbing another ball, she took aim again. 'How late are you?' she asked Sam, letting fly with another deadly assault.

'Eight days,' said Sam, wincing as the hard ball made contact with the Nigel substitute's head.

'Could be the start of the menopause,' suggested Allie, spitting on her hands to try again.

'I'm only thirty-four!' protested Sam.

'My dear girl, it can start when it damn well pleases, any time after thirty-one. I myself am only thirty-nine,' said Allie mendaciously, and hurled her penultimate projectile.

Fran's face muscles twitched as she struggled to bring her expression under control. It got harder as the years went by.

'But at the merest *whisper* of a hot flush I put myself on HRT,' Allie continued. 'And look at me – yesss!' she cried, as the coconut finally admitted defeat to her last ball and fell from its cup.

'Thank God for that! I was beginning to think we were here for the weekend,' said Fran, helping the fairground pentathlon champion back on with her jacket while juggling her other trophies. 'Can we go home now?'

'Who ate all the candyfloss?' demanded Allie sternly, having been handed an all-but-empty wooden stick among her winnings.

'Me,' said Sam guiltily, wiping the sugar from her mouth. 'Sorry, I just couldn't stop. I don't know why – normally I can't stand the stuff.' Her face was suddenly stricken with alarm. 'Gosh, I hope it isn't a sign that I'm preg–'

'It's a sign that you're hungry,' Allie interrupted her firmly. 'And I'm not surprised. Personally, I'm starving.' She lifted her nose, scenting the air like a scavenging fox. 'Hot dogs,' she announced, striding off decisively, leading the way. 'On me.'

Sam made a small moue of dissent, but Fran linked her arm and propelled her along in Allie's wake. 'It's no use even *thinking* of contradicting her,' she said apologetically. 'Better men than us have perished in the attempt. Besides,' she continued, attempting a cheering joke as they picked their way through mud and straw, 'you'd only be sitting at home feeling sick with worry for maybe no good reason. At least this way, eating fairground hot dogs, you'll have every reason to be ill.'

However, having circumnavigated the dodgem rink and the big wheel and finally finding the hot dog stall, they discovered that Allie had evidently had other ideas, for she was nowhere to be seen.

'Well I'm damned if I'm actually going to participate in my certain death if the Queen of the Night isn't here to command it,' said Fran, eyeing the food with suspicion from their place in the queue, and scanning the heads of the nearby dodgem car drivers for signs of a Kiss Me Slow hat.

'I suppose we could get her one, and pretend to have eaten ours already,' supplied Sam, adept as always at taking the conciliatory course. But before the words were out of her mouth Allie had joined them, bubbling over with her news.

'I'm just about to start a new affair!' she crowed, startling the rest of the food queue into keeping a respectful distance between themselves and her.

'Not the boy on the Waltzer! Tell me you haven't been back there. He's barely seventeen!' Fran scolded her.

'No, I haven't,' mused Allie, her eyes lighting up. 'But it might not be a bad idea. She did mention something mechanical would be involved.'

'Who did?'

'Gypsy Brenda,' said Allie, pointing over their heads to a caravan, and reading from a sign. ' "Psychic Consultant to the Stars. As seen on TV." I crossed her palm with a five-pound note, and it was worth every penny.'

'Oh! A fortune teller!' exclaimed Sam, and shoving the tin of tomato soup and the bottle of cider into Allie's arms, she was gone.

'Now look what you've done,' said Fran, liberating the cider as they watched Sam move at a speed they had been unaware was in her gift. 'She'll try anything rather than do a pregnancy test.' She took a hefty swig from the bottle and handed it over to Allie, making a face. 'God, I haven't drunk that stuff since I was a student. Now I remember why.' The queue shuffled forward a couple of paces towards the hot dog stand, taking Allie and her inexorably with it.

'Anyway, back to me,' said Allie unequivocally, not, apparently, having Fran's scruples about the cider, which disappeared at a rate of knots down her throat before she began. 'Gypsy Brenda told me that a new man was just about to come my way, out of the blue! Hot and steamy, apparently – I can't wait! She said it'll start with an accident – some kind of mechanical failure or something.' She paused to reflect on the possibilities while she laid waste to the rest of the cider. 'A repairman?' she mused, wiping her mouth on the back of her hand. 'Why not? It has been known . . .'

'And when is this supposed to happen?'

'Any minute. She asked me if I'd met anybody already, as in, if it hasn't happened yet it's just about to. She said he'd be a bit of a surprise. Not my usual type.'

'What does she mean by that, I wonder?' Fran challenged her, with eyebrows raised. 'Everything's your type.'

'Mm,' conceded Allie. 'Except bald, of course. And short. Or wearing glasses. Apart from that, I am happy to say, I am entirely without prejudice.' To Fran's horror, it was now their turn in the queue. 'Three hot dogs, please.'

'Make that two,' Fran countermanded her. 'I like living too much.'

'Don't be so prissy,' Allie admonished her. 'As you were,' she instructed the stallholder.

'Onions?' came the bored reply.

'The whole works,' said Allie greedily. 'Onions, ketchup, mustard – but hold the botulism.'

While Fran looked Death in the face and saw it was a sausage, Sam was gazing intently, with bated breath, at her own palm, which was currently being scrutinised by Gypsy Brenda.

'What do you see?' she prompted impatiently. 'Is there a baby?'

'You'll have three children,' said Brenda, hedging her bets.

'Oh my goodness! But, am I pregnant now?'

Brenda dropped her hand for a moment as she took a swig of tea from a pint mug. 'I'm a clairvoyant, love, not a gynaecologist,' she said phlegmatically, making Sam blush with embarrassment. 'But – there's something here about new beginnings. Could be a baby, I suppose.' She looked at Sam shrewdly. 'I could probably tell more with the crystal ball.'

'Try it!' urged Sam.

'It'd be an extra ten pounds, love,' Brenda warned. 'Takes it out of me more, does the crystal.'

Sam rooted round in her handbag and produced a note from
her purse. 'Okay?'

'Okay,' Brenda sighed, as if reluctantly, and tucking the
money away in the folds of her skirt she removed a silk scarf from
a crystal ball and gazed within its milky depths. 'I'm still getting
this woman who's important to you. She's in here now, beck-
oning you. Long dark hair.'

'Yes, well, I can't think who that'd be,' Sam said dismissively,
'as I told you before. Are you sure you can't see a man? Fairish,
wavy hair, hazel eyes, about five foot ten?'

'Ah,' said Gypsy Brenda, the mists clearing. 'There he is now.'

'Is he?' exclaimed Sam excitedly, peering into the globe
herself.

Brenda nodded. 'Large as life. Standing behind the woman.'

Sam was getting irritated now with this unwelcome female
apparition. 'Can't you just ignore her, and concentrate on him?
What does he say?'

'Nothing of any importance, love,' said Brenda dismissively,
enshrouding the globe in its silk covering again. 'But she says to
tell you she's waiting.'

'Well, thank you,' said Sam stiffly, feeling distinctly ripped off
as she rose to leave.

'The trouble with seeing the future, dear,' Brenda counselled
her, 'is that at the present time you may not know all the possibilities that are about to come your way, so it may not make any
sense to you just now. I'll leave it with you. You'll meet her soon,
I guarantee. That woman's your destiny, in some shape or form.
I can see her standing beside you now.'

'Right,' said Sam, spooked despite herself, glanced anxiously
at the empty space at her side. 'Well, goodbye.' She struggled
with the caravan door handle and, for a horrible moment, found
she couldn't leave.

'I'll get that, dear,' Brenda sighed, getting up heavily from
the couch and joining her. 'Sticks sometimes. You have to have

the knack.' She delivered a swift kick to the bottom of the door and yanked the handle. 'There you are.'

Freedom! 'Thanks,' said Sam, and she escaped gratefully down the caravan steps. 'Shall I send the next one in?'

'No, I'm done for tonight,' said Brenda, following her out to take down her sign. 'I'm shutting up shop. I'm drained.'

'I'm sure,' said Sam, more politely than she felt. This foolish enterprise had drained fifteen pounds out of her. 'Well, must get back to my friends.'

'Wait!' Brenda commanded, dropping the sign and rubbing her forehead. 'There's another message – not for you. For your friend.'

Sam halted her steps, spinning round, her interest galvanised again. 'Which friend?' she asked eagerly. 'Nigel?'

'Not unless that's a woman's name,' said Brenda. 'It's another woman, close to you.'

Sam sighed impatiently. What was she, a psychic message service? And why all these dratted women?

'Tell her that great gains come sometimes disguised as great loss,' warned Brenda portentously.

'Who?'

'I dunno, love, that's for you to find out,' said Brenda wearily, massaging her temples. 'But they're saying to tell her to weather the storm. Remember to pass that on when the time comes.'

'Okay,' said Sam, turning back to scan the crowds in vain for Fran and Allie. 'I'll remember. Goodnight.' She retraced her steps back to the hot dog stall, where there was no sign of them. A chill wind had started up, and she drew her coat around her for warmth, feeling distinctly piqued. *Was* she pregnant? Perhaps there really was nothing for it but to do the wretched test. And if she were? Was there any way at all that Nigel could be persuaded to leave his wife and three growing children, who he knew and loved, for herself and a new baby?

'Well,' announced a woman's voice at her side. 'It isn't exactly the London Eye, but we saw the whole of Long Throssle and its environs by moonlight.'

Sam jumped, still aware of the ghostly female presence Brenda had seen next to her. It was Allie, of course. Who else did Sam know who could make ordinary English place names sound so lewd?

'Sorry?'

'We've just been on the diminutive Big Wheel,' Fran explained drily. 'Panoramic vistas. We saw you having a good old chinwag with Gypsy Rose Lee outside her caravan. What did she have to say for herself?'

'Nothing of much use,' admitted Sam. 'Shall we go home now? It's getting very chilly.'

'Hot toddies at mine, then,' said Fran, linking arms with both her friends as they walked back across the field and out onto the road to the pub.

'Come on, give,' Allie commanded Sam. 'What did Brenda the Bringer of Glad Tidings tell you?'

'She did see Nigel,' said Sam, making the best of it. 'In her crystal ball.'

'Gosh, you didn't stint yourself,' said Allie admiringly, explaining to Fran, 'The crystal ball's extra. I settled for the tea leaves myself. Much better value. You get a hot drink thrown in.'

'But she kept seeing this woman, and insisting that she was more important somehow.'

'Oh. Are you bi?' asked Allie, as one from Sam's acquaintance might say, 'Do you take sugar?'

'No!' Sam protested, her cheeks flushing hotly in the dark. 'Heavens! Absolutely not!'

'What else?' Fran prompted her, quelling Allie with a sideways look. 'What was all that outside her van, when you were leaving?'

'Some other woman,' said Sam dismissively. 'A friend of

mine, apparently, who I'm to remember to warn when the time comes.'

'When what time comes?' Allie pressed her. 'And which friend? It could be you,' she continued to Fran. 'I told you you should see her.'

'Stuff and nonsense,' said Fran comfortably, kicking a stone down the lane. 'What was the warning, Sam? "Beware the ides of March", or was it something more prosaic?' She glanced up at the sky as a couple of raindrops fell on her face, and urged her friends to hurry along. 'The only time I've ever visited a psychic was in a spiritualist church when I was at uni,' she continued. 'I'd gone out of curiosity with a friend who wanted to find out whether her boyfriend was cheating on her.' Fran laughed at the memory. 'And all the psychic kept banging on about was someone's dripping tap, and somebody else's leaking roof.'

'Yes, it was a bit like that,' agreed Sam in a disappointed tone, drawing her collar up against the falling rain. 'I'm to tell a friend to weather the storm.'

'That's definitely me then!' cried Fran, breaking into a sprint, as with a clap of thunder the heavens opened and emptied themselves thoroughly on Long Throssle.

Time would tell her how right she was.

Five

Sam, not a great drinker, and soaked to the skin, elected not to come in for hot toddies, but to drop Fran and Allie off and go home.

'I've got to do some viewings tomorrow,' she told them by way of excuse as they got out of her car and ran for the cover of Fran's porch. 'No rest for the wicked!'

'If she's wicked, then I am the Devil incarnate,' Allie said, waving her off. 'Hurry up with that damned door, I'm saturated.'

'Yes, oh Dark One, I obey,' Fran replied, finally finding her key in her pocket.

Two hot toddies later, Allie was consenting to stay over for the night. 'You're right, I suppose,' she said, nursing the warm drink in her hand. 'It's not that I couldn't drive, perfectly safely in fact, but with the stupid law insisting you lose your licence . . .'

'Oh, I love drunks who think they can drive safely,' said Fran. 'Paul's always the same, too. I practically have to arm-wrestle him for the car keys after we've been out to a party.'

'Shall I put the kettle on?' asked Allie, deciding not to take offence.

'If you like. Why? Do you fancy a cup of tea?'

'No, you idiot, I want another one of these,' said Allie, holding out her empty toddy glass and making no attempt at getting up herself. 'Since I'm grounded, I might as well be floored while I'm about it.'

Fran grinned, and took the glasses into the kitchen. It was fun having Allie to stay, particularly since Paul had been away so long. She hadn't realised she was so lonely for company. And having an evening, just girls together, reminded her of the nice bits of her old single life, when she'd been between marriages. Reminded of Paul, she was also reminded of her earlier prognostication, and after returning with replenished glasses to the living room she went over to check the answer phone, where the digital display announced one call.

'What did I tell you?' Fran asked, as Paul's voice came into the room. 'Sod's Law. As soon as I'm out, he calls.'

'Aah! Isn't that nice – he loves you,' said Allie, listening to him signing off.

Fran smiled, feeling a warm glow inside. She loved him too. She wished she could tell him that now, in person. Still, only another week, she comforted herself, and then they'd have the whole weekend together. She must remember to buy some smoked salmon and bagels for next Saturday brunch. They would have a feast in bed.

'Do you think she *is* gay?' Allie asked her now, surprising her out of her nice reverie.

'Who? Sam?! No! Why? You heard her – she's been with Nigel for – what was it? Seven years?'

'Exactly,' said Allie, as if that proved her point.

Fran returned to the sofa and to her drink. 'There's some logic missing in the middle there – you'll have to fill me in.'

'Why would a woman hang around for seven years, waiting for a man she can't have?' Allie challenged her impatiently. 'He couldn't have made it plainer, could he, that he will never leave the wife and kids?'

'Hope springing eternal?' suggested Fran. 'She thinks she'll wear him down? Or maybe she's just in for the long haul. Thinks he'll come to her once the children have left home.'

'It's clear you've not done therapy,' said Allie dismissively.

'If you had, you would be looking for the unconscious motive.'

'Neither have you. Have you?' Fran leant forward, interested now.

'I had a few sessions with a Mr Fox in Marylebone after The Bastard left me,' Allie admitted, alluding to her once true love by another name, which didn't smell as sweet.

'Really? I had no idea.'

'I thought I was going mad. I was crying on tube trains, openly, like a woman possessed. Mr Fox helped me to see that it was, on the contrary, a sign of sanity to be distressed.'

'I could have told you that for free. In fact, I seem to remember that I did.'

'Yes, well, water under the bridge,' said Allie, closing the subject with an airy wave of her hand. 'But young Sam, now . . .'

'Yes?'

'Mr Fox would ask her why she puts obstacles in her own way. Like picking a married man.'

'Some things you don't pick, exactly,' Fran offered. 'Sometimes you just see somebody, and bang, that's it.'

'Mr Fox would suggest that things don't go "bang" for no reason. And even if they did, they wouldn't stay banging for seven years. Although, of course,' said Allie, laughing at her own double entendre, 'I imagine that's exactly what they have been doing.'

'Very funny. What's your point, Dr Ruth?'

'Well, a woman who was frightened of being true to her sexuality might unconsciously choose a man she couldn't have – it would solve all her problems at once. Dating a man would save her from having to confront her lesbianism, but dating a *married* man would save her from having to have a proper committed relationship with a member of the opposite sex.'

'You're losing me now,' said Fran, studying her hot toddy. 'Or perhaps it's the Scotch.' She yawned, and stretched her shoulders. 'Time for bed?'

'Heavens! What an invitation!'

'Not with me, you idiot!'

'Well in that case, no,' said Allie, pretending to pout. She held up her empty glass. 'Another one of these.'

Fran trundled through to the kitchen once again. 'We'll regret this in the morning,' she said, doling out the whisky.

'I have rarely regretted anything in the morning,' rejoined Allie, calling through from her position on the comfortable sofa, 'when weighed against the fun of the night before.'

'*You* haven't slept with a woman, though, have you?' Fran checked as she returned with the booze.

Allie lifted one eyebrow, stretching out her legs and examining her pointed toes. 'These shoes are ruined,' she said.

'You haven't!' exclaimed Fran, taking this as an admission of – well, not guilt exactly. That wasn't in Allie's repertoire. 'Who? When?'

'Oh, I can't recall names,' said Allie. 'It was so long ago. Somebody's girlfriend, at a party. He was called Harry, I seem to remember. We had a little dabble à trois.'

'You are full of surprises, even after all this time,' said Fran admiringly. 'Is there anything you haven't done?'

Allie shrugged and smiled. 'I draw the line at animals.'

Fran spluttered into the remains of her hot toddy, choking on a laugh. 'For which, I am sure, the farming community of Little Langton are truly grateful,' she said when she had recovered, and they giggled naughtily like little girls who'd been allowed to stay up at a pyjama party for far too long.

In her bijou cottage a few miles down the road, thoughts of sex were keeping Sam awake too. She had thought that she was tired enough to sleep when she'd cleared her bed of the dozen fluffy toys which decorated its surface by day, and pulled back the sheets to slip inside alone. But the sound of her own heart beating had kept her awake as she had tried to drift away into the bliss of unconsciousness, and now she was lying on her back, staring at the ceiling, going over and over things in her mind. The subject under review was, what would she do if she were pregnant?

In Scenario A, Nigel left his wife and children and came to live with Sam in her cottage. That was her favourite story, and she spent some time moving things around the house in her mind, turning the small spare bedroom into a nursery, hanging pretty mobiles and switching on Beatrix Potter night lights.

Scenario B had them buying another house together (one Sam had her eye on over in Radcliffe Parva, which had a large garden with an orchard – perfect for growing children), since Nigel was used to a lot of space, and he always complained her cottage was too cramped. This, too, she moved into her mind, pulling out that hideous fifties fireplace to reveal the inglenook behind, scraping off layers of horrible old wallpaper and painting colour washes onto clean new plaster.

Scenario C, or the Nightmare Scenario as she had come to call it, was that Nigel insisted on her having an abortion under threat of never *ever* seeing her again. Tonight, however, to her surprise, her imagination refused to be enslaved by the now-familiar image of her as victim, lying alone on a narrow metal bed in a white operating gown, powerless, crying, waiting for the new life to be scraped out of her against her will. Perhaps it was after spending time in Allie's company this evening, she mused, for there was a woman who would never do anything she didn't want to do.

So Scenario D had been born in the early hours of the morning, and was taking shape, with refinements and deletions and mental notes to herself of things which needed more research, as the hands on her alarm clock crept ever closer to the time that it would ring. The new plan was bold and shocking. She would have the baby and abort Nigel.

Six

Fran had been absolutely right, and despite her denial of the
night before Allie had to concede the point, if only to shut her
up and get her to make the goddam coffee. Yes, it was true. This
time, even when weighed against the fun of the night before, she
did in fact regret the hot toddies. Well, not all of them. Perhaps
only the last two or three. But men with hammers had moved
into her head this morning, and were rather irritatingly clanging
them against the pipework of her brain.

'Sure you don't want a fry-up?' Fran teased her, grinning
despite the obvious pain behind her own eyes as she ground the
coffee beans.

But currently, Allie was beyond the reach of humour. 'Sure
you're as funny as you think?' she asked, glowering. 'Pre-
caffeine, I don't think so.'

Clearly it was not going to be the most convivial of breakfasts,
thought Fran, loading a tray, but what the hell? They would have
it in the garden anyway. She led the way out of the back door to
her favourite morning spot, a table and chairs on the kitchen
patio, and Allie followed haplessly in her wake, her nostrils
twitching in a futile attempt, it seemed, to get some of the coffee
inside her with all possible speed. Conversation, such as it was,
was one-sided and repetitive.

'Milk?'

'Coffee.'

'Sugar?'

'Coffee, coffee!'

But after half an hour or so of silence, and the required amount of caffeine, Fran witnessed a remarkable transformation in her friend. 'Wow,' she said, when it was over. 'That was like watching Spencer Tracy morph back into Dr Jekyll from Mr Hyde. I swear to God I just saw your fangs shrink.' She knew that it was over when Allie smiled at her instead of snarling.

'I've been thinking about the breakdown,' she said.

'*Breakdown?* I thought you said you just had a couple of sessions with your Mr Fox of Marylebone?'

'Not that kind of breakdown, idiot. The mechanical breakdown, as seen by Gypsy Brenda.'

'Ah, of course. There had to be a better reason for your new good mood than just sitting in a pool of sunshine in an English country garden on a summer's morning with one of your oldest friends.'

'Which is also very pleasant,' Allie conceded, toasting her with her coffee mug. 'No, I was wondering which of my appliances is about to go bung. I've only just replaced my washing machine and microwave, so I doubt it will be either of them.'

'You don't think you're perhaps placing just a tad too much faith in her prognostications then?'

'I can dream, can't I?' asked Allie tartly. 'With my run of luck with men recently, it's all I have left to amuse myself.'

'I hadn't realised it was so bleak,' said Fran. 'What happened to—' She cast about in her mind for the name of Allie's last young beau. 'Robin? I thought you liked him?'

'Oh that was aeons ago. The holidays were over. He had to go back to school,' said Allie wearily. 'No,' she added quickly, seeing a look of shock pass over her friend's face, 'not literally – give me some credit.'

'Did I utter one word of censure?' asked Fran disingenuously, hurriedly rearranging her features.

'He just started to get on my nerves. Too enthusiastic about everything, too full of childlike wonder. Fine in the bedroom, of course – almost, one might say, flattering. But completely inappropriate at the Ivy, for instance.'

'You took him to the Ivy? What happened?'

'I went to the loo, and when I came back he was trying to get Sue Townsend to autograph his napkin. Adrian Mole, apparently, was his childhood hero. She was very gracious about it but to me it signalled the end.'

'So which of your appliances do you think will lead the way to the next rocky road to love?' asked Fran.

'I don't know. I was wondering about the car,' mused Allie, and she stood to drain her coffee mug. 'Which is why I really should be going. I've got some work to do today, and if my schedule is going to be interrupted by breaking down on the way home followed by – who knows what?' She smiled at the thought of what that might be. 'Then I should get started.'

Fran was disappointed to see her go, not least because she had been looking forward to asking Allie her opinion on the current situation at work. Since overhearing the girls in the lift, it had been at the forefront of her mind. 'Things are so quiet at Q&A, there's talk of cutbacks and lay-offs,' she ventured now quickly as Allie strapped herself into her seat belt in her car. 'What do you think?' By way of answer, Allie tapped the side of her nose and winked.

'Meaning?' asked Fran.

'Meaning that I happen to know that the company's best account handler—'

'That would be you, false modesty having no place here?'

'That would be me, indeed,' Allie smiled. 'I've just hooked another big fish. Or will have, if you creatives don't balls it up on the proposal.'

'Who? What?' asked Fran, already sharpening pencils in her mind.

'You'll find out tomorrow. I mentioned to Ben that I thought *your* input, specifically, would be valuable – I know you think he favours the boys over you.'

'There's hardly any thinking involved,' said Fran dismissively. 'My head has been pressed against the glass ceiling for so long, it's now permanently flat on top. Ben – Creative Director! Comes in as a junior, and two minutes later he's running the show. And he just keeps me at writing long and tedious copy for direct mail shots. I never get the sexy new campaigns since he took over.'

'I know,' said Allie, cutting her off. 'You've told me a couple of times before.' She switched on the engine and put her Audi in first gear. 'Sounds all right,' she said, disappointed.

'So what's the product?' asked Fran.

'Wait and see. Now stop hanging on to my car and let me go – you're reminding me of the clinging little Robin. My destiny with an AA mechanic awaits me.'

Fran obediently let go of the car, and waved as she watched Allie roar off down the village street, scattering children and churchgoers in her wake. If she drove like that all the way back to London it wouldn't be an AA man she'd be needing to mend the car – it would be a pit-stop mechanic, to change the burnt tyres.

Turning to wander back to the house, the whole of Sunday yawned emptily ahead of Fran. How to fill it? Now she'd finished decorating the last room, she was at a loss to know what to do next. But as she stepped through the front door the ringing telephone supplied an unexpected diversion and half an hour later Fran, now smiling happily, decided to change into her gardening clothes to spend the rest of the day pottering. It had been Paul calling, sounding uncharacteristically soppy and romantic, to remind her, he'd said, that he really loved her and was missing her. So sweet. *And* he'd said yes to the herringbone path. So by the time Fran was back outside hoeing the herbaceous border with a grin on her face, all now being right with the world, she had phoned Archie to tell him to get on to Jack Blackmore without delay, concerning the subject of the recycling of the bricks of his old outhouse.

The rest of the day passed pleasantly in a procession of small physical tasks, and Fran's thoughts were little troubled by the future of her job. On the contrary, warmed by her conversation with her husband, and kept company in the garden as she was by feathered parents busy feeding their young fledglings, her thoughts turned first to Sam and her suspected pregnancy, and then before she knew it, seamlessly, to images of herself with child. In fact, so stealthy was the progression of these pleasant, idle thoughts that, in her mind, she was standing in her kitchen helping her firstborn bake a cake for its fifth birthday and wiping flour from is dear little nose, before she caught on to herself and left off her hoeing in confusion. But after a couple of moments of complete surprise a feeling of absolute clarity took its place, and everything at last made sense. For hadn't this been her master plan, forged so long ago? To find the right man, to build the nest, and then to fill it? The right man was indubitably found, the nest was built. The time was ripe and, at thirty-five, so was Fran.

Seven

Later, thinking back, Fran came to see that Sunday as her last-ever moment of happiness, but, human nature being what it is, at the time she just took it for granted and assumed more would be coming her way. With the benefit of hindsight and searing experience, when she wasn't busy blaming herself bitterly for not seeing Doom bearing down on her with a capital D, she came to demand of herself why she hadn't savoured every moment of that day while happiness had still been available. She vowed, once it was lost to her, that if ever happiness should stray across her path again she would seize it in her arms and hug it to her for as long as possible, nurturing it, feeding it, making it feel appreciated and welcome. Never again would she blithely assume it was her due.

On Monday morning, still thinking of babies (and the fun she would soon have getting pregnant) she arrived at work to find Ben, in his role of Creative Director, calling his troops together to announce there was a new client, to cheers of relief all round. The great shock for Fran, however, as she gathered up her notebook and pens to join them, was that, once again, she was not chosen to be among their number.

'Er – not you, Fran,' Ben told her, as she and Willie were just about to go through the door of the conference room where they were to gather for the briefing. 'I really can't spare you from writing the direct mail copy just now. I know, I know,' he continued, seeing the look of fury on her face, and chancing a bit of flattery to smooth the way, 'but you've only got yourself to blame. You're absolutely the best we've got. Nobody sells financial products like you.'

Fran glared at him in fury, then turned to Willie. 'Sorry – you seem to be on the losing team with me,' she said, her cheeks colouring, embarrassed for this to be happening in front of all the boys who were now taking their seats at the conference table.

'Actually, no,' Ben continued blithely. 'Come through, Wills.'

With a hapless shrug and apologetic smile at Fran, her erstwhile partner joined his confrères, leaving Fran completely exposed as the solitary unwanted guest. All eyes were on her.

'You won't mind working alone for a few weeks, will you, Fran?' Ben asked, as if he cared; not waiting for an answer, he closed the door.

In a daze, Fran turned slowly and walked back to her office, running the gauntlet of the sympathetic looks from the juniors in reception, which only made her feel worse. She sat at her desk alone, stunned beyond words, working her way slowly through a spectrum of emotions which ranged from red-blooded vengeance to pale abject misery. What to do? How could she turn this around? And how could she remain here, always overlooked, watching the rise and rise of boys such as Wills? In a nutshell, she could not. Her hand reached for the phone to call Allie.

'He's dumped me,' she said, cutting to the chase, dispensing with such formalities as hellos.

'Paul?!' asked Allie in astonishment, recognising her desolate friend's voice at once.

'Of course not!' Fran snapped. 'Ben. He's kept me on direct mail. It's boys only for this new effing contract of yours, apparently, whatever the hell it is.'

'But he can't have – that's absurd!' said Allie. 'The new effing contract, as you have it, is for baby clothes for God's sake! That's why I was so confident he'd use you.'

'Well there you go,' said Fran bleakly, but nevertheless, an appealing solution now started to form in her mind, making her deaf to Allie's words of condolence.

'I'm leaving,' she said, suddenly and decisively, interrupting Allie mid-flow, and, phone still in hand, she started emptying her desk into her bag.

'You're what? Don't be ridiculous! Without first finding another job?' protested Allie. 'You're crazy. Wait a while, calm down, think this through . . .'

'I have. I'm finished. It all suddenly makes sense,' Fran said, her voice now sounding energised and determined. 'I would have left anyway, in a few months. This just makes it all happen a bit quicker, that's all. Not a problem – it'll give me time to sort things out.'

'Sort what out?'

'I'm going to have a baby.'

'You're pregnant?!'

'Not yet, but I will be soon.'

'You're giving up your job to fuck full-time?' said Allie incredulously. Even to the likes of her, that sounded a mite extreme.

Fran laughed, excited now by the idea of how her life was about to change. 'You see, put like that it sounds fun, doesn't it? Anyway, enough of me. How about you? Did you break down and get serviced by your mechanic on the way back home, as promised?'

'No I didn't,' said Allie. 'And don't change the subject. What will you do for cash?'

'Paul's business couldn't be doing better,' Fran answered blithely. 'He can keep us for a while. And I hate this job. I never meant to stay in it forever, even when I quite liked it. I've got an unfinished novel I'd like to go back to, and I can tout round for some freelance stuff – articles for magazines, maybe, or the Little Langton local rag, come to that.'

'Fine,' said Allie. 'In due course, terrific. But plan first, get

some commissions while you're still drawing your salary. Apart
from anything else you'll go out of your mind with boredom on
the second day at home.'

'Not me,' said Fran giddily. 'I shall be in pig heaven. Speak
later. I'm out of here.'

'Wait – don't move – I'm coming down!' Allie shouted into
the receiver, and hanging up, she raced for the lift.

Feeling more fully alive and in control than she had in ages,
Fran took great pleasure in writing the succinct copy for her
letter of resignation, which took the form of a Post-it note stuck
onto Ben's office door. It said merely, 'Ben – Up yours. Best,
Fran.' For a final flourish, she scattered the whole of reception
with an armful of her direct mail paperwork, to the amazement
of the receptionist and the junior account execs.

'Can't get much more direct than that,' she said to them,
flushed and grinning. 'See you!'

Out in the hallway, the lift which she had called to take her
away disgorged Allie, who barred her escape. 'I can't allow you
to do this,' she said, still panting from her speedy arrival. 'Not
until we've talked things through.'

'Okay,' said Fran, pushing past her to join her in the lift.
'You've got two floors to give me three reasons to stay.' She
pressed the button for the ground floor, and folded her arms in
anticipation.

'One,' said Allie, 'money. You simply cannot live off a man –
it's too dangerous. What if Paul were to leave you?'

'He won't,' Fran said firmly. 'He loves me to bits, and we're
going to make babies.'

Allie rolled her eyes in despair. 'Haven't we both learnt to our
cost how fragile love can be?'

'Things are different now. I'm sure of Paul.'

'Fine. I just hope that continues to be the case,' warned Allie.
'So, two – self-respect.'

'What – I'd have greater respect for myself if I stayed here for more abuse? I don't think so,' rejoined Fran, enjoying herself now. 'And three? Oh – too bad, we're here,' she said, as the doors opened to the ground floor and she walked, exultant, out of the lift for the last time.

Allie followed her, accepting defeat. 'You're absolutely sure about this?'

'I've never been surer of anything in my life,' Fran grinned. 'Already I feel better than I've felt in years.' The lift having disappeared immediately again on its upward journey, she pressed the button to summon its return for Allie.

'Where has this baby thing come from all of a sudden?' asked Allie.

'I'm thirty-five, I'm hardly being impetuous. And I've always wanted children, you know that – that was one of the reasons I wanted to move out of town, and chose that house. I just got side-tracked doing it up, and it stopped being at the forefront of my mind. Till Saturday night when Sam said she might be pregnant, I suppose.'

'Any news from her?'

'Not yet. I mean you're right, if I could have borne staying on here a while longer, it would undoubtedly have been better, but as things stand I'd be doing myself a disservice, coming in here every day to be insulted. Surely you can see that?'

'Mm,' said Allie, although at that moment it was clear that she could not see much besides the very pretty youth in overalls who had just entered from the street and was making his way over to the lift.

'Are you thinking mechanical failure?' Fran asked her impishly.

'Mm,' said Allie again. The lift arrived and the doors opened, and she turned to smile at him warmly. 'Going up?' she asked in mock innocence, for Fran's amusement.

He nodded his assent, returning her smile, and together they got in.

'Wouldn't it be terrible if the lift were to get stuck?' teased Fran, as the doors started to close on her beaming friend.

'Simply dreadful,' agreed Allie, and winked broadly before she disappeared from view.

Left alone in the foyer, Fran looked for the last time at the place which had been her home for the whole of her working life, and breathed a deep sigh of relief. She was getting out! It was nothing short of a miracle. She felt almost giddy with elation, as if she had just got a job rather than that she was walking away from one. She glanced at her watch, thinking about times of trains home to Little Langton, then, realising it was still so early and that she had the whole day at her disposal to do with what she wished, she thought shopping might be good. She must start researching nursery furniture and baby clothes, and buy books on how to bring up children wisely. And since, in future, she wouldn't be visiting London quite as often as she had, she should take advantage of being in town for the day and begin immediately. She turned from the lift and crossed the foyer to the front doors and to her great escape, eagerly planning her shopping route and making mental lists.

Which was how she didn't come to notice that the light on Allie's ascending lift indicated that, after a brief sojourn at the mezzanine, it had stopped around the third floor and wasn't budging.

Eight

The next day, Archie, incurious and phlegmatic as ever, merely nodded when Fran told him she was taking some time off work – she couldn't face telling him the whole story – and handed her a chisel and a wire brush. Since she was at home she could help with the herringbone project, and while Archie broke up the old concrete path to make way for the new, Fran sat beside the huge pile of Jack Blackmore's bricks which had been dumped in her garden, to chisel off the mortar and clean them up for reuse.

After having been buried alive in the slipperiness of words for a decade and a half, floundering after the right adjective, searching through the thick mists in her mind for the pieces of the jigsaw which would make the perfect selling phrase, there was great satisfaction in this physical labour, and she felt she was indeed, as she had prophesied she would be to Allie, in pig heaven. It was so simple, to take up a brick from one pile, to chip away at it and scrub its face, and to put it down, clean and perfect, in another. Sitting between two stacks of bricks on the third day, chisel in hand, the new pile growing neatly while the chaos of the other came steadily under her control, she felt she was as content as she had ever been. How wonderful it was to be able to look at the fruits of one's labours and see immediately what one had achieved in a day. How deeply satisfying to know at once whether one had done a good job. The brick was either still dirty, or now clean. There was no endless self-criticism and interminable repolishing, no nervous waiting to see if the client approved – just one brick after another, taken up and worked on, passing from the jumble at her left side to the order on her right.

And with one's body engaged in physical labour, one's mind was free to wander pleasantly, flitting from place to place with all the lightness of a butterfly, unfettered by responsibility, without fear of being chided for lack of productivity. When had she last allowed herself the unalloyed joy of letting thoughts pop into her mind, she asked herself, to circle round lazily, and then go straight out again if they lost their appeal? Wasn't this what the mystics called karma yoga, distracting the mind by *doing* instead of *thinking*? Ah yes, the dignity of labour, the majesty of honest toil . . .

She was kidding herself of course. The thoughts which mainly popped into her mind were all about the injustice at work, her hatred of Ben, her fury at Willie, her outrage at having been insulted and passed over again and again; and none of these thoughts 'circled lazily', but sat and festered, boiling within her, erupting onto her face in a rather nasty rash of spots. She was still too stunned to tout for the freelance work she had talked to Allie about, and her self-confidence was at rock bottom. (Or so she thought. There was, alas, still worse to come.) She felt, in her current state, that she could no sooner present herself at the offices of *Little Langton & Greater Thrapsford Clarion* than she could telephone the features editor of the *Guardian* and demand a three-page spread in the weekend section.

Allie, the only friend who knew what she had done, had since been curiously silent, and Fran was in no hurry to call her just now, to hear again that she had made a mistake. And she had told no one yet about her impulsive departure from her job – not Paul, not her mother, not Sam. She wanted to get her story straight in her mind before she shared it. She knew they would understand her anger, but she doubted whether any of them would approve of her impulsive reaction. Perhaps she *had* been too hasty? But whenever that thought entered the arena she immediately showed it back to the door, rapidly replacing it with images of nursing a newborn baby, exhausted but complete, gazed on proudly by Paul, or of pushing a pram through the village, stopping every few yards to be congratulated and for her baby to be admired.

Come to that, she thought, she would probably be pushing her baby side by side with Sam, the two of them sailing down the pavements of Little Langton like an armada of motherhood, discussing such pitfalls as nappy rash and colic, and the terrors of the medieval-sounding croup (Fran had of course already started frightening herself with the baby books she had bought on her shopping jaunt in town). So she was ill-prepared for Sam's dramatic, unannounced arrival that Wednesday night, and the news she had to impart.

'I'm not!' were Sam's first words, delivered on Fran's doorstep at eleven fifteen, washed up on a spring tide of tears, and Fran, already befuddled by sleep after another hard day's labour, just stood in her pyjamas and stared.

'Not . . . ?' she asked after a moment, rubbing the sleep from her eyes, her wits scrambling into emergency mode for the call to action stations.

'No,' Sam sobbed, and not waiting for an invitation she pushed her way past Fran into the living room, knocking over the umbrella stand as usual and upending a potted palm.

'Leave it,' Fran told her, not altogether generously, since she feared worse mess would result from Sam's frantic scrabbling at the soil on the rug while wailing about her clumsiness. 'It really couldn't matter less. Sit down. Have a tissue. Tell me what on earth's been going on. Brandy?'

Whether Sam wanted one or not, the idea seemed suddenly appealing to Fran. 'Brandy,' she said decisively. Diving at the sideboard she found the bottle and two glasses, which she quickly filled, and which were just as swiftly emptied – Fran's down her throat, Sam's down her front.

'Not to worry,' Fran soothed her, dabbing at Sam's jumper with a tissue already sodden in tears. 'Plenty more where that came from. Now what's all this about?'

What is was about was that Sam's pregnancy had apparently been more real in her imagination than in her womb. Her period had come that evening, completely out of the blue, as she was sitting watching television, knitting tiny yellow bootees.

'It wasn't a miscarriage?' Fran checked, starting to get alarmed about her own fecundity and the massive gamble she had taken on proving to be effortlessly fertile herself. But no, said Sam, it was just the normal period, abnormally ten days late. And when she thought about it, and if she was totally honest, it wasn't all that uncommon in fact. Her body had often reacted like this in the past when she was under a great deal of stress.

'The stress being in this instance . . . ?' Fran asked, unaware that there had been any pressure in Sam's life recently, except, of course, for the usual.

'Nigel,' Sam supplied, practically spitting the name, finishing Fran's unspoken thought.

'Okay,' said Fran, trying not to sigh and not to glance at the clock. 'What's the problem now?' She bent forward to grab the brandy bottle to recharge their glasses; they were obviously in for the long haul. 'Look – I'm going to pour you another cognac, and I'm going to leave it here on the table. When you want some, tell me, and I'll feed it to you myself.'

'I want some,' said Sam immediately, and Fran brought the glass to her lips as one would to a baby, wiping away the dribbles when she'd done.

'So,' said Fran, settling back into the cushions to listen to her bedtime story, nursing her own glass. 'What's new?'

'Nothing really,' Sam admitted, taking a deep breath. 'Nothing different from the norm. It's just – I don't know – lately I've been thinking about Christmas.'

'In June?' asked Fran, willing to follow the plot if she could.

'Yes, in June!' Sam retorted, as waspishly as Fran had ever heard her. 'You couldn't know, being married – it's easy for you, you don't have to make plans in advance. I suppose you just sail blithely up to Christmas week, and the biggest decision you have to take is "goose or duck?". It isn't like that when you're single. And holidays are the same. You aren't tortured with wondering, "Who will I go with, where shall I go?" Last summer holiday I went to a health farm, even though I didn't need to lose weight – by the time I got there I'd already lost it with the worry about going alone. And last Christmas I just spent on my own, indoors, watching telly and eating Marks and Sparks pre-made pudding from its plastic cooking bowl.'

'I invited you here!' protested Fran. 'You said you were going off to your mother's, and afterwards you told me what a jolly time you'd had!'

'I know,' said Sam, shame-faced. 'I lied. I didn't come here because I couldn't face watching another couple play happy families, knowing that Nigel was doing exactly that in his own home with his wife and children. And I didn't go to my mother's because I couldn't bear to hear all my aunties and my grandma and my mother's neighbours and, let's face it, the family dog, ask me yet again when I'm going to find a man and settle down.'

'I see,' said Fran, feeling guilty now for her own connubial bliss. Never had she heard Sam utter such an angry outburst, nor heard her complain as bitterly as she was doing now. Clearly, she thought, Sam's outward, sunny nature – which Fran had never thought to question – was kept in place at some considerable internal cost. What else did she not know about her friend's true feelings? And almost worse – how now was she to tell her about her own plans to increase the size of her apparently accursed 'happy family'?

'More brandy?' she asked, at a loss to know what to say, and Sam nodded glumly, looking up at her with huge tear-filled eyes.

'I'm sorry,' said Sam, coughing as the burning liquid bit her throat. 'I'm being horrible.'

'Not at all,' said Fran gallantly. 'I can quite understand, and you should have felt able to tell me all this before. If you felt you couldn't, then that was my fault, and I should apologise to you.'

Sam rewarded her with a warm and instant smile, looking much more like her normal self. 'You're a good friend,' she said, hugging her. 'I don't know how I used to manage before you moved here. All my old friends are married and have kids, and hanging around them, I just used to feel such a failure. You're right – I should have taken you up on your offer of having Christmas dinner with you and Paul. It's lovely seeing the two of you so happy together, and unspeakably churlish of me to resent it.'

Fran returned her smile, feeling more than a little uncomfortable about her own secret plans. 'So how did Nigel take the news that he was off the hook?' she asked, to deflect the conversation away from herself.

'Oh, he was *delighted* of course!' said Sam, her happy face again transformed for the worse by anger. 'He's so *ecstatic* with *relief* he even promised me a *weekend away* in a couple of weeks, which is practically *unheard* of, because it's really *difficult* for him to organise, what with his *family commitments*. And he reckons he'll see me this Saturday night. At *my* house, of course, *behind closed curtains*, tucked away out of sight, for which I'm expected to be *overwhelmed* with *gratitude*! We hardly *ever* go *out* together, for fear of being *seen*,' she continued spitefully, spitting the words so venomously that mere italics can only hint at their murderous toxicity.

'You don't think that now might be the time to call it off?' asked Fran tentatively. 'Since he's evidently never going to change his mind?'

'I was going to if he insisted on me having an abortion. I decided on the night of the fair. I'd made my mind up to finish it.' The wind went out of Sam's sails immediately, and her shoulders sagged, defeated. 'I should, shouldn't I? I should call it a day.'

'We-ell,' said Fran with hope in her voice, but she couldn't bring herself to be so brutal as to jump on this suggestion with the outright, unqualified approval she felt. 'You did say it's been going on for seven years, and if he hasn't changed his mind in all that time . . .'

'Seven years,' echoed Sam. 'He's had the best years of my life. I was only twenty-seven when I met him! How could I find another man at my age now?'

'Thirty-four is hardly—'

'Dead,' supplied Sam. 'Finished. Over the hill. Past my sell-by. Dried up and useless. Unwanted goods.'

'Thirty-four!' repeated Fran, louder now, with outrage in her voice, since she was thirty-five. 'It's nothing! No age! You're in the prime of your life! Any man would have you, and think himself blessed! You're attractive – lovely, in fact – great figure, nice hair, wonderful personality—' She was silenced by Sam's look, which was somewhere between pity and contempt. 'What?' she asked after a moment of being thus contemplated.

'You haven't been out there for a while, have you?' Sam challenged her.

'Out where? What, out looking for a man?' Sam nodded. 'Well no, obviously, not since I met Paul,' Fran conceded, 'but that wasn't *so* long ago.'

'How long ago?'

'Just a few years. I was coming up to thirty when we started dating.'

'Twenty-nine,' said Sam, as if this proved her point. 'More brandy, please.'

Replenishing their glasses, and helping Sam to hers, Fran was not about to give up. 'You're not saying, surely, that a woman in her thirties has no chance of finding a man?' she challenged her, tipping rather too much brandy into her friend's mouth in her annoyance.

'You have *heard* of Bridget Jones, have you?' asked Sam with uncharacteristic sarcasm, emboldened, no doubt, by the cognac.

'Yes, and she got her man in the end.'

'Oh, that was in a book!' Sam scoffed. 'She had to have a happy ending. It isn't like that in life. Look around you, open your eyes! Men prefer their women young! And you and I, in our mid-thirties, only seem young to fifty-plus men now!'

Fran felt herself bridle at being included in such a group of losers, but couldn't say so for fear of being cruel to her friend. *She* wouldn't have any trouble getting a man her own age, she was sure. She'd always only had to look at a guy she fancied to get him scurrying over to her side, eager to please. She took another swallow of brandy and pursed her lips.

'I suppose, to be fair, it's all to do with primal instincts and survival of the fittest,' Sam continued, going down her well-worn track of rationalising the unpalatable. 'A fundamental urge to procreate with the youngest and most promisingly robust and fertile-looking females in the herd. They probably can't help themselves, don't even stop to think how insulting it is to women their own age. And of course, there aren't many of them around. By the time they're in their mid-thirties, all the best ones have already been snaffled up – they're married with children, like Nigel.'

'And how old is Nigel now?'

'Forty. Which is still considered young for a man, of course. He'll probably be thinking of trading me in soon for a younger model.'

'So pre-empt him – finish with him first,' said Fran, stifling a yawn. It wasn't the first time she had recommended this course of action.

'I might,' said Sam, sticking out her chin defiantly.

'So do it.'

'Mm,' said Sam, shutting down the cranial pathways which would lead her to good sense, and flitting back into la-la land. 'What are you and Paul doing on Saturday night – he's back on Friday, isn't he?'

'Yes,' said Fran. 'I don't know. Haven't made any plans in case he's knackered, or got loads of work to do after his trip.'

'Terrific!' Sam returned, cheering. 'Why don't you come to me and let me cook you both supper?'

'Well, that would be lovely, but didn't you say you were seeing Nigel on Saturday night? Or are you going to tell him to stuff it?' Fran asked optimistically.

'I might jolly well do exactly that,' Sam threatened bravely.

Fran checked once again, to be absolutely sure. 'So it'll be just us and you?' Though she had never met Nigel, never laid eyes on him in fact, she knew she didn't want to spend an evening in his company. What kind of a man ratted on his wife and children for seven years, and tried to force abortion on his mistress? Not the kind she would want to break bread with, certainly.

Sam smiled brightly. 'Shall we say seven thirty for eight?'

Fran nodded, trying to look pleased. After not seeing Paul for so long she would have liked to snuggle up with him for the whole weekend, popping out of the bedroom only as far as the kitchen to take on more supplies, but if Sam was really going to finish with Nigel, she would need some moral support. 'Sure,' she said generously. 'Seven thirty it is.'

'Wonderful!' said Sam. 'I hardly ever entertain, what fun! But enough of me,' she continued brightly. 'How are you? Have you been off sick? Josie Bradshaw told me she'd seen you in your garden yesterday when surely you should have been at work?'

This was certainly the downside of living in a small community, thought Fran: the jungle tom-toms beat you to it every time.

'Actually, I quit,' she admitted.

'You're *kidding*!' Sam exclaimed, pouncing on this new bit of gossip to further deflect attention away from herself. 'How exciting! Have you been head-hunted? What's the new job?'

'There isn't one,' Fran admitted. 'As yet. I'm reviewing my options,' she hedged, 'thinking things through. Taking a break to reassess.'

'I see,' said Sam. 'Well – good for you! You haven't been happy there for some time now. What are you thinking of doing instead? Something allied, or are you thinking of retraining? Lots of people our age do.'

Fran had had enough for one night of being made aware that the road to maturity for a woman ended in a cul de sac in her thirties. All this talk merely confirmed her view that it was high time she started planning to have babies before it was too late and she really was 'dried up and useless' as Sam had inaccurately described herself. But now obviously wasn't the time to share her news with Sam, however annoying she was being.

'I'm not sure,' she said finally. 'I might do a short course in creative writing. I used to want to be a novelist when I was at uni – this advertising lark was only ever meant to be temporary, to get some money behind me before I made a start.'

'Gosh, yes!' said Sam enthusiastically. 'You could be our own Joanna Trollope, writing up our village lives!'

'Mm,' said Fran, now taking her turn at not wanting the jolt of reality to disturb her pleasant, and perhaps impractical, fantasies. What if she had no talent? She hadn't even looked at her old half-started novel yet this week, and that was most likely because she already feared the worst about her creative writing skills. 'Anyway,' she continued firmly, '*anything* will be a blessed change from that wretched office and those awful boys. Even if I had to go out cleaning for a living I'd have more self-respect and more job satisfaction than I've had in ages!'

She laughed, not realising at that moment that she would live long enough, even at her advanced age, to have those words come back to haunt her.

Nine

At last it was Friday, and Paul was coming home. And this was auspicious, since Fridays were sacrosanct in their relationship. Along with their wedding vows, they had also promised each other at the beginning of their commitment always to spend Friday evenings at home, no matter what, to talk over anything which might have arisen in the week. As Fran had told Sam on the night of the fair, they had both learnt from their earlier marriages that effective communication was the key to a healthy relationship, and so they had both sworn that nothing should be swept under the carpet if there was the remotest chance that it might re-emerge later to cause trouble.

It had been hard at first, both of them having been used to choking resentments down and bottling anger up, but they had stuck at it, and, in the early days, learnt much about each other and themselves which had profited them both. They had swapped stories of their childhoods, told each other of their terrors, shared their worst moments, warned each other of their fears, confided their wildest hopes. Gradually, as they gained confidence in the process, they had also dared to voice their complaints of each other's behaviour, to listen without interrupting, to acknowledge the other's concern even when it did not accord with their own view, and to reassure and accommodate new ideas. In this way, uncomfortable and embarrassing subjects had come under their joint scrutiny and, no matter how much they might have dreaded mentioning them, had been dealt with kindly. And because of this effective and regular cleansing,

as time had rolled by there was less and less to fear from a Friday
night in and more and more to look forward to. For, lately, they
had initiated a new codicil to their rules of engagement.

They had always had a fabulous dinner, which they took turns
to cook, and they had always made an effort to dress up – this
had been decided at the start. If they were to take each other seriously and keep their love alive, they had felt, they should
formalise the proceedings with elegant ritual for fear of sliding
into companionable TV dinners on the couch (which is what
Fran felt, among other things, had sown the seeds of destruction
for her first marriage), or wearing baggy joggers and towelling
socks (which Paul had found to his cost to be the giddy limit to
his former connubial bliss). So, for the last several months, if
there was nothing cataclysmic that either needed to discuss (and
nowadays this was usually the case), they dressed attractively,
fed magnificently, flirted outrageously, and afterwards they
made love.

Rising early on this particular Friday morning to make a shopping list for the evening's feast, which was her turn to cook, just
thinking of the lovemaking to come made Fran feel weak at the
knees. For this time, as nice as it always was, it wouldn't be just
a matter of having sex for mutual gratification or selfish lust.
This time it would be made all the sweeter by its primary
purpose of begetting a baby. It would be like starting all over
again.

Finding to her amusement that she had been absent-mindedly
humming Madonna's 'Like a Virgin' as she was going out to her
car to drive to the shops, the smile was swiped almost immediately from her face by the arrival of another car in her driveway,
and was replaced with a long-suffering sigh. It was her mother,
Rachel, turning up, as always, out of the blue, pursued by whatever demon she had invented to torment her, and arriving at the
very worst time.

'Darling!' she cried through her open car window, 'Thank

God you're in! I was dreading you might already have gone off to work.'

Well, that'll be the first bone of contention, thought Fran wearily, my job – or lack of it. For as much as she had found with Paul that things were the better for being openly and honestly discussed, with her mother she had discovered the exact opposite. Rachel's crises were best managed with large doses of light inconsequential talk from Fran's side and a keeping of her own counsel. She had long ago stopped trying to get kindly maternal advice from her, learning to her cost on countless occasions that with her mother, contrary to the old axiom, a problem shared was a problem doubled.

'What a – lovely surprise,' she offered mendaciously, swiftly rearranging her features into a welcoming smile. 'Come in. I was just about to make coffee. I'm – working from home today.'

'I'm not keeping you?' Rachel wherrited, climbing out of her car nonetheless and following Fran back into the house. 'You're sure I'm not in the way? Not stopping you getting on with something more important? Because I could go, and come back later if I'm holding you up. I know you're always busy,' she added, in a hurt and complaining tone, which was pretty rich, thought Fran crossly, since she had never, ever failed to drop whatever she was doing the very moment her mother demanded her attention. There was always the worry at the back of her mind that this time it might be serious, even though all other occasions had proved to be the false alarms of a woman born to be a martyr.

'Not at all,' she murmured in return through clenched teeth aching from duplicity, and she returned her shopping bag to its hook and took the kettle to the tap.

'This parlour palm looked an awful lot healthier when I gave it to you,' Rachel complained, returning from the living room where she had strayed, and breaking off the one dead frond which Fran had been too busy to notice since its fateful collision with Sam. 'But of course, the way you and Paul overheat your house, I suppose that's hardly a surprise. You poor thing. Aren't you?' she crooned to the plant, in a tone far more sympathetic than any she ever employed for her daughter.

Fran bit back an acid remark, and decided to get down to the nitty-gritty at once. If she were to be able to accomplish her over-ambitious plans for this evening's feast, she would need to get this over in half the time that it usually took. 'How are you?' she asked, wilfully turning the key in the floodgates and bracing herself for the deluge which would now gush forth.

'Dreadful,' her mother obliged her at once. 'Quite frankly, at my wits' end with worry. I've been turning it over and over, and I can't come up with a solution. I've hardly slept in days.'

'Oh dear,' said Fran soothingly, on automatic pilot since, in her experience, she knew there would be quite a lot of this wittering before Rachel would cut to the chase. 'Hot milk, or cold?' she enquired politely as she filled the cafetière, never suspecting for a moment that such an innocent question could touch the very core of Rachel's current distress.

'Milk?!' her mother retorted, as panicked as if she'd been asked whether she'd care for poison in her coffee. 'No milk at all! Black, I'll take it black! I'm back on the cabbage soup diet for my sins. Which is what this is all about, of course, and why I'm now in such a state.'

'Right,' said Fran, bewildered. 'No sugar then, I take it?'

'Oh, if you insist, just a spoonful,' sighed Rachel.

Stirring sugar into the black coffee, Fran didn't even bother to wonder what pleasure her mother imagined it might give her to be doing so, but merely waited with dread for her story to unfold. For now she knew Rachel was on another diet, she also knew that her stepfather would somehow be involved, and she always felt uncomfortable about acting as her mother's marriage guidance counsellor – a role which had been thrust upon her since her own father had left for the office one day when Fran was still at primary school, and failed to return.

'He complains that my dress is too tight to fasten, and then he goes and organises this,' Rachel complained, ever unfairly persecuted, not even bothering to mention her current husband by his name. 'And I swear I hadn't put on an ounce anyway. He was just being clumsy as usual, and broke the zip by being too rough. Of course, *he* can never be in the wrong.'

Which makes two of you, thought Fran. Or four, if we include Daddy and the awful creep you married and divorced on the rebound, post-Dad, pre-Roger.

'So when I told him off for ruining my favourite frock – he didn't just break the zip, he actually tore the material too! – he has to let himself off the hook by accusing *me* of being to blame, for being too fat!'

'Which is ridiculous,' supplied Fran, because it was. Anyone in their right mind would look at Rachel and agree that a whippet carried more excess flesh.

'Thank you, darling,' smiled Rachel, appeased for a moment, both by her daughter's support and the inrush of sugar to her system, which always cheered her. This was a woman who could eat and drink exactly what she wanted, anxiety crunching up the calories and keeping her slim, where others needed treadmills and diets. 'But nevertheless, if Roger says I'm fat, then fat I must be,' she continued in a long-suffering and satisfied tone.

'So . . . ?' Fran prompted her, for fear her mother would now stray to one of her other favourite subjects – the fact that Fran had put on weight since she had been so happily married to Paul. Over the years, she had had all the dire warnings from Rachel that she could take about letting herself go to seed. 'He says you're fat, you go on a diet, and . . . ?'

'And he invites the Harrisons for supper tomorrow!' Rachel proclaimed in outrage, practically glowing with oppression and abuse.

'The Harrisons,' echoed Fran, none the wiser.

'Bernard and Cecily Harrison. They're gourmands!

Epicureans! Gastronomes! And she is a cordon bleu cook!'

'I see,' said Fran, relaxing at last. The usual fuss about nothing, then. And of course it was. What could be more devastating to her mother's peace of mind in her uneventful life, what else could require such immediate filial attention and sympathy? Rachel was here to agonise over recipes, not death, not destruction, not divorce. No matter that her daughter was facing *real* drama at this moment, that she had left her job because of the continued abuse she had been suffering at work, that she was being forced to re-examine her life and rebuild it, that she was about to throw herself on her husband's financial generosity . . . Rachel's imagined crisis must come first. And would she, Fran – for she was mature enough to acknowledge that it took two to tango, and she could not ignore her own part in this ridiculous one-sided continuum – would she never learn that, whatever she feared her mother might cry one dreaded day, to date it had only ever been 'Wolf!'?

Her justified anger, however, was somewhat mollified by how easy it would be to deal with this present drama, and after they had consulted Delia and Madhur and Jamie for flashy but non-fattening dishes, Rachel was soon packed happily back into her car with merry waves and grateful kisses. And, it being an ill wind, Fran had also managed while sorting out her mother's menu for the next day to refine her own for that evening. Where she had been going to serve the aphrodisiac oysters *cru* with a little Tabasco on the side, she was now going to coddle them in eggs and stock and serve them as *chawanmushi*; the fillet of lamb would now be daubed with a *duxelles* and served *en croûte*; and instead of the planned three-kinds-of-chocolate mousse, she'd be damned if she'd duck out of the challenge of Grand Marnier soufflé suprême.

She smiled and hummed all the way to the shops and back and on her return, as she weighed this and blended that, kneaded dough (she'd even decided to make her own poppyseed rolls) got out the best linen and polished the silverware and crystal in preparation for her feast of seduction, she looked through the kitchen window at the gorgeous new herringbone path which Archie had now begun, and pictured her husband's home-coming.

She'd be wearing her black dress when he came through the door, the one with the plunging neckline which never failed to arouse him, and, as a tease, she wouldn't even let him kiss her until he had been upstairs to shower and shave and change into his evening suit. When he came down again, looking gorgeous, smelling sublime, he would be led by the passionate chords of Rachmaninov out onto the terrace, lit by candles, where she'd be waiting, champagne flutes in hand. She'd kiss him then, and together they would sway to the music, his arms around her, his face nuzzling at her neck. Impatient for what came next, even in her imagination, she rushed them through the meal at the flower-bedecked table in the dining room in a series of rapid mental snapshots as he saw each dainty dish she had made for his pleasure: the *chawanmushi* brought his incredulous delight, with its subtle flavours and silky mix of textures on the tongue; the lamb *en croûte*, glazed with egg and decorated with pastry letters which read 'Eat Me' had him smiling naughtily at her with thoughts of how he'd like to do exactly that right here and now; and when she brought in the soufflé, perfectly risen, light as a feather, oozing with the flavours of vanilla and orange liqueur, he was quite overwhelmed. Now she was ready to tell him her plans as they sat gazing at each other with loving eyes across the length of the table, sipping Cointreau from iced glasses. 'Time to make babies,' she said, and smiled at him, as one of the thin fragile straps of her dress slipped down her arm. He was on his feet in a trice, unable to wait any longer, picking her up in his arms, wordlessly carrying her upstairs . . .

A phlegmy cough at the door brought her back to the here and now, making her jump. It was Archie, telling her he'd be on his way and would see her again on Monday. Heavens, if it was that time already, she needed to get a move on with the mushrooms. She laughed at her fantasy, romanticised as it was like a scene from a film, and dropped a dollop of butter in a cast-iron pan. Perhaps the reality wouldn't be quite as seamless as that, she thought, now feeling rather nervous about the soufflé, but at the very least, when he saw to what pains she had gone to prepare his homecoming feast on this Friday evening of evenings, her darling Paul would feel so spoilt rotten, he wouldn't know what had hit him.

Ten

Lying well over on her side of the bed, with Paul curled up and out for the count snoring softly behind her in the dark, Fran tried, without much success, not to feel deeply disappointed and resentful. It was hardly surprising he'd fallen asleep so early, she told herself, acting devil's advocate on his behalf – he'd looked absolutely shattered when he'd finally arrived home at a quarter to ten, having missed his intended flight. The dinner, of course, had been ruined, although not from any culinary fault of her own. She'd held off actually cooking the prepared dishes when he'd first phoned from Berlin to tell her he'd be late, and things still might have been retrieved. But when he'd come in, shattered, even later than he'd said, looking pale and overworked and fraught, all he'd wanted was a whisky and water and scrambled eggs on toast before falling into bed. To sleep.

Of course he was apologetic when she showed him all the trouble she had been to, but it still didn't make him any hungrier – for the feast, or for her. And it would have been silly to force him to appreciate oysters delicately poached in stock, cocooned in a savoury custard, when all he could face was a bog standard light snack and oblivion.

'Can't we have it tomorrow night?' he'd asked ruefully. 'It seems a shame for me to be falling asleep over such a fantastic spread, and I could really do it justice then.'

But of course they could not, Fran having already committed them both to dining at Sam's, at which news he'd groaned. 'I was hoping for some time on our own,' he'd said.

'No more than me, I suspect,' she'd replied tartly, sweeping the stove top of waiting saucepans and jamming sliced bread in the toaster for his blasted scrambled eggs. 'It's Friday night! Our night in! And there's so much I've been wanting to tell you.'

'Like what?' he'd asked, yawning, sipping his whisky and sitting down heavily at the kitchen table in his travel-worn suit, his hair looking greasy, a day's stubble showing dark on his chin.

'Doesn't matter. We'll talk about it in the morning,' she'd said, dumping his plate of eggs in front of him. She was unwilling to unburden herself, under these unromantic circumstances, of the tale of her hasty walkout from work, and her subsequent rationalisation of it into a scheme to start a family with him this very night. 'How were things for you?'

'Hectic,' he'd said, his eyelids drooping already with the effects of the Scotch. 'But productive, I hope.'

She'd been moved then, sufficient to make her rouse herself and change her mood to one of a more generous spirit. 'You look knackered,' she'd said, her hand covering his, and she'd kissed him affectionately on his cheek, the familiar smell of his skin going straight to her heart. 'Shall I run you a bath?' Even then she'd thought that all might not be lost, had allowed herself a brief fantasy of candles floating in the sink, their soft light reflected in the mirror, of aromatic oils scenting the water, of washing him so tenderly that he'd be overpowered by lust.

But, 'No thanks, I'd probably fall asleep and drown,' he'd quipped in a tired voice, and heaved himself to his feet. 'I'll just have a quick shower and turn in.' He'd plonked a kiss on the top of her head, and shuffled towards the stairs. 'Sorry, love. But I'm completely and utterly shagged.'

Which was more than Fran could say for herself, she thought with some irony, as she turned over, still wide awake, to lie on her back an hour later, aching with thwarted desire, and watched the moon disappear behind inky black clouds through the latticed window of their bedroom. True to his word, Paul had fallen fast asleep as soon as his head had hit the pillow, and no amount of tender touches, soft murmurs, winding of her limbs around his – nor indeed, frantic, frustrated squirming up against him followed by her whole tongue in his ear, which used to do the trick every time in their early days – had had any effect whatsoever. Letting out her tension in a heartfelt sigh, she rolled over on her side and snuggled up to his back, hoping that sleep would come to take her soon too. Tomorrow morning would be better, she told herself, think about that.

To cheer herself up while she waited to nod off, she pictured herself creeping softly down to the kitchen when she woke, and bringing back a tray of smoked salmon, cream cheese, and bagels to bed, with two glasses of the chilled champagne which was still biding its time in the fridge. How decadent! And they could stay in bed the whole day if they wanted to – they didn't have to be at Sam's until seven thirty. When was the last time they'd done that? She couldn't remember. The Christmas before last? The holiday in Greece? Heaven forfend that the romance should go out of their lives at their early age. They used to stay in bed for the better part of most Sundays before they were married. She felt herself getting aroused again at the thought, which certainly wasn't going to help her get off to sleep. She turned her attention firmly back to the breakfast tray, and had rearranged it several times in her imagination, having quite a tussle over the inclusion of chopped red onions (which Paul loved, but which would linger unappealingly on his breath) before she finally replaced them with cornichons and sun-dried tomatoes, and, thus satisfied, her busy mind slowly shut down and was reconciled to slumber, perchance to dream of the morrow. She'd wear her sexy black silk nightie, she decided sleepily. Or maybe the suspender belt Paul had bought her as a naughty joke last year, together with her Wonderbra? And high heels? Come in carrying a riding crop and play dominating games? Or more virginal, given the occasion? The white lace negligée, with nothing on underneath?

In the event, when she finally woke, exhausted, at nine thirty, it was to hear Paul calling her to join him downstairs. Dragging her towelling dressing gown on over the old T-shirt she had slept in, her face still creased from where she'd slept, her hair a mess, she finally found him outside on the terrace, fully dressed, having made them both bacon and egg sandwiches.

'Hi,' he said, already stuffing his into his mouth. 'You were out for the count. Did you come to bed late?'

'No, I followed you. Don't you remember? But I couldn't sleep. I was feeling a bit frisky, it being Friday night.'

He leant over to put his hand on hers. 'Yes, sorry about that, mate.'

'That's okay.' She smiled. 'There's always the rest of today.'

'Ah,' he said. 'Actually, I'm going to have to go into the office.'

'You're *kidding*!'

'Just for a few hours. There's so much to catch up on after having been away.'

'Can't Katie do it?' Katie was his PA. Rather attractive. Young. Big breasts. But apart from that, quite a nice girl.

'Not on her own. We talked about it on the plane back home, and agreed that we'd need to do it together.'

'Katie went with you?' Now this was news. She scanned his face for signs of guilt. She'd always had her doubts about Katie.

'I told you I was taking her, that I was going to move her up. She's a bright girl.'

'You said you were thinking about it.'

'Well, I thought about it, and she came. And a good thing too. There were too many meetings for me to handle on my own, so Katie covered some of them for me. Did a great job. We got a lot of interest. But now we need to follow it up, quickly, so we don't lose it. I want them all to open their e-mail first thing Monday morning and see our specs and quotes.' Paul's company,which he had started up only two years ago, was something to do with tailor-made computer software for businesses – Fran had given up trying to understand exactly what he sold some time ago, getting lost in acronyms and arcane language. She knew this trip had been a make-or-break kind of a do, and she knew too that he'd been thinking for some time of taking a partner.

'Have you made Katie a partner, then?'

'Not a full partner, no. But I've offered her a nice package, and she's taken it. We're going to interview potential new PAs this week. Which is another reason to get ahead of ourselves today.'

'Couldn't you do it tomorrow?' Fran pressed him, seeing all her plans go out of the window.

'Katie's got something on tomorrow, apparently.'

'Well, you've got something on today,' she countered, trying to sound alluring, but aware that, fresh out of bed and dressed as she was, she looked rather less than seductive.

'What – dinner at Sam's?' he said, chomping into his sandwich. 'Don't worry, I'll be back ages before that.'

'No. Servicing your wife.'

'Oh. Right,' he said, swallowing the last mouthful and swilling it down with coffee. He glanced at his watch and stood up, offering his arm, attempting a gallant smile. 'Well – I reckon I could be half an hour late.'

'Not quite what I'd had in mind,' she said, thoughts of passion completely deserting her. 'There's – some stuff I want to tell you first. We haven't had our Friday night debrief, remember.'

'Okay.' Paul sat down again, apparently to listen, but his energetic posture and jiggling foot weren't exactly conducive to sharing such delicate confidences. 'So what's up?'

Fran took a deep breath, and faltered. 'I feel a bit pressured like this, to be honest. I'd thought we'd have time to talk properly.'

Now Paul looked anxious. 'I'm sorry. What's happened? What's wrong?'

'Nothing, nothing. Well, things *have* happened,' said Fran, on her back foot, 'but nothing's wrong, as such.'

'So . . . ?'

'Oh, Paul – I can't do this now, like this. Go to work. Come back as soon as you can. We'll talk about it then.' She waved at him to go, and he stood up, but hovered, unwilling to leave it there. 'It's – something and nothing. Good news, really, I think. But I'd rather talk about it when we've got more time.'

'I could call Katie if you like,' he offered. 'See if she could come in tomorrow after all? It was only some wedding she had to go to, I think.'

Now Fran felt churlish. 'No, no, you can't ask her to do that. You go off and do what you have to do, and, if there's time, we'll have our chat before dinner with Sam. And I'm sorry, by the way, about arranging that for this evening without first talking to you. But she's finished with the grisly Nigel at long last – or said she was going to when she called round the other night.' They both raised their eyebrows in mutual acknowledgement at how often they'd heard that said. 'I know,' she continued, 'but this time she sounded serious. Things have been happening on that front too, while you were away. So I reckon she'll have done it, and be in need of our moral support.'

'That's okay. Poor old Sam. She's a lovely girl – she deserves better. Of course we'll go and cheer her up.'

'And less of the "old" tonight. She's decided she's over the hill,' Fran said, smiling now.

'At thirty – what is she – three?!' Paul laughed now. They were back on familiar ground and they'd both relaxed.

'Four, actually.'

'Oh, well, in that case, yes, I see what she means!' he joked.

'Will she be all right to do the cooking do you think, what with her Zimmer frame?'

'I expect she'll manage,' Fran smiled. She loved it that Paul was never less than sympathetic, and was completely comfortable with her female friends. Her first husband, Mike, had been a man's man, happier among his own kind at a football match or propping up a bar than discussing women's problems.

Paul bent to kiss her, and she smelt the spice of his aftershave. He looked so handsome this morning in his Levi's and polo shirt, the sunlight bouncing off his hair. She held on to him for a little too long, and could feel his anxiety to be off.

'I've really buggered up, haven't I?' he said, as she pulled away from him finally, suppressing a little sigh of longing. 'I'm really sorry about last night.'

'I'll get over it,' she said graciously. 'Now go ! Hurry! If you're not back by mid-afternoon *at the latest,* I shall come down to the office and take you right there, at your desk, Katie or no Katie!'

'I'll do my best,' he called, already hotfooting it round to the front.

Left alone in the back garden, listening to the sound of his car driving him away until it had faded completely and all she could hear was birdsong, she wondered how to fill the next few hours. Well, she needed to tidy up the kitchen from last night's aborted feast, freeze what could be frozen, chuck away the rest. And then? It was a lovely day. Too nice to waste indoors, if it were to be spent on her own. So. She could either clean up some more bricks for Archie, or finally face her insecurities and fetch down that old incomplete novel, bring it out of the darkness and into the sunshine to read . . .

No contest there then, she swiftly decided. Kitchen first, then bricks.

Hours later, wiping the sweat from her brow and sucking the thumb which she'd clouted with the mallet for the third time, she glanced at her watch. Impossible! It was already five o'clock, and still no sign of Paul. She stomped back up the garden to the house, angrily slapping mortar dust off her clothes as she walked, and punched his office number viciously into the kitchen phone to give him a piece of her mind. Enough was enough. She'd been as patient as she was prepared to be. So he was having a crisis of success. Big deal. She was having a crisis of being unemployed and having the creeping terrors that she'd acted rashly. She needed him, now. She needed to talk things over, she needed his reassurance that she'd done the right thing, and she needed his body in her bed, all before they went to Sam's in a couple of hours.

His office phone rang and rang, and was finally picked up by his machine. Katie's voice, purring politely to say that messages, if left, would be dealt with pronto. Fran froze, her mind racing anxiously, coming up with images she couldn't bear to view. What on *earth* was going on, and where could he be? Surely he wasn't bonking Katie? Was he? She checked herself, astonished at how quickly she was unravelling into the suspicious serially-cheated-on wife she'd been with her ex-husband Mike. Hadn't she prided herself, only a week ago, on how things had changed now she was with Paul? Of course he wasn't having an affair with Katie. He wasn't the type. After all, hadn't he suffered enough himself from his ex-wife Helen's faithlessness? Hadn't he and Fran bonded so quickly in their early days together because they had been helping each other recover from the hurt and rejection of being dumped? And hadn't they both sworn then that they could never, ever, hurt anybody as they had been hurt, by doing what had been done so cruelly to them?

Nevertheless, she'd call him on his mobile and find out where the hell he was. If that was switched to divert, then she'd – what? It didn't bear thinking about. Disintegrate? Rend her clothes, gnash her teeth? Die? She'd got herself into such a state now that she'd misdialled twice before, at one and the same time, his phone rang and she heard his car pull into the drive.

'Hi – I'm sorry, bloody computer crashed – I've just got home,' he said through the phone.

'I know,' she said. 'Okay.' How daft did she feel now? And how quickly she'd reverted to the sad tortured victim she'd once been! Ridiculous! She glanced up at the clock – there was still time – and caught her reflection in the kitchen window. Old work clothes covered in mortar, her hair like a haystack, dirt smeared across her face. Throwing down the phone, she raced upstairs to the bathroom, turned on the shower, stripped off her dusty clothes and, just as Paul's key turned in the front door, plunged herself under the hot spray.

'Hi!' she called out, quickly shampooing her hair, but what with the noise of the shower she wasn't sure if he'd heard. With a bit of luck he'd come up in a moment – preferably the moment when she'd got the blasted shampoo out of her blithering eyes. She tilted her head back and let the warm water run over her face, sighing with pleasure. Ah, this was nice. But there was one thing that would make it nicer. How long since she and Paul had showered together? Ages. When they had lived together in her London flat with its small immersion heater, they used to do it all the time. Where was he? She turned off the shower for a moment and cocked her head to listen for him.

'Hi-i!' she called again.

'Hi,' came the flat reply from downstairs.

Pissed off about the computer, by the sound of it. Perhaps not the best time then? But hey, what the hell, worth a shot . . .

Dripping soapy water across the bathroom floor, she went to the door. 'I'm having a shower,' she called down.

'Okay,' he called back, which was not the required response.

'What are you up to – want to join me?' she invited him, per-severing.

'No, it's all right – I'll have mine when you've finished, take your time.' He was in the kitchen, clattering about.

'Paul?'

'I'm getting a drink,' he said, sounding tetchy. 'Want one?'

'G and T,' she called finally, giving up on the idea of hanky panky in the shower. 'In the bedroom?' She waited for á moment for another response but there wasn't one, save for the sound of ice being cracked out of its tray and the chink of it being dropped into glasses.

Returning to the shower and switching it back on full blast, she found it had lost all its former sensuous appeal and was now merely an efficient way of getting clean. She decided to take her time anyway as instructed, hoping that in the meantime Paul's drink might help improve his mood. Bloody computers, breaking down and spoiling everything. God – she hoped that didn't mean he'd have to go in tomorrow as well. At this rate she'd be menopausal before she managed to get her husband's full attention!

She wound a towel round her wet hair, pulled on her bathrobe and went into the empty bedroom. 'Paul?' she called.

'Yes! Sorry, just coming,' he shouted back, still downstairs, still clattering about.

She toyed with the idea of stripping off and lying in a provocative pose on the bed, ready for his arrival, but just as quickly decided against it. In his present humour he probably wouldn't notice anyway, and then she'd feel even more idiotic and let down than she felt now. The times were clearly out of joint. There she was, hot to trot, needing the reassurance of a good seeing to (quite apart from needing what that good seeing to might bring), and there was Paul having a stupid work crisis. Sitting down at her dressing table, briskly towelling her hair dry, getting herself into a pother of righteous indignation, she suddenly reminded herself of her silly, self-absorbed mother, which brought her up sharp. Listen to yourself! she thought in disgust: whining and whingeing like a spoilt little girl, just like you swore you'd never be. And all because you can't have what you want *now* this *minute*. Where's the panic, what's the rush? She could hear Paul downstairs, finally leaving the kitchen and mounting the stairs, ice cubes tinkling in glasses. Bless. They just needed to talk, that was all, and take their time. How was he to know how desperately vulnerable she felt after her dramatically eventful week about which, so far, he had heard nothing? She could have told him on the phone while he was away. Her choice not to. And if she had, whatever problems he was having now would be taking second place – of that much she was certain. Hadn't he always been sympathetic and supportive when she needed him?

He arrived in the doorway with their drinks on a tray, and, evidently having found the smoked salmon in the fridge, had draped some over bite-sized crackers, topped with olives. 'Canapés,' he said, with an attempt at a smile. He looked awful.

'What's the matter?' Fran asked him, shocked to see his normally happy face weighed down with worry.

'Nothing. Tired still, I suppose. Here – your gin.'

'Thanks.' She'd been going to clink glasses with him but he had turned away before he'd noticed her offered gesture, to plonk himself down heavily on the bed.

'So,' he said, swallowing down a large slug of his drink. 'What's new with you?'

Where to start? 'Quite a lot, actually.'

He kicked off his shoes and lay back, his arms under his head, staring at the ceiling. 'Uh huh?'

'But maybe this isn't the time? Did the computer crashing really bugger you up?'

He rallied then, heaving himself up to lean on his elbows. 'No, no – just a bit of a bore and a waste of our time, but nothing disastrous. Sorry. I'll be back to normal tomorrow, probably. Just still feel like I've been run over by a truck.'

'Poor you. It's been a big three weeks for you, dashing about all over Europe, you must be shattered. So things really went well?'

'As far as one can judge at this stage. Lots of enthusiasm and promises of contracts. I'll feel happier once we've done the paperwork and they've all signed on the dotted line. But yeah, overall, I reckon we did really well. Be having to take on another couple of programmers if everything sticks.'

'Fantastic.' And great timing, now that she was going to rely on him to bring in the money single-handed.

'So come on, tell me what's up. Obviously something's been going on. Everything okay with Archie? The path's looking great.'

'Oh, Archie's the bright spot, as usual,' she smiled. 'No trouble there. Finished inside a week ago, ahead of schedule. Unheard of!'

'The living room looks nice. I was just looking at the wallpaper when I was down there. Didn't notice last night, I'm afraid. He did a good job.'

'No, I did,' said Fran, feeling proud.

'You decorated the living room?!'

'Yup.'

Paul stood up then, and came over to give her a hug. 'Oh, God, aren't I horrible?' he said. 'Moaning on about me being tired, when you've been here, going off to work in town, coming back and slogging away at night . . .' He felt her body stiffen in response. 'What?'

'I haven't been going off to work in town. Not this week, anyway.'

'How come? Haven't you been well?'

'No, no, nothing like that.'

'So, what? You took some holiday time off? That's all right. Things have been slack there anyway, haven't they?'

'This is my big subject,' she told him, pulling back out of his embrace to look up at him, her hands on his arms. 'This is what I need to talk about.'

'Okay,' he said, and sat back down on the bed to give her some space. 'I'm all ears.'

Now she had his full and undivided attention the story of her being passed over at work yet again all came out in a rush and, in the telling, she was surprised to hear how hurt and rejected she still felt about it.

Gratifyingly, Paul was incensed on her behalf. 'That's outrageous! Couldn't you get them on sex discrimination or something?'

'No,' she said. 'Ben would just make it sound like he was already doing me the most massive honour. He'd give them the bullshit he gave me, about how I'm the best writer of direct sales copy for the financial services we handle and how he needed to keep me at that.'

'I know I should know this, but just explain to me again what that means?'

'It means I can string more than two words together. It means I spend my days writing pages of prose about insurance policies, for instance, describing them in detail. Or ISAs, or tracker funds.' She rolled her eyes. 'It's the unsolicited junk mail that we all get sent, and it's the bread and butter of a medium smallish firm like ours. But I hate it. It isn't what I went into advertising for – it's not sexy, it's not glamorous, it's not very creative.'

'Not like coming up with slogans and campaigns,' offered Paul.

'Exactly.'

'Well, there's no point doing something you don't like,' he said sympathetically. 'So what are you going to do – keep your head down at Q & A while you sniff around, apply elsewhere?'

'Too late for that,' she said. 'I walked out.'

'You quit your job?' He sounded shocked.

'Yes.'

'Because you've been offered something better elsewhere?'

''Fraid not.'

'You've quit your job and you don't have anything to go to.'

'That's it.'

'Was that wise?'

There was something of the headmaster's study about this: having to explain away giddy actions in a saner moment to a calm, reproving authority. She laughed uncomfortably, suddenly acutely aware how this unilateral action of hers affected them both. She'd never lived off a man before, despite having been twice married. 'Probably not.'

'So what are you going to do? Apply elsewhere? Are there jobs coming up that you know about?'

'Not really, no. I thought—' But that was the problem, wasn't it? It now occurred to her that she hadn't *thought* at all, she had *felt*, she had acted rashly on a welter of emotion, on a sea of hormones. And who, again, did that remind her of, Mummy dearest? *I left my job so I could get pregnant* suddenly sounded ridiculous, but it had all seemed to make such good sense before. 'I thought maybe I could try to get some articles, or short stories, placed in newspapers, magazines, that type of thing. A complete change of direction,' she offered. Paul said nothing. He was listening intently, with a quizzical expression – presumably for the words, yet to come, which would explain everything, which would help the penny to drop. 'It wasn't just the job, although I really did hate it for ages. It was – everything. You know, commuting every day, spending hours on the train, battling on the underground,' she continued, floundering now, unable to say the words which would reveal her as archetypal preying woman, robber of men, hunter of seed, succubus.

'So who are you gong to target?' Paul asked, ever practical. 'Have you been working on some articles this week?'

'Not really, no. I've been helping Archie do the path, catching up on the gardening, that kind of thing.'

'This is so unlike you,' he said finally, evidently having given up all hope of elucidation. 'I've always thought of you as being driven by work, like me. Surely you'll go crazy hanging around here with no colleagues to bounce off, alone all the time, having to be self-motivated? And it's a fairly precarious way of making a living, isn't it, being a freelance writer?'

'Yes,' she said, stung. This really was not going at all as she had hoped. She should have prepared the way a lot more, had discussions about money at their weekly chat sessions. They didn't even have a shared bank account. When the bills came in, they just divided them and paid half each. What would it do to their relationship, having her financially dependent on him? Already she felt like a mendicant, and frankly it was early days.

But surely, she reasoned, as a married man, Paul must have assumed that some day he would be cast in the role of provider? They had talked, when they'd decided to get married, of having a family once they were settled. Reluctant and vulnerable as she now felt, the subject of her wanting babies must be broached. She just wished he'd be the one doing the broaching. She took a slug of her gin and tonic for courage and joined him on the bed, sitting at the foot end, facing him. She'd have liked to lie on top of him, kiss his neck, start on this baby-making business there and then, but there seemed to be such distance between them.

'Anyway,' she began, taking one of his feet to massage, working her hands up his leg.

'Tickling,' he said, moving his leg away and glancing at his watch. 'Suppose I'd better take that shower now.'

'We've got ages,' Fran protested. 'Finish your drink, relax.' Was he annoyed? Resentful? Was he thinking, *Here I've been, working myself into the ground, dashing around Europe, and she's complaining about commuting to London?* Maybe. So she must put it into context, help him understand. 'The thing is,' she began again. 'I'm thirty-five. Not getting any younger.'

'Still,' he said, attempting a smile, 'bit early for a mid-life crisis, isn't it?'

'It is and it isn't,' she said elliptically. 'And anyway, it isn't so much a crisis as a – a crunch point. A reassessment. A regrouping. A rethink.' God, she sounded like a thesaurus. 'The fact of the matter is, we've finished the house . . .'

'Yes . . . ?'

Why was he being so obtuse? 'We've built the nest.'

A look of – what was it – horror? Heaven forbid! – crossed his face, which he struggled to replace with surprise. 'You don't mean – you're not . . . ?'

'No, no, I'm not pregnant.' Yet. And at this rate it wouldn't be any time soon. 'But I want to be. And we always said, didn't we, that – I mean, it can't come as that much of a shock, surely?'

'No,' he said, sitting up straight now. 'Not a shock, but a surprise, certainly. I suppose my head's been in the firm, I've had other things on my mind, I haven't given this a thought. Not recently. I mean, these things ought to be planned, discussed.'

She was getting cross now, her defensiveness turning to attack. 'I've been trying to discuss it with you ever since you came home.'

'It's not that I'm anti, as such,' he explained, chilling her blood. 'It's just, well, what if the business doesn't take off right away? What if the contracts don't come in? With neither of us actually being employed, both of us working for ourselves – I mean, how could we afford it? Kids cost money.'

'Other people manage,' she said huffily. 'Maybe "these things" as you call it shouldn't be thought about too much. Otherwise one might never feel ready.'

'I just think, perhaps, that we should wait a while longer. A few weeks. A month or two, let's say. To make absolutely sure that we're in good enough financial shape to – take the plunge. And in the meantime it'll give you a chance to set things up for your career change. Get some stuff written, start sending it out, see what reaction you get, find out if it's feasible.'

He made it all sound so businesslike. Where were his feelings? 'You do want children, though, don't you?' she pressed him.

Silence. He appeared to be having an inner struggle. 'Sure,' he said finally. 'I suppose so.'

'Paul!'

'I told you, you've taken me by surprise. My head is elsewhere. Surely you can understand that? At the moment, the business is my child, and just now it's learning to take its first steps. I have to watch it, encourage it, bring it on, like a responsible parent.'

Put like that, Fran started feeling very irresponsible indeed. 'You think I acted rashly over my job, don't you?' she asked, her head lowered, her insecurities hanging round her like a slipped halo. 'I should have put up and shut up and bided my time. I should have got some writing work lined up first. Or at least found out if I *can* write about anything other than financial products.'

'Of course you can. Hey, if you were that unhappy, then you did the right thing,' he said, chubbing her leg. He bent forward to give her a friendly kiss, and she put her arms round him, desperate for a hug. 'You'll be all right. You'll be great,' he said to reassure her, stroking her hair. 'Don't worry, love. Everything will turn out okay.'

She smiled at him gratefully then and allowed him to slip from her arms to go to the shower. But left alone on the bed her insecurity returned, and she wondered, was it her he'd been trying to reassure, or himself?

Eleven

Driving over to Sam's, Paul wanted to hear all about the evening she'd turned up to tell Fran about finishing with Nigel. What had occasioned such militant talk, he wanted to know, after all this time? There was a companionable closeness between them in the car, made possible only by the fact that, after his shower, where he had presumably given himself a talking to, Paul had returned to the bedroom in a more giving mood, and had made love to her very sweetly. Having craved his physical attentions for what had seemed an eternity while he'd been away, she hadn't even minded when he had first checked with her that she was still on the pill. He was right, after all. It would be irresponsible to rush into starting a family, and she could see that he was under enough pressure at the moment, worrying about his firm. As he had said, in a month or two he would have a clearer idea of how things were going, and that really wasn't so very long to wait.

So, with his warm hand (when it wasn't needed for driving) now resting on her thigh, her body fulfilled, her emotions calmed by the catharsis of lovemaking, she managed to make quite a funny story out of Sam's nocturnal visit, emphasising the slapstick of the overturned plant and umbrella stand and the spilling of brandy, downplaying the reason for Sam's upset, the phantom pregnancy. No way was she about to endanger this welcome return to marital bliss by the mention of babies playing their part in the destruction of relationships.

'So how did Nigel take it? Has she phoned you with the gossip since she told him it was over?' he asked Fran, still chuckling at the image of her feeding cognac to Sam, wiping away the dribbles, as she had listened to her tale of woe.

'No, she hasn't. Saving it all for tonight, I expect,' Fran replied.

So they were both more than a little surprised, not to say gob-smacked, when they arrived at Sam's cottage a few minutes later and the door was answered by Nigel himself, playing the genial host.

'You must be Fran and Paul,' he told them, smiling, offering his hand. 'Nigel Ford-Roberts. Nice to meet you at last. Come in, come in.'

He was much less attractive than Sam's descriptions of him had ever led them to believe, his shirt buttons straining over his budding paunch, his hair with the usual Number One cut that balding men currently believed gave them street cred. As they followed him through to Sam's living room Paul threw Fran a querying glance, at which she could only shrug in helpless confusion.

'Samantha's in the garden – picking herbs, I believe,' said Nigel, grinning, as if this were a huge joke. He gestured towards the drinks cabinet as if he owned it. 'She'll be in in a moment. Wine? Gin? Vermouth? Sit down, please – make yourselves at home.'

'White wine, thanks,' said Fran, affronted by him instructing her to feel comfortable in her friend's house where she had felt perfectly at home for eighteen months, thank you very much. She started to feel furious with Sam. What on earth was she up to? Why was *he* here? Where were his marching orders? She raked through the conversation of the other night looking for clues, for a possible misunderstanding on her part, and she remembered Sam's bitter complaints that Nigel and she never spent time in other people's company, for fear of his infidelity to his wife getting out. She remembered too that Nigel, in his relief at not having been made a parent for the fourth time, had offered to see Sam on a Saturday night, in what had always been considered hallowed, untouchable family time. So here they all were for a cosy foursome. It was *the* Saturday night. A malignant suspicion started to form in Fran's mind that perhaps Sam had never even entertained the idea of finishing with this – this adulterous twit. That maybe it had all been a ruse to get Fran and Paul here for this deceitful imitation of two normal couples having dinner together. But was it really possible for Sam – innocent, naive, straightforward Sam – to be so devious? There was one way to find out.

'Thanks,' Fran now said, attempting a smile as she accepted her glass of wine from Nigel. 'I'll just pop out and see if Sam needs any help.' She swapped a quick look of complicity with Paul, and left him to it. Poor man. As she went out through the kitchen door she could hear Nigel enquiring if he played golf. Well, that conversation would be brief.

She found Sam at the bottom of her garden deadheading a climbing rose, putting off this dreaded moment, she supposed. Tough. It was here.

'Sam!'

Sam started guiltily at the tone of her voice and whipped round, cheeks flushed with embarrassment, ripping her hand on a thorn. 'Ouch! Fran! Hi! I didn't realise that was the time!' Sucking her bleeding finger, she downed tools and joined Fran on the path.

'What's going on?' Fran demanded *sotto voce*. 'Why is Nigel here? I thought you were going to finish with him last week?'

Sam couldn't meet her eyes. 'I know. I did finish with him, on Thursday. But he was devastated, simply devastated. He called me last night, and came round, and . . .'

'And you took him back.' There could not have been more contempt in Fran's voice as she said it.

'Just pro tem. Till I find somebody else.'

'How's that going to happen? You don't look for anybody else!'

'No, but I will, I will. I've been thinking about maybe joining an agency, or putting an advert in the paper.'

'Great. I'll help you write it now.'

'Oh, Fran, don't be beastly! I know you must think me weak and pathetic, but I was so lonely!'

'You were only on your own for a day! Jesus! You have to bite the bullet, give it a chance!'

'Easier said than done when you still live on your own at my age,' said Sam. 'You don't know what it's like, coming home from work to an empty house and a meal for one. And I think it's worse in the summer than the winter – the evenings are so long.'

'I know exactly what it's like,' Fran snapped. 'Paul's just been away for three weeks if you hadn't noticed, and he's practically been away more than he's been here this year!'

'How *is* Paul?' said Sam, seizing the opportunity to turn the conversation away from herself. 'Is he here? Was it lovely to see him? When did he get back?'

'Last night, late,' Fran replied tetchily, not wanting to go down that road at all. 'And don't think I haven't noticed you changing the subject.'

Sam turned to her then, taking her hands in her own, her large liquid eyes begging for understanding. 'Don't be cross with me, Fran, please. Let's all try to have a nice evening together. I will sort things out, I promise. And I have made a start – don't tell Nigel!' She glanced behind her towards the living room window, and seeing Nigel looking back at her, with Paul at his shoulder, she waved and called 'Coming!' She turned back to Fran, grinning like a naughty schoolgirl. 'Oops! Better take those herbs in and get on with the food.' She stooped down to pick up her basket of parsley and chives and threaded her arm through Fran's. As they walked back towards the house, Sam leant in to whisper, 'I sent off for an information pack, on Thursday, to a dating agency, and it arrived this morning! Shall we have lunch on Monday? I'll need your advertising skills to help me decide what to say about myself.'

Despite herself Fran was disarmed, and felt guilty now at having been so tough on her friend. 'Yeah, okay. Look – it's not that I think you're weak and pathetic, it's just that I can't stand Nigel making you so unhappy, having it all his own way.'

'I know. You're a good friend. And it's so sweet of you to come tonight, when Paul's only just got back. I really appreciate it.'

They had arrived back in the kitchen where they found Nigel putting ice in a water jug, making further covert conversation impossible.

'Couldn't find any fizzy water in the fridge, darling, so we'll have to make do with tap. I'll put some sliced lemon in, shall I?' he asked, masquerading as the good husband. Which might just about have been bearable, thought Fran crossly, unable to bring herself to watch as Nigel's pudgy arms possessively encircled her friend's waist, if Sam had been his wife.

She found Paul slumped on a sofa in the living room, still looking tired and stressed, but he attempted a smile when he saw her.

'Sorry about that,' she said in a low voice, settling next to him. 'So how did you make out with Wee Willie Hague?'

She'd lost him. 'Who?'

'Haircut Harry. The Bald Bastard. Knobhead Nigel.'

'Oh,' said Paul, frowning, 'he's okay. Don't be so hard on him, give him a chance.'

Fran was surprised. 'You *like* him?' She wouldn't have had him down as Paul's type at all.

Paul shrugged. 'I daresay he's finding this pretty embarrassing.'

'Tough! He should have thought about that before he started cheating on his wife. Embarrassing? That's the least of it!'

Paul shot an anxious glance at the door and shushed her,

getting up to wander over to the drinks cabinet to freshen his glass. 'More wine?' he said, in an attempt to normalise things.

Fran looked at him, puzzled and still cross. 'You'll be telling me next to make myself at home,' she complained.

For somebody so accident-prone and clumsy, Sam managed to present a more than passable meal, and apart from her crisis over the vegetables being more charred than chargrilled, she appeared to relish the occasion, playing at being Mrs Ford-Roberts II. Fran, still grumpy and out of sorts, felt like an outsider, an observer, as she listened to the three of them hop from one light conversation to another, never settling anywhere which might prove dangerous to the evening's delicate status quo. Had she bothered to listen properly she could have learnt more about Paul's work than she had ever managed, hitherto, to understand, as he was breaking it down into easily digested bite-sized pieces for her fellow technophobes, Nigel and Sam. But all she heard was a background blur of safe – and, to her, this evening – uninteresting subjects, while she gave her attention to the inside of her own head.

From time to time, when her opinion was politely sought on some other anodyne subject, she had to force herself to snap back into the present, to smile and nod and agree. Wasn't Cornwall fantastic? Yes it was. Weren't they doing well for weather this summer? Yes they were. Didn't the new motorway spur road cut oodles of time off their journeys? Yes it did.

But throughout all this she was mulling over Paul's reaction to the baby idea, and the more she mulled, the less reasonable she felt. At the time she had been on her back foot, defensive, feeling strangely guilty and selfish, but now she asked herself why? All right, so she had felt a bit naff about her impulsiveness over quitting her job, had dreaded telling him, but leaving that aside for a moment, what was so wrong with wanting to start a family when you were married and settled and in your mid-thirties? And whereas before she had been prepared to think that Paul was being grown-up and sensible while she was being immature and irresponsible, now she just thought of him as sounding middle-aged. Over-cautious, like her father had been. A killjoy, even. Where was his excitement about finishing the house? Why hadn't he grabbed her in his arms, jumped on her, giggled like an excited kid, why hadn't they snogged and cuddled and made whoopee?

But what was worse, really, and what now occasioned this unflattering reappraisal of her husband's behaviour, was the memory of the image, pushed down at the time and minimised by her, quickly covered up and changed by him, of his initial look of horror when he had thought for a moment she was pregnant. Again and again she replayed that look in her mind, trying to pin it down, trying to understand it. Why had he been so horrified? What was all that nonsense he'd spouted about perhaps not being able to afford it? People on low incomes had babies and managed, for God's sake. Even, dare she say it, unemployed people like herself sometimes had the temerity to breed! So what if Paul's business didn't take off quite as quickly as he hoped, so what that she'd left her job? It might mean, at worst, that they would have to cut down on some luxuries, but with their skills and contacts they'd never be down-and-out poor.

Try as she might, she could not come up with a single plausible reason for that momentary horrified look which had flashed across his face. Nothing seemed to fit. Unless, of course, it was he who was having the mid-life crisis? Perhaps he was feeling reluctant to grow up, had a Peter Pan complex as some men did, and felt, however unconsciously, that becoming a father would mark the end of his youth? It was possible, she supposed doubtfully, scrutinising him now as he chatted pleasantly to Sam and Nigel over coffee, but most unlikely. It would certainly reveal a side to her husband she hadn't known before.

However, when the time came for them to leave, as the host

couple stood in the lighted doorway of the cottage seeing their guests out, swapping pleasantries, Fran was shocked to hear something which made her doubt that she knew Paul half as well as she'd complacently thought.

'I'll see what I can do about the club,' Nigel said to him as they were shaking hands goodnight, 'and give you a call.'

'That's very kind of you,' Paul told him, 'and thank you both for a lovely evening.'

'What club?' asked Fran, completely mystified, when they were alone again in the privacy of their car, driving home.

'What? Oh – Thwaitstone Golf Club,' Paul said nonchalantly. 'Nigel's a member, and he's going to try to get me in.'

You could have knocked Fran over with a feather. 'Golf? *You* join Nigel's golf club? But you hate golf! Overgrown schoolboys hitting stones with twigs, you say.'

'It's where a lot of business is done,' said Paul, quietly aloof. 'There's a good deal of potential contacts to be made at Thwaitstone.'

'Blimey,' said Fran, taking this in. Well, that was the Peter Pan theory clearly out of the window, then. How much more grown-up could you get than that? 'Who'd have thought? You in plaid trousers.' She laughed at the image. 'You'll be baring your breast and joining the Masons next!'

'That's a possibility,' Paul agreed. 'I've got some feelers out in that direction, actually.'

'Blimey,' said Fran again, beginning to see him in an entirely different light. If he was prepared to make these sacrifices, joining boys' clubs and wearing silly clothes, maybe he really was worried about his business taking off? In which case, by comparison, her own impulsive walkout from work seemed like irresponsible, adolescent pique. Was that what Paul thought too, she wondered guiltily? Was it he who was maturing, she who longed to stay a little girl?

★

But later, looking at herself in the bathroom mirror as she applied her face cream, getting ready to join Paul in bed, she rejected this unflattering, immature image of herself. For surely little girls wanted to *be* babies, not have them? And in the maturity stakes, didn't wanting to be a mother beat wanting to be a Mason into the proverbial cocked hat? Which left her right back at square one, still none the wiser why he'd looked so horrified when he'd thought for that brief moment she was already with child. How would she have felt about his reaction if she *had* been pregnant, she wondered now, getting angry all over again. Pretty bloody awful, was the answer. Rejected. Unwanted. Mistress turned madonna. A millstone round his neck.

Well, it was no good staying in the dark, fearing the worst, getting resentful. Hadn't they vowed when they married never to repeat the big mistake they had both made in the past, of letting the sun go down on their wrath? She would have it out with him now, she decided, snapping off the bathroom light – get it out into the open for better or worse.

Which would have been great, had she not on her return to the bedroom found Paul already curled up, snoring softly, dead to the world.

Twelve

⟡

Waking on Sunday morning, ready for a row, Fran was astonished to see Paul standing by the bed with a breakfast tray, the Sunday papers tucked under one arm. He'd found the bagels and toasted them, spread them thickly with cream cheese, and topped them off with smoked salmon. There was coffee, freshly squeezed orange juice, and a kiss.

'This is fantastic!' said Fran, completely overwhelmed, her need for confrontation now forgotten. 'Have I missed something we ought to be celebrating? Our anniversary? My birthday? World peace?'

Paul laughed and set the tray down on the bed, settling beside her for their breakfast banquet. 'No, I just woke up feeling so much better – less tired and a lot less cranky.' He gave her a rueful glance. 'I've been a bit self-obsessed since I got back, haven't I? Sorry, love.'

'Listen, you are one hundred per cent forgiven,' said Fran graciously, cramming a bagel into her mouth. She felt so much happier than a moment ago. *This* was more like the Paul she knew. They feasted happily in companionable and greedy near-silence, after which he astonished her with the offer of a massage. An hour later, every cell and fibre of her had been smoothed and soothed into a state of bliss, and Paul got into the bed beside her to cuddle up, their bodies automatically fitting together like two halves of a whole.

'Will there be anything further, madam?' he asked.

'Mm,' said Fran, snuggling up to him, and promptly fell asleep.

When they woke again a couple of hours later they pottered companionably around the house and garden together, discussing things still to be done, admiring what had been achieved. Gradually, during the course of that glorious afternoon of brilliant sunshine and cloudless blue skies, she felt more confident, more comfortable with her decision, more aware of her potential and what she might achieve. And now she felt more relaxed, it seemed churlish to challenge Paul about his initial bad reaction to having a baby. She realised she had been rushing things unnecessarily since he'd arrived back home, driven by her own fears. Naturally he was frightened about taking this life-changing step, for clearly she wasn't exactly taking it in her stride herself.

She also realised, with a sense of surprise, just how guilty she'd been feeling about leaving her job so precipitously, and how that had paralysed her. Now, comforted by Paul's affection and reassured by his friendly presence, she felt more daring, more up for the challenge. Why stop at articles? Why not have a go at short stories, poems, start to plan another novel, try her hand at writing for kids?

As the shadows across the garden grew longer, Paul suggested having supper and a drink down at their village local, where they found to their amusement that a quiz night was planned, and they were co-opted onto what proved to be the winning team. Thus a perfect evening ended a perfect day, and when they returned home it was to flop into bed together, to cuddle up again in each other's arms, and to drift into a peaceful, restful sleep.

After Paul had gone to work the next morning, tactfully not asking Fran how she intended to fill her day, she lay in bed looking at the ceiling pondering that very question. Should she start work on a novel or attempt something smaller – a short story, perhaps? After all, she needed to earn money sooner rather than later, and a novel could take her years to complete. Look what had happened the last time she'd tried to write one – she'd ground to a halt less than a quarter of the way through and then abandoned it altogether in a pother of self-doubt. She couldn't afford to do that this time. This time she had to stick at it, see it through to the end, finish the bloody thing. And even that wouldn't be enough. Then she'd have to tout it round publishers, try to get them to give her a huge advance to fund the writing of her next book, enough to live on for another year or two. And for them to part with that amount of cash, it would have to be popular, have an instant appeal, have the clear potential to sell thousands and thousands of copies . . .

In less than half an hour, lying there in bed, she had managed to banish all trace of her enthusiasm and optimism of the day before and replace it with anxiety and dread. What if she slogged away at writing a novel for the next couple of years (or three!) living all the time off Paul, having drained her paltry savings in the first few months, and then it failed to sell? She'd have wasted all that time and achieved nothing, earned not a sou. The embarrassment! The shame! And then what? Tail between legs, three (or five!) years older, trying to get her old job back, humble enough now to be grateful for the chance to write copy for direct sales? No, no, it was too huge an undertaking, too massive a gamble – and with *Paul's* money, not her own! To even think of embarking on this foolish project, she must be utterly convinced before she wasted a minute of her time that it was going to be a winner, that it would take the publishing world by storm.

Okay then, she challenged herself, work it out, think it through. Define the properties of a best-selling novel. It must be – what? Gripping. A page-turner. Accessible. The lead character should be empathic, recognisable to the reader. She should be . . . She? Or he? Could she write a male character? No, don't put obstacles in your way right at the very start, stick to what you know. *She* must be likeable. Funny? Fran quailed. Could she write comedy? How would she know – there certainly hadn't been many laughs in financial products. All right, forget the comedy. It would be a drama, or a tragedy perhaps? A thriller! Or a crime novel: they sold in scads. Look at Patricia Cornwell, she must be as rich as Croesus! So, her heroine would be a . . . a . . . Give her a name, for God's sake, all this heroine this and heroine that! Sheila. Susan. Suzanne – better, more dash. Suzanne would be a – well, not in forensics, that had been covered. A private detective? Oh very original, hardly been done at all. An ordinary woman who somehow gets caught up in a drama? Think, think!

An ordinary woman – good; called Suzanne – yes; who is out walking one day, minding her own business, when suddenly, from out of nowhere . . . What is her own business? Is she employed? A housewife? A mother? Married? Divorced? Hopelessly in love with the wrong person? Happily settled with five kids? Kidnapped – maybe she's kidnapped! There she is, Suzanne, an ordinary woman, walking down the street one day, minding her own business, thinking about what to feed the kids for tea, when suddenly a car screeches to a halt and two masked men leap out and bundle her into the back seat – or the boot? Bundle her into the boot and drive her to . . . How old is she? Five kids, she's got to be in her thirties, certainly. Okay. Thirty-something Suzanne, an ordinary mother of five kids, is on her way to the village shop, when . . . Or town? A city street? London? No, village. Town. Make your sodding mind up, does it really matter? Suzanne, thirty-something, mother of five kids, village street, minding own business, car screeches, men jump out, Suzanne bundled into boot and driven to a remote . . . Is she attractive? What does she look like? What colour's her hair? Irrelevant, it doesn't matter, stick to the big questions!

So. Opening chapter – Suzanne, mother of five, ordinary, village street, minding business, car, men, bundled, boot, driven, remote hideout, blindfolded (what was this, a haiku?), pushed into a cold room, left alone because, because . . . what? Why is all this happening to her if she's so damned ordinary? Ransom? She'll have to be rich then. *Rich* thirty-something Suzanne. So why's she doing her own shopping for the kids' tea – wouldn't she have a nanny to do that, or an au pair at the very least? No, keep her ordinary. Not rich, not ransom. So. She's – witnessed a crime? And they know that she knows who they are and what they've done? Which is what? A murder? Robbery? Blackmail? Come back to that later. Mistaken identity? But, what if . . . ? No.

Fran slid down the bed and pulled the covers over her head, willing herself to think the story through calmly, fighting down a rising tide of panic and hopelessness about having writer's block on the first day of her new career. Rethink, rethink, rethink. The problem was definitely the bit about the heroine being ordinary. Strike that. She's not ordinary. She's extraordinary. Thirty-something extraordinary Suzanne, walking down the street. What was so bloody extraordinary about the stupid effing woman then? She's . . . what?! Nothing, she's nothing, thought Fran sulkily. Thinks she's so bloody fascinating pottering down to the village shop to buy tea for her five kids, but who's interested? Does she really think masked men are going to waste their time on her? Dream on, Suzanne. That's about as likely as me coming up with a best-selling plot.

Well terrific. Now even her own inner voice had stooped to the lowest form of wit. And why not? She had been an absolute fool, blindly holding her nose, hang the consequences, and gaily stepping off the cliff. Of *course* she had fallen. Of course she had landed with a crash. Any idiot could have foreseen that. Except an idiot like her. What a mistake she had made, what a terrible, terrible mistake. To walk out of a well-paid job with nothing but the woolliest of plans, relying entirely on a supposed talent which she clearly didn't possess. Why? Why? Why? If only she could have her time over again, if only she could turn back the clock. Was it too late? Was there anything she could do to inveigle her way back in to Q & A? Maybe she should call Ben, see what kind of a mood he was in, be conciliatory, take the blame, laugh it off as a touch of the hormones, tell him how much she was missing direct sales? Because in a spooky way, she was. How spoilt she'd been, without even knowing it, to be able to go into work each day and to be *told* what to write about. That was obviously the hard part about this writing lark, the old blank canvas of the mind. If absolutely any colour was possible, any shape, where did a person begin? In an agony of self-doubt is where. Huddled under the bedclothes with a pillow over one's head, apparently.

What if she hadn't been so quick to take offence at Ben? What if she had taken what he'd said about her being the best writer of direct sales copy as a compliment, not as an insult? At least she could derive some pride from that, being the best at something. Yes. She should bite the bullet, call Ben. Or not. Maybe she should call Allie first. Get her to sound things out, lay the groundwork for a rapprochement. Allie . . . Where had she been since Fran had walked out a week ago? Why hadn't she phoned to see how she was? Did she hate her? Had she written her off for being foolish and impulsive and beyond the pale? Maybe their friendship was really only based on work, on being in the same firm? Suddenly Fran felt terribly alone, drowning in a cold sea of hubris. Her best and oldest friend had given up on her, and her husband thought she was selfish and irresponsible. What the hell had she done? Why had she wilfully trashed her own life?

She fought her way out of the covers for air and lay on her back, staring at the ceiling again. She'd come full circle with nothing to show for it. She felt exhausted by defeat, her limbs felt like lead, her head ached from indecision. A storyteller – her? Ha! Her brain started to shut down, to shrink away from any more self-criticism – not listening, I'm not listening. It was very tempting to just go back to sleep, to drift away from this horrid start to the day, to take refuge in the arms of Hypnos, the most attractive of all the Greek gods. Yes. Perhaps that was a better idea. Sleep on it. It was still early. She peeked at the clock. Well – it wasn't that late, anyway. Just have a little nap now, and wake again refreshed, start the day later revivified, write this off as a rehearsal. And who knew – maybe she'd have a dream, find a useful starting place for a story. She hadn't been doing too badly, after all, until the logical, critical side of her mind had started kicking in and carping. Maybe, if she just had a little zizz now, unwound a bit, she wouldn't feel that her only option was to crawl back to Ben, cap in hand . . .

Two hours later she was ripped from an entirely dreamless sleep by the shrill ringing of the bedside phone. She blinked and looked at the clock. It was almost midday! Jesus! She sat bolt upright, firing on all cylinders with high-octane guilt.

'Hello?' she enquired in a small, shocked voice.

'Hi, it's Sam. Are you all right?'

'Fine, yes, miles away,' she dissembled, rubbing her eyes till they stung.

'Oh heavens – I haven't disturbed you at your writing have I?'

If only. 'No, no, what can I help you with?'

'Lunch? That is, if you're still up for it? We didn't decide where. I've got a bit of a full day, so would you mind coming to Market Harborough? Say Dino's, at one?'

'Yeah, fine. See you there.' Bloody hell. Lunch already. Outside, she could hear Archie whistling and bashing bricks into shape in the garden. And what had she achieved with her morning? Nothing. Sweet FA.

She leapt out of bed and flung herself under the shower. She'd only just make it to Dino's in time. God, what a waste of a day! And what would she say to Paul when he got home tonight, knackered after a full day's work, and asked her what she'd done? Well, I lay in bed for a while and depressed myself, then

I went to sleep, then I got up and went out for lunch. How happy would he be about that, when he was working himself into the ground at the moment? Dashing back into the bedroom, towelling herself dry on the run, she saw that the linen basket was overflowing with Paul's washing from his trip. She could at least do that, put a load in before she left, race back and hang it out to dry. If she was lucky with the weather, she might even time it so he arrived home to find her ironing his shirts, being virtuously, selflessly productive. She pulled her clothes on at record speed, foregoing make-up, grabbed her handbag and an armful of whites and threw herself down the stairs to the kitchen, startling both herself and Archie, who had come inside to make himself a cup of tea.

'Thought you was back at work,' he said awkwardly, embarrassed to be found with her kettle in his hand.

'No, I'm working from home at the moment,' Fran lied, equally embarrassed, shoving the washing into the machine. 'That's what I was doing this morning. Upstairs. In the study. The time just flew and I've got to go into Market Harborough now. Anyway, help yourself to tea. Sorry, I should have made you some myself. Shall I do it now, bring it out to you?'

'No, you're all right,' said Archie in alarm. He was gasping for a real cuppa – the last thing he wanted was some of her Pearl Grey or that Lapland Joujong, whatever the bugger were called. 'He's back then,' he added, grasping at straws to distract her as he noted Paul's shirts and underwear disappearing inside the drum. 'You'll be pleased about that.'

Fran smiled and switched the machine on. 'Yes, it's great. He loves the herringbone, by the way.'

'I know,' said Archie, 'I seen him when I got here first thing. *He* were dashing about an' all. Meks me glad I'm retired, seeing you young folk having to run everywhere on the double. Anyway, off you go. I'll be right.'

'Well,' said Fran, stuck for a response and feeling even worse

now for being less productive than a retired person. 'See you
later then, probably. Help yourself to biscuits or whatever.
Anything you need fetching back from Harborough?'

'Not for me, no. But you could help hubby out and tek his
suits in. 'Ere y'are,' he explained, as Fran looked puzzled, and
he lifted up a bag which was draped over the back of one of the
kitchen stools. 'He were gooing to tek 'em to the dry-cleaners
but he forgot in his hurry. I just spotted the bag when you come
down. I were thinking I could drop them off for him missen
when I'd finished, help him out like.'

'Archie, what would we do without you?' said Fran gratefully,
taking the bag and whizzing past him to run outside to her car.
Now when Paul came home and asked her what she'd done with
her day, she could truthfully point out that a good part of it had
been spent doing chores for him. She felt better already, more
virtuous and less of a failure. 'Just don't ever finish the path!' she
yelled over her shoulder to Archie. 'I'd miss you too much!'

'No fear of that!' Archie chuckled, shouting back. 'I'm here
for the duration!' When he was sure she was gone he eyed the
tea caddies by the kettle dubiously and lifted their lids, sniffing
them suspiciously. Perfumed – yek! Old bonfire – phwor! What
was in this last one? Could it be . . . ? It was! Bog standard bags!
At last. A decent cup of tea in this house! He rubbed his hands
together in anticipation and looked around. Now where the
bleddy hell did she keep her white sugar?

To her amazement, and with some degree of pride, Fran found
a parking spot right near Dino's with ten minutes to spare before
she had to meet Sam. Incredible, what a woman! She'd just have
time to dump Paul's suits off now, and maybe even collect them
this afternoon if she used their express service and did a bit of
shopping after lunch while she waited. The thought cheered her
enormously. This was more like her old self – Fran Holdaway,
time manager extraordinaire. She was exhilarated by having

driven, if she said it herself, quite brilliantly, her foot flat down, weaving through the country lanes like a professional rally driver, accelerating round bends. Allie would have loved it.

She grabbed the bag from the passenger seat and set off for the dry-cleaners, keeping an eye out for Sam. Thinking of Allie again, now she was in a better mood, she felt ridiculous at having assumed earlier that her friend would have ditched her so easily. There would be some perfectly reasonable explanation as to why she hadn't been in touch all week. Fran would have to watch that now she was to spend her days alone – the quick and easy descent into paranoia and despair. Imagine, having one bad morning, and thinking she was entirely hopeless! Ridiculous! This was her first-ever attempt at being freelance, and she must learn as she went, putting mistakes down to experience, not seeing them as proof of her inadequacy. She must be kinder to herself, give herself more leeway.

Today, for instance, she had learnt that she must get up first thing, get dressed, work at her desk, not lie around in bed. She must give herself a structure, protect herself from failure, set herself easier targets. And tomorrow she would attempt something more easily achievable – a short story, perhaps, or an article. Nobody could be expected to write an award-winning novel from a standing start. She needed to build up her confidence, practise her craft, keep up her spirits. Perhaps she should dig out that old Louise Hay self-help tape she'd bought when she was recovering from her first marriage, stick up some bracing Post-it notes to herself, start talking to herself in mirrors. She grinned at the thought. 'I am beautiful. I am successful. Everything is working out perfectly.' Yes, why not? All of it was absolutely true.

Thus, smiling, optimistic, cheerful, she stepped jauntily into the dry-cleaners, where life as she had known it was about to come to an end.

Thirteen

Sam had almost finished her lasagne by the time Fran finally arrived at Dino's, entering like a zombie and plonking herself down wordlessly, her cheeks pale.

'Sorry, I ordered, I was worried about the time,' Sam explained, mopping rich bolognese sauce from her lips with her napkin, embarrassed to be caught pigging out alone. She signalled to a waiter, then turned back to examine Fran more closely. 'Are you all right?'

'Yeah, fine – time of the month,' Fran replied, attempting to pull herself together. She had been wandering the streets in a daze, had sat on a bench staring into space, her mind feeling numb and feverish by turn. 'I'll just have a white wine,' she told the waiter, rejecting the proffered menu.

'Have you taken anything?' Sam asked her. Fran really did look awfully pale, which wasn't helped by the fact that she wasn't wearing a scrap of make-up. 'I think I might have some paracetamol somewhere in my bag,' she said, scrabbling around under the table.

'Don't bother,' said Fran. The waiter arrived with her wine, which she gulped down like water. She leaned forward, eyes bright. 'Tell me – what would Nigel's wife do if she found out he was involved with you?'

Sam's search for pharmaceuticals ended abruptly, her cheeks now as pale as Fran's. 'Margo?! How? She mustn't – ever! Why? What have you heard?'

'Nothing, nothing,' said Fran tetchily, which was true. It wasn't what she had heard, but what she had seen which had brought her to this current state of unravelling.

The manageress on duty at the dry-cleaners was an assiduous woman, and she had insisted on a meticulous search of Paul's pockets before she would take charge of his suits and allow Fran to leave the premises with her ticket. 'We had a woman come in here last week claiming to have left a hundred pounds in her jeans,' she'd explained. 'Caused no end of a stink at head office, threatened lawyers and all sorts. So now it's our policy to make a thorough examination of all incoming garments, on receipt.' She had been flushed with triumph when her investigations had produced a folded hotel bill from the buttoned-down back pocket of a pair of his trousers, and practically cock-a-hoop when she discovered the gold earring in his linen jacket. 'That could have caused untold damage to our machine,' she admonished Fran, blithely unaware of the utter devastation she was bringing to Fran's marriage. For the earring wasn't hers. And the bill, from a hotel in Berlin, was made out to Mr and Mrs Holdaway, and dated last week.

There could only be one explanation, of course. She'd worked that out as she had blindly wandered the streets. That little bitch Katie had seduced him. She'd kill her when she saw her. She'd scratch her eyes out, pull out every tinted hair from her head, pour paint stripper on her car. She'd have her sacked, send her packing, insist on her replacement being male. But how *could* Paul have succumbed – notwithstanding Katie's big tits and twenty-something skin – after all he'd said about faithlessness when his ex-wife Helen had broken his heart? How could he have contemplated, even for one moment, committing this heartless, hurtful crime? And what had yesterday been about – the breakfast, the massage, the affection? Guilt, she supposed. God, no wonder he'd freaked about having a baby. At least his dick had a sense of shame.

'Look,' she snapped now, cutting of Sam's anxious wittering about what Nigel would do if Margo were ever to find out, and signalled for another glass of wine. 'This is hypothetical, not real. If Margo were to find a – hotel bill, for example. Made out to Mr and Mrs Ford-Roberts, when she knew for a fact that he'd been away on his own? What would she do?'

'That happened once,' said Sam, shamefaced. 'After we'd been away to London for a couple of days. But Nigel blustered it through. Got angry about the inefficiency of the hotel staff, rang them up and screamed at them in Margo's hearing, told them he'd sue for defamation of character, said they could pay for his divorce, and for the therapy his children would need when they were older. Then he put Margo on the phone, and they apologised for their mistake.'

Fran was gobsmacked. The barefaced cheek of it! Would Paul attempt that, to bully perfectly innocent people into making specious excuses for his crimes? 'But what did the hotel say?' she prompted, needing to be prepared. 'They knew what they knew, surely? They could have exposed him for the liar he was.'

'Well,' said Sam, looking shifty. 'In actual fact he hadn't phoned the hotel, of course, he'd phoned me. I didn't know what on earth he was up to at first, but then I caught on, realised what he was after. So when he put Margo on the phone I apologised on behalf of the hotel, as if I was the manager.' She pushed the rest of her lasagne away from her, having lost all appetite now. 'It's not something I'm proud of.'

'Jesus!' said Fran, her eyes narrowed dangerously, glaring at Sam with as much hatred as if it were *she* who had been to bed with Paul. 'Not proud of having lied to her about the hotel. But what – proud of having fucked her husband?!'

Sam, stung by the malevolence of her attack, swept the restaurant anxiously for eavesdroppers. 'Please don't,' she whispered, her voice trembling. 'I know it's wrong. I've told you how badly I feel about it. And I did finish with him last week.'

'For twenty-four hours! He was back in your knickers by Saturday night!'

Sam gripped the edge of the table with nervous hands, looking as if she would explode into tears on the spot. 'Fran! Why are you doing this? I told you I was joining an agency. I thought we were meeting today to try to fill in the form?'

Fran steadied herself, gulped back more wine, bumbled an apology. 'Sorry, Sam, sorry – I didn't mean to attack you. I'm . . . it's . . .'

'Your period,' supplied Sam magnanimously, relieved to be off the hook, eager to be friends again. 'Don't worry – I'm the same. Only it's usually the week before, with me.'

Fran smiled a vague acknowledgement, not really having heard, her mind busy with its own agenda. 'Actually,' she said, 'It's because I'm stuck on something I'm writing. About marital infidelity. About how tolerant a wife should be if she discovered something was up. You know, should she forgive and forget, turn a blind eye type of thing? I mean if it had been just a one-off fling. Would it be – immature of her to get a divorce, ruin what had been a perfectly good marriage, leave somebody she really loved, just because he'd made one mistake?'

'Oh, I see,' said Sam, flattered now to be called in as an expert witness to give evidence to a writer. 'Well, it would depend, wouldn't it? Is this for an article, by the way?' she checked apprehensively, 'I won't be quoted, will I?

'No. For a novel.'

'Fran! How exciting! So you're doing it – well done! Tell me the story so far. What have you got? Anything besides the hotel bill?'

'An earring,' Fran supplied dully. 'In his jacket pocket.'

Sam gasped. 'Oh! This is uncanny! This could be my life!'

'*Margo* found an earring too?' asked Fran, almost giving herself away. 'I mean, in addition to the bill?'

'No, she didn't,' Sam admitted. 'But she might have done

once, a long time ago. It was early in our relationship, when I still believed Nigel might leave her. He kept saying he'd tell her about us, kept saying he'd ask for a divorce, but that he had to find the right time – he couldn't do it while little Alice had chickenpox, or when Dan fell off his scooter and ended up in A and E, or when Margo had her cervical cancer scare.'

'No, I don't suppose he could!' exclaimed Fran, outraged on Margo's behalf. 'Jesus! Poor woman!'

'Oh, it was all lies,' said Sam dismissively. '*I* was sympathetic too, when he told me. But then I found out it was all nonsense, just excuses to fob me off.'

'*How* did you find out?' asked Fran, sarcasm giving her voice a nasty edge. 'What did you do – bribe her gynaecologist?!'

'No, she got pregnant with Jocelyn,' Sam said stiffly, still hurt after all these years by that ironic turn of events. 'And when I asked him if she'd have to have an abortion because of the cancer, he didn't know what I was talking about. He'd forgotten his own lie.'

'God, how can you stay with such a lying cheating bastard?!' Fran exploded. 'To lie about a thing like that, to say his wife's got cancer! Has he no shame at all? Have you no pride?'

'Apparently not,' Sam said quietly, biting her lip and lowering her eyes. She glanced at her watch. 'I'd better be getting back to the office.'

Fran threw herself back in her chair, aware suddenly of her aggressive posture. Talk about in Sam's face – she had practically been within biting distance. Again she soothed and apologised, again she signalled for more wine, despite the fact that it was having zero effect on calming her down. The more she drank, the more wired she felt, but hey – what the heck. She slugged back another half-glass in one and wiped her mouth with the back of her hand. 'It's just that I feel so angry for you,' she lied. 'You must have been so hurt, so let down – betrayed.'

'Mm,' agreed Sam, mollified. But in fact she had felt nothing.

She seemed to have an automatic erase button in her head concerning hurtful events, had developed it as a child. No matter
how people provoked her, once they'd explained, she could
always see their point of view, and then it seemed wrong not to
forgive and forget. But strangely, sitting here now in the restaurant, years after the event, it was quite exciting to hear Fran
getting angry on her behalf. She *had* been treated badly by Nigel,
and it felt good to have that acknowledged, a validation of her
sacrifice of suffering.

'We'll find you a nice one, a better one than Nigel,' Fran continued. 'We'll write that copy, advertise your wares. They should
be so lucky to get you.'

'Great,' Sam smiled, and signalled to the waiter that she
wanted to pay. 'Only I don't think there'll be time today. I've got
a viewing in fifteen minutes.'

'My fault for being late,' said Fran, putting her credit card into
the arriving waiter's hand without even a glance at the bill, 'so
my shout.'

'Oh no, but honestly! I ate, you didn't!' Sam protested, searching her bag for her purse. 'Here we are – let's go Dutch at least.'

'Absolutely not,' said Fran firmly, and pushed her money
away, not entirely philanthropically. 'Anyway, you were saying.
Margo nearly found your earring, back in the old days, when
you and Nigel were first together?'

'Oh, that, yes,' said Sam, looking sheepish. 'Well, as you say,
it was a long time ago. I was tempted to . . . But I didn't do it in
the end! . . . It's not something I'm proud of,' she ended lamely.

Fran hadn't realised until now quite how often that phrase was
on Sam's lips. It was almost like her catchphrase. Did Katie say
that to *her* friends, she wondered in horror? Did she sit around
in restaurants with her girlfriends, complaining about Paul's
behaviour, with the same stupid, self-deprecating, masochistic
expression on her face, like Sam? 'Didn't do what?' she
prompted, trying to keep her voice light and encouraging. She

felt like a detective or a forensic psychiatrist, gathering material to understand the psychological profile of the Other Woman. Knowledge was power. She needed to know how she was made so she could break her.

'It was when Nigel kept saying he'd tell Margo but the time wasn't right. After a while I realised that, left to him, there would never be a right time, so I thought that I'd give things a push.' Sam stopped, colouring a warm shade of guilt. 'It's not—'

'Something you're proud of,' Fran supplied impatiently. 'But anyway, go on.'

'Well, one night, he'd been round at mine and we'd—' Sam glanced round at the nearby tables to reassure herself that she wasn't being overheard. 'Been to bed,' she mouthed, without giving it voice.

'You'd what?' asked Fran, squinting in an unsuccessful attempt at lipreading.

Self-consciously, Sam mouthed it again.

'Oh, been to bed,' Fran repeated at full volume. 'And?'

'Quietly!' Sam warned. 'I have to be so careful!'

'Course you do,' agreed Fran. 'Sorry. Hang on.' She signed the credit card slip which the waiter had brought over, and dispatched him again with an imperious 'Thanks.'

Sam stood up. 'Walk me to the office and I'll tell you as we go,' she said quietly, unwilling now to trust Fran's discretion in this busy local restaurant.

Uncharacteristically dominant, she led the way out into the street where the thrum of the lunchtime traffic would mask her words, and following her, Fran wondered if Katie's life was now so cloak and dagger. There was some small amount of satisfaction to be had if so, if her rival had to live her life in the shadows, skulking from restaurants, choosing her confidantes with care. But not enough, Fran decided dismissively. Punching her in the face might bring more overt pleasure. Kicking her shins till they broke. Pulling her teeth out without anaesthetic . . .

'I'm only telling you this to be a help with your novel,' Sam was saying. 'I wouldn't want you to judge me harshly for a crime I didn't, in the end, commit.'

'Course not,' said Fran, and feigned a conspiratorial smile. 'And I really appreciate it. It must be so hard, being you.'

Returning her smile, reassured again, Sam innocently picked up her story as they walked. 'So, because he was late going home that night he was already nervous about Margo being suspicious, asking awkward questions and so on. I mean, he often uses the excuse of working late at the office, but at half past midnight! She was hardly going to swallow that this time!'

'No!' said Fran. 'Not unless she was a fool.' Like me, she thought, cursing herself for her naivety, fulminating silently inside. Working late at the office! Having to go in at the week-ends! How could she have been so blind, so trusting, so stupid? Traipsing over Europe for weeks at a time, shacked up in hotels with his bit of fluff, pretending to be hard done to! She'd kill him when she saw him. She'd rip his liver out, eat it while he watched. 'So what excuse was he going to use this time then?' she enquired in a deceptively pleasant voice.

'Well, being in the Masons helped – it's all so secretive any-way, he can often get away with quite a bit if he says he's had an emergency meeting at the Lodge.'

'Ah, yes, of course.' Of *course*!

'Anyway, while he was showering in the bathroom, I suddenly got this terrible temptation to force his hand. I crept out of bed and put one of my earrings in his jacket pocket. I thought, if Margo really is suspicious, she'll start searching round soon and she'll find it, and then he'll have to come clean.'

'*You* put the earring in his pocket?' Fran was gobsmacked, speechless, her breath had been taken away. Such treachery, such unspeakable spite, such a BITCH! Had this been a message from Katie then, a gauntlet flung down, jewels scattered in her path to grab her attention? God, the little cow must have been desperate to dare to do that. Didn't she realise that now she was dead?

'But I took it out again!' Sam protested. 'I couldn't go through with it! It's not something that I'm—'

'Proud of,' Fran supplied automatically. They were standing at the kerb, waiting for the little green man to give them permission to cross to Sam's office. 'Well, thanks for that,' she said suddenly, falsely bright. 'That's been a real help to my story.' She grabbed Sam for a perfunctory kiss, surprising her. 'I'm going to leave you here – got a few errands to do. Have a good viewing. Speak soon. 'Bye.'

Sam stood for a moment, stricken, watching Fran stride away purposefully down the street while she herself was left stuck at a crossroads. Well, wasn't that just like her life! She felt as if she had been giving damning evidence at her own trial this lunchtime, rather than lunching with a girlfriend. And she'd seen a side to Fran which she had never before suspected – judgemental, critical, angry . . . She blinked back tears. That was that, then. A friendship destroyed. Quite clearly Fran was disgusted with her, as she had every right to be. She tried to summon up every ounce of determination and resolve as she stood there on the kerb, the world going about its business in a blur around her. She *would* finish with Nigel – even though he had been sweetness itself at the weekend. It was totally untenable for her to live like this, hating herself and being hated by her best friend. The very next time he called her on her mobile she would end it there and then, on the phone. No meetings, where he could twist her round his little finger again, tell her his pretty little lies. She would be firm, curt, decisive, final.

Bracing her shoulders, sticking out her chin, she stepped off the pavement into a screeching of brakes and a volley of insults, and swiftly stepped back again, pantomiming her apologies, shaken to her core. She hadn't been watching, hadn't been paying attention, she could have been killed. Was it a sign? Hadn't fate just given her a second chance? But to do what? Why had she given away all her dirty secrets, revealed her disgraceful behaviour which she normally kept hidden inside? For clearly Fran was going to distance herself in the future, would disappear from Sam's life as quickly as she'd disappeared into the crowds just now. And if she finished with Nigel, she'd have no one.

No, now was not the time. She would wait and see if Fran ever called her again, wait for her to make the first move. If she did contact her, and proved her friendship, then Sam would sever the cord which held her to Nigel, however painful that might be. She felt a terrible pang, like bereavement, deep inside, and her eyes filled again. She didn't know whether she was grieving the loss of her lover, or of her friend.

Fourteen

❧

Fran was on her way to Leicester, to Paul's office, to a show-down with him and the Little Bitch with the Big Tits, belting along the A6 as if her life depended on it (which, after all, it did) when just past Great Glen she became aware of the flashing blue lights in her driving mirror and, cursing, she was hauled over to stop at the side of the road. She waited tensely, her hands clenched on the steering wheel, as the burly police-man lumbered out of his car towards her. God, it was so unfair! She was shaking, charged with too much adrenalin, and she felt dangerously close to unravelling. Whether that would take the form of rending her clothes, gnashing her teeth and wailing, or clawing at the policeman's throat with vixen-like screams, she just couldn't say. She controlled herself with great diffi-culty. It wouldn't do to let him see she was on her way to commit murder. She rolled down the window and attempted a smile.

'Yes, officer?'

'Would you get out of your vehicle, madam, please.'

'Of course.' In so doing, she flashed as much leg as possible, and stood close to him, looking up into his eyes, chattering away like a vacuous girl. 'Don't tell me I was speeding? Oh heavens, I'm so sorry. I think maybe there's a fault with the instruments – something electrical? The petrol gauge has been acting all funny too. Yesterday it was on empty, and when I went to fill it up this morning, it was already full!'

Instead of being charmed by her, which had been her intention, he took a step back with a small moue of distaste. 'Have you been drinking, madam?' he asked gravely.

Shit! He sounded as censorious as a founding father of the Plymouth Brethren. Just her luck! 'A small glass of white wine with my lunch,' she admitted, trying not to breathe on him again.

'If you'll remain by your vehicle I'll just fetch the breathalyser,' he said.

She watched him walk away, and for a moment was tempted to fling herself back into the car in an attempt to escape. With a supreme effort of will she forced herself to stay put, and glared, with hate-narrowed eyes, at the gawping drivers of passing cars as they went by unhindered by the long arm of the law. Why me? she wanted to scream, Why not you? She sank back to lean against her car, her mind working feverishly. How much *had* she had to drink? A couple of glasses of wine – or had it been three? Was that enough to convict her of drunk driving? And what were her rights? Could she refuse to breathe into his infernal machine, or would that count against her if it went to court? She just wanted this to be over as quickly as possible, to be on her way again to confront Paul and kill Katie. But what if she was over the limit? Presumably then she wouldn't be allowed to drive anywhere. She'd be bundled into the patrol car, and then what? Thrown into jail? Banned from driving? She needed this about as much as she needed her husband's floosie to be sending her declarations of war home in his pockets. Her lower lip trembled at the injustice.

Policeman Plod was back at her side, asking for her driver's licence and vehicle registration documents, which test she passed with flying colours. Licence in handbag, log book in glove compartment, so far so good.

'Now if you'd blow into this tube, madam.'

She bent her head to the task. Here goes nothing, she thought, and puffed precisely that into the breathalyser. His response was an old-fashioned look.

'Did I do it wrong?' she asked disingenuously.

'I think you'll find you actually have to breathe *out* for the machine to function at its optimum performance, madam,' he replied with heavy irony. Clearly he'd seen it all before.

'Look,' she said, prevaricating, hoping against hope that any delay, however minimal, might give her system a chance to get rid of the alcohol. 'I did say I'd had a glass of wine, didn't I? With lunch? But I also had some sherry trifle – which wouldn't have been *drinking* as such, would it, because it was *eating*. In fact, I didn't give it a second thought until now. I just hadn't made the connection. And who knows how much the chef used? Say if he'd been liberal? It might have been enough to have brought me just over the limit, and surely that wouldn't have been my fault. Would it? I couldn't be punished for eating dessert?'

Plod regarded her, unruffled. 'Are you saying that you don't want to breathe into this breathalyser, madam?'

Her heart leapt with hope. 'Do I have a choice then?'

'Within limits. We could go to the station if you'd prefer.'

'Not necessary, officer,' she said quickly, and wished she hadn't picked words so full of sibilants just sitting there, waiting to be slurred. She closed her eyes and blew, feeling utterly, utterly defeated, and handed over the damning evidence of her guilt. Until this moment, the tremendous shock she had suffered on discovering incontrovertible proof of Paul's infidelity had made her feel speedy and aggressive, but now that the whole world had shown it was against her, she was on the verge of simply dissolving into tears and wailing.

'You're lucky,' said Plod, in what sounded to her like a disappointed voice. 'It's amber.'

'Is that good?' asked Fran tremulously.

'Put it this way,' he said, 'The last bloke who tried the old sherry trifle routine on me was so full of booze he got banned for two years. Whereas you get off with a warning.'

'Oh thank you, thank you!' Fran gasped, and turned to get back in her car.

'Ay!' said Plod, 'You haven't had it yet.' He bent down to her eye level to fix her with a serious stare. 'Don't ever, ever let me catch you at it again. I'm the one who has to scrape your victims off the road.'

'I won't,' she said gratefully, blinking away her tears, and turned the key in the ignition. 'I'm a real stickler for drink-driving myself, officer. Honestly, if it hadn't been for that trifle—'

'Don't push your luck, Mrs Holdaway,' he said, cutting her off, and handed her documents back through the window. 'I'll be watching for you.'

Fran, chastened, couldn't bring herself to meet his eyes as he waved her out into the flow of traffic, where she made herself settle down to a sedate, law-abiding forty-nine miles an hour. This enforced curbing of her bat-out-of-hell instincts had the sobering effect of a short black coffee and a long cold shower, and the nearer she got to Leicester, the more she doubted the wisdom of her mission.

She had been so wild with rage when Sam had told her about sending the earring to Margo that she hadn't been able to think beyond storming into the office to confront Paul and beat Katie to a pulp. But now, as she drove through the outskirts of the city centre, only minutes from his office, scanning the streets for somewhere to park, she quailed at the image. Apart from anything else, she had never hit anybody in her life, and she doubted she could do it, even in self-defence. She was no hell-cat, no karate-kicking heroine. She was Ordinary Fran, unemployed housewife, doer of DIY, used to pottering to the shops, minding her own business – more likely to be the one who was bundled into the boot of a car, not the one doing the bundling. So wouldn't it be better to wait until she had Paul on his own tonight, to reason with him calmly, and get him to give up his affair?

But did she still want him after this, she wondered. Was she big enough to forgive and forget? Could she ever trust him again? Could she rid her mind of the unwanted images of him playing Mr and Mrs in a hotel in Berlin, of his kissing and canoodling with another woman in a queen-size en suite? She didn't know. But just thinking of his betrayal made her see red again, and ready to kill. Even if she didn't take him back afterwards, she would have the dog in the manger satisfaction of having lashed out at the cow who had dared to eat her hay.

Providence appeared to approve her renewed resolve for vengeance, for just as she despaired of ever finding a place to park within a fifty-mile radius, a van pulled out from the kerb a few yards ahead, and she slipped her car effortlessly into the generous space it had left. She was practically outside Paul's office. Without waiting for doubt to enter her head again, she grabbed her handbag which bore the evidence for the prosecution, Exhibits A and B, and sprang out of the car and up the outer steps of the building, to press the entryphone bell. She waited impatiently for a response, her body like a coiled spring, ready to leap up the two flights as soon as she was admitted.

A mellifluous voice greeted her. 'Software Solutions, hello?'

It was The Cow. Fran choked back a stream of invective and announced herself through gritted teeth.

'Oh! Hi Fran!' The buzzer sounded and the door yielded to Fran's aggressive shove. The Cow sounded shocked to hear her, with gave Fran grim satisfaction. Had she caught them at it? Were they panicking, struggling back into their clothes even now? The thought fuelled her feet, and she pounded up the stairs taking them two at a time, until another thought had her pounding back down them again. Shit! She'd forgotten to lock her car.

Two minutes later, the wind already out of her sails, she was back on the doorstep ringing the bell.

'Hel-lo?'

She felt like an idiot. 'It's Fran.'

'Fran? Didn't I just let you in?'

'Yes, but then I had to go out again because I'd— oh just press the damn buzzer, will you?'

A merry laugh. 'Sure.' *The supercilious bitch.*

Mounting the stairs for the second time, Fran was past the peak of her physical powers and down the other side ('*Must* start jogging,' went through her head, which self-criticism was about as welcome at the moment as this false entrance). Panting slightly, she hauled herself to the top and finally made it past Paul's logo and into his office to arrive glaring at – nobody. She faltered, completely wrong-footed.

'Hello?'

'Oh, hi Fran!' The Cow called from the direction of the tiny kitchen. 'I'm just putting the kettle on. Fancy a cup?'

'No thank you.' *I've come to kill you, you stupid bitch!* 'Where's Paul?'

Katie emerged, cup in hand, looking shifty. 'He's – out of the office today.'

'*Out* of the office? Out? I thought the two of you had a lot of catching up to do *in* the office after your trip?'

'Yes, well,' said Katie, and bit her lip. 'How are you? I've not seen you for ages. You're looking great.'

Lying cow. Okay, two could play at polite chit-chat. 'How was your wedding at the weekend?'

'My wedding?'

A hit, a palpable hit! Fran had known in her bones that must have been a lie. It had just been an excuse for Paul to see her on Saturday. *Go on, punk, get out of that!*

She did. 'I'm not getting married till October.'

Now it was Fran's turn to falter. 'You're getting married?'

Katie grinned. 'Yup. I finally tamed Steve. Well – early days to know. But at least I lassoed him!'

Convention demanded a response, however grudging, and however puzzled. 'Congratulations.' What was going on here? Was this another lie? And if so, what was the point? Why send her earrings by pocket post, and then, when she arrived, hot to trot, pretend that everything was normal?

Fran tried another tack. 'Sorry to hear about the computer crashing. Steve must have been as pissed off as I was that you and Paul had to work Saturday after being away for so long.'

She was rewarded by a fleeting look of puzzlement as great as her own had been a moment before. 'Mm,' said Katie, and starting looking through her desk drawers. It was clearly a diversionary tactic to cover the fact that she was unable to meet Fran's eyes. Time to move in for the kill.

'Looking for this?' Fran asked with a voice of steel, and held out the earring on the flat of her hand.

'What's that?' Katie parried, playing for time, her head still under her desk.

'The message you sent me.'

'Message?' Katie repeated, reappearing slowly, her cheeks flushed.

'Your earring,' said Fran with contempt, covering the short distance between them and shoving it under her nose. 'That I found in Paul's pocket.'

Katie cowered in her seat beneath Fran's dominant position, looking up in a semblance of innocence. 'Fran – look – honestly, it's not mine.'

Fran curled her lips into a cruel sardonic smile. 'No, of course not. He probably just – what? Found it in the street and decided on impulse to bring it home? And what about *this*?' She produced the hotel bill like a rapier from her side and held it to her adversary's face. 'Enjoy your break in Berlin, Mrs Holdaway?'

With difficulty, Katie pushed her wheeled chair backwards and stood up, keeping out of arm's reach. 'Fran,' she began awkwardly.

'*Mrs Holdaway* to you, you little bitch!' Fran exploded. She was shaking with rage, the hotel bill trembling in her hand as she pursued Katie round the small office. 'The *real* Mrs Holdaway! The stupid one! The one you think you can cheat, and steal from, and lie to!'

Reversing, defensive, Katie was at a distinct disadvantage, and she stumbled against the office furniture, almost falling. 'Fran, please!' she implored, recovering her balance and backing still, her hands held in front of her face to ward off the inevitable blows. 'Listen to me! It wasn't me! It was—' Wild-eyed, suddenly she turned tail and bolted across the office to the loo with Fran in hot pursuit. The door slammed shut in her face, and the key was turned in the lock from inside.

'Come out here, you coward!' Fran cried, raining blows against the flimsy wood in her frustration. 'If you're so bloody innocent, what have you got to be afraid of? Hey? Huh?'

There was a small sob from behind the door by way of response.

'Go on!' Fran challenged her whimpering foe. 'Surprise me! Who are you going to blame? If it wasn't you sharing my husband's bed in Berlin, then who?' She rattled the doorknob to focus Katie's attention, and followed it up with a hefty kick to the door. 'I've got all the time in the world, Katie. There's no escape.'

'Fran, honestly, you're making a mistake,' Katie stammered in a tiny voice. 'You need to talk to Paul,' she finished lamely.

'*Don't* tell *me* what I need to do with *my husband*!' roared Fran, punctuating her words with more kicks. 'Or so help me God, I'll kill!' To prove it, she rammed the door with her shoulder, and Katie sobbed again.

'Why send me the sodding earring if you didn't want me to

know?' Fran demanded, shouldering the door again. 'Yes, I know all your pathetic little mistressy tricks – I've been taking advice from a professional!' She rubbed her shoulder, bruised now from all the battering, and looked around for a better instrument. But what was she thinking of? She was Extraordinary Fran. She couldn't be seen, and therefore had the upper hand. 'I've got a gun here, Katie,' she said, grabbing a stapler and clunking it against the door. 'I'm going to count to three, and then I'm going to fire it.'

'Fran!'

'One.'

'Fran, please, I beg you!'

'Two.'

'It wasn't me!'

'Thr—'

'Helen!' Katie screamed. 'He was with Helen!'

The shock at hearing that name after so long, combined with the adrenalin that was surging through her veins and the manic physical exertion she had been expending, nearly floored Fran. She felt dizzy, her vision dimmed to grey, and she staggered back to lean against a desk.

'Helen?' she repeated, dazed. Paul's first wife? Impossible!

'I'm really sorry,' whispered Katie. 'I told him I didn't approve. She came out to join him. She was with us for most of the trip.'

A sound came out of Fran's mouth which was something between a gasp and a hiccup. She felt sick. She had gone cold all over, but her skin was sticky with sweat. She dry-heaved.

'Fran? Are you okay? Fran? I'm coming out now,' Katie said bravely. She unlocked the door and peeked around it. What she saw was the crumpled husk of the betrayed wife, and risking life and limb, she approached her, her hands fluttering with the desire to give comfort and the fear of being hit.

'Is that where he is now? With her?' Fran asked hollowly, and Katie nodded her confirmation.

'I'm so sorry,' she said again.

Fran nodded dumbly, her face white, and staggered back the way she'd come.

'Fran?' Katie called after her anxiously. 'Don't you want to sit down for a bit? Are you all right to drive?'

Her would-be assassin paused for a moment in the doorway, and without turning, mumbled, 'Thank you, Kate. Sorry about—' She shrugged hopelessly, and was gone.

Fifteen

Fran remembered nothing of the drive back to Little Langton even before she had started on the brandy, which she did as soon as she was through her front door. The second thing she did was to phone Paul on his mobile to scream at him to come home *now*, but he'd put it to divert, so she had to content herself with screaming impotently to his answering service. Between then and the time the phone finally rang, the level in the brandy bottle had mysteriously gone down by half and dusk had fallen.

She whipped round at the sound – she had been pacing the house for hours, it seemed, unable to settle, like a caged and dangerous animal – and her eyes gleamed with rage. Crossing the room at speed, she pounced on the receiver, and lifted it, saying nothing.

'Hello, it's Mummy. Frances? Are you there?'

Jesus *Christ* Almighty!! Anything but this! Fran swallowed hard and tried to steady her voice. 'Hi – Mum, listen, it's not a good time.'

'Oh, sorry, are you cooking?'

'Mm.'

'Well it won't take long, and it's why I've called, actually. Those recipes we found, Frances – for the meal with the Harrisons? – were an absolute *triumph*! You should have *heard* their praise! And *slimming*? We've been eating nothing else since, and I've already shed four pounds! Honestly, Frances, you should be doing the same.'

'Mum—'

'Now don't get touchy. You know as well as I do that you've
been putting on weight ever since you said "I do" to poor Paul.
Anyway, what I need now are some more recipes,' Rachel rolled
on, oblivious of the blow she had just delivered. 'Roger's
complaining he's bored to the back teeth. Honestly! I try to
please him on one issue, and then I find I've offended him on
another! Men! What would you do?'

Castrate them? thought Fran, full of her own agenda, but
instead managed to say again, 'Mother – it's not a good time.'

'Oh dear,' Rachel complained in an injured tone, 'I always
know I'm in trouble when she calls me "Mother". What have I
done now?' she whined. 'If you don't want me to call you, you
merely have to say!'

If only it were that easy Fran would have said it unequivocally
and with heartfelt passion now, but she knew from experience
this was a hollow offer. 'I'm expecting an important call. About
work,' she extemporised. 'I'll call you tomorrow.'

'You won't be able to get me tomorrow,' Rachel interjected,
'because I—'

But before she could launch herself fully into the complexi-
ties of her engagement diary, Fran interrupted her firmly and
loudly with, 'Mother, *please*!' and the phone went dead in her
hand. Terrific. As if she needed more trouble, she had just alien-
ated the woman who was supposed to be a girl's best friend. But
then again, of course, in Rachel's case . . .

Fran returned the receiver to its cradle, and refilled her glass,
feeling even more wretched. She still couldn't absorb the knowledge which had come her way today. Paul back with Helen?
Impossible! After all her betrayals of him, after all his hurt, after
all he'd said? And she was older, for God's sake – no man left
his wife for an *older* woman, surely to God? Unless of course his
wife had grown so fat that even her own mother was repulsed
by her. Pacing up and down again, she caught sight of herself in
the mirror which she'd bought and hung after reading an article

about *feng shui*. So much for going with the flow. Mirror mirror on the wall, who is the dumpiest dumped wife of them all? *You, fat face. Look at you – have you weighed yourself recently? No? I rest my case. And those jeans you heaved out the other week – it wasn't really because you didn't like the cut, was it? It was because they didn't fit any more. They made your arse look like a barrage balloon and you couldn't pull the zip up. Look at your thighs, woman! What bloke could be expected to be turned on by the size of them? Only a pervert with a fetish for hippopotami!*

Almost immediately, the phone rang again, stopping her mid-swig, but instead of striding over to snatch it up she waited for the answering machine to click in, for fear it was Rachel ready for Round Two of the Heavyweight Mother and Daughter Contest.

It was Allie. 'Fran, darling lovey heart,' she began, which almost tempted Fran to answer, but she held her ground. It was so good to hear a friendly voice, but she couldn't talk to anybody until she had cleared things up with Paul, for better or for worse. After all, it was just conceivable (to a person grabbing at straws) that Katie could have been lying. Maybe she had been spurned by Paul, and she'd been getting her revenge? He could be working hard right now – or queuing up with the Masons to bare his breast.

In the meantime, Allie was still banging on into the machine, hogging the line. '. . . I've been a v. bad friend – you must have thought I was dead! I *have* been thinking of you, but from a prone position. What am I saying?! I've been in *every* position since we spoke! He is *fantastic*! I can't believe my luck! And you know what I'm like about work – obsessive! – but I even rang in *sick* last week, told them I couldn't get out of bed – which was absolutely true, of course, but not for the reasons they thought!'

There was a muffled male voice in the background, and Allie called 'Coming!', then the male voice again, saying something which sounded like 'What – already?', and an explosion of laughter from Allie before she lowered her voice to whisper excitedly into the receiver. 'He shags like a *stallion*! Don't ask me how I know, I've had a rather eclectic past – just call me Catherine the Great! But get this, Fran – the weirdest thing – you know what *I'm* like about men – fuck 'em and forget 'em. But I think I might be *in love*! Me! And it *was* all to do with a mechanical failure, just like Gypsy Rose Lee said – and you were there! When you walked out of Q&A and I got back in the lift? We consummated in the *elevator*, stuck between two floors! Not the pretty boy in the dungarees who you saw – he got out at the mezzanine and Trevor got in. You should have seen my face! Remember the clairvoyant said he wouldn't be my type? Well, just *wait* till you see him! And everybody in the office knew about it, because apparently there's a *surveillance camera* in there, and they were all in Security, watching us in black and white! By the time they winched us up, the usual suspects had gathered round the lift doors and we were *applauded* as we came out, still adjusting our clothing! Anyway,' she continued, at last beginning to wind down, 'there is limited appeal in dishing the dirt to a tape recorder without your accompanying oohs and aahs. *Call me*. Hope everything's going well in the freelance world, by the way. Big kisses. Speak soon. 'Bye.'

Despite herself, Fran had actually smiled during Allie's breathless monologue, and she was reminded just how much she'd missed her. But then Paul walked through the door, sheepish, eyes cast down, and Fran didn't feel like smiling again for a very long time.

Sixteen

Though they talked for some hours, Fran and Paul might have been speaking in different languages for all either of them really understood of the other's frame of mind. Paul, though anxious about this meeting with Fran, was feeling the elation of having fallen in love with Helen (again), and intoxicated by the winds of change which he could feel almost palpably blowing fresh and invigorating against his skin. Fran, sensing the same winds of change, felt battered, chilled to the bone, abandoned, betrayed, shocked, bewildered, and as if one of her limbs had been severed.

The misunderstandings began from the very first moment, as soon as Paul was over the threshold. His present wife, speechless with rage, paralysed with terror, watched him cross the room with an abject air and a strange half-smile, eyes downcast, to sit in his usual chair, where he studied his hands for a moment and finally said, 'Fran, we've got to talk.'

'You bet your fucking *life* we've got to talk!' was the immediate shouted response, which was emphasised by Fran's brandy glass hitting the wall just behind his head. Well, at least she'd got eye contact now. He was looking at her like a startled bunny.

Recovering himself and addressing her in a slow and reasonable voice, as one would a dangerous, unpredictable hysteric, he began again, 'I know I'm late, and I'm sorry. I want to tell you why.'

'I *know* why, you pathetic, miserable cretin!' Fran screamed. 'You're back into necrophilia! You're shagging Helen again!'

The startled bunny was now staggered. 'How do you know? Has she called you? I *told* her not to – I *said* I was going to talk to you tonight.'

Without warning Fran suddenly retched, and she fled to the downstairs cloakroom. It was as if she'd been punched in the gut. She didn't know what she'd been expecting, but nothing as final as this. Screaming, certainly. Shouting, of course. Insults hurled like sharp objects – but with her doing the hurling, not him. Then apologies, recriminations, promises, an attempt at renewing their vows; a procession of peace offerings on plates of gold (including Helen's head), the offer of a second honeymoon in a tropical location . . .

Instead, she now knew what every cheated person in the world feared most – they had been talking about her in their bed. She had become an inconvenience. She needed to be tidied out of their way. She was a small problem which needed to be solved. She wasn't even their enemy, since she was already vanquished. She was a corpse, waiting to be buried. A casualty of war littering the battlefield, destined for an unmarked grave. There was no dignity in this.

Neither was there dignity in her present position, blinded by tears, pressed against the porcelain on her knees, spewing up cognac which, by a miracle of sanitation, would now be converted into water. And wasn't that just like her life? Only minutes ago, her cup had overfloweth – she'd had a job, a marriage. Now she had dust.

Paul had followed her and was standing over her in a tremulous semblance of concern, offering her a dampened towel, enquiring into her health. For a moment, seeing red, she wondered how she had ever been able to love him, how she had ever been taken in. Nevertheless she snatched the proffered towel. The worst she could do to him under the circumstances was not to say thank you. She felt impotent and undefended, rejected and unloved. And fat, of course. For why else would this have happened, if false notions of contentment hadn't turned her to sodding seed?

She rinsed her mouth in the hand basin and washed her hands and face, and then waddled back into the living room, followed haplessly by Paul, agonisingly conscious of thigh rubbing against thigh.

'Would you like some water?' he asked.

'Wine,' she said hollowly.

'Do you think you should?' he began, but was silenced by her look, her eyes boring into his like poisoned gimlets. 'White?' he suggested, on his way swiftly to the kitchen, fearful of being impaled.

'Whatever,' she said, and on his return she said, 'Why?'

He sat then, a safe distance away, conscious, it seemed, that he had just handed her another missile. He'd brought himself a glass too, and emptied it before speaking. 'I never got over her,' he said simply. 'And I'm truly, truly sorry, Fran. I wouldn't have hurt you for the world.'

'Bullshit,' Fran snapped. 'You have.'

'I know,' he conceded, 'and again, all I can do is apologise. I know you're hurt and angry – you have every right to be.'

'You think this is angry?' stormed Fran, standing as if propelled from an ejector seat. 'No, *this* is angry, Paul!' And suddenly she had the many hands of Kali, goddess of destruction, sweeping surfaces of what once had been ornaments but which now were a salvo of ammunition, hurtling through the air at astonishing speed, all aimed at Paul's head.

Discretion being the better part of valour, he hid behind his chair and, when he could finally hear her sobbing instead of screaming, he peeked out to check the All Clear. The room was wrecked. And so was their marriage. Fran was defeated, cowering, her anguished cries cutting him to the bone. He watched her in silence, at a loss to know what to do, twinned opposing instincts impelling him both to rush forward to comfort her, and to flee from the house, to get the hell out.

'I—' he began. 'Fran?' he began again. 'Sweetheart?' He had only ever seen one person as utterly destroyed as this in his entire life and that was he himself, after Helen had betrayed him for the first time. It brought him no comfort that the boot was now on his own foot. He would rather have cut it off than it offend him like this. Frightened as he was, the instinct to offer comfort won over his craven impulse for flight, and cautiously he approached Fran, testing her reaction to a hand on her back, then an arm round her shoulders, now her face, wet with tears and contorted with grief, pressed against his chest.

'It's all my fault, Fran,' he said softly, rocking her, his arms around her. 'It's nothing to to with you.'

'It's – every – thing – to do – with – me,' she sobbed, as though winded. 'It's me – who's – left – like – this.'

'I know, I'm sorry – I meant—'

She pushed herself from his embrace, still gripping his arms in her hands, and looked at him, the meniscus of her tears defying gravity, hanging like crescent moons beneath her eyes. 'Why did you pretend?' she asked him. 'What was Sunday supposed to be about? Nothing but a last-ditch stand?'

He paused for a fraction, then dumbly nodded his head. The least he could give her was honesty now, however late and unwelcome it might be.

'I really thought you loved me,' she said, so numb now she was beyond all feeling except emptiness. 'You made me feel guilty. I thought that me wanting a baby was irresponsible compared to you wanting to join the Masons to improve your position at work. I blamed myself for making you angry, for quitting my job. But all along it was that you were appalled I'd given up my livelihood just as you'd decided to dump me, wasn't it?'

Her voice was so dull now, so devoid of life, that this sounded less like an angry accusation and more like a person checking stock. Paul cleared his throat, his lips half-forming words and then rejecting them. Finally he said, 'Helen came out to Europe on an impulse. I had already seen her a couple of times before, and we had been speaking on the phone since – well, for quite a while, to be frank.' Honesty was one thing. The kind of candour which would have him admit now that Helen had, in fact, first phoned him on his mobile during his honeymoon with Fran, could only bring more pain. 'I thought when I met you – well, when we decided to marry – that I was over her completely. But I wasn't. When she said she wanted me back, when she apologised, when she said she'd made a terrible mistake – at first I told her it was too late. Then . . .'

'You realised it wasn't,' Fran supplied. 'You thought, fuck the fat one – I'll have the ancient one back instead.'

'Helen is no more ancient than you are fat,' Paul felt bound to demur. 'Have you been talking to Rachel recently?'

Fran nodded, and the shared intimacy, the reminder of a common enemy, of their old mutual support for each other, raised a weak smile from them both.

'Can't you change your mind again?' Fran asked simply, humbled.

Her vulnerability tore at his heart. For a moment he weighed in his mind staying, and going, and almost gave way. But the winds of change were calling him still, whispering of fresh pastures, of a new life with Helen, his one true love. 'I know in my heart that you're twice the person she'll ever be,' he said, which sounded to Fran's ears like the empty flattery it was, 'but I can't seem to change. I've tried, and failed, and brought you down with me. She's—'

'A bitch,' Fran offered. 'And you like it rough.'

'Maybe,' Paul conceded, since it cost him nothing to agree.

'And she's like your mummy, and you want to stay a little boy.'

'Possibly,' he said, a little stiffness now entering his voice.

'Which is why you don't want babies, because then you wouldn't be an only child – you'd be forced to be a father and grow up.'

'I don't know if I can go along with that,' he countered, his ego having taken offence.

'Which is why Helen is perfect, because she's dried-up and menopausal, whereas I am fertile and fecund,' Fran continued, her ego having decided to build itself up.

'She's forty-*eight*!' Paul remonstrated.

'A crone,' Fran agreed.

'I don't think it's right to attack somebody who isn't here to defend themselves,' Paul said sanctimoniously.

'So where was *I* when the two of you were in your hotel bed in Berlin?!' Fran stormed, the truce now clearly over. 'Wasn't *that* an attack on *me*? Or did you somehow strangely think, little boy, that by putting *my name* on the bill, it kind of made it all right? Is that it, Peter Pan?'

'I didn't put *your* name on the bill,' Paul shouted back, changing in an instant from her champion, the white knight, into her enemy, the black. 'I put Helen's!'

'*Who* is Mrs Holdaway? Her or me?!'

'Both of you!'

'But you *divorced* her!'

'She never changed her name.'

'I don't give a flying *fuck* what she calls herself. I am Mrs Holdaway!'

'You're the *second* Mrs Holdaway – she's the *first*!'

After that there was nothing left to say or shout, and Fran didn't even have the energy to throw things as he walked towards the front door.

'I'll call to collect my things at your convenience,' Paul said in a small voice.

Fran nodded. 'I'm having the house,' she said quickly, raising her voice once again. 'Don't think for one minute that I've done all this work for *you* to capitalise on!'

He hovered in the doorway for a second, then turned to face her. 'That's fair,' he said. 'Agreed.' Turning back, he went out of the door and disappeared from her life.

And thus it was, ironically, that while thinking she was standing up for her rights, proud that even in this weakened state she could assert herself, believing she had just defended her own property from thieves, the second Mrs Holdaway had set the scene for her own destruction.

Seventeen

Now followed a period so dark, so full of negative energy, that it was as though Fran had been swallowed by a black hole. The phone remained silent, and no visitors came to her door. Her two best friends Allie and Sam were both, for their different reasons, waiting for her to call them, and her mother had taken offence at her tone. For this Fran was grateful. She felt she would never be ready to face anybody ever again, so full of shame was she, so low was her opinion of herself. To be rejected by two husbands: to be twice divorced at thirty-five! She had never guessed before quite how repulsive she must be, how unappealing, how unattractive, how disappointing as a wife.

After Paul had walked out of the door she had first hit the bottle and then hit the deck. She'd woken from a dull stupor in the early hours of the morning to find her head under the coffee table and her feet on it, in the most extraordinary contortion which would have defied even the supplest and most practised of yogis. Since she was still completely blotto, however, she thought nothing much of it, but staggered across the living-room floor, crunching broken ornaments on her way, mounted the stairs, fell down them, mounted them again, and finally made it to the shameful emptiness of her marital bed, where she found oblivion once more.

When she finally woke again sunlight was streaming through her bedroom window, blinding her and making her wince from the pain in her head. Outside, she could hear the sound of Archie scraping metal trowel against unyielding brick, hear him loading the wheelbarrow and trundling it with its squeaking wheel, hear his loud and cheerful tuneless whistle. Her first instinct was to leap out of bed, to throw open the window, to lean out and scream at him to *shut the fuck up!*, but a nanosecond later another instinct stilled her, and she froze into a foetal position under the bedclothes. What would Archie think if he knew she was at home a second week running? She still hadn't admitted to him that she had left her job. And what would he say if, when he came in to make his tea, he wandered into the living room, and saw the carnage of the chaos she had wreaked, which she suddenly remembered with a sickening jolt? She didn't want *anybody* to know the extent of her failure as a human being, least of all Archie, who to Fran was the quintessence of normality, decency, and a quiet, ordered family life. In comparison to Archie she felt depraved and disgusting, a thing that must be hidden, cursed above all cattle and above every beast of the field, made to slither on her belly and eat dust all the days of her life; it was she, not the serpent, who was the cause of all sin.

Lying there, huddled in the darkness under her duvet, she just wanted to die, to disappear. For after all was said and done, how hard was it really to be a successful human being, and how had she come to flunk such easy tests? Adult entrée into society required the successful commission of two simple tasks, and she had failed them both utterly. One was honest toil, which she had rejected, and the other was the finding of a partner, who she had been rejected by. She felt shunned, as if she had been cast out of Eden for fear of upsetting the others, an abomination. She would have lain quietly in her bed until she died of starvation, if it were not for the dread of being discovered by Archie. She didn't want his pity, she couldn't face his concern, and she definitely didn't want the whole of Little Langton to know that at Number 84, The Avenue there lived a woman who was so unattractive and so vile that two husbands had fled from her embrace. What to do?

Suddenly she remembered that carte blanche of excuses, the sick note, and eventually she dragged herself from her bed, discovering as she did so that she was still wearing most of yesterday's clothes. She pulled them off, staggering against the chest of drawers as she tugged at her trousers, hopping on one leg, and noticing now the small cuts on her feet, the purple bruises flowering on her shins, the puzzling stiffness in her shoulder (for, since the shock of Paul's abandonment of her the evening before, she had forgotten completely the image of herself as human battering ram, pounding against Katie's toilet door). Slowly, painfully, she drew on her pyjamas and her dressing gown and padded down the stairs.

The devastation of the living room was even worse than she remembered. There was not a surface she hadn't cleared of missiles, not an ornament she hadn't broken, not a picture hanging on the wall still straight and square. The brandy bottle was on its side on the floor, having discharged the little she had left in it onto the carpet. The whole room stank of booze, and her stomach heaved at the memory. The darkness of the heavy velvet curtains, still drawn, enshrouded her in gloom.

Carefully, she picked her way across jagged glass and broken ceramics to the kitchen, where the glare of the sun made her shield her eyes and gasp with pain. Half-blinded, she groped across the surfaces for her shopping jotter and a pencil, and she scribbled a note to Archie, telling him of the sudden and virulent virus that had stricken her in the night, forcing her to take time off work. The doctor had been consulted on the phone, she wrote, and had told her that for a speedy recovery she must have absolute rest and quiet, so would Archie please take the week off? In an attempt at warding off any well-meaning interference, she added a postscript that she had everything she needed, that she was being well looked after, that at this moment she was probably sleeping and shouldn't be disturbed, and that anyway, she was dreadfully contagious and would be for at least a week, and she couldn't bear it on her conscience if Archie caught her lurgy.

Ducking down beneath window-level she crossed the kitchen, bent as a hairpin, and reached her hand up to prop the note against the kettle just as Archie came in for his tea. It was hard to say who was the more startled as he banged the door open against her crouching form.

'I'm *sorry*, me duck!' Archie exclaimed, recovering himself as he helped her up from the floor, 'I din't know you was in!'

Fran rubbed her hipbone, where yet another bruise was now forming, and kept her gaze on the ground, shielding her face with her arm as she handed him the note. 'I'm sick,' she said. 'Don't come near me!', and she backed away to open the fridge and take refuge behind its door.

'You look terrible!' said Archie. 'You goo back to bed, I'll bring you wharrever it is you want.'

'No!' Fran cried. Anything but that he see the living room! 'I've got it – juice! Here!' She waved it at him, wild-eyed, forgetting to hide her face. 'I've had the doctor. Read the note. I'm contagious – don't come near me! And I just need peace and quiet. I'll see you next week, probably. No need to worry. I'll call you when I'm better. But if you don't mind packing up just now? It's the noise, Archie, my head! I just can't bear the noise!'

'It ent meningitis, is it?' asked Archie in concern. 'My Hilda had that two year ago. Y'ought to be in hospital if it is. I could run you down in me van, if you like.'

'No, no, just a virus, just some bug. I'll be fine if I'm just left to sleep.'

Archie was unconvinced, reluctant to leave her in what looked to him like a near-death condition. 'Have you took owt? Will Paul be coming home early to look in on you?'

'Yes! That's right! Paul will be here soon. He's going to pick up my prescription and bring it home. Honestly, Archie, I'm sorry but I really do think you should go. What if you caught it and got sick?'

'Doon't worry about me, me duck. I've never had a day's illness in my life. Strong as a bleddy ox I am,' Archie grinned.

'But what if you carried it, and gave it to Hilda? Or to one of your grandchildren?' In her desperation for him to be gone, Fran was grasping at dirty straws. 'Apparently it can be lethal to older people – especially those who have had meningitis, so they say. And young children are particularly prone – it can make them deaf, or stunt their growth!'

'Has it been on the news?' asked Archie, stunned to hear of what must surely be a terrible new plague, but nonetheless backing now towards the door for fear of taking death home to his family.

Fran could almost hear the shrill sirens of the health authorities bearing down upon her once Archie had spread the story of her dangerous illness. Why wouldn't he just go? The more he made her lie, the worse it all sounded. 'No, it's not an epidemic, just a few isolated cases. I picked it up in London, from work. The doctor said if I just quarantined myself, that I could save an outbreak in Little Langton. He was most insistent about it. So go, Archie, go!' She flapped her hands at him and he retired to the other side of the door, still hovering, watching her through the glass.

'Are you sure there's nowt you want, duck?' he mouthed, his face wreathed in concern.

'Not a thing. Goodbye!'

'I'll just pack me tools up then,' he pantomimed, and Fran nodded in relief. As soon as he had turned away from the window she looked at the carton of juice in her hand and rejected it in favour of white wine. Hair of the dog, or nail in the coffin – either way she didn't care, she just wanted oblivion back in her life. Grabbing bottle and corkscrew and a half-pint glass, she fled back from whence she'd come, where she lay in bed, swallowing great gulps, until she heard Archie's van start up, and then recede into the distance. Alone at last.

And that was how she stayed for the rest of the week, sometimes weeping, always drinking, occasionally sleeping. The phone rang twice during that time. The first time was three days later, which woke her from a desolating dream. If her ebb had ever been lower she certainly hadn't known it, and she was at a point of such hopeless despair that she would have taken Paul back like a shot if he'd offered. She lay on the couch, silent in the darkness of the living room whose closed velvet drapes had remained undisturbed since the night Paul had left, counting the rings and waiting for the machine to click in. Finally it did, and its smug outgoing message informed her and whoever else was listening that Fran and Paul Holdaway were unable to take the call, but that they would return it as soon as ever they could if the caller would just leave a message after the long tone. The long tone came and went, and then Paul started speaking. Fran was up and across the other side of the room, the receiver in her hand, before he had completed his opening phrase of, 'Hi, Fran, it's—'

'Paul!' she said. 'Hi! Sorry, I was – outside. Gardening.'

'At this time?' he asked, puzzled.

She glanced down at the clock on the video recorder, and saw it was 22.36. 'Well – watering,' she offered.

'After all the rain we've had?' he said in surprise. 'Or did it miss you?'

'Yes. It's been completely dry here,' she said in some annoyance. 'But I don't imagine you've called to ask me about the weather?'

'No,' he agreed. 'I was wondering, actually, if it might be convenient for me to come over tomorrow night?'

'Tomorrow? Of course! What time?'

'Seven-ish?'

'See you then!'

She ended the call quickly, terrified that he might prick this brief bubble of happiness by saying he was just coming to collect some of his clothes. She wanted him back so badly, she ached with longing to see him, her rage was a thing of the past. She would be conciliatory, she would surprise him with a nice meal, she would be dressed to kill. She would be apologetic for having been rude about Helen, for getting so angry, for having thrown things at him. She gazed at the room is dismay. The broken ornaments were still lying where they had landed, and other stuff had now joined them on the floor – dirty glasses, empty bottles, cigarette packets, overflowing ashtrays, ice-cream cartons, biscuit wrappers, the foil containers of microwaved food. For three days Fran had been bingeing and living like a slattern, and now suddenly that was over and she was galvanised into action. By four in the morning every surface gleamed, the sticky patches on the carpet had been scrubbed on hands and knees, four black plastic bags had been filled with detritus and shoved outside by the bin. Living-room ornaments were at a premium, of course, but she solved that by hunting through the house for any surplus, rearranging dressers and windowsills upstairs to hide the gaps, and spreading them out sparsely downstairs in a new hybrid style which she dubbed in her mind 'Victorian minimalism'.

By the time she finally got into her bed (which due to her cleaning frenzy she had, on sudden impulse, stripped of its crumby, coffee-stained sheets and replaced them with her best lace-edged Egyptian cotton) she felt better than she had in ages. This, of course, was partly due to the fact that, since she'd been doing housework till the wee small hours, she hadn't had the time or the inclination to consume so much alcohol, but it was also because she felt the satisfaction of achievement. Honest toil, it appeared, was back in her repertoire.

She woke late, but without a headache, and it was a pleasure to walk through the living room, where everything was now arranged just so, into the sparkling kitchen, where she decided to breakfast on solids for a change. She hadn't done a grocery shop for ages, and the fridge and the cupboards looked decidedly bare, so while she chewed her muesli and waited for her egg to boil she made a list of provisions. She decided on salad niçoise with seared, fresh tuna and a home-made vinaigrette flavoured with herbs from the garden for supper with Paul – one of his all-time favourites, and a dish which was more or less flung together at the end, so it wouldn't look as if she'd been to a great deal of trouble on his behalf. Conciliatory was one thing; desperate, quite another. She had more eggs in the fridge and enough potatoes, and there was lettuce aplenty in the vegetable patch, but she would need to buy green beans, black olives, tomatoes, a tin of anchovies, some tuna steaks, and some fresh crusty bread, which meant a trip to Market Harborough. The thought of going out, and worse, going into Harborough where she might bump into people she knew, brought her up short, and she temporarily lost the will to live, staring into space, her heart pounding. By the time she rescued her egg from the pan it was hard-boiled, and anyway she'd lost her appetite, but, rallying, she put it on one side for the salad. Waste not want not, she told herself. Everything has its place, and there is a place for everything. So butch up, get dressed, and get out of the house *now*.

Showering was a joy without a hangover, she rediscovered, and as she luxuriated in the powerful stream of hot water she decided to pamper herself with a total body exfoliation and a hair treatment, which had the added benefit of putting off the fateful hour when she must venture forth into the wide world. An hour and a half later she was depressed again, sitting in front of her dressing-table mirror, wondering where on earth to start with her ravaged, puffy eyes. She couldn't possibly go out looking like that – it was too obvious she'd been crying non-stop for days. She felt hugely tempted just to go back to bed and give up on the day, felled by the first hurdle, but with a great effort of will she rallied herself again and compromised. There was only one thing for it, she realised with relief – she must lie down quietly for a while with cucumber slices balanced on her eyelids.

This she did, pottering down the stairs and back again with the last of the cucumber (mental note: buy some more while out at the shops), and sinking back onto her bed with an exhausted sigh. That was better. Naturally she was tired after her night-shift cleaning. She shouldn't rush things, she told herself – she should treat herself like the invalid she had pretended to be to Archie. After all, she had had a tremendous shock, and that was as physically draining as running a marathon, or completing an assault course, or being in a car crash – more so, probably.

However, after all her recent activity and the accompanying sense of achievement, this felt wrong and lazy and under-achieving. She suddenly remembered her Louise Hay tape. Here she was taking care of her body, which was good in itself, but she was doing nothing for her inner self-nourishment – she could be doing both at once, multi-tasking her way back to health. She struggled up once more and went down to the living room, where she went through her entire CD and cassette collection in vain, before a dim memory floated into her mind of having shoved Louise Hay into the bottom drawer of her study desk back in the days when she thought she wouldn't need her again. Ho ho. Back up the stairs to find the tape, back down again for the forgotten cassette player, back on her back on the bed, the tape now playing, the cucumber slices balanced in place. Aah. She breathed out, concentrating on relaxing her mind and releasing the tension in her body, and woke again at five o'clock feeling like –

Shit! Five o'clock?! Too late for the shops now – what would they eat? What a miserable failure she was, what a worthless idiot, what an abject, lazy, stupid fool. And why had she been attempting all this pathetic achieving? It wasn't for herself, it was for Paul. *Two* strikes against her. Motivating yourself for somebody else was worse than not motivating yourself at all. And what had possessed her to think that he was worth the chase? Paul would never have her back – he was in thrall to Helen. And anyway, after all he'd said and done, Fran wouldn't take him back now if he begged her on penitent knees over a bed of hot coals.

Get real, she told herself bitterly, angrily peeling a slice of cucumber off the back of her neck. Fran, Roman, countryman, lend me your stupid cloth ears – he's coming to collect some clothes and to argue about the record collection, not to praise you. You're dead. The ides of March have been and gone. You were stabbed in the back by this bastard and you're wondering what to *feed* him? Try arsenic, belladonna, gall! Where is your sodding pride, woman?

Galvanised now, and fuelled with anger, she sat once more at her dressing-table mirror to make her face up. This is for *me*, she told her reflection, not for him, but she glared at herself nonetheless while she applied her mascara, just to let herself know that she was on her case – there was still the matter of what to wear, and she'd be buggered if she'd let herself choose anything special. Let him take her as he found her. Gardening, probably, in her oldest clothes. Yes, she'd be deadheading the roses when he arrived, devil-may-care. Certainly she would not be picking lettuce and herbs for his supper. Let him starve. Let him eat worms.

An hour and a half later, having been through her entire wardrobe, she was dressed by Liberty's in smart casual, and her bed and the floor were adorned with all the other outfits she'd rejected. She stood in the middle of this mayhem, viciously blaming Paul for having made her make a mess after she'd already cleaned up so beautifully earlier in the day, and was about to start putting the discarded clothes away again when she heard his car in the drive. How *dare* he – she checked her watch – how dare he be on time?

Closing the bedroom door firmly behind her, she ran down the stairs and into the kitchen, her heart beating wildly (how *dare* it?), splashed a lot of gin and a little tonic into a glass and, gulping it at a gallop, dashed out to the garden, secateurs in hand. She was still panting heavily, trying to look nonchalant while lopping off perfectly formed buds and blooms, when Paul appeared through the garden gate.

'Hi there,' he called. 'Hard at work, as always!'

'Oh,' said Fran, feigning surprise. He looked gorgeous, damn him. 'Is it that time already? Do you want to get yourself a drink? I'll be with you in a minute.' She needed time to control her breathing and to speak sternly to her heart which was leaping about girlishly in her breast, playing peek-a-boo round her ribs and batting its eyelashes.

'Sure,' said Paul after a moment's hesitation. 'Shall I get one for you too, and bring them out here?'

'Well, if the sun really is past the yardarm,' Fran replied, her voice full of false virtue while she surreptitiously nudged her empty gin glass into the shrubs with her toe, 'then yes please. G and T for me, thanks.' She waited tensely as she listened to his footsteps fade into the kitchen, and breathed out a tremulous sigh. She really wasn't feeling as strong as she'd hoped for this meeting. It would have helped if she'd known what it was to be about. Should she be preparing herself to forgive him, or forget him – or, feeling the weight of the secateurs balanced nicely in her hand, for something far more proactive in the punishment department perhaps? She shook herself to rid her mind of that image – too grisly by half – and noticed finally that she had denuded one of her best rose bushes of its finest blooms. Put the secateurs down, she told herself firmly, and go and sit at the table on the patio. Stay alert! Play it cool! Your unconscious desire to wreak vengeance is getting out of hand and far too close to the surface.

Since Paul had walked out of her life and into Helen's, when she hadn't been howling in agony or drunkenly unconscious, Fran had been trying to imagine her way into the inside of Paul's head. Where was the attraction for him to return to somebody who had hurt him so badly, not once, but on several occasions? Why did he want an older woman? What did he see in her that made him blind to her wrinkles and sagging muscle tone? What, essentially, did Helen have that Fran did not? She couldn't figure it out. She knew that she herself was no great beauty, but neither was she hideously unattractive – there were still some days when labourers shouted their appreciation of her from their scaffolding, which wasn't bad for thirty-five. And from what she'd seen of Helen in snapshots Fran doubted that *she* would occasion such badinage when passing by construction sites.

So what did Paul see that Fran could not? Hadn't he complained endlessly about Helen's short temper, about her bitchiness, of how she ground him down, battering his ego, making him feel less of a man? Fran started to fill up with rage again, which at least felt more assertive than the girly palpitations she'd been suffering since his arrival. Was it that simple – that Paul was a masochist, that he preferred rough treatment at a woman's hands? Was that where Fran had gone so terribly wrong – that she hadn't been horrible enough to him? Should she have loved him less and tortured him more? And if that were the case, why the hell had she left the secateurs in the rose bed?

When Paul finally emerged from the kitchen, drinks in hand, he found her sitting outside, mumbling to herself.

'What?' he asked.

'Nothing,' she said hastily. 'Shopping list. Reminding myself.' She hadn't realised until then that this new habit of talking to herself was actually voiced out loud – she'd thought she was having an interior dialogue, not muttering to herself like a mad woman. She started to fear for her sanity. Only a few days on her own and she was already losing it. She suddenly felt very vulnerable and sorry for herself. What she wanted most, she realised, even more than she wanted to be snipping bits off her soon-to-be-ex-husband's almost perfect body, was to be cuddled by him. She wanted him to tell her it was all a mistake, a bad dream, that he had temporarily lost his wits, but found them again now. She wanted him to beg her to be allowed to come home to her. Or just ask. Or even hint.

'Couldn't find any nuts I'm afraid,' he said now, handing her a glass. 'Cheers.'

She bit back the obvious response. It was too early to go on the attack. 'No,' she said instead. 'I've been a bit busy to go out shopping. Sorry about that.'

'Been writing?' he asked pleasantly, as if they were old acquaintances and they were catching up on their lives.

'Mm,' she said, burying her face in her gin.

'That's terrific!' He sounded relieved, as well he might, she thought bitterly. The little masochist doesn't want to think of himself as being the one who dishes out the hurt. He's the poor baby who gets punished by Mummy, not the grown man who breaks a woman's heart. 'Are you working on commission then?' he asked hopefully.

'Why?' Fran snapped suddenly. Of all the uncomfortable places he might prod her at the moment, reminding her of her unemployed status and failure as a writer was about as low as it got. 'Are you calculating how much you might be stung for maintenance?'

Paul sighed self-righteously and stared down at his knees. 'I had hoped we might be able to have a calm and reasonable discussion,' he began.

'I am perfectly calm,' Fran spat icily, 'and my question, under the circumstances, was perfectly reasonable. I imagine you are here to discuss the division of the spoils?'

It was Paul's turn to bury his head in his gin for a moment, then he put down his glass and took out some papers from his jacket pocket. 'Okay. If you want to plunge right in, we'll talk about the practicalities. You want the house, so—'

'I'm having the house, no question!' Fran blazed.

'That's what I'm saying!' he protested, in a voice which suggested that he had done nothing to provoke her opprobrium. 'Look – I've been doing some sums.' He laid out the sheets of paper on the table between them, and pointed to a row of columns. 'This is what we both put in for the deposit, here's what we've both contributed to the mortgage repayments—'

'*I've* spent all the money on the renovations!' Fran challenged him, her eyes unable to focus on the swimming figures on the page. 'I've bought all the paint and stuff, I paid for the carpets and the curtains and most of the extra furnishings.'

'I *know*, it's all here in *this* column,' said Paul, raising his voice and stabbing at the document. 'And we've both been paying Archie's bills as they've come in, more or less equally—'

'Bollocks!' Fran shouted. 'I've paid far more of his bills than you! And I paid for his materials as we've gone along! Who paid the timber yard? Who bought the bathroom stuff and paid for the kitchen? Me!'

'And the months you did that, *I* paid the mortgage, *and* paid the other bills – gas, electricity, council tax, food – it's all down here in black and white. I've been through all my bank statements, Fran. I'm trying to be fair.'

'*Fair?!*' Fran leapt up, too enraged now to continue being sedentary, spilling her drink. 'What's fair in your book, Paul? Sneaking off round Europe to cheat on me? Pretending you were over Helen when clearly you weren't? Marrying me as some kind of experiment, to test the strength of your feelings for her? Making a fool of me? Lying through your teeth?' Not waiting for his reply, she stalked into the kitchen to replenish her glass.

Paul sighed again, and gathering his papers, followed her inside on leaden legs. She was pouring gin with shaking hands, blinded by tears, weeping with rage. Steeling himself for possible attack, he gently took the bottle from her hands and held her to him, where she sobbed against his shoulder. 'I'm so sorry,' he said softly. 'So very, very sorry to have hurt you like this.'

'Then why *did* you?' she hiccuped through her tears, pushing herself out of his embrace. She was furious that she was crying now, when she wanted to be screaming at full pitch and attacking him with her fists. 'Why are you *doing* this to me? Don't I count? Doesn't it matter about Fran, as long as Paul and Helen are happy?!'

Before she knew what she was doing she had kicked him on the shin, eliciting a satisfactory yelp of pain. Startled, he looked at her with fresh eyes, and backed towards the door as she advanced. 'Is this how you like to be treated?' Fran taunted him. 'Does she tie you up and beat you, or does she just break off little pieces of your heart? What is it that you like, you naughty boy? Tell me, and I'll be happy to oblige. You've always said that Helen hurt you – what's your preferred instrument of torture? Blunt, or something sharper? Like a knife?' She lunged towards the cutlery on the draining board and in the same instant Paul legged it outside, scattering his carefully prepared accounts in his wake.

'Yes, that's right, run!' Fran screamed as she pursued him across the patio, round the trestle table, and out through the garden gate into the front drive to his car, the hastily grabbed weapon gripped in her outstretched hand. 'Or so help me God I'll *kill* you!'

She skidded to a halt as, after fumbling with his keys, he leapt into his car, and she stood like an Amazon on the attack, her blade held high, her eyes gleaming with triumph, watching him drive away. *Victrix ludorum!* All hail Extraordinary Fran!

When she was finally satisfied that he wasn't coming back she dropped her pose and turned to look admiringly at the house she had just fought for. You and me, babe, she thought – or perhaps she said it out loud – it was getting difficult to tell. Don't you worry, I'll defend you to the last with my trusty—

Looking down now at the weapon in her hand, she noticed that her husband had fled from death by spatula.

It was official, then. She had definitely lost the plot.

Eighteen

Let us be kind and draw a veil over the next few weeks for Fran, for no wounded animal, slinking off to their lair to lick their wounds, enjoys spectators. It is enough to know that where she had, over the previous twelve months, cut down from thirty cigarettes to a mere five, she now found she could manage two packs a day. Easily. In the short term, until she was forced to go out to forage for fresh supplies, she also discovered that she could develop a taste for cooking sherry, a forgotten bottle of raki from some half-remembered holiday, and something at the very back of the drinks cabinet called Parfait d'Amour, which looked like methylated spirits. And, since her nocturnal forays to twenty-four-hour supermarkets were witnessed by sleepy youths doing the night shift, it would not break a confidence to reveal too that her appetite for chocolate and cakes swiftly returned to the record levels of her adolescent years. Phone messages were not returned, and Archie, when he came back to his herringbone project, was fended off by notes left on the kitchen table, telling him she was fully recovered and busy at work in London, whereas she was in fact skulking silently about the house in unwashed clothes, or asleep in her locked and darkened room. Post was forwarded, unopened and unread, to a carrier bag under the sofa. Her novel was unearthed from a dusty box in the study, opened, read, and torn in two. The bathroom scales were re-located to the dustbin. More than this, as the politicians say, it is not in the public interest to know.

Neither will I be persuaded to indulge the prurient by cutting over to the bedroom of Allie's Bloomsbury flat during this period, save to say that she was continuing to enjoy the attentions of her new beau and, as a consequence, she was becoming both remarkably happy and astonishingly fit.

Instead, we will turn our attention to Sam for a while, whose life had taken the most extraordinary turn. We left her, as you will remember, feeling judged and rejected by her best friend Fran. Since then she had been meaning to finish with Nigel, had been meaning to get round to filling in the application form to join the dating service, but time had gone by and she had done neither. She fobbed herself off, when the guilt got too much, with the excuse that work had gone manic, and that just as soon as ever things slacked off, she would be onto it like a shot. Of course, deep down, she didn't believe her own excuses and – needless to say – it was not something she was proud of. The fact was she did not have the courage to change, but since she also lacked the courage to think things through honestly to a definite conclusion she could not admit this to herself. Instead she was aware of a vague feeling of self-hatred, a sense that she was not being quite true to herself, an uncomfortable feeling of inauthenticity.

But at least these feelings were familiar. They had been her secret companions for as long as she could remember. As a child she had striven to be a good girl, outwardly cheerful and obedient, while learning to keep her meetings with depression clandestine and hers alone. As an adolescent she had grown tormented, forced to lie awake while others slept undisturbed, provoking fresh eruptions of acne with every toss and turn. Images came into her mind, alone at night, unbidden and unwanted – images which filled her with terror and with dread. For what ailed her was something so entirely unacceptable that she would have died rather than admit it, even to herself. Nevertheless she knew in her bones that she was different, and in the whole of human experience there is nothing more terrifying than that.

However, sometimes, by a miracle, things change. Some are born self-accepting, some become self-accepting, and others have self-acceptance thrust upon them. Fortunately for Sam, since she had fallen at those first two hurdles, she was about to discover that she belonged in the third category.

It was a Tuesday morning – a Tuesday morning which started deceptively like any other but which, by lunchtime, proved itself to be irrevocably unique. There she sat, smiling, behind her desk in the Market Harborough branch of Parry and Eastlake's Estate Agency extolling the virtues of 145 Cubbitts Road to a newly married couple, the Blounts, when change with a capital M burst through the door. It was Margo, Nigel's wife.

As Sam was clearly busy, her colleague Lynne innocently greeted her as she rocketed in, and so it was she, rather than Sam, who unwittingly provoked Margo's unconventional salutation, 'Are you the tart?'

'I'm sorry?' Lynne asked, doubting her own ears (she had been suffering from tinnitus for a fortnight, since attending the opening of a Leicester nightclub, so this was nothing new).

'Samantha Talbot?' Margo challenged her, growing more specific, cutting quickly to the chase.

Sam, hearing her name, but engrossed in discussing the finer points of underpinning with Eddie and Maggsie Blount, glanced over, unaware of the danger she was in, and reassured her un-recognised arch-enemy that she would be with her in a minute. For though she had once seen a blurred snapshot of Margo, taken with the kids at the seaside some years before, her cursory glance told her nothing more now than that this was a well-heeled prospective client, nicely turned out, who would probably be looking for a family home in the three hundred thousand plus bracket.

Margo, however, was more in the mood to confront than to

buy, and once her quarry had identified herself she lost no time in covering the distance to Sam's side.

'You and I have to talk,' she asserted, in a voice which brooked no argument.

'Certainly,' said Sam, still smiling. 'If you wouldn't mind just taking a seat.'

'And shoving it where, exactly?' asked Margo, favouring the direct approach. 'What's your preference?'

Looking to Sam for guidance, but seeing only incomprehension and fear spreading across her features, the Blounts, on the brink, it had seemed, of closing their deal, excused themselves on the basis that they really ought to go away and think it over. Their decision was no doubt helped by Margo who, feeling the need to elucidate her grievance to all at large, pointed at Sam as they were gathering their things and shouted, 'This woman is an adulteress! Yes, you, bitch! On your feet – you're coming with me!'

Before Sam could demur, or Lynne could reach the phone to call for police back-up, Margo had grabbed the object of her opprobrium roughly by the arm and dragged her to the door, bouncing the Blounts from her path.

'Where are you taking me?' asked Sam in alarm, shooting a desperate, meaningful look over Margo's shoulder towards Lynne, imploring her with that glance to act immediately on any information this query might elicit.

'To lunch, of course,' Margo replied, sounding deceptively sweet. 'To Chez Jean-Paul. Isn't that where you're meeting him today?' Her tone changed, however, as she apprehended the look of complicity between Lynne and her intended prey, and further, saw Lynne's hand straying towards the phone. 'Do you *want* this in the papers?' she challenged Sam, in a voice edged with steel. ' "Local estate agent breaks up homes?" '

'No,' Sam quickly conceded, blushing now under the narrowed-eyed scrutiny of Maggsie Blount. 'Don't worry,

Lynne, I'll be fine. It's just a misunderstanding. I'll be back after lunch.'

'She'll be late,' added Margo, and bundled her out of the door.

Under normal circumstances Chez Jean-Paul was Sam's favourite restaurant, saved for absolute treats. It was here she had celebrated her anniversaries with Nigel, and it was here he always brought her when he needed to sweeten her up after letting her down. Their arrangement this Tuesday had been for the latter reason, since she had awaited his arrival at her cottage until eleven thirty the previous Friday night before finally admitting to herself that he wasn't going to show. On Saturday morning he had e-mailed her at her work address, apologetic, promising this lunch by way of recompense, and hinting that if this were not enough, he would also bring along a present besides. Little had he suspected that, as a result of sending the e-mail from his children's home computer, he had left a trail which Margo would follow. And for Sam's part, much as she adored surprise gifts, she would gladly have foregone this one, who was presently smiling at her brightly across the table for two with frostily glittering eyes.

'Champagne?' asked Margo, with worrying gaiety. 'I think one should, don't you? Celebrate this thing in style.' Caring not a fig for Sam's choked reply (nor, indeed, for Sam's surreptitious head turns, every now and then, to shoot wild, apprehensive looks over at the door) she selected and ordered the most expensive bottle on the menu, and watched with pleasure as it was poured.

'To new horizons,' she proposed, raising her glass to Sam. 'Whatever they may prove to be.'

Sam, unsure of the etiquette in a situation such as this, declined to echo her sentiments for fear of giving more offence and said instead, 'I'm so sorry.'

'Are you?' asked Margo, undaunted. 'But you shouldn't be. I

couldn't be happier, in fact. I've been trying to catch him out for ages, the slime ball, but he's always been clever at covering his tracks. I suppose you know you aren't the first? Nor indeed – and I'm sorry, this might come as something of a shock – are you the only one now. He wasn't with *me* on Friday night when he stood you up, contrary to what he told you in his e-mail. So I can only assume he's cheating on us both at the moment. I *think* her name is Gilly, since he's been murmuring it in his sleep of late and, if the rest of his nocturnal ramblings are to be taken at face value, she is apparently handsomely endowed in the mammary department. Know anyone who fits that description?'

Sam was torn between being gutted and outraged, but she could hardly appeal to Margo for her sympathy, and she simply answered 'No,' in a small pale voice.

'Of course we could always get Jean-Paul out of his kitchen and ask him for verification,' Margo continued, evidently enjoying herself. 'Since Nigel appears to favour his establishment above all others. He always brings me here to celebrate our major milestones – my birthdays, our anniversaries, his guilt. I imagine it is the same with you, and therefore the same with Gilly? Shall we ask Jean-Paul – get his opinion, as a man – what it is that she's got and that we, apparently, lack? Or shall we just assume that it is, as Nigel mutters in his sleep, the thought of drowning in her "big milky jugs" that outweighs both our charms?'

Not unnaturally Sam was rendered speechless by the barrenness of choices presented to her. She certainly didn't favour discussing her replacement with Jean-Paul, and neither did she want to think about this Gilly's superior breasts. Furthermore, frightened of Margo's controlled rage as she was, she also found herself admiring her. She was so self-confident, so sure of her right to behave exactly as she chose, so enviable. It was a confusing moment indeed. It did not, however, last long.

'Well, well, well,' Margo drawled next, looking over Sam's

shoulder with evident satisfaction. 'Here comes the old Jugs Man himself.'

To Sam's horror she waved to him to alert him to their presence, and beckoned him over to join them. Since Sam could not bring herself to turn round to look at him, she had to rely on Margo's reaction to ascertain that Nigel, clearly, was reluctant to do so.

'No, don't slink off, Nige!' she called out with specious joviality, occasioning several disapproving looks from more sedate lunchers. 'Come over here and satisfy your harem!'

Taking advantage of the delay while Nigel assessed his options, saw the hopelessness of his situation, and reluctantly obeyed Margo's command, Sam drained her champagne glass to fortify herself against what was to come. Inside, she was seething at Nigel's faithlessness, but it was not in her normal repertoire to make a scene. Nor did she feel, under the circumstances, that she could justifiably give rein to her rage at this moment – for what were her feelings of outrage compared to his wife's? She felt all at sea, both angry and guilty at one and the same time, unable to trust what might come out of her mouth if she gave vent to it. Watching Margo, who was refilling their glasses and calling the waiter to bring another chair, she resolved to say nothing unless called upon to do so, until she felt either calmer or drunker, whichever came first. Since she seriously doubted that she would now ever feel calm again during her lifetime, she gave her full backing to the latter possibility, and drained her glass again. She knew by the rising trajectory of Margo's eyes that Nigel had arrived behind her, even before she heard his falsely jovial, 'Well, well. What have we here?'

'A threesome?' Margo offered, smiling dangerously. 'A double date? Every boy's wet dream? Or every errant husband's worst nightmare? We must be led by you in this, darling. We haven't your wealth of experience to draw on.'

By way of an answer, Nigel choked on a half-laugh, half-sob, and Margo immediately ordered him to sit down lest he 'fainted or messed his pants'. Once he was ensconced uncomfortably at their level, fussing with his attaché case, unable to meet their eyes, a tight silence enshrouded them all for a moment, which Margo, taking up her menu, broke at last.

'Well, isn't this nice? Shall we order? What do you normally have as a starter when he brings you here, Sam? The terrine, the smoked duck? Personally, this summer, I've been going for the chilled minted pea soup. Nigel – oysters? They *are* meant to be an aphrodisiac and let's face it, as Sam and I both know, you need all the help you can get. What's the matter – cat got your tongue? Never mind, lover boy, leave it to me.'

While Margo went through with the charade of giving their order to the waiter, Sam watched Nigel struggle to regain his composure. His brain was clearly at full stretch to come up with a plausible-sounding story, since his eyes were practically bulging with the effort and little frowns kept creasing his fore-head as he evidently rejected various ideas. She had never noticed before how shifty he looked when he was about to lie, but seeing this familiar expression on his face now she realised with shock just how many times he must have deceived her in the past. She decided then and there that if Margo didn't kill him first, she would.

By the time the waiter had been dispatched to the kitchen, Nigel's brow had cleared and a little pout had formed itself on his lips. Apparently he had made his decision, and Sam could tell from the sudden pressure of his hand on her knee beneath the table that he was relying on her for back-up. Now this was going to be interesting. Could it really be, as his hurt expression suggested, that he was going to go for 'wounded and misunderstood'?

He cleared his throat. 'It seems to me,' he began, but Margo, at that moment, was calling loudly for more champagne.

'Oh, sorry!' she said, affecting surprise. She turned back

to give him her full attention, her elbows on the table, her chin resting on her hands. 'You're ready. I thought perhaps you might need longer to come up with a story for this. What were you saying? It seems to you . . . ?'

A braver man than Nigel might have quailed under Margo's ironic, beady gaze of faux-innocence, thought Sam, but then, there was always a thin line between bravery and foolishness.

'I've been sitting here trying to puzzle things out,' Nigel began again, starting with unquestionable truth, and working his way swiftly thereafter towards his usual lies. 'And I can only assume, darling, that not only have you spoiled my big surprise for you but worse, that you have somehow made the most ridiculous assumption.'

'Sorry to interrupt again,' said Margo, raising her hand for him to stop. 'But which "darling" are you addressing here – Sam darling or Margo darling? It's a small point, but unless you make yourself absolutely clear as you go along one or other of us, like the silly girls we are, might continue in our ridiculous assumptions.'

A look of sadness passed over Nigel's face. It was a look which Sam had seen many times before, and in the past it had worked its magic as it was intended to do, turning her feelings of legitimate anger into unaccountable guilt. But this time she saw it with fresh eyes. This time, she saw right through it.

'Okay,' said Nigel, changing his tack from 'wounded and misunderstood' to 'hurt and angry' at a stroke. 'Let's have it out. You think don't you Margo, that Miss Talbot and I are having some kind of affair?'

'Do you know, I do. Is that very silly of me?' asked Margo, wide-eyed in a similitude of dumb bimbo.

'Very silly,' he confirmed with a patronising smile. 'Particularly when you hear what has really been going on here, eh, Miss Talbot?'

Dropping her pose of impending brain death, Margo

pounced on this immediately before Nigel could expand. 'Perhaps, then, Miss Talbot would like to tell me, to save you the trouble? By the way – I don't know why you're being so formal – I call her Sam, and she doesn't seem to mind. Would *you* like to say what has really been going on, Sam?'

The two women locked eyes, and for the first time in her life Sam did not back down. Instead of cowering under Margo's mocking, green-eyed gaze, Sam took strength from it, and it became clear to both women in the look that passed between them that they had formed an alliance, however uncomfortable, and that Sam was now prepared to go hunting in a pack.

'No, I'm sure that Nigel will tell it much better than I could,' Sam replied, mimicking Margo's posture, chin on hands. They both turned their gaze simultaneously, as if by tacit agreement, in Nigel's direction. The fool looked mistakenly relieved.

'Quite right,' he blustered, 'since it *is* my surprise. Or it was to have been, at any rate. Miss Talbot – or Sam, if you prefer – have I got that right?' he checked with Sam, now varnishing the gilding on the lily.

Two pairs of raised eyebrows were his only reply, and he was glad of the interruption which was occasioned by the French waiter bringing their first course and fussing with the cutlery and plates.

'Mm, lovely,' said Margo, tasting her soup. 'No, sorry – go on.' She put down her spoon and returned her full attention to him, as did Sam.

'I was about to explain—' said Nigel, preferring to study his oysters rather than either of his companions.

'Would you like some Tabasco with those, or are you spicy enough?' Margo asked, disingenuously solicitous, as if she cared less. 'Sorry – I've interrupted your flow yet again!'

Nigel summoned up his last reserves of injured dignity to eye her coldly. As Sam knew from experience, this normally accompanied the playing of his final trump card, so clearly he still thought that he could win. Or was it just that the rest of his hand was so barren, she wondered? Despite the fact that the scent of his blood was now curling appetisingly around her nostrils, she was intrigued to hear what fiction he was about to pluck from thin air.

'In your rush to apportion blame, to suspect my motives, and to accuse me of heaven knows what, you may have missed the fact that this lady is an estate agent,' he now told Margo in a frigidly triumphant tone. 'You have complained for some time now, have you not, that our house is too small—'

'Oh!' exclaimed Margo, throwing up her hands in mock despair and raising her voice to appeal to the restaurant at large. 'You thought I meant the *house* was too small! How funny! No, darling, it was your *penis* I was complaining about – the house is just fine.'

Sam muffled her reaction in her napkin, but among the rest of the diners there was an audible intake of breath. Margo had her audience's full attention. She smiled.

'But do go on. Were you about to say that you're moving out to make more room for me and the children? When? Where to? How exciting! Where shall I have your things sent?'

'Margo!' barked Nigel. At least he attempted to bark. In reality it came out as more of a yelp. 'You are being deliberately provocative. Enough!'

'You're absolutely right, darling,' agreed Margo equably. 'We've all had more than enough. Or rather, I think that I can speak for myself and for Sam?'

Sam nodded her unequivocal assent, her eyes never leaving Nigel's.

'But as for – what's her name? – Big Jugs?' She appealed to Sam in a pretence of forgetfulness.

'Gilly,' Sam supplied, spitting it in Nigel's face. He had a look of half-smiling, pop-eyed vacuity about him, suggesting that his brain was now in total meltdown.

'Gilly, of course,' Margo continued. 'Perhaps *she* may still have some – what would you say – some milk of human kindness left?' And without a word of warning, nor indeed the merest twitch of a muscle preparing itself for action, she upturned her plate on his head.

'Waiter!' she cried. 'There's a toad in my soup!'

She turned to acknowledge Sam's burst of surprised laughter and, beaming broadly, added in a triumphant shout, 'And where the *devil* have you got to with our champagne? There are two thirsty women here needing to celebrate!'

Nineteen

After Nigel had left Chez Jean-Paul, leaving a trail of minted green goo in his wake ('I told you he was a slime ball,' Margo commented, as she flicked at the mess on his chair with a napkin), the strangeness of the occasion really hit home to Sam. For here she was now, elated and close to hysteria, having colluded in the public humiliation of her (ex) lover, drinking a second bottle of champagne with his wife. As the hubbub died down around them and Margo, declining the management's kind and perhaps foolhardy offer of more soup, started tucking in to Nigel's oysters, Sam put down her glass and reached under the table for her bag.

'Mrs Ford-Roberts,' she began, rather formally.

'Miss Talbot,' Margo responded with twinkling eyes.

'I'd just like to say – and I *know* that words cost nothing – but I'd like to say anyway that I am most awfully, dreadfully, truly sorry. And if there is *anything* that I could *ever* do for you, anything at all, by way of recompense—'

'Does that include committing hara-kiri?' asked Margo, swallowing an oyster whole. She barked a surprisingly good-natured laugh at the change in Sam's expression and said, 'Just a joke, Sam. And yes, there is something you can do for me, right now this minute. Put down your handbag, pick up your fork, and start demolishing that smoked duck salad. It looks delicious – far too good to waste – and there is absolutely no fun at all to be had in lunching alone. Besides,' she confided, in a quieter voice, pouring more champagne in both their glasses, 'I'm paying for this on Nigel's card, and I'm not leaving here until we've had at least another bottle of this. It's eighty smackerooni a throw!'

Sam smiled back bravely and toyed with her salad. Having offered to do anything to please Margo, there was nothing she could do now but to sit this out, even if it meant that she would have to endure an inevitably scathing, opprobrious, attack. It was only fair that she should give Margo this satisfaction. After all she had done to wreck this woman's marriage, it was nothing less than her due, and Sam's just desserts.

'So tell me about yourself, Sam Talbot,' Margo instructed her. 'Explain to me how an attractive girl like you – no, don't blush! You are! – became entangled with such a louse as my husband.'

Before Sam could scramble together an answer which wouldn't insult Margo about her own choice of husband, his soon-to-be ex-wife answered for her. 'Of course, you could ask the same of me,' she said candidly. 'He is an odious creature at best – dull-witted, and devastatingly unattractive. I never, ever fancied him, not even when I agreed to marry him.'

'Then why did you?' asked Sam, genuinely curious, emboldened no doubt by the champagne. A moderate drinker, she had already sunk four glasses, and her speech, like her vision, was well on the way to being blurred. 'That is, if you don't mind me asking?'

'Curiously, I don't,' Margo assured her, her own speech starting to sound similarly affected. 'It was for a rather silly, adolescent reason, I fear, and certainly not something on which to base one's entire adult life. So I have only myself to blame. I say,' she digressed suddenly, regarding Sam's plate with greedy eyes, 'are you going to eat that duck, or just rearrange it?' Without waiting for a reply, she reached over and helped herself. 'Outrageous table manners, but I'm starving,' she said, her mouth full. 'I always get ravenous after a good row. Mm – it's delicious. Where was I?'

'Have it all,' said Sam, passing over her plate. 'You were saying marrying Nigel was an adolescent mistake. What happened? Were you pregnant?'

'Good grief, no! Like a fool, I married him before I'd found out what a dud he was in bed. No, I did it to annoy my father. He couldn't stand the sight of him. Shrewd man, my old dad, but I didn't see that at the time. An absolute out and out bigoted, bombastic patriarchal bastard, but perspicacious on the Nigel question, I have to give him that. Although it was probably more a matter of "it takes one to know one". Anyway, the old bugger wouldn't have him in the house, so I eloped.'

'How romantic!' breathed Sam.

Margo rewarded her with an old-fashioned look. 'Yes. And let that be a warning to rebellious girls everywhere. Before I knew it, I'd got two kids and a house and husband to look after – I was as trapped as I'd been in my father's house.'

'But you have stayed together all these years,' Sam reminded her. 'And you had another baby with him later. There must have been *something*?'

Margo nodded. 'Of course. There was the mortgage, the school uniforms, the utility bills, the food.'

'I see your point,' said Sam. 'And, of course, he is the children's father – I suppose you've had to think of that.'

'Indeed,' Margo agreed. 'Although, for the amount the children actually see him, I don't imagine they'll notice our divorce for some time. He's hardly ever at home. Not really interested in family life, apparently. Still, you're right, I had intended to try and stay with him till they were all old enough to weather it. But when I found he'd used Dan's computer to send his love letters I just saw red. It occurred to me that if I stayed with him any longer just to give the kids a dad, their mum would go completely off her rocker. A woman can't sit silently on that amount of rage for too long without imploding, or committing murder. Which might have been fun,' she mused.

'Oh no,' said Sam, empathy sharpening her witticisms. 'The soup was *much* funnier.'

Margo's face cleared, and she burst into laughter. 'Yes, I suppose as blunt instruments go, you can't get much blunter than green pea soup. God, though, his face! I wish I'd had a camera! I'd have sent it out as this year's Christmas card!'

A casual observer would have thought, looking at their table, that these two laughing women were old friends, so delighted with each other did they seem at that moment. For Sam's part, she admired Margo enormously. Once she'd stopped being so terrifying – and also because the champagne was working its magic on both of them – Margo came across as a warm and expansive woman, full of irony and intelligence. And very, very attractive. What on earth was wrong with Nigel that made him want more than this?

The same thing, apparently, was on Margo's mind. 'Nigel's a bloody fool,' she said, wiping away her tears of laughter and looking at Sam appraisingly. 'What did he want Juggsie for when he had you? You're beautiful.'

Sam blushed. 'I'm not,' she protested. 'Not as beautiful as you! You're absolutely lovely. Gorgeous.'

For a moment they regarded each other in mutual admiration, their faces softened by smiles. 'Bet you say that to all the girls,' Margo said finally.

'No I don't!' Sam protested hotly. Alarm bells rang in her internal self-defence system – alarm bells she had installed so long ago that she couldn't even remember doing it. She looked round now for the waiter and signalled him over.

'More champagne!' said Margo. 'Good idea!'

'No,' Sam checked her, fishing her handbag out from beneath the table again. 'I was going to ask for the bill. I think, under the circumstances, that I should pay.'

'Nonsense – it's Nigel's shout most definitely,' Margo countered airily, waving at her to put her purse away and holding out the empty bottle to the arriving waiter. 'Another one of these, please,' she said. Turning back to Sam, she continued, 'You wouldn't spoil my holiday, would you? The children are with my mother for the week, and it's not every day I get to behave completely irresponsibly and drink myself under the table at lunchtime on champagne. Or lunch with my husband's mistress, come to that.'

'Ex,' said Sam firmly, blushing again.

'Besides, I don't care if we skip the main course, but I'm absolutely not leaving here until I've had pud!'

Despite a huge, Pavlovian impulse to leg it out of there as fast as she could, Sam leant back in her chair, almost glad that she was not to be allowed to. There was something about Margo which made her feel better, on some deep level, just by looking at her. Let alone when she opened her mouth to speak . . .

'I'm sorry?' Sam said suddenly, realising at last that Margo must have asked her a question. 'Sorry,' she said again, shaking her head. She was having some difficulty in focusing. 'I think I'm a bit squiffy. I don't usually have more than two glasses and not even one, normally, during the day.'

'I said, "Anyway, enough about me, let's talk about you,"' said Margo. 'You were going to tell me about yourself before I interrupted you. Are you married?'

Sam shook her head.

'Sensible woman,' Margo complimented her. 'But not *that* sensible, come to think of it. What the hell did you see in Nige? You know, by the way, that's not his real name, do you?' she asked, interrupting her line of enquiry yet again.

'Nigel?' slurred Sam. 'Not his real name? Why? What is it? What's he change it for?'

Margo shrugged. 'He's a fraud through and through. Nigel Ford-Roberts. What a silly confection. He was born Barry Wigley, apparently, from Stoke-on-Trent. My dad had him investigated by a private detective after we'd married, just to show me what a fool I'd been. And I *was* a fool. When he showed me the detective's report, I just thought it made old Bazzer all the more glamorous, having a hidden past.'

'But what did Nigel – Barry – say when you confronted him?' asked Sam, bemused. Either the conversation had taken a surreal turn or this daytime drinking was even more dangerous than she'd thought.

'Came out with some old bollocks about having been a police witness in some big case in the past – stood up to be counted even though it threatened life and limb, blah blah. Had to be given a new identity afterwards for protection. *Boy's Own* stuff, all very derring-do.'

'Did you believe him?'

'No, I don't think so, not even for a minute. But what could I do? I wasn't about to admit to my father he'd been right. The banal truth of it was that he just decided to reinvent himself.' Margo brightened as the next bottle of champagne arrived and she dispatched the waiter to bring her the dessert menu, taking over his pouring duties for him. 'But then again, if you were Baz Wigley from the Black Country,' she said, mimicking the accent, 'maybe you'd do the same. Still, Nigel Ford-Roberts. Takes the bloody biscuit, doesn't it?' She laughed, enjoying the joke at her own expense, and eyed the proffered list of puddings greedily. 'Hm, tricky choice. What are you going for, Sam?'

'I don't know that I can,' said Sam apologetically, trying to read the menu while the words swam about on the page. Her eyes now seemed to her to be working independently of each other, relaying everything to her brain in duplicate. 'I really am feeling rather muzzy with the wine. Perhaps some coffee.'

'Double espresso for my friend, treacle pud and custard for me,' Margo told the waiter. Hearing herself described as Margo's friend, Sam felt quietly pleased. She would like to be this woman's friend, she thought to herself, although she didn't feel as if it were her place to suggest it. More likely, she supposed, they would never see each other again. Unless, of course . . .

'What will you do about the house?' she asked, in her professional capacity. 'Will you have to sell it and move somewhere smaller so that Nigel can buy his own place?'

'Oh God, I hope not!' Margo declared, looking worried now for the first time. '*I* bought that place with the trust money from my father, and it's in my name. Let him move in with Juggsie, for all I care – that is, unless you still want him?'

'Absolutely not!'

'I suppose I'll have to take advice from a solicitor, if I can find one who's not in Nigel's sodding Masonic Lodge.'

'I know a couple of good ones,' Sam offered. 'Quite a lot of my work these days comes through divorce.'

Margo's mood of euphoria had evaporated now that she'd been alerted to the practicalities of getting rid of Nigel, and even the arrival of the treacle pudding failed to revive it. Not that it stopped her eating – she spooned huge chunks of it into her mouth as she talked, but with no obvious enjoyment.

'I mean, if we had to move somewhere smaller, where would we put the animals?' she asked herself out loud.

'What have you got?' Sam asked her. Nigel had always been stingy with details about his home life.

'A horse, three ponies, a donkey, two retrievers, a labrador, a Westie, five cats – the kids are as animal-mad as me. Oh, and Mr Piglet joined us, of course, after Alice had seen *Babe*. He's grown rather, since, but he still expects to live inside with us – won't even look at his sty. And if you promise not to tell—' Margo dropped her voice, and Sam leant forward to catch the confidence. 'There's also Cecil and Cecilia. Sheep,' she mouthed, looking around her to check they were unheard. 'Had to hide them from the MAFF men, in the bathroom, during the foot and mouth. The kids and I tracked down the vaccine over the Internet and we medicated them ourselves. Poor creatures have never even met another sheep. Think they're people. Or dogs. Scruffbags had just dropped her litter when we got Cec and Cec, so she was in a rather maternal mode when they arrived.'

'Heavens, yes, that is rather a lot of livestock,' Sam agreed enviously. Margo had just described her own fantasy family home. 'I can see why you need the space.'

The restaurant had emptied around them without them noticing, and two waiters were tossing a coin to determine which one of them would have to take his life in his hands and present the bill to the dangerous Soup Woman, as Margo had been dubbed in the kitchens. Dragging his heels, the loser approached them now.

'So sorry, mesdames, but we must close,' he said, dumping the bill on the table and taking a quick step back. He half-ducked pre-emptively as Margo reached into her handbag, but all she chucked his way was Nigel's credit card.

Sam glanced at her watch. 'Crikey! It's four o'clock!'

'Fun, wasn't it?' said Margo, rallying, looking at the bill. ' "Drinks – two hundred and fifty-nine pounds" – oh dear, Barry isn't going to like this! What shall we give them as a tip, would you say? They've shown remarkable forbearance. Round it up by another hundred or so?' She scribbled on the credit card slip with a flourish and handed it back to the astonished waiter, who bowed as he received it.

'Madame! Thank you very much!'

'Our pleasure,' Margo smiled. 'I say, be a good chap and find us something to bung up this bottle, will you? Can't leave this lovely champagne behind.'

'But of course!'

Late shoppers dodged out of the way of the two inebriated women who emerged at a tangent, champagne in hand, onto the street outside Chez Jean-Paul. Margo, who had looked and sounded remarkably sober inside, staggered as she breathed the outside air, and grabbed Sam's arm to steady herself. 'More piss' shan I shought!' she laughed. 'Walk you to your ossiffe. See a cab on way, flag it down.'

Arm in arm like old friends, they wove their way unsteadily down the small side street towards the main drag, two steps forward, one step back, and in this way they were making reasonable progress until Margo tripped over a perfectly flat paving stone. Time telescoped, and it seemed to Sam as if she witnessed their joint descent in slow motion, hours going by before they hit the deck to land in a tangle of limbs on the kerb, where they finally rolled to a stop.

'Meant to do zhat anyway,' said Margo with defiant dignity, eyeing the disdainful passersby. 'Free country. Fancied a shit down.' Blinking slowly, she looked round for Sam, finally sighting her below. 'Oops! All right there, unnerneath me, or d'you wan' a go on top?' she giggled.

'Bit heavy,' Sam grunted, and they struggled to sit up.

'Loss zhe effin' champagne,' Margo commented, noticing the broken glass around them, and the wine trickling into the gutter.

'Blood!' said Sam in an appalled voice, examining her hands. They were covered in it.

'Cut y'self?' asked Margo solicitously. 'Is it bad?'

'Can't look, I'll faint.'

With a huge effort (and a couple of false starts) Margo heaved herself to her feet, and dragged Sam to hers. She peered round to get her bearings. 'Go back Jean-Paul's,' she decided. 'Nearer zhan ossiffe. Clean you up, see if you need stishes.'

The world had gone very grey to Sam as they staggered back the way they'd come. She was convinced she could feel her life's blood ebbing from her veins in pints during the short walk back to Jean-Paul's, and she doubted she would still be alive, let alone conscious, by the time the waiter answered Margo's loud banging on their door.

'Merde alors!' he exclaimed at the sight of them, and helped Margo to half-carry Sam inside. Together they propped her up over the basin in the Ladies, and carefully washed away the blood until the water finally ran clear.

'But there is nothing!' said the waiter, astonished, peering at Sam's unblemished hands. 'Not even a scratch.'

'That is the mos' curioush thing I have ever sheen,' Margo agreed, after a hazy, double-visioned examination. 'Lookerzat, Sam – absolute bloody miracle. 'Stonishing healing powers you've got there.'

Sam forced herself to open her eyes, and couldn't believe them when she did. The non-existent wound she had imagined obligingly stopped throbbing at once.

The waiter gasped, staring in horror at the floor near Margo's feet. 'I will call an ambulance at once!' he said, and disappeared rapidly.

'No nee' for zat,' Margo shouted after him. 'But you could get us a cab! Bloody dangeroush out zere today, isnit, Sham, what with the pavemensh coming up to grab you? Drop you at your ossiffe on my way home.'

'Oh, God, Margo – it's you!' Sam exclaimed, pointing a trembling finger at the ever-widening pool of blood on the floor.

And these were the last words she spoke before she woke again in the ambulance to find herself staring at Margo's bare and lacerated bottom, a paramedic in attendance.

Twenty

It is to Sam's credit, having offered over lunch to do anything in her power to help Margo at any time, that not for one moment (and this even before she'd got the colour back in her cheeks) did she think of shirking her duties. Despite the fact that she had an aversion to blood and hospitals and injections that was practically phobic, she bullied triage staff to attend to her friend before they even looked at the student who had poked a Malteser up her nose for a laugh and was now laughing no more, or the man who had, he asserted, had the one-in-a-million, freakish misfortune to fall backwards onto a torch when he'd come out of the shower, resulting in a three-volt light now twinkling from a place where his mother used to think that the sun shone.

Having once elicited the doctor's ministrations, Sam insisted on being close by (that is to say, inside the cubicle with them, but sitting with her head between her legs and facing the other way) while they examined Margo's wound and came to their conclusions about the depth of the gash and the possible damage to muscle. By the time they had cleaned the wound, fished out the stray bits of broken glass, sewn it up with fifteen stitches, equalised the pain between Margo's two buttocks by administering an anti-tetanus shot into the undamaged one, and lectured her sternly about not even *thinking* of trying to move, let alone stand or do chores, for at least a week, for fear of tearing the stitches and doing further damage to the muscle, Sam had made up her mind irrevocably to take a holiday from work in order to look after her. Which was the easy part. The hard part began when she tried to get Margo to see the wisdom of her decision.

'I'm perfectly all right,' the reluctant invalid instructed her in irascible tones as she was helped to cross her own threshold. It has to be said that Margo was not at her best, having had the indignity of travelling from the hospital in the back seat of a minicab at a most unusual angle, and since the deleterious effects of the champagne had now spread upwards from her nether regions to add pain and confusion in her head.

'We can have an argument if you like, but I'm not going to back down,' said Sam firmly, taking the bossy tone of the doctor who had told them both, in no uncertain terms, how catastrophic any stretching of the wounded muscle might be, and she bravely overcame her queasiness to reiterate his graphic description of stitches stretched beyond their capacity, of tearing tissue, and of the resultant further damage to Margo's gluteus maximus. 'Who is going to feed the animals if not me? You said yourself the children are with your mother. If you do everything the doctors say, complete rest for a week, and then *possibly* a little pottering about the house for another two, then it'll all be over within a month. But if you disobey their orders – you heard them as well as I did – you could be in for *months* of convalescence, and maybe even *irreversible damage.*'

'I just want to be left on my own,' Margo complained, frowning, limping towards a sofa.

'You're just feeling hungover and that's why you're cross,' Sam countered blithely, on her way out to explore the kitchen. 'I'll be back in a moment with a cold compress and a lovely drink of water. You just try to find a comfortable position, and *stay in it.*'

'You've missed your vocation,' Margo called after her spitefully. 'You could have been a sergeant major in the army, or a torturer.'

'Be as nasty as you like,' Sam encouraged her, returning with a smile and her hangover remedies, and dodging nimbly round

Mr Piglet (an inaccurate soubriquet since, judging by his enormous size and weight, his youth was well behind him) who had arrived in the sitting room to see what all the fuss was about. 'Leave Mummy alone, Mr Piggy – don't snuffle her bottom! – she's not very well,' she admonished him familiarly, scratching him with uncanny instinct behind his ears in his favourite spot, thus winning a place in his heart. 'You're not going to change my mind, Margo, and I am not going to leave you. Am I, Mr Piggy? No I'm not.'

'Oh that's right, turn my animals against me,' Margo grumbled, but with a softening around her eyes as she watched Mr Piglet roll over on his back at Sam's feet, trotters in air, thus obligingly facilitating easy access to his large tummy. 'He's such a tart, that pig – no fidelity at all,' she carped, the affection in her voice belying her bad humour.

'So,' said Sam happily, after taking the edge off Mr Piglet's appetite for abdominal scratching. 'You must tell me about everybody's requirements.' Apologising to him for this interruption to service, and promising him that there would be more where that came from just as soon as she got a free minute, she dived into her handbag and emerged, pad and pencil in hand. 'Horse and ponies,' she prompted.

'Ponies live out in the summer,' said Margo, wincing as she tried to adjust her position, and admitting to herself as she did so that looking after livestock simply wasn't within her gift at this moment. 'So they don't need feeding, but they've got to have clean water. Just check them over at least once a day, clean their hooves and so on. Ever done it?'

'Oh yes,' Sam reassured her, contentedly starting on her list. 'I had ponies when I was younger, and I sometimes exercise Linda Browne's hunter for her when she's on holiday or has too much work. Ponies' names?'

'The skewbald's Dinky, chestnut's Ginger, and the palomino's called Princess.'

'Horse?'

'Jumping Jack. He's out in the field with the ponies and Ralph in the day.'

'Ralph?'

'Donkey. Vicious kick – don't get behind him. Vicious bite, too, so don't get in front of him either. If he likes you he'll let you know in his own time and in his own way. If he doesn't, you'll find out sooner rather than later. Jack needs putting in his loose box at night, two scoops bran, one of oats, plus hay net. Same in the morning before you let him out. Needs mucking out of course, clean water, fresh straw – and exercising. What are your hands like?'

'Gentle – not hard.'

'Good, because he'll throw you if you go hanging on his mouth.'

'Dogs?' asked Sam, cocking her head on one side, having heard the sounds of muffled barking from somewhere outside.

'Christ, yes. I shut them up in the barn before I left for lunch. You'd better let them out when we've finished. Tin each, twice a day. Cats, three-quarters of a tin each.'

'And lastly, Cecil and Cecilia? Where are they, by the way?'

'Probably on my bed or on Alice's,' said Margo. 'They're lazy little buggers. The biggest part of your job with them is to try to persuade them they are *outside* animals, and that that is where the grass is to be found. If you start pandering to them and bringing it in to them like Alice does, you'll be sunk without trace.'

'I'll start with them first, then,' said Sam, pocketing her notebook in a businesslike way. 'Need anything else before I leave you?'

'More painkillers.'

Sam looked at her watch. 'Not till eight o'clock,' she said crisply, and disappeared to take up her shepherding duties, pursued by Mr Piglet.

'Fascist!' Margo shouted after her with feeling.

'Sticks and stones,' Sam carolled back smugly.

As grouchy as Margo was feeling, she had to admit that Sam had a remarkable way with animals. Only moments after she had gone up the stairs she was descending them again, this time with Cecil and Cecilia preceding her and Mr Piglet rather bossily bringing up the rear. They swept past Margo in a regal procession, Sam chatting to them in her reasonable way, extolling the virtues of an outdoor life, and out through the kitchen door where the grass, Sam assured them, really was greener. Perhaps Margo nodded off for a while, but it seemed to her that she had just closed her eyes for a second, and when she opened them it was to find Sam sitting on the sofa opposite her, covered in cats who all looked as if they had swallowed the cream, the four dogs curled up and pressed as close to her as they could get, and Mr Piglet snoring happily at her feet. A delicious scent hovered in the air.

'There you are,' said Sam, seeing Margo awake. 'You can have your pill now if you want it. Everybody's been fed except us. Cecil and Cecilia have decided to try sleeping outside tonight, just to see if they like it. Jack's in his loose box, fed and watered – we thought it was rather chilly, so we decided he'd wear his coat. Ponies are all present and correct, and with clean hooves – actually they looked rather dry, so I put some neat's-foot oil on them. I hope that's okay? And when Ralph saw them having *their* nails varnished, of course, he had to have the same. We didn't discuss Mr Piglet's food, but he kindly showed me where the kitchen scraps are kept. So, could you face a little soup? I hope you don't mind, but I found the chicken in the fridge and popped it in a pot – should be ready now. Can I tempt you?'

Margo blinked, then smiled despite herself. 'Abso-bloody-lutely,' she said. 'You any good with kids?'

★

The days that rolled by were the happiest of Sam's life. She cleaned, she cooked, she fed and watered and rode, she groomed, she shopped, she gardened. And she laughed. A lot. Margo, once you knew her (and had stopped trying to steal her husband), was an absolute hoot, and not at all frightening. A companionable intimacy quickly developed between them, and reluctant invalid though she was, Margo wondered sometimes if she had not died and gone to heaven.

'You can see why men want to marry,' she said to Sam one afternoon, tucking in to cheese scones, still warm from the oven, dripping with melting butter. 'It's wonderful having a wife.'

Sam blushed. 'I just love pottering,' she said self-deprecatingly. 'Ooh – must remember to turn the lawn sprinkler off after we've had this.' While she'd waited for the scones to bake, she had filled her time productively with a little light gardening.

'You see, that's one of the differences between the sexes right there,' Margo told her.

'More tea?'

'Yes, great.' She held out her cup for a refill and wriggled to find a comfier position from which to expound her hypothesis.

'Mind your stitches!'

'Mind your business! My arm has gone dead.'

'Then wait!'

Sam took the cup from her, hauled her forward, plumped her pillows, rearranged her limbs, massaged the muscles in her arm. 'Hair wash today I think,' she said, looking at her patient critically, and handed back her tea and supplied another scone. 'Now then,' she continued, settling back in her own seat 'The difference between the sexes . . . ?'

'*And* she reminds you where you left off,' Margo mused to herself. 'Yes, right, difference between the sexes. You bake, clean, muck out, manage the livestock, nurse a grumpy invalid—'

'You're not grumpy, you're just in pain.'

'Console, buoy up people's egos, wash, iron, weed, mow,

remember to water the lawn – achieve the near bloody impossible in communicating with spoilt sheep and dangerous donkeys – and *you* dismiss it all as pottering. If a man were to be doing this – if such a man could even be found! – he'd have elected committees, formed steering groups, divided up labour, appointed managers, leaving *him* free to think about the noughts on his productivity bonus cheque – and complaining all the way that he's under the most intolerable pressure at work. Phone,' she said, interrupting herself, hearing the chirrup of Sam's mobile coming from somewhere in the depths of her bag.

'Sam Talbot?' Sam said sweetly into the phone, before her face creased into a furious frown. 'No,' she said firmly. 'No, don't even . . . Absolutely not. You must be *kidding*! That is my business, and nothing at all to do with you . . . No I don't. Ever . . . Never . . . Well, if you do that, I shall call the police. Just try me,' she warned icily. She snapped her mobile shut and bit viciously into a scone.

'Nigel?' asked Margo.

Sam nodded, still too angry to speak.

'Thought it had gone a bit quiet,' said Margo. 'Juggsie chucked him out then, has she?'

'Presumably,' Sam agreed. 'He's been to my house, called in at work, wanted to know where I was. Wanted to stay in *my* cottage – said he was going to let himself in! I'll have him done for breaking and entering if he tries that on – trespass at the very least! Thinks he can wheedle me round!'

'Does he know you're here?' asked his wife.

'No. Nobody does.'

'Then he'll be here next,' said Margo prophetically. 'Trying to wheedle me.'

'Do you want him to?' Sam felt obliged to ask in doubtful tones. Margo's reply was a withering look. 'Good,' she continued, reassured. 'Because I've been doing a bit of digging about his finances, actually, on your behalf. Based on some stuff

Nigel let drop over the—' She checked herself from saying 'years', since she still hadn't admitted to Margo how long her affair with her husband had actually lasted, and said instead, 'Time we were together. You were saying the other day that he'll more than likely make himself out to be broke, and since his dealings are so dodgy, you won't be able to prove he's lying.'

'And?'

Sam looked guilty, but defiant. 'I borrowed Dan's computer to surf the web, and I dug around in Nigel's papers. I found some accounts and their numbers and – tried out a couple of passwords I thought he might have picked.' She blushed and lowered her eyes.

'I think I can imagine,' Margo said drily. 'And "TITS" worked the magic, did it?'

'"NIPPLES", actually,' said Sam. The brief silence before they caught each other's eyes was rudely ended by a burst of raucous laughter from them both. By the time they had recovered, tears running down their cheeks, the sound of Scruffbags and his pals' chorus of barks outside announced the arrival of Nigel's car.

'Bang on cue. He is *so* predictable!' marvelled Margo.

'Unlike me,' said Sam, standing, with fire in her eyes.

'What are you going to do?'

'You'll see,' said Sam, and so as to ensure that Margo did, she pushed her on her sofa over to the window for a grandstand view.

'God, he looks a sight,' said Margo, peering over the windowsill. 'Is that still the green pea soup on his jacket?'

'Soon be clean again,' said Sam elliptically, marching out of the room. 'I assume you don't want to speak to him – I'll tell him your lawyers will be in touch, shall I?' she called back.

'Better hire some then, hadn't I?' said Margo, more to herself, since Sam had disappeared from view.

Sam's head popped back round the door. 'Actually,' she said, blushing again, 'I've sort of already done that on your behalf. Liz Samuels – one of the solicitors I recommended? – is coming round to see you in the morning. Forgot to say.'

Margo laughed and shook her head. 'You are the most remarkable woman it has ever been my extreme good fortune to meet,' she said.

Sam blushed a darker shade of scarlet, her eyes alight with pleasure. 'That's – mutual,' she stammered. 'More than.'

'Nigel alert, Nigel alert!' Margo warned her, glancing out of the window and ducking back down into her sofa. 'Go to it – give him hell!'

The scene that unfolded through the wide screen of her front window kept Margo amused for many a year. Although she had heard the phrase said many times before, never had she witnessed anybody's jaw actually drop, as Nigel's did when he encountered his ex-mistress emerging from his ex-wife's home. 'Plummet', in fact, was a more accurate description, as she had great pleasure in telling many dinner tables over the years to come.

But that was only the start of the surprises Sam had in store for him. Ignoring him completely at first, she ran quickly through the lawn-sprinkler to the paddock, opened the gate, and called. Ralph came trotting out immediately, head aggressively down and, seeing the excitement, was joined at a gallop by Ginger and Jack. Cec and Cec arrived immediately at a brisk trot from the back garden, rounded up and followed by Mr Piglet, and even the cats appeared in a phalanx, spearheaded by Mother-of-All. The dogs, who had been barking and wagging their tails at Daddy, now flung themselves to the ground and growled. For when Sam talked to the animals they not only talked back, but organised themselves, under her leadership, into a formidable fighting force. At least that is the version of the story with which Margo liked to entertain her friends later, and who am I to suggest she might have exaggerated just a touch?

A terse conversation took place between the two-legged creatures at the head of the waiting troops, the one with the green stains on his suit spluttering and backing towards his car, the one in the flowered skirt advancing, hose in hand, having disconnected the sprinkler attachment which was used for peacetime duties, and thus commandeering it as water cannon, weapon of war.

'No bloody camera *again*!' Margo complained, chortling, as she thumped the back of the sofa in her glee and with scant regard for her injuries, knelt up for a better view. Though Nigel had made it to the safety of his car, there was no hiding place – Sam had the hose through the driver's window, running to keep pace, as he drove like a bat out of hell from the place that he used to call home, pursued by a posse of over-excited animals. Unable to contain herself any longer, Margo struggled with the catch on the window and flung it open to shout her exultant congratulations to her general and troops.

What she also told her friends later, with no embellishment at all, was that it was at that moment – looking at Sam, hose aloft, flushed, breathless and triumphant, surrounded by her cabal of happy creatures, all caught beneath the rainbow-sparkling spray – that she knew she had fallen headlong and hopelessly in love.

For Sam's part, since she had been refusing to acknowledge her Sapphic instincts for the whole of her life, it took a mite longer to admit to her ex-lover's ex-wife that her feelings were reciprocated. Indeed, she put up a spirited (and almost convincing) defence for a good half an hour before she found herself kissing Margo with the same ardour and enthusiasm as a parched and dehydrated desert dweller might, when at last she discovers an oasis.

Twenty-One

As has been noted before, Archie Scaysbrook, Builder ('Clean and tidy. No job too small'), that solid rock of middle England, was not a man who, in the normal run of things, suffered either from insatiable curiosity or from flights of fancy. But it was at around this time he found himself to be in an absolute welter of conjecture and an agony of mental confusion. Things weren't right with the Holdaways. The pieces didn't fit. He couldn't help feeling – and he finally confided as much to his wife Hilda one evening over their TV dinner (she were a bugger for her *Coronation Street*) – that sommat were most definitely up at 84 The Avenue, Little Langton.

This feeling of unease, of course, had started the day he had found Fran at home suffering from the mysterious and deadly contagious virus, although that in itself hadn't so much aroused his curiosity as his sympathy. She had looked bleddy chronic, as he had told Hilda when he'd arrived home unexpectedly early and announced that, due to a new plague in London, he was stopping home all week. But when he returned to work on the herringbone the following Monday at seven thirty prompt, expecting to find Fran over the worst and convalescing (and therefore, perhaps, up to a little light companionable cleaning of bricks), there was no sign of her at all. Even more curiously, when he decided it was time for his cup of tea a few hours later, the kitchen door would not yield to his key. Peering over the edge of the glass, he could just make out that it had been bolted from the inside. Now that, as he explained to Hilda, were an uncommon occurrence.

Nevertheless, he had carried on as normal that day and the next, albeit occasionally scratching his head as he tried to puzzle it out. But by the Thursday morning, not having seen Fran for ten whole days and disturbed, therefore, by an uncharacteristic and driving curiosity, he had arrived at her house at six a.m., hoping at least to see Paul and thus have his mind put at rest. His best-case scenario (suggested by Hilda) was that Fran, being a young and normally healthy young woman, had made a quick and full recovery and was now back at work, commuting to London as per. His worst nightmare, fuelled by the mystery of the bolted door, was that she had been took so bad she'd been hospitalised. But even at that early hour this bird had caught no worms. There had been no sign of Paul – nor even of his car, come to that.

Friday had come and gone, still with no sight nor sound of them, and it had been followed by another listless, anxiety-filled weekend. As he was quick to remind Hilda and their sons and daughters-in-law and grandchildren that Sunday lunchtime over their roast dinner, it weren't as if he were a necky bugger normally, but surely they had to admit it were a bleddy rum do. Over lamb and three veg and sticky toffee pudding, each member of the Scaysbrook family was challenged in turn to solve the conundrum, but though a few hypotheses were offered, not one of them could come up with an explanation that stuck. Indeed young Darren (number two grandson, aged eight, a devotee of *Brookside*) was given short shrift when he suggested that the Holdaways had probably just run out of money and had done a moonlight flit to avoid paying Gramps what he were owed.

The fact of the matter was, Archie had a soft spot for the girl. She'd brought the sunshine back into his life when she'd got him out of retirement. She had a sweet nature and she were a good worker, and in the eighteen months they'd worked together, sometimes side by side, he had come to feel quite fatherly towards her. He'd always hankered for a daughter, but in his youth had bred four fine sons before Hilda had wearily called a halt.

Halfway through the next week, still getting up every morning to go to Fran's house to work on the garden paths (though now with dragging feet), Archie's discomfort was dark indeed and Hilda could bear to witness it no more. By the time he arrived back home that night she had phoned all the local hospitals, and ascertained that Mrs Frances Holdaway was not a patient at any of their establishments. She had even rung up Mrs Daly, the receptionist at the Little Langton Group Family Practice, a woman renowned for keeping things medical close to her chest, and persuaded her to break a lifetime's observance of patient confidentiality to admit that Fran was not on any critical list of hers. Further, Hilda got her to take the unprecedented step (by reminding Mrs Daly that membership of the same WI was thicker than water) to ask Drs Batty, Copthorne and Patterson if they had heard word of a deadly disease now spreading its way out from London. They had not.

'What d'yer make o' that, then?' Archie asked her, now even more confused.

By way of an answer, all Hilda could do was shrug. She didn't like to state the obvious; that clearly Fran had lied.

But neither did she like an unsolved riddle, nor indeed did she like the effect the same riddle was having on her husband. Thus it was, that evening, as she sat knitting in front of the telly and pondering the question from every angle, she suddenly said, 'What's that estate agent girl called – the one who's her friend? Why don't you go and see her and ask her what's up?'

And so it followed that the next morning Archie put on his best bib and tucker and went into Market Harborough to pay a visit to Parry and Eastlake's to see Sam, who – guiltily admitting that she knew no more than Archie about Fran's whereabouts since she'd been 'rather busy with – some other things' – dug into her memory and her address book and called Allie at *Q&A*, who in turn assured them both that she herself was rather puzzled, having left several messages for Fran over the last couple of weeks, not one of which had been answered. A three-way conference call on Parry and Eastlake's speaker-phone soon amounted to a council of war, and as a result Allie urged them to go immediately to Fran's house and break down the door. But since neither Archie nor Sam was by nature as bold or confrontational as Allie in their approach to problem-solving, it was agreed finally that all three of them would convene that afternoon (or just as soon as Allie could 'find the fucking place again') at 84 The Avenue, Little Langton, armed with the necessary for breaking and entering.

As it transpired, it was a posse of six who gathered in Fran's front drive. Naturally, wild horses wouldn't keep Hilda away from this foolhardy action: if there was a danger of Archie getting into trouble with the law as a consequence of a casual suggestion of hers, she'd need to be on hand to help him talk his way out of it. Margo, of course, felt by this time that any friend of Sam's was a friend of hers, so there was no question but that she would be present – quite apart from the fact that she wouldn't have missed out on the excitement for the world. And Allie, joined as she was now at heart and at hip, brought Trevor, the much-vaunted stallion.

'Right,' she said as she sprang out of her car, not even bothering to ensure she had brought it to a complete halt, leaving Trevor to apply the handbrake with the unconcerned, automatic air of one who had become used to taking care of such things. 'What's the plan?' she demanded, striding over to the others. 'And who's got the hammer?'

The sight of her gravity-defying breasts – which (with the aid of her Wonderbra) looked as if they were struggling out from her black leather décolletage, desperate for air – had at least three of the party pop-eyed in a rather provincial way (Sam had seen it all before, and Trevor, of course, had seen even more, so the surprise was certainly not theirs). But, rallying quickly, Hilda nudged Archie, and Archie wordlessly held up his hammer and chisel, and with another rather sharper nudge even managed to rehang his jaw back on its hinge. Margo, as a recent convert to the beauty of the female form, and never one to be bashful, simply stared openly in frank admiration, wearing, as Sam chided her later, a boyish grin.

'This is my boyfriend Trevor, by the way,' said Allie to the assembled company, as the short, balding, bespectacled forty-something joined her at her side. 'And I'm Allie, Fran's friend.'

'Hilda,' said Hilda. 'And Archie, my husband.'

'Builder,' added Archie, by way of explaining his existence.

'Hello, Trevor,' said Sam. 'This is Margo, my – friend.'

'Not *the* Margo, surely?' Allie marvelled. 'Of Nasty Nigel fame?'

'The same,' said Margo, offering her hand.

'More of this later, frankly I'm intrigued,' Allie told her, eyeing her with new interest. 'But for now, action stations. You've already tried phoning and banging on the door, I take it?'

'Banged on the door every day last week,' said Archie.

'And we just tried phoning her now,' said Sam. 'We could hear it ringing inside, but nobody answered.'

'Okay then,' said Allie. 'So shall we break down the front door, or try round the back?'

It was quickly decided by a unanimous vote that the back door would be the preferred route of entry, away from the prying eyes of the good folk of Little Langton and their constabulary – but that, alas, was where their unanimity ended. Having swarmed en masse through the garden gate and round to the back of the house, Allie was all for the quick smash and grab approach to the glass in the door, whereas Archie favoured a more restrained method, carefully removing putty with his chisel. After all, as Hilda pointed out in his defence, he'd be the one who'd have to mend it again later. Allie paced up and down in an excess of nervous energy, urging the Scaysbrooks that every second wasted could mean the difference between life and death for her friend, and Sam shushed them all nervously and reminded them of the neighbours. But Trevor mooched across the lawn and turned back to look at the house for any signs of life, and what he saw interested him.

'I say,' he whispered urgently, returning to Allie's side, 'there's one set of curtains drawn upstairs, and there's a window open in that room. Could it be her bedroom? Do you think she might be in there, if Archie said she was ill?'

While Archie progressed painstakingly slowly with the putty and Hilda tidied up behind him, the two younger couples trooped down the lawn to Trevor's observation post, and Sam confirmed that it was indeed Fran's bedroom window.

'But if she is still sick and in bed, where's Paul in all this?' demanded Allie.

'And if she has been in bed all this time, why didn't she ever answer – or at least call out – when Archie knocked at the door last week?' added Sam. 'Or indeed, pick up the bedroom extension when I called her just now?'

'Soon find out,' said Margo practically. 'Isn't that a ladder lying there by the side of the house?'

And so began a two-pronged invasion on Fran's privacy, with Archie busily (but tidily) attacking her downstairs door, and Trevor manfully climbing up an almost vertical (and most definitely vertiginous) ladder to her first-floor window. Both men were watched anxiously by the four women who would form the second wave of the rescue mission once access had been gained. All six felt sick with their unspoken imaginings of what advanced state of decomposition Fran's body might be in when at last they found her. Not one of them came anywhere near the truth.

Upstairs in her room, cocooned in a jumble of unwashed bedlinen, unaware that she was about to be rescued, Fran finally started swimming towards something approximating conscious-ness. Her descent into the unrelentingly grey pits of hell had been rapid and complete. She had resolutely ignored the phone, and made herself deaf to Archie's frantic knockings at her door, which had finally subsided. She hadn't washed, or combed her hair, or cleaned her teeth – nor, indeed, been dressed in outdoor clothes – for as long as she could remember, although that wasn't saying much. She could remember nothing of the days that had passed since Paul had left, due to the fact that she hadn't been of sound mind, let alone sober, for one of them.

It wasn't as if she was an out-and-out coward or that she hadn't tried to surmount the mass of awful problems that faced her. For instance, for a technophobe, she had shown extreme courage in working out the problem of how to get her booze (and such food as she was eating) without being seen by the neigh-bours. She had sat at the computer for hours until she'd worked out how to access Sainsbury's ('making life taste better') Online, and had even browsed their 'Best of Healthy Living' page while she waited for her wine order to be delivered.

And there had been a spirited rally halfway through the second week when she had woken, at some indeterminate time of the day or night, to find herself eyeing the bag of her un-opened mail, since her head was apparently jammed under the living-room sofa. Once she'd managed to unjam her head and get the rest of her body more or less upright, she decided there and then that enough was enough, and that it was high time she tackled reality. Unfortunately, the kind of reality she found in each of the envelopes she opened was far too real for any woman, let alone one whose heart was as broken and whose self-confidence as shattered as hers.

First came the unpaid bills for the mortgage (colossal!) and the utilities (gargantuan!), and the store cards (moving swiftly on!), followed by the smug letter from Ben at Q&A (don't go there!) regretfully accepting her resignation.

Next had come the unlooked-for answer to a question which had been puzzling her on and off as she had grappled with the computer, regarding the subject of why two of her credit cards had recently refused to do the business at Saino's. Swiftly following that came the terrifying realisation that her other cards wouldn't perform the magic for much longer either. Coming face to face with the size of her debts and her overdraft, with no hope of earning any money ever again to put things straight, her thoughts had turned darkly and drunkenly to suicide. Leaving no note (who would care, after all?) she had lain for a good ten minutes on the kitchen floor, her head in the greasy oven with the setting turned to MAX, before, sweating and swearing, she had remembered it was electric. Undeniably that had been a low point, but after drinking the last bottle of wine from her current stock she had remembered her car in the garage and the hosepipe in the garden, and putting them together and jamming rags under the doors, she had turned on the engine and awaited her fate. Which had been to find the petrol gauge on empty.

The only change she made to her life after that was to take a cheaper path to oblivion. She switched from wine to cider.

Thus it was that when she woke in her darkened bedroom on this fateful day, she looked like even death had given up on her. After struggling to toss back the bedclothes she lay inert for a while, listening for more evidence of the sounds she'd thought she'd heard outside and which she'd thought had woken her. However, her concentration being at an all-time low, she gave this up after a few moments, unable to remember what she'd been doing or indeed if she'd been doing anything at all. Rashly, she decided that she needed a drink and groped around on the floor by the side of the bed where she had a dim memory of stashing a bottle. No luck. *Shit!*

With grim determination she forced herself out of bed to go and look downstairs, but staggering towards the bedroom door in the dark, she fell over an empty bottle and barked her shins – *double fucking shit!* – so she crawled on hands and knees over to the window, dragged herself upright on the curtains and, swaying slightly, viciously pulled them open.

Through the window, face to face, eyeball to eyeball, Fran and a balding, bespectacled stranger at the top of a ladder both screamed at once, but remarkably both held their ground. After that it was only a matter of moments before Archie pounded into the room behind her with Hilda on his heels, swiftly followed by Allie and Sam, and Fran found herself back in the bosom of her friends, her troubles – if not halved – at least shared.

Twenty-Two

Since Fran was first speechless and then incoherent, it was decided that the talking could wait until order was restored. While Sam reintroduced her to the notion of toothpaste and soap and shampoo, and Allie searched her wardrobe for something more presentable than the costume they'd found her in (a string vest and an old pair of Paul's boxer shorts), Archie mended the kitchen window, and Hilda marshalled Margo and Trevor on a clean-up campaign of the house. By the time Fran, washed and brushed and wearing cheerful colours, came down the stairs to make her embarrassed entrance into her own living room, four bin bags of empties had been collected and put outside for recycling, surfaces had been scrubbed and bleached, hoover and mop had been wielded, and coffee was about to be served.

'So what's all this about?' demanded Allie, settling into the sofa next to Trevor. 'I left you, as I remember, about to make babies, finish a novel, and seize the world of freelance journalism by storm. I take it that was a no go?'

Fran nodded, her cheeks reddening, unable to look any of them in the eyes. They all looked so healthy, so robust, so capable. By contrast, even though she'd now been scrubbed up, she felt like a worthless piece of detritus they'd dragged from the gutter.

''Ere you are, me duck,' said Hilda maternally, pressing a mug of strong coffee into her shaking hand. 'Black, two sugars. It's hot – mind you don't scald youssen. Can you manage? Tek it steady.'

Being spoken to kindly by a motherly woman overwhelmed Fran in a bout of self-pity, and tears glistened in her eyes. In the whole of her life her own mother had never even noticed that Fran was a separate human being with her own set of problems and desires, let alone addressed her in such cosseting tones. Seeing the tears sparkling on her cheeks, Archie felt uncomfortably in danger of adding his own. He cleared his throat manfully and stood up, making towards the door.

'P'raps better be mekking tracks, Mother,' he suggested awkwardly to Hilda. 'Now we know she's all right. Leave her to talk to her friends.'

It was on the tip of Hilda's tongue to ask him what exactly they were then, if not friends, seeing as they'd just done a fortnight's housework in less than a hour, but looking at her husband she could see that their proposed exit was meant as much for his benefit as for Fran's. Never could cope with big emotions, couldn't Archie, drat the wretched man. How was she going to get the rest of this story now? But Fran, struggling bravely to control her tears, was of the same mind as her.

'You're all my friends,' she said humbly. 'And I owe you an explanation. And an apology to you, Archie. Because I can't pay your bill at the moment. I'm sorry. I'm broke. I'm destitute. It's all over. I've fucked up completely. Excuse my language. Sorry Hilda.'

'I have heard the expression,' Hilda assured her, striving for a worldly air, and made meaningful eye signals to her husband to sit back down.

'Doon't know what you want to get youssen in a state about me for,' Archie said gruffly as he settled uncomfortably on the edge of the chair. 'I towd you at the time I were happy to do it for nowt. I doon't say whar I doon't mean. Did it for me own pleasure. Nowt to do with you. Forced the 'errinbone on yer is what I remember.' He was alarmed to note that the more he said, the more Fran cried. 'Ay, ay, now then duck,' he said awkwardly, looking to Hilda for guidance. 'Steady on. I'm trying to mek you feel better, not worse!'

Sam mopped Fran's face with a tissue (a nice reversal of the last time she was in this room) and put her arms round her. 'Sometimes when things are going badly, it's people saying kind things that makes you most upset,' she explained kindly to Archie, who felt like demonstrating the veracity of her words himself, right there and then.

'I need a drink,' said Fran, blowing her nose.

'That, my dear friend, is exactly what you don't need at this moment in time,' Allie overruled her firmly. 'Repeat after me the first step of my unique one-step programme: "I am not an alcoholic, I'm just going through a bad patch." Your turn. Go on.'

'I am not an alcoholic, I'm just going through a bad patch,' said Fran obediently, smiling weakly despite herself.

'Excellent,' said Allie approvingly. 'A good old-fashioned firm denial works every time – or at least it does for me. And it saves having to do the other eleven boring steps AA apparently insist on. It also means that, after a short period of abstention' she consulted her watch, 'in polite society that's when the big hand's on twelve and the little hand is on six – you may put your new resolve to the test. By that time, we'll all be gagging for a drink, I suspect. So,' she continued with her go-get-'em approach to tricky situations, 'we're all sitting comfortably and now you can begin. This is Trevor, by the way, and that is Margo over there. What the fuck – sorry Hilda – has been going on here?'

And so, without the aid of alcohol to lubricate her tale, Fran told the story of her husband's betrayal, and her friends ooh-ed and aah-ed in all the right places, and all of them agreed that Paul had better not show his face to them again or they would be honour-bound to amputate parts of his anatomy that he'd find he couldn't live without.

'But he's given you the house, at least,' Sam checked with her.

'Yeah. And the mortgage,' agreed Fran morosely, 'which is

huge. Even if I still had my old job, I couldn't manage it on my own.'

'But it's something to sell,' said Allie, 'to clear your debts.'

'Never!' said Fran. 'I've killed myself to get this house looking this beautiful. So has Archie. I love it. It's mine, it's my home. I'll never give it up, ever. Never. No way.'

'Feisty, but impractical,' Allie commented, and consulted her watch again. 'Well, well, great timing. I don't suppose you've got anything to drink?'

Hilda and Archie, fending off Fran's protestations, elected themselves to be the foraging party at the nearest supermarket, and while they were gone in search of a picnic supper Trevor, Allie, Sam and Margo all got down on the floor among Fran's unpaid bills and bank statements to assess her current situation. By the time they lifted their heads again they could confirm that it was bleak and it was dire.

'Sorry,' said Fran crossly to Trevor, who had just told her the difference between what she'd got and what she owed, 'but who are you?'

'He is my mechanical failure, my stallion, and my man,' said Allie, proudly, drawing him to her. 'He is also an ace accountant. Take it from me – if he says you're stuffed, then you're stuffed.'

Fran eyed him with frank amazement. Surely – short, bald, bespectacled, an *accountant*, for God's sake, called *Trevor* if you please – he was everything that Allie didn't like in men?

'I can see what you're thinking,' said Allie, 'and yes, I am pleased to say that I have recently overcome my erstwhile prejudice in certain areas concerning looks. To me, this man is beautiful, and I love him. So sue me for inconsistency.'

Trevor grinned. 'My wildest dreams made flesh,' he said, nodding towards Allie, and he leant over to shake Fran warmly by the hand. 'Trevor Calder, pleased to meet you. Take heart, old friend of my pomme d'amour – and, I hope, honoured new friend of mine. I'm living proof that things can only get better.'

'What a coincidence, so am I,' said Margo, beaming at Sam, and followed Trevor's lead in offering her hand to Fran. 'Margo Ford-Roberts. How do you do.'

'Not—?' began Fran, looking to Sam, agog, for confirmation.

'Nasty Nigel's soon-to-be ex-wife, yes, the very same,' Margo provided warmly. 'But now, happily reformed and reborn as Sam's lover. Isn't life strange?'

In the gobsmacked silence which followed, Sam bit her lip and examined the pattern on the living-room rug with great attention.

'Well fuck my old pumps, am I psychic or what?' demanded Allie, the first, as always, to recover the use of speech, peppered though it was with profanity. 'Just call me Gypsy Fucking Brenda.'

'Well,' said Fran bleakly, looking enviously at her two best friends, both happily in love. 'I'm glad it's going well for somebody.'

'And it will for you, too – soon,' promised Sam, her cheeks still scarlet with embarrassment. 'You'll see.'

Her words of comfort were proved true almost immediately by the return of Archie and Hilda bearing the first solids that Fran had eaten in far too long. In less than half an hour, the motley party was seated at a candle-lit table outside on the patio ('This calls for a celebration!' said Sam), tucking in to a feast of the best that Little Langton could provide (as selected by the Scaysbrooks). Back at last in the land of the living, basking in the warmth of her very good friends, Fran conceded that being made to repeat Allie's 'I am not an alcoholic' mantra before being allowed to join the others in a glass of wine was indeed a small price to pay.

Twenty-Three

Over the next critical few days, Fran's rescue party made sure between them that she wasn't left on her own until they were certain she was over the hump. She was forced out of bed each morning by at least one of them and given simple and achievable tasks round her house, and while she was being kept amused and employed in this way, Trevor and Allie were hard at work making sense of her finances and rationalising them accordingly. By shopping around for better mortgage rates and putting all her credit card debts into one account, in one day Trevor saved her a year's worth of interest. Allie, having read Ben's high-handed and curmudgeonly letter ('. . . I enclose a cheque for £1,431.19 in full and final settlement, this representing the balance of your salary for the part month you worked, and any holiday entitlement accrued'), took great pleasure in improving that amount threefold ('she's going to sue the shit out of you, you little wanker – we're going all the way to Europe with this. Oh and by the by – Accounts have been doing an audit – they want you to provide them with rather more details concerning your expenses. Will that be a problem?'). Sam had been busy researching a top-secret rescue project of her own, about which there had been several phone calls between herself and Allie, and now, the following Saturday, the three women were convened at Fran's for a strategy meeting. Since Fran had been behaving herself, champagne was being served in the rose arbour.

'I'd like to propose a toast,' said Fran, lifting her foaming glass.

'First step statement first,' warned Allie.

Fran heaved an irritated sigh. 'I'm not an alcoholic, I've just got an annoying friend who drives me to drink.'

'Funny,' said Allie, arching an eyebrow at Sam. 'Clearly much better. You may continue.'

'To the two best friends a woman has ever had, I give thanks. I owe you my life, my sanity—'

'Your liver,' Allie added, 'And pancreas.'

Eyeing her viciously, Fran continued. 'I was in a very dark place, and you brought me back from there. I salute you. I will always be in your debt, and anything I can ever do for either of you, just say it and it will be done.'

Allie and Sam swapped a conspiratorial look. 'Funny you should mention it,' said Allie, producing a bundle of papers from her bag and dumping them on the table.

'There is something, actually,' said Sam, adding papers of her own.

'Oh dear,' said Fran, looking at the figures crawling down columns and swarming over the pages. 'Looks like maths home-work is about to come my way.'

'That,' confirmed Allie, 'and a lesson in life's harsh realities, I'm afraid, girlfriend.'

'You see, the thing is,' Sam started gently, placing a calming hand on Fran's arm, knowing how she was going to react to her plan, 'Allie and Trevor have worked it all out, and though things aren't as bad now as they looked a week ago – in fact they're heaps better, aren't they Allie?'

'Tons better, oodles, better in scads.'

Fran reached nervously for the bottle. 'I'm not an alcoholic, I just have a strange feeling I'm going to need a bracer,' she argued, raising her voice to quell Allie's reproving look.

'The thing is,' Sam continued brightly, 'there is a bit of a shortfall problem at the moment. Until you get another job, of course, and have some money coming in. Or finish your novel and sell it for millions!'

'I tore it up and binned it,' said Fran. 'It was crap.'

'I stuck it back together and read it,' said Allie. 'And you're absolutely right. No salvation there.'

Fran glared at her malevolently, in shock. 'Did you go through my knicker drawer as well?'

'God, yes,' said Allie. 'Who still wears high leg in this day and age? Get thongs. Banish VPL. It's almost a religion with me.'

'Okay, I can't write fiction and my knickers are too big. Anything else you'd like to share with me, or can we cut to the chase?' Fran demanded sulkily. 'And don't think I don't know what's coming. The answer's still never. Ever.'

'We don't think you should sell the house, if that's what you're thinking,' Sam offered soothingly.

'You don't?'

'Absolutely not,' Allie confirmed. 'It's your only asset.'

'She builds me up, and then she knocks me down,' Fran complained to herself.

'In the financial sense, I meant,' Allie added. 'In the warm and wonderful human being department you are, of course, in a league of your own.'

'What we're talking about is a short-term solution,' Sam told her, trying to swing the conversation back in the direction she had been working on all week. 'A slight readjustment for a year, perhaps, or even six months if things go well for you on the job-hunting front.'

'Six months . . . a year,' mused Fran. Her eyes opened wide in alarm as the penny dropped. 'You want me to rent it out! No way! Tenants in my beautiful house? Drunken parties? Stains on carpets? You must be mad!'

'May I remind you of your toast and the promises made therein?' Allie warned her with narrowing eyes.

'I retract my toast,' Fran challenged her. 'I had my fingers crossed behind my back the whole time.'

'You really needn't worry about damage being done by tenants,' Sam assured her. 'Naturally, with a beautiful home like this one, we're not talking students.'

'What are we talking then?' Fran demanded.

'A corporate let,' said Sam. 'Big money. Responsible tenant with high-flying job.'

'Great. And where do I live in the meantime? In a tent in the field?'

'We don't know yet, do we? That's up to you,' said Allie practically. 'Depends what you decide to do next for a living. Maybe you'll need to come back to London, rent a place there.'

'Over my dead and rotting corpse,' said Fran.

'The one we found last week in your bed?' Allie challenged her. 'Yes, she was clever. Got her finger on the pulse, that one.'

Fran looked morosely from one friend to another, and allowed her glance to fall finally to the papers they'd produced between them on the table. 'Looks like I'm beat then,' she concluded sadly.

'Not beat, exactly,' Sam said encouragingly.

'Retrenched,' offered Allie.

'Pragmatic,' offered Sam.

'Stuffed,' said Fran.

That evening they were invited over to Margo's for dinner, where they were joined by Trevor (and by Mr Piglet and various cats and dogs, but not Cec and Cec, since they had found, as Sam had promised, that living outside could be fun – at least in the summer), and where the finer points of Fran's capitulation were negotiated. But first, once she'd got over the surprise at having to share her leg room under the dining table with a pig, Allie wanted to know details.

'Did you both know you were gay all this time?' she demanded of her hostess and partner as the five of them did damage to poached salmon. 'Or is it that Nigel is a one-man Lesbo-making machine?'

Margo laughed. 'I wouldn't want him to take all the credit, but yes, I'm sure, in my case he helped.'

'By finding you a girlfriend and test-driving her?' Allie teased.

Sam flushed and choked on a bone.

'Oh, I'll always be grateful to him for that,' Margo assured her, patting her lover on the back and demanding to examine her throat. 'I'd have to say, rather immodestly perhaps, that his taste in women is peerless. But no, I meant rather by making me see that my life was intolerable as it was.' Having seamlessly fished out the bone from Sam's craw without even interrupting herself, she kissed her better and continued, 'Happily, I now realise by comparison that I hadn't the faintest idea, before Sam, of how wonderful a relationship could be, and what it is like to love and be loved.'

Sam, though embarrassed, was flushed now with pleasure and, try as she might, she couldn't repress the sunny, beaming smile which warmed her face.

'I take it then,' Fran said to her (a little acidly, perhaps, due to envy), 'that this is finally something you *are* proud of?'

'I – well, yes – I suppose so,' she stammered. 'Actually, I *had* known all my life that I was gay. Or feared it.'

'Feared it? Why?' demanded Allie. 'Surely it's acceptable now? The small ads are filled with "bi-curiouses" – reading them used to be a hobby of mine,' she added quickly, for Trevor's benefit. 'In my darker days.'

'Oh, mine too,' he assured her with a grin.

'Feared it,' Sam continued, since she had given this much thought (and since she had drunk far more wine, under the circumstances, than she was used to), 'because it may be very chic in London, for example, or in artistic circles perhaps, for a woman to love another woman, but in the rest of the world people still find it shocking. Even perverted, or blasphemous. You should hear my parents on the subject.'

'Have you told them?' Fran asked her incredulously, having once had the dubious pleasure of briefly meeting these two bastions of traditional values. 'How did it go?'

'We're – working on that,' Margo answered for her.

'They've cut me off,' said Sam. 'They never want to see me again, nor ever meet Margo.'

'Oh well, every cloud . . .' offered Fran, feeling guilty for mentioning it.

'My feelings exactly,' Margo agreed. 'And on the plus side, my kids are ecstatic. It's a close-run thing as to who loves her more.'

'So you've got everything you've ever wanted in one fell swoop,' said Fran, feeling envious again. 'Someone who loves you, and a ready-made family all at once.'

'Yes, I'm truly lucky and blessed,' said Sam, and sensing her friend's feelings of bleakness added, 'just as you will be, honestly, I promise. Because, although I've lost my parents . . .'

'For the moment,' Margo prompted her.

'I've gained a family,' Sam concluded. 'And I feel complete now, for the first time in my life. Not just in the contented sense, but because I finally feel – joined up. Whole. I'm a joined-up person at last.' Looking at the softness on the two women's faces as they gazed into each other's eyes, nobody doubted it for a moment.

'Yes,' agreed Margo, tearing her gaze away, 'It's like that for me too. I saw a play once, years ago, at Derby Playhouse, and a phrase from one of the lovers always stuck in my mind. "You join up my present with my past," she told him. I can't remember now who wrote it – isn't that awful? – but I do remember that it was directed by Terence Armstrong, before he made it big.'

'Terence Armstrong,' marvelled Allie. 'Now there's a blast from the past.'

'You knew him?' asked Margo the theatre-goer, her eyes alight with interest.

'Had him,' Allie replied airily, then, remembering she was now a partnered-up woman, turned to reassure Trevor. 'Not a patch on you, tiger.'

'I've heard the one about Terence Armstrong about a thousand times,' Fran complained. 'When are you going to tell us about you and Trev? Dish the dirt, girl.'

It was Trevor's turn now to blush and to beam, and he, like the others, made himself comfortable to hear his pomme d'amour tell their story.

'You know all this,' protested Allie. 'I told it all to your infernal answering machine.'

'Yes, well, I wasn't at my most receptive just then,' Fran admitted, her eyes darkening at the memory. 'Remind me of the details?'

So Allie pitched in to her tale, starting with the fair at Long Throssle and Gypsy Brenda's prediction, and ending on the floor of Q&A's lift.

'The thing is, she gets claustrophobic,' Trevor explained with a twinkle, in mitigation of their precipitate coupling. 'And she was about to go into a full-blown panic when the lift got stuck. We managed to speak to the engineers on the phone, and when they said it'd be a couple of hours before they could get us out, I thought she'd implode. Then I suddenly remembered the bottle of Scotch in my briefcase, which I'd bought – in anticipation of another loveless evening – on my way into work.'

'"Another loveless evening"! Listen to him!' Allie chided. 'His poker-playing pals were coming round.'

'Well, those chaps can get pretty brutal – it's no picnic,' Trevor bantered back.

'Hm. Well, neither of us has had a loveless evening since, have we, my little long throssle?' Allie purred smugly, which frankly made Fran want to puke.

'Oh dear,' she commented drily, 'don't tell me you've both started doing everything as a couple and forgotten your boundaries and your own individual pursuits. That will never do.'

'Of course not,' Allie riposted. 'He still plays poker with his chums, but I get to have my way with him before they come and after they've gone. Believe me, I know the importance of him having his own private time. Apart from anything else, he needs the rest.'

'Look,' said Fran tetchily, her Envy Meter having now gone off the top of the scale, 'enough of bragging, Allie. Why don't you just gloat?'

'Oh my goodness!' exclaimed Sam suddenly. 'That's it, of course! Fran, *you're* the friend I have to remember to tell!'

'There's more?' asked Fran dully. 'To be honest, sitting here this side of the table as I am, the only single surrounded by adoring happy-ever-after couples, I don't think I could take any more good news – unless it was mine.'

'But it is!' squeaked Sam, beside herself now since she was the bringer of joy. 'And look how right Gypsy Brenda was about Allie's and Trevor's mechanical failure! And when she looked into the crystal ball for me, she could see a Woman With Dark Hair, standing beside Nigel.' As if providing incontrovertable evidence, she gestured towards Margo in triumph. 'Woman with dark hair, see? "She says to say she's waiting for you – that woman is your destiny," she said.'

'And this has to do with me how exactly?' Fran complained. 'You got Margo, Allie got Trevor, Helen got Paul.'

'Don't you remember, Gypsy Brenda had a message for a friend of mine, about something that would happen in the future? "Tell her that great gains come sometimes disguised as great loss. Tell her to weather the storm." It's you, Fran, to a T! Something fabulous is going to come your way soon, some great gain, some wonderful thing!'

'Yeah, right,' said Fran darkly. 'A corporate bloody tenant. Lucky me.'

And in the prophetic stakes, as it later transpired, she had hit the nail more or less bang on the head. But first there were one or two obstacles that had to be negotiated.

Twenty-Four

It was decided, in order to spare Fran's feelings (and because neither Sam nor Allie trusted her not to put a spoke in the wheel of her salvation) that Fran would be out when Sam showed her house off to the woman from Cresco. Unable to make herself too scarce, she had been walking in her field at the back of the house ready to leg it up the garden just as soon as Sam gave her the wave to say all was clear. When it came, Fran astonished both her friend and herself at how fast she could run when she tried.

'What did she say?' she demanded, breathless, skidding to a halt on the patio. 'Did she like it?'

'Loved it,' Sam confirmed happily. 'And I've negotiated a really good price.'

Fran's face fell. 'Shit. It's real, then. When does she want to move in?'

'No, Fran,' Sam explained patiently yet again. 'It's not for her. She just vets properties for companies. It's for a new CEO they're expecting at Cresco.' She consulted her notes. 'Jeremy Sinclair. Apparently he's a really high-flyer, been head-hunted from London. That's why he's looking to rent for a while – it's all finally happened in a rush – I think they were despairing of finding somebody with the right qualities for the job.'

'But they managed,' Fran said morosely. 'Damn them. How long have I got?'

Sam swallowed hard. 'A fortnight.'

'Two weeks?' cried Fran. 'But that's impossible! That's too

soon. I mean, I haven't got used to the idea yet. Two weeks? It can't be done!'

Sam put her arms round her and gave her a hug. 'I know things are bleak now,' she comforted her. 'But honestly, they will improve. You just have to weather the storm for a while.'

'Where?' demanded Fran. 'Where am I going to weather it while Jeremy Sinclair trashes my house? I've been through the budget Allie and Trevor have done for me – I can't afford to rent so much as a cupboard, even with the money I'll get from letting this place. And where am I going to put all my furniture and things?'

Sam was dreading this bit. 'Oh, that's not a problem. You're letting it furnished,' she said, in as casual a tone as she could muster.

Fran sprang out of her embrace. 'No way! You must be crazy! Somebody sleeping in *my* bed, putting coffee rings on *my* side-board, eating out of *my* fridge? You're kidding! Do you know what I went through to choose all these things? Have you forgotten the agonies I had tracking everything down to make it perfect?!'

'Of course not,' Sam soothed her, wishing that Allie was there to play the hard cop. 'And you did a wonderful job, which is why it's worth so much in rent. That's what's saved you now: your great taste, and your cleverness and talent in doing it up.'

'Some salvation,' said Fran bitterly. 'I'd sooner starve.'

'Maybe we should call Allie,' Sam suggested, despairing of her own ability to push this crucial stage of negotiations through to its satisfactory conclusion. 'Get her and Trevor to come up again this evening for supper and just go through the figures again?'

'No thanks,' sniffed Fran. 'It was bad enough last Saturday, watching them panting over each other, practically drooling. Or do I need to remind you how *you* used to feel when you were single, having to watch other couples being happy?'

Sam looked stricken. 'Oh dear,' she said. 'In that case I think perhaps I've done the wrong thing.'

'What now?' Fran demanded. 'What else could you do?'

'I told Margo to come over here with a picnic lunch, to celebrate. She'll be here any minute. I thought maybe it would be nice to—'

'Hello-o!' Margo called to them as she came through the garden gate carrying a hamper.

Sam took Fran's hand and gave her an apologetic look. 'I'll ask her to go, shall I – and just leave the food?'

'No,' said Fran relenting. 'I'm being a bitch. Hi Margo!' she called, as she led Sam back up to the house. 'Surprise! Guess what – I'm homeless! Let's eat, drink and be merry!'

Lunch in the garden was a sombre affair, with Fran maintaining a brooding silence while she wrestled with her inner struggle against herself, and Sam and Margo trying to keep up a light, pleasant, and positive conversation without coming across as a sickeningly contented couple in love.

'See, if I can't afford to live anywhere else, even with the rent from here, it doesn't work,' Fran said, suddenly cheering. 'So, although it was a great idea of yours, Sam, I think we'll have to come up with something else.'

'But we've thought of everything else, haven't we?' Sam asked in despair. If she couldn't carry this off, Allie would kill her.

'Well no, not everything,' Fran began slowly. 'I mean, I appreciate that it's a good idea of yours to use the house to make money – that as Allie says, it's my only asset. But thinking about it now – I could do B&B, couldn't I? Then I'd be living here too, kill two birds with one stone. Save on me renting somewhere else, and I'd be here to supervise.' Her eyes narrowed in jealous pain as she imagined strangers touching her things with sticky fingers, treading on her carpets with muddy boots, not cleaning the bathrooms after they'd used them. 'To keep things neat and tidy.'

'It's certainly a thought,' Margo said, surreptitiously putting a restraining hand on Sam's thigh under the table. 'But then again, do you think that you'd get enough guests staying to cover your costs? How much did you say Cresco was prepared to pay, Sam?' she asked deviously.

'Fifteen hundred.'

'Fifteen hundred, gosh. A month?'

Sam nodded, seeing the way her lover was going with this. 'How much would you say you'd charge a night, Fran, for bed and breakfast?'

'I don't know. What do you think?' asked Fran, pleased that they were taking her seriously. 'It's a nice place, great setting. Thirty quid?'

'Sounds reasonable,' said Margo. 'Let's see – how many thirties in fifteen hundred? Is it fifty? I don't know, I get lost with the noughts.'

'Yes, it's fifty,' Fran confirmed.

'Fifty guests a month,' mused Margo, waiting in vain for Fran to work it out for herself.

'Well, I grant you, it'll be hard work. And I'd have to buy more bed linen and towels,' said Fran, who had brightened immeasurably at the thought. 'But it would be worth it in the long run, wouldn't it? It would give me a job, and somewhere to live.'

'Yes,' said Margo slowly, not enjoying her role of the voice of reality. 'But do you think we get that flow of tourists here in Leicestershire?'

'People touring through,' Fran suggested optimistically.

'Fifty a month? In Little Langton? That would be one point six people staying every day of the year, wouldn't it?'

'I could advertise,' Fran offered petulantly, aware now that she was losing her audience's enthusiasm for her new business plan.

'Shall we call Allie?' suggested Sam, reaching for her mobile. 'See what she thinks?'

'No,' said Fran in a small hopeless voice. 'Okay, bad idea.'

'What's the worst thing for you about the corporate rental?' Margo asked kindly, pouring her another glass of wine and quelling Sam's objections with a look. 'Bad patch,' she mouthed silently to her lover, while Fran's attention was elsewhere, gazing with regret at her garden.

'What – besides everything?' she answered finally, her eyes glistening with unshed tears. 'Not living here, in the place that I love. Not being here to defend it and keep it looking beautiful. Maybe having to go back to live in London to do a job I'll hate just in order to afford the rent of a bedsit I'll loathe. And what about my lovely garden?' she challenged them both. 'Who'll look after that, after all my hard work to reclaim it from jungle? You can just see a male CEO having the time or the interest to do weeding and watering, can't you?'

'I tell you what,' Sam offered, not for one moment even suspecting what would result from her rash suggestion, 'I could call Melissa back, at Cresco, and tell her that he has to have a cleaner and a gardener as part of the deal. Doesn't Archie's wife Hilda do cleaning? We could suggest her if you like. Look what a good job she did here when we all came round.'

'That's a good idea,' Margo said approvingly, shamelessly steering Fran to a similar point of view. 'Hilda would be perfect.'

'She's got enough clients,' said Fran, quashing the idea with some finality. 'I know, because I asked her only recently if she'd like to come and work for me. And who'd do the garden? It isn't as if I haven't tried to get local help with that too.' But though her words were all negative, there was something about her manner that seemed to be fostering a new germ of optimism.

'We'll leave it with you to think about, then,' said Sam, looking at her watch and tidying plates. 'Sorry – I've got to run. Another viewing. I'll call you this evening – I'm afraid Melissa needs a definite by tomorrow morning, latest – and if I've got to persuade her to fork out extra for staff I'll need to give her due warning.'

'Perhaps, this afternoon, you might visit the local shops and look round for notices in their windows advertising cleaners and gardeners,' Margo suggested brightly to Fran as they took their leave, in the manner of a mother who is used to motivating recalcitrant adolescents from slothful ennui.

'Yes, good idea,' agreed Fran, all businesslike now. 'In fact, why not just take it as read, Sam. Get the cleaner and gardener clause put in to the contract and I'll sign it tomorrow. You're both absolutely right – it's the only solution. All I'll have to sort out then is somewhere for me to live. Fairly locally, I mean. I really would sooner die than go back to the Smoke, and it'll be cheaper to rent round here, won't it?'

'Ye-es,' said Sam doubtfully, who had already combed through her books of properties to let on Fran's behalf, and found nothing she could possibly afford. 'I'd offer you my spare room, of course, but I've decided to sell my cottage and it looks like I've got a buyer.'

'Congratulations,' said Fran warmly. 'Are you going to move in with Margo?'

Sam and Margo nodded guiltily. It was no fun being ecstatically happy when one of your friends was so low.

'That's great,' said Fran, unexpectedly cheerful. 'Leave the pots, Sam, I'll do them – won't take me a jiff.'

'Shall I bring the papers round tomorrow evening, then?' Sam checked, putting down her cargo of plates and grabbing her handbag.

'With a bottle of champagne?' added Margo, whose scars from her last tango with that drink were now healed and forgotten.

'Super!' said Fran. 'See you then.'

★

Going out into Fran's front drive to their separate cars, Sam and Margo congratulated each other on a job well done.

'Great wheeze about getting somebody in to look after the place, darling. Well done,' Margo told Sam as she kissed her goodbye.

'No, well done you,' Sam demurred happily. 'I could never have swayed her without your support. And I was dreading telling Allie that I'd failed.'

But when she finally found time to call Allie at her office later that afternoon, she found that Fran had already beaten her to it.

'Yes, she rang me an hour ago. And by the way, good work,' Allie congratulated her. 'I don't know how you did it, but she actually sounded enthusiastic when she phoned. Said we'd make it a celebration – we're all invited round a week on Saturday – her last evening in the house. Astonishing how she's come round. It was an inspired idea of yours about the cleaner and gardener – it really seems to have tipped the balance.'

Sam finished the call feeling pleasantly fulfilled. Praise from Allie was praise indeed. But of course neither of them knew then precisely how far Fran's balance had been tipped, nor what plot she was hatching, even at that moment, with her old pal Archie.

Twenty-Five

Though Sam was more than happy to take the credit for performing a miracle, she was nevertheless a little nervous, as the two weeks rolled by, about whether the not-so-small details of Fran finding a cleaner, a gardener, and somewhere to live, were being attended to. Melissa at Cresco had reluctantly agreed to stumping up the cash to pay the staff, but she was absolutely adamant that it would not be their responsibility to hire them, nor to check their references, nor to replace them if they left. If that was what Mrs Holdaway wanted, Mrs Holdaway could damn well sort it herself. When Sam relayed this information to Fran on the phone, she was greeted with a merry laugh, and reassured that everything was going perfectly.

'So you've found a gardener?' Sam pressed her.

'Yup, and the cleaner – don't fret!'

'*And* somewhere to live?'

'Yes. Archie's found me somewhere. Quite close by.'

Sam's professional interest was aroused. 'Great! Where? Can I see it?'

'It – needs work,' Fran told her. 'We're doing it up. I want you to see it when it's perfect – surely you can understand? Anyway, got to go. You can imagine how much there is to sort out and organise.'

'Isn't there anything I can do to help?' Sam asked pathetically, now feeling left out as well as anxious.

'Absolutely. Bring a bottle with you on Saturday. Let's party! See you then.'

★

Standing on Fran's doorstep that following Saturday evening, waiting for her to answer the bell, Margo squeezed Sam's arm. 'Relax darling, I'm sure she'll have everything taped down, just as she said.'

'But what if she hasn't?' Sam insisted. 'What if she's just been fobbing us off and doing nothing? There's no room to manoeuvre, we're right at the edge – she *has* to be out of here tomorrow, or I am dead at Cresco. And they're a really good client of ours. Mr Parry would kill me if we lost them.'

'He could hardly kill you if you were already dead, sweetness,' Margo joshed her, trying to lighten her mood. Sam rang the bell again. Again there was no answer.

'Where the hell is she?'

'If the worst comes to the worst, which I doubt,' said Margo, showing rather more confidence in Sam's friend than Sam could muster herself, 'then she could squeeze in with us till we find her somewhere.'

'Mm,' said Sam absently, as she peered through Fran's living-room window. 'You don't think she could have done a bunk, do you?'

She was about to try the garden gate when they were joined with the usual squeal of brakes and slewing of wheels, by Allie and Trevor arriving post haste in the drive.

'We actually found the fucking place first go this time!' Allie called to them ebulliently as she threw open her door, leaving Trevor, as always, to turn off the engine and lock up. 'In under an hour and a half. What's up?' she demanded, finally registering the alarm on Sam's face.

'She's not answering,' Margo told her, trying the doorbell again and adding calmly, 'she's probably just in the shower.'

'This gate to the garden's locked,' Sam announced, looking ashen. 'It's never been locked before, except when she's out. 'A feeling of terror had replaced her anxiety, and she rattled the gate again, pushing against it with all her strength.

'Shit. Not again,' said Allie, the colour draining from her face too. 'You don't think . . . ?' She could no more bring herself to finish the question than Sam could make herself answer it. It all seemed too horribly familiar, too similar by half to the last time they were all here.

'Fra-a-an!!' Allie bellowed, and getting no immediate answer save for the ferocious barking of the next-door neighbour's dog, she turned to Trevor and challenged him to climb over the gate.

'Need a leg up?' asked Margo, used to things horsey, as Trevor gazed up at the obstacle which was a couple of feet taller than himself. Lacing her hands together, she invited him to put his foot in them and was counting to three for the big heave-ho when suddenly the gate opened beneath him, and there at last was Fran.

'Hi there,' she said, a little out of breath, but apart from that looking healthy and happy enough. Indeed, she looked better than any of them had seen her for ages, dressed in her finest, beautifully made up, and elegantly coiffed. 'Thought I heard something. Sorry – hadn't realised the time – I was down at the bottom of the garden.'

'Thank heavens for that,' Trevor said smiling, breaking the heavy atmosphere. 'I think I'd just mastered the theory of how to get flung up and over the gate, but I was rather worried about the descent.'

Fran laughed. 'Why didn't you just come through it, rather than over it?'

'It was locked,' said Sam accusingly, feeling a little bit silly and rather over-dramatic now.

'Of course it wasn't,' said Fran, although Sam could have sworn that she looked shifty as she did so. 'It just sticks some-times. Anyway, now you're here, let's go in the quick way,' she continued, leading the way past them to her front door. 'Come on, come in, cocktails all round – I've made margaritas!'

★

In the living room, the group's mood lightened considerably as the first jug of margaritas was drained and the second was begun. 'We're going to eat in the garden,' Fran assured them as Allie fanned herself with a coaster. It was the hottest day of the summer so far and outside the heat of the sun was undisturbed by so much as a whisper of breeze. 'But I thought we'd start the party off in here first. Say goodbye to the place. Trevor! Not on the coffee table – not without a coaster – it'll leave a ring!'

'Sorry,' said Trevor, embarrassed, rescuing his glass. 'It isn't wet, I made sure.'

Sam and Allie exchanged a worried glance. Fran was going to have to get used to a lot worse than that after her tenant moved in the next day. But to their pleasant surprise, she apologised for overreacting.

'Just polished in here,' she explained. 'Wanted everything to be nice for Mr Sinclair. But I can give it a quick whip over in the morning.'

'Well let's go outside now then,' Margo suggested, standing and bashing the sofa cushions she'd been sitting on back into shape. 'Save us mucking up anything else.'

Fran seemed curiously reluctant for them to go into the garden, but she was forced to bow to the general consensus as they started to file out past her towards the kitchen. 'Okay,' she said, scampering in front of them and cutting them off at the back door, wielding the jug of margaritas. 'But let's just top up everybody's glasses first – make sure this party goes with a swing!'

'Quite strong, isn't it?' Sam said, suppressing a hiccup. 'Just half a glass for me.'

'To the brim for yours truly,' commanded Allie, pushing forward her glass and eyeing Fran suspiciously. 'I have a horrible feeling you're preparing us for something out there, and I'm damned if I want to face it sober.'

Fran grinned, striving for an innocent expression. 'To that,' she proposed, and clinked her glass against Allie's. 'Bottoms up! Come on then, if you're coming,' she continued, leading the way outside, and sitting down at the patio table, she gestured for them to all to join her.

'Something's fishy,' Allie complained, eyeing the few small dishes of crisps and nuts on the table. 'I can smell it.'

'Prawn crackers,' explained Margo, taking her literally, and helping herself to a handful.

With a roll of the eyes, Allie ignored her. 'I know you,' she said accusingly to Fran. 'Why isn't it set up out here for a feast? You can never resist, with your napkins and candlelight and umpteen canteens of cutlery. What's going on?'

'We're having a barbecue. I've set up further down the garden,' Fran told her, trying to sound casual. 'We'll go down there later, when we're hungry. It's such a fag to keep coming back up here for more booze.'

'No more than the fag of carting plates and knives and forks all the way down there and back again, surely?' Allie challenged her, unconvinced. She had no idea what skulduggery she was expecting, but she knew Fran well enough to know by her mood that she had something up her sleeve. Otherwise this would be a wake, with Fran wailing and gnashing her teeth about leaving her beautiful house.

'Okay, you've caught me out,' said Fran, unruffled. 'I've compromised my standards just for one evening. It's paper plates and plastic cutlery at the barbie tonight.' Eyeing the now-empty jug, she stood up. 'Is that the margaritas finished? Shall we open Sam and Margo's champagne?'

'You're up to something, Holdaway,' Allie began. 'I can feel it in my bones. Look at me when I'm accusing you!'

But Fran, glancing over towards the garden gate, attuned from habit to the sound of his car pulling into the drive said, 'Oh shit. That's Paul, come to collect his stuff. I'd forgotten all about him. I've had to empty wardrobes and shelves for the tenant.

Sorry – he was supposed to come earlier, but he rang to say he was running late.'

Allie's eyes sparkled. 'Forgotten, my arse,' she said. 'So that's what you're up to. Well, don't worry, old friend, we won't disappoint – will we, boys and girls? Let's give him a welcome he won't forget.'

'No, really,' Fran protested, 'he should have come and gone already before you got here. I didn't mean—'

'Of course not,' soothed Allie. 'But since he's here now,' she continued, stalking over to the back gate, the look of battle in her eye, 'I really must tell him how much I've been thinking about him.'

Paul had been dreading seeing Fran. When she had phoned him to say she was having to move out of the house for a year because she couldn't afford the mortgage on her own, he had been stricken with even more guilt than he already felt. Having put it off till the last possible moment, he was now squaring his shoulders to face her at the front door, dithering between ringing the bell and using his key, when he heard his name called from the direction of the garden gate.

'Hello?' he called back, but receiving no answer, he walked over to check. 'Hello?' he called again, going through into the garden.

'Hello!' Allie greeted him, having rapidly regained her seat after luring him here. 'Surprise! Isn't this nice?'

'Allie!' Paul greeted her, with fear in his voice. 'How are you? And Sam. Hi. Sorry I'm late, Fran – I didn't realise you were having company. You should have said.'

'Oh! Blaming the victim! How original!' Allie said warmly, in a confusingly complimentary tone.

'I'll start bringing your stuff downstairs,' Fran told him, backing towards the kitchen door in an effort to lead him to safety. She felt very torn about him at this moment. As much as she would have liked to hear Allie decimate him, he looked so uncomfortable and embarrassed she also felt strangely protective of him. Habit, she supposed. But what was more, he was not meant to be the evening's star turn, whatever Allie thought. She had been leading up slowly to revealing her secret plans to her friends, and now she'd got enough booze inside them she wanted to get on with it.

Paul made to follow her. 'Oh no, don't go yet!' Allie commanded him, stopping him in his tracks. 'You haven't met Trevor, the new man in my life.'

Fran couldn't bear to watch. 'I'll make a start then,' she said again, and disappeared into the house. If he didn't have the wit to follow her, he was definitely on his own.

'Pleased to meet you,' Paul said politely, then gestured after Fran. 'Excuse me, I'd better—'

'And Margo, the new woman in Sam's.'

'How do you do?' asked Paul, struggling to cover his surprise.

'Margo, Trevor – this is Paul. The little shit who betrayed our good friend Fran,' Allie continued, in her best hostess voice. She smiled to see his discomposure. 'Went back to his first wife – doesn't that just chill your blood? How is it, living with Helen again, Paulie? As fabulous as you used to say it was?'

Paul regarded her coldly with injured dignity. 'In fact, if it's any of your business, we're not living together at the moment, Allie,' he said. 'I'm renting a flat on my own. We're taking things slowly.'

'She's not up to her old tricks again, is she?' Allie crowed delightedly, clapping her hands in glee. 'Not reeling you back in then dangling you on a string?! How simply dreadful for you! But then, I said to Fran at the time that you would rue the day . . .'

Knowing there was nothing he could say to this woman that she wouldn't be able to twist around to insult him, Paul walked to the kitchen door in silence – a silence which was soon ended,

however, by Allie hissing and doing a slow handclap during his
long lonely exit from their lives.

'Ouch,' said Trevor when Paul was safely inside.

'Can't stand faithless husbands,' said Allie dismissively. 'I let
him off lightly. How's yours, by the way, Margo?'

'Not as sorry as that one looks,' said Margo, pouring more
champagne.

Sam's eyes glistened with tears in the gathering dark. She'd
always been fond of Paul. Poor Fran, she thought. And poor
Paul. 'He did look as if he was actually rueing the day, didn't
he?' she said sympathetically.

'Good,' said Allie without any sympathy at all, and raising her
glass and her voice, she proposed, 'May he rot in Helen.'

When at last they heard Paul's car leaving, however, and Fran
rejoined them outside, even her most loyal defender examined
her anxiously to see how she'd reacted to seeing Paul finally
removing his things from their old love nest.

'Well,' said Fran flatly, as she sat down rather heavily. 'So
that's that.'

Empty words of condolence and calls for courage flitted into
all their minds, but were left unspoken – however good for her
in the long run this might be, they couldn't expect her to see that
just now.

'He's not having a good time with Helen, though,' Sam
offered into the silence, unable to resist offering some words of
comfort.

'Isn't he?' asked Fran, brightening, leaning forward with
interest. 'How do you know?'

Allie watched her friend critically and looked daggers at Sam,
who, oblivious to the danger, continued, 'He's living on his own
in a rented flat. She's playing with him again.'

'You're kidding!' Fran exclaimed. 'What a bitch!' She leant
back in her chair, staring into the distance. 'Well, that explains

a lot. He seemed really down when he came in to take his stuff.'

'That was probably more due to me,' claimed Allie robustly, trying to change the mood. 'I cut up a little bit rough on your behalf.'

'I can imagine,' said Fran. 'Poor old Paul.'

'Poor old Paul nothing!' Allie protested angrily. 'And stop looking so dreamy-eyed! He'll always be in that woman's thrall – it's what he likes, quite evidently. He'll never be free of her, but that's his choice – don't make it yours.'

'Hey,' Fran countered, 'give me a little credit. As gorgeous as he is – even you've got to admit he's handsome?'

Allie shrugged dismissively. 'In a boyish sort of way. I sometimes wonder if there's not a picture of him somewhere in an attic gathering wrinkles in his stead.'

Fran smiled. 'Anyway, you've got nothing to fear from me in that direction. I've learnt my lesson there, as painful as it was.'

Margo, experienced in the horrors of being the betrayed wife, leant over to take her hand. 'It does get easier with time,' she assured her. 'And things change in the most unexpected ways. I mean, look at me – I lost a husband and gained his mistress! Who won there, I ask you?'

'My God!' Fran told her, her sense of humour returning. 'Don't wish that on me. You haven't seen Helen!' With an air of finality and of a subject closed, she stood up and made for the kitchen. 'I'll get the food and we'll go down to the barbecue, shall we?' she offered.

The party rallied itself to join her and help in the carrying down of the provisions.

'So it's over?' Allie pressed her gently, needing her mind put at rest, as they walked together down the herringbone path through the gathering dark. 'And you're okay?'

'Absolutely,' Fran reassured her bravely and decisively, and added for good measure, 'Besides, he farted in his sleep. I'd have had to get rid of him eventually.'

Allie's delighted and dirty laugh was cut short as they came at last to the bottom of the garden, and she beheld Fran's well-kept secret in the field beyond, in all its glory of festooned lights and red-checked picnic cloths.

'What the flying *fuck* is that?' she demanded, turning on her friend.

'It's a horsebox,' said Margo helpfully.

'It's Casa Nova,' twinkled Fran.

Twenty-Six

When Sam had first met Fran she had been excited and flattered that this fascinating woman from London's fast lane had wanted to be her friend. She had reminded her then of the racy set of girls – to whom she had been barely visible, being such a goody two-shoes – who had sat at the back of her class at school and tried to subvert every lesson. They had seemed so sophisticated and witty, so unimpressed by authority, as they openly chewed their gum in corridors, or compared their tattoos in the loos, or laughed together behind the bike shed at secrets to which Sam would never be privy. She had longed then to be among their number, if only for a day, had envied their irreverence and complete disregard for propriety and how things *ought* to be. So being picked to be in Fran's gang had seemed an unexpected, exciting privilege eighteen months ago. She had finally made it to the back of the class.

Now, however, crammed into a converted horsebox listening to Fran's excited telling of her tale, Sam began to wish fervently that she had never met her. Didn't she realise that this kind of behaviour was completely and utterly out of order? Had she no conception of the kind of hot water she was getting Sam into? Couldn't she see that this was anarchy run riot? Evidently not. And nor, apparently, did the others. While Sam played and replayed her imminent sacking from Parry and Eastlake's in glorious Technicolor in her mind, Fran demonstrated all the features of her new home to an ever more impressed audience. Here were the storage heaters that would keep her warm through the winter, this is how the table folded back into the wall when not in use, here was the sofa – hey presto, now it's a bed, here's the immersion heater for the hot water, the clever storage space here and here . . . The fact that the electricity was being supplied from the main house through a cable buried all the way down the garden, thus meaning that she would be stealing from her tenant, was the very least of it. By the time Sam found her voice again, they were all trooping out of the groom's door of the antiquated horsebox and down the three wooden steps which Archie had built for easy access, to sit outside on campaign chairs beneath a string of coloured lights, Trevor and Margo having elected to be the chefs at the barbecue.

'But why a *horsebox*, for Pete's sake?' she asked at last in exasperation.

'Just what I thought in my darkest hour,' Fran admitted exuberantly, refilling everybody's glasses. 'I'd asked Archie originally if he thought it might be possible to *build* something in the field in the time available – I'd been picturing a little house made out of wood, or breezeblocks perhaps – but he pointed out that we'd have needed planning permission for a permanent structure, and we'd never have got it because of the field being classed as agricultural land. But then – well, you know what Archie's like, he's a wily bugger – he grinned and said to me, 'There's way's round it though, me duck. They can't stop you *parking* on yer own land, can they?'

'I'd like to get to know Archie better,' Allie said. 'Sounds like a man after my own heart.'

'Ooh ar, me duck, he is an' all,' Fran told her, doing a creditable impression of Archie's Leicestershire accent. 'Ooh yer blizzard, ar.'

'Ooh your what?' asked Allie, laughing.

'Blizzard, me duck,' Fran repeated, showing off, and giggling.

'Ooh yer sausage,' Margo contributed, throwing another lamb chop onto the barbie.

'Ooh yer sausage,' Fran nodded, 'ooh yer beauty. They've got words for every occasion – you'd be surprised at the inventiveness of Leicester folk in their attempts not to swear.'

'But – not that I'd have liked it any more, you understand – but why not a caravan at least?' Sam demanded, doggedly determined to stay on track. 'Or even a Portakabin?'

'Money,' said Fran. 'And availability. Old Portakabins, apparently, never die. They just go on working for the NHS and the Department of Education, even when they're knackered and on their knees. And the only caravans we saw that were big enough were far too expensive. Then Archie found this, on a farm in Houghton on the Hill. It's ex-Army, apparently. Been standing in a field for years, being used as a hen coop. You should have seen the state of it when Archie finally managed to get it here. I thought I'd die. Up shit creek – literally! But it was an absolute gift, and Archie relished the challenge. The farmer said that if we could shift it, we could have it for free.'

'You don't mean to say it actually goes?' asked Trevor, who was interested in motors.

Fran nodded. 'Archie's second son Phil is a wizard with engines. He had it all to bits, and finally got it back in the right order, and bingo – we drove her here. Free accommodation, and conveniently close to the house.'

'But that's my point!' said Sam, her patience sorely tried. 'Why do you need to be on the doorstep? You can't police your tenant all the time. He's paying through the nose for the privilege of living in your house, and he's entitled to some privacy. I can't go telling him that the owner lives at the bottom of his garden – he'd never wear that.'

'Don't even think of telling him I'm the owner,' Fran said firmly. 'It would only complicate things.'

'Then who the hell shall I say you are?' Sam demanded.

'Me, me duck?' Fran asked her with a wicked smile. 'Doon't you worry, gel, I'll introduce messen.' She looked round them all, revelling in the suspense, before revealing her last and most outrageous secret. 'I'm Mrs Mop.'

'You're who?' asked Allie, choking on her wine.

'I'm 'is cleaner an' gardener.'

'No!' said Sam.

'Ooh ar, me duck,' Fran assured her.

'Ooh yer fucking blizzard!' Allie drawled appreciatively, and they all laughed except Sam.

After the barbecue when they'd all gone home, having first helped her to clear up and tidy the furniture back into Casa Nova, Fran congratulated herself on a successful evening's work. She'd been dreading Allie's response most of all, but she, it turned out, had merely been amused at her friend's gall, and apart from commenting rather drily, 'I thought you left Q&A to *write* fiction, not to live it,' had been more enthusiastic than Fran could have hoped; it appealed to her sense of anarchy, she'd said. Sam had tutted, of course, and droned on for a good hour about how *outrageous* her scheme was and how much hot water she'd be in if this *ever* came out at work, but in the end Margo had helped persuade her how lucky Jeremy Sinclair was to have such a highly motivated person to look after the place.

'It'll be a labour of love,' she said.

'No it bloody well won't,' Fran had corrected her. 'He'll pay the going rate.' After that, she'd had to overcome Sam's next objection – that over her dead body would *she* be the one to negotiate Fran's wages – but eventually she was mollified enough (more likely pissed enough) at least to wish her luck for the next day.

Retiring for the last time for the foreseeable future to her own bed in the Big House, as she now thought of it, Fran snuggled down under the duvet to enjoy a good night's sleep. As much as she still disliked the idea of having somebody else living in her beautiful home, now she had worked so hard with Archie getting the horsebox shipshape she felt quite excited at the prospect of moving in. On that light, warm summer's night, with the soft breeze breathing gently through the open window, even her dreams reflected her new-found optimism and sense of adventure. She was in a time long, long ago, on holiday on the shores of a Scottish loch, before her father had left them. Granny and Gramps were there and they showed her how to make a hammock out of string. There was a primus stove, its flame an iridescent blue, and her smiling mother was making tea. Fran stood in the shallows, the crystal-clear water, warmed by the sun, lapping round her legs, her dress tucked up in her knickers. Dad was bending down, his hand guiding hers, teaching her to skim flat stones across the glassy surface of the loch. He said she was his princess. Her heart was bursting with happiness, and in the dream there seemed to be an intense significance about everything: the colour and shape of the stones, the soft curves of the hills beyond, the transparency of the water, the blue flame of the primus, the hammock made from knotted string. There was an urgent sense that she must remember this, that she must store up these images intact, that they were some kind of key to something which would become clear at some future time, when all would be well and all would be well and all manner of things would be well.

For the first time in weeks, she woke refreshed and happy. For the first time since he had left her, she hadn't dreamt of Paul.

Rising luxuriously late, she breakfasted ceremonially for the last time on her kitchen patio with food bought specially for the occasion, hang the expense – ripe purple figs and strawberries, warm croissants loaded with unsalted butter and apricot jam, Blue Mountain coffee, freshly juiced pineapple. There would be

time enough for austerity and thrift in the coming months in her
mobile stable. Looking round at her burgeoning summer garden
and the lovely red herringbone path which guided the eye to
travel further, following its gentle curves, she complimented herself on having learnt, in a very short time, to take care of herself
and to treat herself well. Images from her dream came up to greet
her, and she was surprised to remember that childhood camping
holiday, which had lain untouched in her memory for so long.
Of course, her dream had been selective. It had picked the best
bits and gathered them all together for one glorious day, had
stopped her mother's whingeing and put a smile on her face,
had shown her an occasion when her father had noticed her and
played – had even made a hammock out of the scarf or shawl
she now remembered her gran crocheting, the steel hook nip-
ping deftly in and out of the coloured wool. In reality there had
also been the usual rows, the tense silences, the compressed lips,
the sharp sting of a slap across the back of her legs. But it was
good to remember at last that there had been some happiness
there.

Reminded now of her mother, she suddenly realised how long
a time had passed since she'd been in touch. She still didn't know
about Paul leaving, or even that Fran had quit her job, let alone
about having to rent out the house and live in a field. But this
wasn't so remarkable. When Rachel sulked and sent you to
Coventry, you stayed there – at least, until she wanted something more. After that it was all smiles, everything swept neatly
under the carpet, nothing learnt at all. Fran sighed. She'd have
to tell her eventually – if only because, in a few short hours, there
would be somebody else's outgoing message on her answering
machine. But not yet. She couldn't face the crisis that Rachel
would inevitably make out of this situation which was already
dramatic enough.

Shutting her mother firmly out of her mind now, she tidied
away her breakfast things, scattering crumbs for the waiting

robin. There were still a few chores to do in readiness for Mr Sinclair, CEO: cupboards to be checked, cushions to be plumped, windows to be cleaned. She stripped her bed and enjoyed the luxury of having an in-house washing machine for the last time in a while. After this, it would be the launderette, she supposed. Unless she was very cheeky (as cheeky as she was going to be with his electricity) and used the facilities when he was out. She grinned to herself, her good humour returning. How would she present herself to him when he arrived, this important corporate man? Did she dare to have fun with him, to pretend the Leicester accent she'd been mimicking last night for Allie's benefit? It *would* be a laugh. She could invent a whole new persona, thus giving him nothing of her true self. It would be a kind of secret revenge. And if he was the kind of man she feared he would be in his position – high-handed, brusque, used to his fawning office subordinates scuttling round to obey his commands on the double – if, in short, he treated her like a servant in her own home, then she would be having the last and longest laugh.

The morning passed pleasantly enough in a round of house-hold chores, and she was buoyed up by the optimism of her dream. Leaving her home no longer felt like a humiliating failure and defeat; it felt instead like the start of a new adventure, like setting out on a camping holiday, packing only the essentials. Humming, she denuded her bedroom of evidence of herself, scrubbed the shower, rearranged ornaments in the living room and, when all was to her satisfaction, took her wet sheets down to her new washing line by the side of Casa Nova and pegged them out to dry. A hammock was a good idea, she thought. She would buy one as soon as Jeremy Sinclair's rent money plumped out the hole of her overdraft. What an enviable life she was about to embrace, she mused – to live in an exciting space which she had helped to design and build, to eat outdoors while the summer lasted, to actually be *paid* to do what she'd always loved the most: tending her garden, cosseting her house. She should have it so rich.

With only the windows left to clean, she allowed herself some time off for a lunch break, basking in the sun in her campaign chair by the van, Radio 3 playing rollicking Strauss waltzes through her Walkman travel speakers, the clean laundry billowing next to her in the breeze. It was good to be alive.

Like Allie before him, the dyed-in-the-wood Londoner Jeremy Sinclair had difficulty in finding Little Langton once he'd left the motorway. But unlike Allie he didn't mind at all about getting lost in neighbouring villages, or driving down the country lanes, seeing for the first time the fields and copses of the Leicestershire landscape, the hawthorn hedges, the horses grazing, the new foals kicking up their heels. He'd always loved the countryside, and often spent his holidays walking, either at home or abroad, enjoying the contrast of a simpler lifestyle for a couple of weeks a year. He was looking forward to taking up the challenges of his new post. He knew that it would be hard work, but he vowed to himself that he would make the most of this location. He turned up his car radio. The Strauss waltzes had finished, but now here was Philip Glass to provide the musical score to this gorgeous film which spooled across his windscreen. On the weekends when he didn't go back to London he'd explore, go for long walks, visit wayside inns – maybe even hire a horse and take it for a hack down some of these bridlepaths he was passing. Life was good, and full of promise, and he mustn't lose this opportunity by burying himself in his work, as he usually did.

Coming at last into Little Langton he consulted the notes from the relocation officer, and found The Avenue without difficulty. Driving past its houses he felt quite excited and impatient to see his own. He'd been sent details, of course, but everything had been done at such speed that they'd been faxed, and the photograph had come out dark and smudged. Counting off the numbers of the houses as he edged the car slowly forward, he came at last to 84 and turned into its drive just as P. Glass ceded the airwaves to F. Poulenc. It was a magic moment, taking his first view of his new home to the stately, declamatory orchestral opening strains of *Gloria*. It was wonderful. It was amazing. It was beyond his wildest hopes and dreams of country living. A manor house for his lordship, complete with leaded lights and an impressive, generous porch, with climbing roses, trailing honeysuckle, gabled roofs – and a woman up a ladder cleaning windows. Good grief! On a Sunday? If this was the cleaner he'd been told about, she certainly earned her keep.

Switching off the engine, and therefore reluctantly cutting off the Westminster Singers and the City of London Sinfonia just as they were getting into their stride, he was astonished, as he stepped out of his car, to hear the cleaning lady carrying on where they had left off, really giving it some welly up her ladder, '*Gloria! Gloria! Gloria! Gloria in excelsis deo!*' He quickly disabused himself that he was having an out-of-body experience when, examining her more closely, he saw the Walkman earphones. That explained why she still hadn't noticed his arrival, then. How funny, and what a coincidence! And what a gift, to have a daily help who sang along to Radio 3! He waited patiently for her to catch sight of him below, but she had now embarked on the jaunty '*Laudamus te*' and he began to wonder if he'd still be waiting until she had sung the final '*Amen*' of '*Qui sedes.*' Not that he minded. Although it was strange to hear just the vocal part on its own without orchestral accompaniment, he was rather keen to hear her try to tackle the high notes of '*Domine Deus.*'

However, that wasn't to be. Having finished the window she was working on she had started to descend her ladder and, coming face to face with him as she was on the last few rungs, the high note she emitted was a scream. She clutched her chest. Clearly he'd given her a nasty shock.

'I am *so* sorry,' Jeremy apologised, his arms spread wide to catch her lest she fall. She ripped the earphones out and came down to his level. 'Jeremy Sinclair,' he explained to her ashen face, 'the new tenant? And you must be Mrs . . . Um . . . the cleaning lady?'

'Mop,' Fran supplied, her brain completely scrambled. She hadn't realised it was so late – or was he early? God, she felt an idiot. How long had the bastard been listening to her?

'Mrs *Mop*?' Jeremy queried, laughing impolitely. 'Surely not?'

'Nickname,' Fran invented quickly, wishing she hadn't started this. 'Mrs 'Oldaway gev it me an' it stuck.' And so was she, now, with her new bogus persona. Although she'd toyed with the idea she hadn't really meant to do it, and wouldn't have, if he hadn't caught her by surprise. 'You're early,' she said accusingly, in an attempt to turn his attention away from herself until she could collect her wits. Not only had he surprised her with the time of his arrival, but also by his appearance. He was not at all the desiccated fifty-something she'd been expecting to see, but a rather attractive man who was perhaps nudging forty. She wished to God she was wasn't dressed in her oldest and baggiest joggers at their first meeting, her hair all over the shop, and not a scrap of make-up.

Apologising again for the shock he'd given her, Jeremy walked with her to the front door.

'What a wonderful house!' he enthused, thereby endearing himself to her the more. 'It's gorgeous! So quaint! Are you going to show me round?'

'Ar, if yer like,' said Fran. She threw open the door and gestured to him to precede her inside.

'Oh!' he exclaimed, seeing the huge fireplace. 'An inglenook! It's like a fantasy! We used to have one when I was a little boy, when we still lived in the country, before we moved to town. I used to have a little stool and sit right there, watching the fire. My legs would go all red and blotchy, but my mother could never persuade me to come out. It felt so safe. And so exciting. Is it original? Was it always here?'

Fran felt herself warming to this man by the minute, and she responded in kind to his enthusiasm, forgetting her accent in her excitement. 'No, it had been bricked in with a mean little Edwardian affair, and then in front of that a grotesque sixties electric monstrosity. I knocked them out and found this.'

'*You* knocked them out?' Jeremy asked her. Was there no end to this woman's industry?

Fran pulled herself up, reminding herself of Mrs Mop's accent. 'I 'elped. The missus. Mrs 'Oldaway, she done it. Ar.'

'And the beams,' said Jeremy, looking up at the ceiling. 'Are they original too?'

'Ar. Boxed in they was. False ceilin' an' all. Mrs 'Oldaway found 'em and stripped 'em down. They'd been painted over. Barbaric, she said.'

'Evidently a woman after my own heart,' Jeremy unwittingly complimented her. 'And look at those stairs – they're oak, aren't they? Can we go up?'

'Don't need me to give yer permission,' Fran said ungraciously, following him up. 'It's all yours now, ent it?'

'I wish,' said Jeremy, as he gained the upper landing and opened the door to the study. 'Gosh, it must have been hard for Mrs Holdaway to move out after she'd worked on it so hard.'

'She weren't best pleased, no,' said Fran flatly.

After they had looked in all the other upstairs rooms and Fran had answered all Jeremy's enthusiastic queries, they went at last into Fran's huge and airy bedroom where Jeremy sat and bounced on the bed. It was a strange moment for our heroine.

'It's ridiculous, you know,' Jeremy told her in his friendly, open manner, as he put his feet up and leaned back against the bedhead. 'It feels just like home.'

'Feet,' said Fran, unable to prevent herself.

'I'm sorry?'

'Shoes on the mattress,' she explained. 'Mrs 'Oldaway wou'n't like it.'

'Of course,' said Jeremy, unoffended, and got up to look at the view from the window. 'What a gorgeous garden! You know,' he continued, turning to her again, 'some places just feel friendly straight away, don't they, as if you've been here before and have finally returned? It so reminds me of my childhood home! Sorry,' he said, mistaking her look of momentary sadness for an expression of bemusement, 'I'm burbling. I'm over-excited, I admit. I hadn't dared to think that I'd be moving to anywhere as beautiful as this.'

'Firm must think highly of you,' said Fran, turning her back on him and leading the way out. Seeing another man lying in Paul's vacated space on the bed had quite unsettled her. She didn't know whether it was the pain of bereavement she was feeling in the pit of her stomach or the stirrings of lust for this really rather gorgeous guy. 'Cup of tea?' she called behind her on the stairs, hoping to calm herself with a practical chore. 'Mrs 'Oldaway left you with the necessaries.'

'How kind of her, thank you,' he said, bounding down the stairs behind her. When they came into the kitchen, his enthusiasm was undiminished. 'Wow,' he exclaimed. 'I'll be able to do some entertaining here!'

'Married are you?' asked Fran, rather more than conversationally, as she clattered spoons into saucers.

'Divorced, actually,' Jeremy told her. 'Amicably. Well, it is now. A couple of years ago.'

'Had an affair then, did you?' she accused him. She could get used to this new person she'd become, completely devoid of tact and the niceties of civilised intercourse.

'In fact no – quite the reverse,' he answered, unruffled. He found her phlegmaticness quite amusing, and rather a refreshing change. 'I was the boring one who wanted babies and forever, but . . . well, I can quite understand that that's all very nice for the man.'

Fran's heart skipped a beat, her head reeling. 'You probably wouldn't say no to a nice slice of me 'ome-made apple pie,' said Mrs Mop, turning a smile on him, for all the world like a latter-day Eve.

Twenty-Seven

Tea, naturally, was served in the rose arbour in the garden, Fran having first briefly excused herself to visit the downstairs cloak-room. Staring at herself in the mirror she despaired, but there was nothing much she could do about her appearance, without a complete make-over, other than to smooth down her hair and nudge her eyebrows back into shape. Back outside, pouring his second cup of tea, she continued to encourage Jeremy to tell her all about his former marriage.

'Yes, it did come as quite a shock,' he admitted. 'I suppose I'd just settled down, taken it as read that we were okay as we were. But Belinda just felt suffocated by it all. I'd never even thought to ask her how she felt about children before we married, I'd just taken it for granted that that's what we'd do. Stupid of me.'

More stupid of Belinda, thought Fran. Was the woman mad? Did she think that men like this, who could talk openly about their feelings, grew on trees? 'More pie?' she asked, taking his plate and plonking another great wedge on it.

Jeremy grinned. 'I shouldn't, but – home cooking! I haven't eaten pastry like this since I left home. Delicious.' Not bothering with fork or spoon, he picked the pie up and bit into it. 'Mm,' he said, 'I feel like I've died and gone to heaven.'

You too? thought Fran, admiring the laughter lines around his eyes. She had an almost overwhelming urge to bend towards him and gently brush the crumbs of pastry from his mouth.

'Actually,' he continued happily, 'you remind me of my mum – she could always draw me out like this.'

Fran's smile died on her lips. 'You've got a piece of pie on yer chin,' she pointed out. If she was going to be a mother to him, she'd model herself on her own dear mater, bring him down a peg or two.

Unconcerned, and unaware that he'd offended her, Jeremy flipped the crumbs into his mouth with his finger. 'I was saving that till later,' he quipped. 'Anyway, enough of me. What about you and Mr . . . Mop? Are you happily married with a fleet of Mopettes?'

'He's dead,' said Fran with feeling. 'No issue.'

Jeremy's expression reflected his embarrassment at his gaffe. 'I'm so sorry. Not recently, I hope?'

'Weeds over his grave. He was a cheat and a liar. Buried and forgotten.'

'Well, good for you,' Jeremy complimented her. He raised his tea cup in salutation. 'Here's to new life for both of us!'

'To that,' agreed Fran, her good humour returning. She was prepared to forgive his unintended insult, preferring to let him off the hook with the thought that perhaps she reminded him of his mother's personality rather than her age. He seemed such a nice man, his mother must be rather special to have brought him up like this. She knew she was in danger of rushing her fences in her mind, but even if nothing actually did happen between them, he'd be good company to have around. 'Bein' yer first night 'ere, Mr Sinclair—'

'Oh, don't let's be formal – do call me Jeremy.'

Fran smiled coyly. 'Jeremy, then.'

'And I'm sorry, I'm sure it's a very good joke when Mrs Holdaway says it, but I'm afraid I really can't bring myself to call you Mrs Mop. What's your first name – may I call you by that?'

'Gloria,' said Fran after a moment's hesitation, picking the first name that came into her head.

Jeremy laughed. 'So you were singing your signature tune when I arrived then?'

'Oh! Ar,' Fran agreed, feeling rather foolish as she realised why Gloria had been the first name to come to mind. 'That's right. Any road, I were goin' to say – Jeremy – seein' as it's yer first night and you won't have got stuff in, p'raps you'd like me to cook for you?' The way to a man's heart, after all . . . 'Nothing fancy – just plain home cooking like.'

Just as Jeremy was going to answer – in the affirmative, Fran was sure – a shrill and petulant voice cut through the air. 'Are you *deaf*?' it demanded.

Jeremy was on his feet in a second, his face transformed with pleasure. Turning, Fran saw a slim, leggy twenty-something, dressed to the nines for London, looking strangely out of place as she came through the garden gate.

'I've been ringing the front doorbell for about an hour!' she complained. 'Jesus!'

'Nikki!' announced Jeremy, running to embrace her. 'I'm sorry, darling, we didn't hear you. I didn't think you'd get away so soon – you said tomorrow.'

'Shoot was cancelled,' said Nikki, eyeing Fran suspiciously over his shoulder. 'Who's that?'

Jeremy led Nikki by the hand back down the garden to introduce her. 'This wonderful lady is Gloria, our cleaning lady. Gloria – this is Nikki.'

Fran forced herself to unpurse her lips. She felt as if she had just been forced to suck a bushel of lemons. 'Pleased to meet you,' she lied.

'Can't we go indoors?' whined Nikki, as she watched a bee disappear into a flower nearby. 'There's insects out here.'

'Of course!' said Jeremy. 'Come and see the house, it's amazing. Leave the pots, Gloria – I'll get them later – and thank you so much for the tea,' he called back to Fran, who was busily stacking plates.

'No trouble,' Fran told him, ignoring his directive and taking the crockery back into the kitchen, unable to abide the thought of a stranger going unsupervised into her home.

As Nikki swept through the house bits dropped off her and landed untidily on chairs and on the floor – her coat, her handbag, a cardboard-backed envelope, a couple of video tapes, her mobile – and Fran followed on behind, picking things up in reproving silence and putting them in a tidy pile, while Jeremy bubbled enthusiastically about the house.

'Isn't it wonderful?' he asked her as she flopped down on the sofa.

Nikki glared balefully at Fran's living room. 'It's like a pensions commercial,' she said damningly.

Jeremy laughed. 'Cosy isn't it?' he pressed her.

'All right if you're a hundred and three,' said Nikki, putting her feet up on the coffee table. 'Can't you get rid of this horrible old furniture and get some new stuff in? It's like a museum in here.'

'Feet,' said Fran, seething inside. 'Mrs 'Oldaway's very particular about this *antique* furniture. No shoes allowed. Coasters to be used for drinks on wood surfaces.'

'Yeah?' Nikki challenged her coldly. 'Well she's not here, is she? And anyway, Jeremy's paying for the privilege. We can do what we bloody well like.'

Embarrassed by her rudeness, Jeremy had wandered over to her pile of stuff and was holding the large envelope. 'Are these the new photos?' he asked, changing the subject. 'Can I see?' Nikki nodded her permission. 'Nikki's in PR at the moment, Gloria,' he explained, leafing through the ten by eights. 'But she's hoping soon to break into presenting – on television.'

Fran suppressed a cynical smile. Of course she wanted to be a television presenter – it was the new wannabe job for the third millennium. Crave the trappings of fame, but have no obvious talents? No problem! Get hired to talk bollocks on TV.

Jeremy was full of admiration for her publicity shots. 'Oh, these are great! Has your agent seen them? Is he pleased?'

'Yeah,' said Nikki, smiling now. 'He's doing a mail-out this week. The video's great too. Should be – cost me an arm and a leg, bloody rip-off merchants. He reckons I come across as really professional. And he says if we don't get a result in the next couple of months, there's loads of new reality TV shows in the offing that he's going to put me up for – you know, like *Big Brother* and that.'

Fran was trying to frame some withering response in Leicesterese when Nikki's mobile rang from the pile of her belongings Fran had tidied.

'Chuck us my phone,' Nikki commanded her rudely, making no attempt to get it herself. Seeing Fran make no attempt either, Jeremy took it over, and got no word of thanks as Nikki clamped it to her ear.

'Yeah? Did they? Well I'll do Miami, but they can stuff Hong Kong . . . Because I won't be working for you then, will I, stupid?'

Tactfully, Jeremy arrived at Fran's side and gently took her arm, walking her back to the kitchen. 'Her PR job by the sounds of it,' he explained. 'She's serving out her notice, gearing herself up for her new career. Thanks for everything, Gloria. As for supper, I think now that Nikki's arrived—'

'There's an Indian take-out in the village,' Fran interrupted firmly, reluctantly leaving her house in the hands of the enemy, her earlier offer now retracted. 'Or a supermarket on the ring road. I'll be in in the morning, as per.'

Beating a retreat back down the garden to her horsebox, she laughed bitterly to herself. To think that she had seen a happy ending coming her way so soon. To think that she'd actually liked Jeremy Sinclair. He was just as bad as the rest of them. Going out with a twenty-something spoilt brat, just like the men Sam had complained about in her darker days. God! What a wanker! No wonder Fran had reminded him of his mother. The man was practically a paedophile. She stomped up the stairs to the groom's door and let herself in to the small space that she would now have to learn to call home. A mirror had the effrontery to throw back her reflection, and she caught sight of her frowning face, her forehead wrinkled, her mouth turned down at the corners.

'I am beautiful. I am successful. Everything is working out perfectly,' she spat at it with vicious sarcasm, before covering it with a tea towel. 'Is there no justice?!' she howled at the top of her voice, alone in her empty field.

Much later, after a lonely evening and a supper for one of beans on toast, she folded up the table, converted her couch into a bed, put on a pair of sensible pyjamas, and climbed beneath the covers. She had meant to relish this first night in her exciting new home, she reminded herself grumpily, and now it was all spoilt. She couldn't get Jeremy and Nikki out of her head. Had they got their feet up in her living room now, cuddled up, watching Nikki strut her stuff across Fran's wide-screen telly? Or worse – were they swapping bodily fluids in her bed? She snapped off the lights and tried to settle, but her curiosity got the better of her and she fished around in the bedside cupboard and pulled out her pair of binoculars. They had been a present from Paul some years ago when she'd mentioned she fancied taking up bird-watching. Now she pushed aside the curtains, kneeling up in bed, and swept the back of the house to spot an entirely different kind of bird.

Her timing was good; or perhaps bad would be another way of looking at it. As she focused on the bedroom window she could see Nikki's willowy shape outlined against the net curtains as she came into the room and switched on the light. After a moment Jeremy joined her and their two shapes briefly merged before they broke apart again and the curtains were drawn. The show was over, but Fran's imagination ran riot.

Sam's message from the fairground clairvoyant came into Fran's mind as she grumpily put aside her binoculars and tried once more to settle down to sleep. Angrily, she turned over and lay on her back, staring tensely at the dark ceiling.

'Okay, Brenda,' she challenged the so-called psychic bitterly, in absentia, 'we've had the great losses. Now where's the great sodding gains?'

Twenty-Eight

Fran woke early and, try as she might, she couldn't get back to sleep. Giving up finally, she got up and dressed; at six thirty she was working in the garden, hacking back plants that had already gone over, pruning shrubs and creepers. The work suited her frame of mind, cutting things down to the shape she imposed on them, training them to obey her will, bringing order to chaos, being in control. But with every snip of her shears she felt even angrier – it fed her rage rather than diminished it.

Jeremy was as surprised to see Fran through the kitchen window as she was to see him when he appeared at her side with his mug of coffee.

'Gloria!' he said. 'What on earth are you doing here so early? And you don't have to do that. There's a gardener comes, apparently, it's in the lease – he'll see to it.'

'I'm him,' said Fran grumpily, not bothering to stop work.

'You're the gardener too?'

'Ar.'

Jeremy watched her for a couple of minutes, then looked at his watch. 'I've made a pot of coffee. Shall I get you a cup?'

'If you like,' said Fran, which was the proper Leicester response to an offer of hospitality. She sneaked a glance at him as he went off to fetch it, admiring the cut of his suit and his freshly washed hair which shone in the early morning sunlight. 'Wanker,' she reminded herself, returning to her vicious pruning. 'Cradle-snatching git.' Snip. Snip.

'Here we are,' said Jeremy, proffering her one of her own mugs. 'No sugar – did I get that right?'

'Ar. Just put it down over there.' Snip.

But Jeremy stood his ground. 'That's a hebe, isn't it?'

'Ar.'

'I'd like to learn more about gardening,' he persevered, evidently trying to be friendly. 'In London I just have a balcony, so I can only grow things in tubs. But I used to love it when I was a boy – I had my own little plot in our country garden.'

'Oh ar.'

'Maybe, while I'm here, you might find time to teach me.'

Here we go again, thought Fran angrily, mistaking me for Mum. 'We'll have to see,' she said, collecting up an armful of prunings. 'Mind out the road – you don't want to mess up yer nice suit.'

'Right,' said Jeremy, conceding ground as she swept past him. 'I'll leave your coffee on the table then, okay? Best be off. First day.'

'Have a nice time then,' said Fran, conceding a little ground herself and at least getting within nodding distance of civility.

'Will you be cleaning inside the house today, Gloria?' asked Jeremy as he emerged back out of the kitchen, attaché case in hand.

'Every day,' Fran told him firmly.

'Okay – great,' he said equably. 'But do you think you could leave it a while before you make a start? Nikki's rather a late riser when she doesn't have to go in to work, and she's having a couple of days off at the moment.'

'Be my pleasure,' Fran assured him.

'See you later then,' he called on his way to the garden gate.

'Tra.'

After he had gone, she stepped back to look at her handiwork and saw that she had rather overdone it in the cutting-back stakes. She had denuded the poor hebe of practically every leaf and it was now only half its original height. Time to sit down and drink her coffee. Punishing Nikki was one thing, but punishing herself by ruining her garden quite another. Sitting at her patio table, she looked up at the sun. Not too hot yet. Her eye roved past Nikki's bedroom window, the curtains still closed. Perhaps a nice noisy gardening chore next, she thought evilly. Like getting out the electric mower and cutting the huge lawns.

By ten o'clock the lawns were like bowling greens, close-cropped and neatly edged, and still the bedroom curtains remained undisturbed. Well tough. Gloria had waited long enough to begin her housework, thought Fran huffily on her alter ego's behalf. She'd change out of her gardening shoes and make a start indoors.

Entering the house, Fran found chaos everywhere she looked. The remains of the Indian take-out littered the kitchen surfaces together with unwashed plates, and in the living room Nikki had marked her patch with her debris like a dog pissed on walls. Her videotapes were on the floor next to an empty wine bottle, and Fran found a half-empty glass sitting brazenly on the sideboard with not a coaster in sight. But what was even more affronting – worse even than seeing Nikki's spiked shoes sitting on the coffee table – was following the trail of her discarded clothes, which became ever tinier and more intimate, as Fran tracked them up the stairs. This was war.

The sound of a vacuum cleaner being wielded at close quarters, none too gently, to the accompaniment of some selfish bastard singing at the top of its stupid yokel lungs, eventually brought Nikki to full consciousness. Furious, she lifted her eye mask and glared at the bedside clock. Ten twenty. Jesus! How dare the bloody woman start so bloody early?! She pulled the pillow over her head and tried in vain to ignore the racket, but when the hoover kept being bashed repeatedly against the skirting boards *right outside the bedroom*, she'd had enough. Grabbing Jeremy's dressing gown, she stormed over to the door and tore it open.

'What the hell do you think you're doing?' she screamed over the noise, her eye mask propped on the top of her head. Making no impression on the impassive, busy back before her, she looked round for the socket and ripped the plug out of the wall. The cleaning woman turned to see what had happened and, seeing Nikki lowering over her, gave a start.

'Ooh, you did give me a turn,' she said and peered at her, framed in the dark doorway. 'It's young Nicola, is it? You look terrible. You off work sick?'

'It's *Nikki* – N-I-K-K-I, and I'm trying to have a lie-in if you don't mind!' spat the young woman whose proud parents, twenty-seven years previously, had christened her Nicola-Jane.

'You doon't want to do that,' the irritating char chummily advised her. 'Too much sleep meks your eyes go all puffy – look at the state of 'em already! What you want's a nice long walk and a good healthy breakfast.'

'What I want is a bit of peace and quiet!' said Nikki, her hands checking the size of her eyelids, but at that moment her mobile rang from somewhere downstairs.

'No rest for the wicked,' observed Fran with a grin, as Nikki went down in search of it, and switched the hoover back on again at maximum power.

When Fran eventually left the house (having spent a great deal of time cleaning in the bedroom for no other reason than to keep Nikki out of it) she found her lying on the sofa in the living room, watching herself on video.

'So you're going to be a telly star, then,' said Fran, watching Nikki pretending she had a personality on the screen, wanging on about herself, direct on camera.

'Have you finished now?' demanded Nikki, not troubling herself to engage in idle chit-chat with the staff.

'Just about,' said Fran, plumping the sofa cushions around her and standing between Nikki and the television.

'Will you *leave* it *alone*?' Nikki snapped at her, grabbing the cushions out of her hands.

'All right, me duck.' Fran took her time to scan the room before going out through the kitchen, while Nikki glared at her murderously. 'I'll be off. Sorry I disturbed your beauty sleep,' she called back after her in a falsely apologetic tone, 'I 'adn't realised you needed so much of it.' She had the satisfaction, as she slammed the back door shut behind her, of hearing herself described loudly in the most unflattering terms. She smiled to herself grimly. It was good to have found a new hobby. Nikki-baiting was going to be fun.

Twenty-Nine

Sam and Margo were having problems with Nigel, and the need to have a chat about that was the reason Sam gave for inviting Fran round to supper. In fact there were a couple of other things which Sam wanted to discuss as well, but she was learning more effective communication skills from her new partner, one of which involved sneaking up on a person when they were un-suspecting, and therefore undefended. At any rate, it seemed to be working now Margo was using the technique on Nigel.

There was the usual mayhem of children and animals at Margo's house when Fran arrived that evening, and she felt like St Francis of Assisi as she walked from her car to the front door, accompanied by two sheep, a pig and three cats. The door was answered by a very young person wearing teddy-bear pyjamas.

'Are you Fran?' she asked.

'Yes. Hello. Who are you?' Fran smiled.

'I'm Jocelyn. I'm supposed to be in bed, but I'm allowed to stay up to see you. You live in a horsebox.'

'Yes I do.'

'Can I come and see one day?'

'Of course. I'd like that.'

'And can I sleep over? Is it true you have to fold the table up to get into bed? And that you've got a shower, and a loo?'

'All perfectly true,' said Fran. 'You're very welcome to come and do a sleepover, but we'll have to ask your mum first. Can I come in?' She followed the young doorkeeper into the house, helped along by the inquisitive Mr Piglet who was snuffling her bottom from behind. Ahead of her, Margo's complaining voice shouted from the kitchen, 'Who let Cec and Cec in?'

'Oops,' said Jocelyn, looking at Fran guiltily with huge sleepy eyes.

'Don't worry,' said Fran. 'I'll say it was me.'

But by the time they reached the kitchen Alice and Margo were having a typical (to them) family discussion about where the two sheep would be spending the night, and the matter of who had let them in was now yesterday's news.

'Okay, I'll ask Sam then,' Alice announced in answer to her mother's assertion that Sam would be cross, having single-handedly trained them up to accept outdoor living. As she flounced out past Fran (she was, after all, fourteen – the perfect flouncing age) she stopped briefly to check her credentials. 'Are you Fran? Is it true you live in a horsebox?'

'I see my legend runs before me,' Fran said drily, as Margo kissed her in welcome and handed her a gin and tonic.

'You're very big in Little Langton,' Margo agreed. 'Particularly with my brood.'

'She says I *can* go and stay with her,' said Jocelyn unwisely, since her mother was now alerted to her presence. 'Can I go this weekend?'

'We'll see,' said Margo. 'Bed.'

'But Fran said,' Jocelyn protested. 'And anyway, I've got a pain in my thumb, so even if I did go to bed, I wouldn't be able to go to sleep yet. I'm in absolute agony.'

Margo suppressed a smile and tried to look stern. 'Oh dear. Well, if your thumb is that serious, perhaps you won't be well enough to stay with Fran so soon.'

'It's feeling a bit better now,' Jocelyn conceded.

'Good. Up the wooden hill, then, to B-E-D. Sleep well. Kiss?'

Jocelyn declined, on the basis that she had been tricked. She did however consent to climb the wooden hill, but only to elicit a fairer hearing from Sam, who was upstairs with Dan, puzzling over his history homework.

'She's settled in well, then, with the kids,' Fran suggested.

'They love her to bits. Good job I'm not the jealous type,' Margo grinned.

It was some time before the livestock had been returned to their natural habitat (after Sam's careful negotiation with Alice), Jocelyn's imaginary pains had been made better with arnica cream and a bedtime story (Sam again), and Dan was confident that he could now tackle the fall-out from Hiroshima on his own. But at last the grown-ups were free to sit down to their supper and dish the dirt. And dirty it was. Barry Wigley, aka Nigel Ford-Roberts, had apparently reverted to type.

'He threatened to take the children?' Fran expostulated, practically hyperventilating in her anger. Sam nodded.

'Lesbians are unfit mothers,' Margo explained. 'At least as far as the law is concerned, as interpreted by Nigel. Of course, it's all a ruse to get more money from me. He was claiming half the house, and contesting the children's maintenance. Reckons he's poor as a church mouse.'

'But that's blackmail,' said Fran.

'Exactly. Charming, isn't it, using his own children as the bait?'

'What are you going to do?' Fran asked them, now very worried on their behalf.

'It's already done,' Margo told her with a naughty grin. 'And it seemed to do the trick.'

'Which is?'

'Why, to give him what he's asked for, of course – to grant him full custody of the children.'

Fran was taken aback. 'Aren't you worried that it'll backfire?'

'Nigel – looking after children? No, not at all. It would interfere with his social life too much. And you would think, wouldn't you, that if he really cared about his children he would have visited them, at least once or twice, since he left them.'

'Well, of course, he claims that he was trying to visit them when he called round here on the day of the hosepipe mis-understanding,' grinned Sam.

'Misunderstanding?' Fran queried. She had heard that story in full, and it hadn't seemed to her that there had been any failure of communication in Sam's piece of direct action.

'Yes,' Sam continued with feigned innocence. 'Apparently he thought I was attacking him with a jet of water, when in fact I was merely trying to wash the soup stains off his jacket. As a friendly act.'

Fran laughed. 'And I thought all that stuff about estate agents being inveterate liars was vicious slander and stereotyping. Any-way, what's happened? Has he responded yet to your offer?'

'He called just before you arrived,' Margo told her, relishing the memory, 'and tried to bluster his way through. I just stuck to my guns – said he could come and get them immediately. And I also reminded him that he'd never, in a million years, organise himself to get a house big enough for himself and the children and their animals. He's staying in a friend's flat at the moment, apparently. And two: if he did get as far as getting custody, the children would drive him completely round the bend within minutes and he'd be begging me to take them back. He never could stand sharing his living space with a menagerie, and you've seen how assertive Alice can be on that subject.'

'So he retracted his threat?'

'He agreed that he would be considering other options with his lawyer.'

'Will you have to sell up here to give him his share?'

'He doesn't have a share,' said Margo. 'I bought this house with my own money – it's in my name.'

'And I did some investigating of his finances – he's got plenty of money stashed away, in fact. He can certainly afford to buy himself another place.'

'What does he do?' asked Fran. The only activity she'd ever heard appended to his name was playing golf.

'Neither of us really knows for sure,' Sam admitted. 'Partly since he's such a liar you just can't trust his answers.'

'And partly because, for my part, I've never really wanted to dig too deep,' said Margo grimly. 'He used to dabble in property, but who knows these days? Porn, perhaps? Exporting arms? One just gets the feeling with Barry-Nigel that if it's dirty and it pays well, he'd do it. Which is why I'm not too fussed about him making maintenance payments for the kids. If Sam and I can manage without his filthy lucre, we will. Besides, we'd be constantly chasing him for payments, taking him to court all the time. Who needs that? God, I should think my old dad is laughing in his grave.'

'So you think everything will be okay?' Fran checked.

'Absolutely,' Margo told her. 'Sam's going to sell her cottage, then we'll buy another one with that money, do it up, and sell it for a profit, and so on. Sam's got the know-how and the contacts.'

'Except,' said Sam.

'Except?'

'My cottage isn't selling,' said Sam, sounding hurt. 'We've had a few people round, but we've only had one offer, way too low.'

'Bad time of year?'

'Perfect time of year – the garden's looking lovely, the sun shines into all the rooms—'

'But . . . ?'

'They don't like the wallpaper, there's only one loo, the kitchen isn't up to scratch, it's too small – which is ridiculous! I mean, it's not a mansion, but its rooms are no smaller than in a lot of other cottages we've been managing to sell.'

'Well,' said Fran, broaching a subject she had never dared raise before, 'it is rather cluttered. You are something of a collector, let's face it, what with your teddy bears and your lace cushions and all your pictures and the Beswick animals – and personally, I did think at the time that you were making a big mistake about the bold flowered wallpaper in such a small living room—'

'Which is why we thought you might be able to help,' Margo interrupted her, seeing Sam's face fall in dismay at hearing her beloved home criticised. 'You've done your own home beautifully. And you've even converted a horsebox with ingenuity, maximising space, making it look really pretty. We were wondering if we could persuade you – perhaps with Archie's help – to do a make-over? For a fee, of course.'

Fran was flattered, but not easily persuaded. 'I don't see how I could spare that kind of time,' she said, after suggesting various ways to improve the cottage. 'I have the cleaning and gardening to do at my place, which is what I'm paid for these days.'

Sam and Margo exchanged the briefest of looks, but Fran nevertheless could see something else coming.

'What?' she asked. 'What? What?!'

'Nothing,' Sam assured her airily. 'How would you say you've been getting on with that during your first week? Everything okay with your tenant?'

'Oh, he's all right,' Fran told them with a glint in her eye. 'In fact, he's more than a bit of all right, if you know what I mean. Or at least I thought he was until I met his odious girlfriend.' She grinned wickedly. 'But I don't think she's going to be a permanent fixture, somehow.'

Again Sam and Margo shared a look, and again Fran demanded to know what was going on.

'Perhaps it might be you who ends up not being the permanent fixture?' warned Margo.

Fran was stricken. 'Because . . . ?'

'I had a phone call,' began Sam.

'Not from Nitwit Nikki?!' Sam nodded. 'What?' demanded Fran. 'What did the little cow tell you?'

It was some time before Sam had reached the end of the catalogue of complaints about Gloria the char. There was the disturbed sleep, of course, and her appearing in the house at odd hours, but then there was the matter of Gloria using all the hot water on purpose so that Nikki couldn't take her morning shower . . .

'She should get up earlier then,' said Fran defiantly.

And the case of the red kitchen hand towel being left in the washing machine on the day that Nikki did her whites . . .

'A complete accident. A bad case of synchronicity,' bluffed Fran, unable to help herself smiling at the memory.

And the comings and goings of Gloria to the sewer manhole cover in the garden, and the terrible smells left lingering afterwards . . .

'I have to empty my Elsan *somewhere*,' said Fran. 'It's not my fault that she insists on sunbathing right next to it.'

And Gloria's unfortunate manner, around the house, as if she owned it . . .

'Well,' said Fran, shrugging. 'Yes. There you are. I do. So—'

'So she wants you gone and a replacement found,' Sam concluded, having now abandoned subtlety as a form of argument.

'The little bitch!' Fran exclaimed. 'Anyway, she doesn't have the power. My contract isn't with her, it's with Jeremy. And besides, she went back to London today, if I'm not much mistaken. She's got an interview with the producers of a new TV show, *Big Brother*-style. With any luck she'll be dropped off on a tropical island the other side of the world soon, and she can drive somebody else mad.' Fran took a slug of wine and stewed in her own juices for a moment, her companions allowing her to think things over without interruption. 'What does Jeremy say, anyway?' she challenged Sam. 'I bet he doesn't even know about any of this. He seems perfectly happy with my services – he even brings me coffee in the mornings if he sees me in the garden when he's on his way to work.'

'He's a very nice man,' agreed Sam. 'He doesn't want any trouble.'

'You've spoken to him?!'

'I had to check with the client,' said Sam sternly. 'It's my job. You're right, he's very happy with the way you're looking after things, but he doesn't want any tension between you and his girl-friend. He's suggested you might cut down your hours – I mean honestly, Fran! Cleaning inside the house for five hours every day!'

'I only charge him for two,' Fran protested. 'He should be so lucky!'

'And he thinks it might be for the best that you don't go in at all when Nikki is in residence, except at times which are prearranged with her, at her convenience.'

Fran spluttered indignantly, but Sam cut her off.

'He's only being this lenient because of you being a *widow* and needing the money, *Gloria*,' she said censoriously. 'And since you brought up the question of estate agents being liars, I might just point out that this estate agent nearly blew your cover on that one when he told me. You might at least keep me up to date on your fabrications.'

'Risotto,' Margo interjected, plonking down plates and break-ing the atmosphere. 'Eat up.'

Fran toyed sulkily with her fork and frowned at the food. 'So what are we saying here?' she demanded. 'Am I on trial, or am I sacked?'

'You're on trial,' Sam said. 'For another two weeks. If you upset Nikki again, it's goodbye.'

Fran was speechless, and her recently defeated dysfunction of binge-eating kicked in straight away. Shovelling risotto into her mouth by the forkful, she maintained an angry silence.

'So you see,' suggested Margo, pushing the salad over towards her, 'doing up Sam's cottage with Archie might be just the thing to get you out of the house, and keep you lucratively occupied.'

Fran helped herself to salad direct from the bowl, stuffing lettuce leaves into her mouth and chewing viciously. 'Archie might not be free,' she said eventually between mouthfuls.

'He is,' Sam said firmly. 'I've checked.'

After Fran had gone home and the pots were washed and teeth cleaned and Sam and Margo were winding their limbs around each other in preparation for sleep, Margo congratulated Sam on being a very good friend indeed. 'Even I believed you about not being able to sell the cottage,' she teased her. 'I hope you haven't learnt too much of Nigel's expertise at manipulating the truth.'

Sam demurred. 'She'd never have gone for it if she hadn't thought she was helping us out of a hole. And besides, we'll get more money for it if we tart it up a bit. It's a good investment.'

'Just be careful you don't over-capitalise,' warned Margo sleepily.

Sam lifted herself on to her elbow and gazed down at her lover. 'Who is the expert in these affairs?' she demanded. 'Who works in property?'

'You, my love,' Margo conceded, adding wickedly, 'Gosh, I love it when you come over all assertive.'

Meanwhile, in Casa Nova, Fran Holdaway lay alone in her converted bed and thought over their offer. Despite disgruntled thoughts about Jeremy and Nikki floating from time to time into her mind, she actually started to feel quite excited by this new turn of events. She reminded herself how contented she had felt, cleaning the bricks for Archie – the dignity of labour, the satisfaction of measurable success. It was an ill wind, she marvelled, which had blown her out of her job in London, wrecked her marriage, moved her out of her home and into a horsebox, and had now plonked her here, about to start anew. She snuggled down under the covers, excited about her new project, re-modelling Sam's kitchen in her mind, adding a second bathroom, getting rid of that ghastly wallpaper.

By and large, she decided, as she drifted off to sleep, though she would never, ever have wished it upon herself, now that the worst had happened and life as she had known it had been wrecked beyond repair, she was actually rather excited.

Thirty

Miraculously, over the next few weeks, everything went so smoothly it was as if events were conspiring to keep Fran in her new mood of optimism and enthusiasm for life. It is a curious fact about human nature that, when things are going badly, we cry to the heavens 'Why me?', whereas when things are going well for us, we accept it as our due. But because Fran had suffered from such a catastrophic run of bad luck so recently, there was not a day now that she didn't wake and count her blessings. Archie and she were getting on brilliantly with Sam's renovations. They worked well as a team, Fran coming up with the design ideas, Archie finding practical and cheap ways of making them manifest. Which was just as well, as Sam had warned them in the strictest of tones not to go over her very tight budget.

And since she was kept so busy on site, Fran didn't have the leisure to fret about her own rented home. Indeed, she was hard pressed even to find the time to fulfil her cleaning and gardening duties at the Big House. She continued to rise very early to work on the garden, dashing to Sam's house after a rushed breakfast to strip wallpaper or paint doors, usually returning home in her lunch break to tackle the cleaning, then back to Sam's again for another session of renovating, before finally arriving back at the horsebox in the evening, exhausted, to catch her breath before the whole thing started again the next day. All this would have been reason enough to think herself blessed – she loved the hard work, the practicality of her chores, seeing the tangible progress made at the end of each day – and it wasn't half bad having a few coins jingling in her pocket either. But fate was being even kinder to her than that. It was giving her cake and letting her eat it. These days Nikki was rarely to be seen, and as a result Fran was spending some very enjoyable time with Jeremy on a fairly regular basis. Or at least, Mrs Gloria Mop was.

She had bumped into Jeremy one morning in the garden shortly after her warning from Sam and, embarrassed, had mumbled her apologies about her over-assiduousness in the house, reassuring him that she would no longer be any trouble. Equally embarrassed, Jeremy had graciously minimised the problem, had brought her coffee, and they had sat together in the warmth of the late summer sun while he told her about Nikki's news. She had indeed returned to London to audition for a new reality TV show and, while she waited to hear if she'd been successful, she was working out her time in her PR job. Emboldened by his friendliness, Fran suggested that now he was on his own again perhaps he would enjoy a home-cooked supper some evening; to her delight he had responded with enthusiasm.

It had been a strange experience that first time, working in her old kitchen to make a meal for a man who would soon come strolling through her front door, back home from the office. It had a curious resonance with all the times she had done this for Paul, which would have been spooky enough, but it was also peculiar, when Jeremy did appear, to have to pretend that this house was not really her domain. She was merely the cleaner, who just happened to know where every-thing was kept. What had started out as a naughty joke now became a problem. She longed to be able to communicate with Jeremy in her own voice – apart from anything else, whenever she started to relax in his company, Mrs Mop's accent started to slip. But that was as nothing compared to the feelings of guilt she experienced, deceiving this very nice man. She was behaving as if she took him for a fool, whereas that was very far from the truth.

That first evening, she didn't know quite how to behave. As his employee, Mrs Mop felt that she should serve him with his meal, and then retire. As his social equal and would-be friend (at the very least) or lover (in her dreams), Fran wanted to share the meal with him, engage him in conversation, find out what made him tick. Fortunately for her, Jeremy had no such class prejudice. When Gloria plonked his solitary plate down in front of him he was most assertive in his desire for her to join him and, opening a bottle of exceedingly good wine, insisted she shared it with him.

He was gratifyingly appreciative of her 'plain country fare' (steak and kidney pudding followed by rhubarb crumble and cream – the woman was no fool), and as the wine loosened their tongues, they found each other's company most amusing, despite the fact that, for Fran's part, she was having to improvise most of the facts of her life as she went along. Since she hadn't previously given a thought to Gloria Mop's history, she was as surprised as Jeremy to hear her story fall afresh from her lips – that she had left school early and had married young, that her husband had been a wastrel, propping up the bar of the local most nights and being no better than he ought to be with the village girls, and that he had met his end while being drunk in charge of a combine harvester, which grisly outcome was no more than he deserved. As Fran spun her tale, the irony was not lost on her that this quickly extemporised story was far more inventive than anything she had ever managed to achieve in her attempts at writing the legend of Extraordinary Suzanne.

Jeremy was sympathetic and sensitive to Gloria's run of bad luck, and therefore didn't press her for too many details. Besides, he wanted to hear more about Mrs Holdaway. What were her circumstances now, where was she, and why had she rented out her beautiful home? He learnt that she was an extremely nice woman, intelligent and witty, and very attractive. She had suffered a similar fate to Gloria with her choice in men, except that they hadn't died. Yet. She had decided to travel, to get away from bad memories, and to find out who she really was.

'Where is she now?' asked Jeremy, impressed by Mrs Holdaway's courage.

'Last I heard she were camping out by a Scottish loch,' Fran told him shamelessly. 'Sleeping in an 'ammock, and catching fish to cook on her fire at night. She's a lot happier with the simpler life.'

'Remarkable,' said Jeremy.

'She is,' agreed Fran.

Over liqueurs, which he insisted they should drink outside in the garden, so uncommonly clement was the weather for so late in September, she managed to draw him out about his feelings for Nikki, and struggled to keep her features looking equable as he sang her rival's praises.

'She's so full of life,' he said, smiling fondly as he described her. 'And so very different from me in the way she approaches things – she's much more instinctive. Where I would debate something endlessly, weighing things up, wondering whether I should do this or that, she just goes in there and grabs it – seizes it by the scruff.'

'Oh ar,' Fran commented drily.

'And she has a wonderful sense of humour – she makes me laugh a lot. You probably didn't see her at her best,' he added, noting Gloria's acid face. 'She's been very unhappy at work, and rather nervous about changing career. I hope for her sake that things work out for her with this programme, although for myself, of course, I'd rather they didn't.'

'How's that?' asked Fran, leaning forward with interest.

'Because if she wins a part in the series, and if she successfully stays in for the duration, I won't see her for several months.'

'Aah, what a shame,' Fran sighed disingenuously. From that

moment on, she wished Nikki all the luck in the world for her new career. 'Is it like *Big Brother*, then, where the public have to vote for them?' If so, Gloria Mop would be spending a fortune on telephone calls once the programme was aired, to make sure that Nikki stayed incarcerated till the bitter end.

'It's similar, but almost a reversal, in fact,' Jeremy told her. 'They get shut up together in a house just the same, but whereas in *Big Brother* it was the most popular members who stayed in each week, with this new programme, it's the one who causes the most trouble who wins in the end. It's called *Housemate From Hell*.'

Gloria Mop let out a yelp of uncouth laughter. 'She'll win hands down!' she exclaimed, but seeing Jeremy's frown she qualified it with, 'What with her acting skills you say she's got. And her sense of humour.'

Jeremy was gracious enough to take her amendment at face value, and agreed that Nikki stood a good chance of staying the course if selected as a contestant, due to her extraordinary inventiveness and sense of fun. And even if she didn't win, she would still have exposure on television that couldn't fail to help in her pursuit of a career as a presenter. Glancing at his watch, he announced that he had an early start the next day, but when Fran made a move towards the kitchen he wouldn't hear of her doing the pots. She had already done more than enough, he told her, in making such a wonderful meal and providing him with good company. When he suggested a payment of two hours overtime for her trouble cooking supper, it was Fran's turn to frown.

'It was a pleasure,' she said, a little coldly now. 'I was off-duty. I'd thought that you might enjoy the company as much as the dinner, seeing as you're a stranger up here, with not many friends yet.'

Realising his faux pas, Jeremy was touched, and said so. He *was* rather lonely, as a matter of fact, and yes, he had enjoyed her company very much. Perhaps, then, she might allow him to return the favour one evening – would she allow him to cook for her? It turned out she would be charmed and honoured, and they smiled warmly at each other as they shook hands goodnight.

'But what am I thinking!' Jeremy exclaimed as Fran made to leave. 'Let me drive you home – I can't have you walking at this time of night!'

Fran shuffled her feet and looked shifty. Although she had not rushed to tell him, since he had taken up residence, that, like the fairies, she lived at the bottom of his garden, she hadn't known for sure that he didn't know. 'That's all right, I tek a short cut,' she told him, sidling out of the kitchen and into the garden. 'Tra.'

Jeremy followed her. 'Gloria, I'm serious,' he said. 'No arguments. I'm taking you home. Come round to the front and we'll go in the car.'

'It's quicker to walk,' Fran protested. 'I'll be there in two ticks.'

But Jeremy was no quitter. 'Fine, then I'll walk with you.'

There was nothing for it but to lead the way across the patio, and to follow the herringbone road, with the aid of her torch, down through the garden.

'So this is why I never see you arrive through the front,' Jeremy said, as his eyes grew accustomed to the dark. 'Do you live across the field at the bottom?'

'Closer than that,' Fran said guiltily. She was more than glad that Nikki was away at the moment. She knew she would have had something very nasty to say about her living arrangements if she'd been there. They had come to the gate in the garden fence, and she tried to shake him off. 'You don't want to get your nice shoes all dirty,' she told him. 'I'll be right from here. Goodnight.'

'Does somebody keep horses here sometimes?' asked Jeremy, peering ahead in the dark at the outline of the horsebox, and ignoring her advice to stay put.

'No, it's where I live,' Fran told him in exasperated tones.

Jeremy stumbled on a tussock of grass. 'You live in a *horsebox*?!'

Putting out her arm to steady him, Fran went on the defensive immediately, terrified that her tenant would find something to say to Sam about this the next morning. 'Mrs Holdaway lets me stay here. It's in our agreement. It's her field. Suits me, suits her.'

'But, Gloria – a *horsebox*? Why not a caravan, at the very least? How can you live like that? It's . . . barbaric! It's feudal! How do you manage in the winter? What on earth can Mrs Holdaway be thinking?'

Fran could have told him, but instead Gloria muttered, 'I'm tough.' However, both her personas were bristling at his comments, and therefore of a mind to show off their inventiveness. Going up the steps of Casa Nova, she switched on the string of coloured lights outside, which she'd hung for the inaugural barbecue. It was a magic moment, as the darkness around them was banished by the multi-coloured bulbs, and the horsebox came alive, as if on a stage. Looking down at Jeremy, whose jaw had dropped in surprise, she was gratified to note he was impressed.

'How come I've never noticed this before?' he asked, looking back and seeing the lights of the house clearly from where he stood. 'It's wonderful!'

'Don't normally use these lights,' said Fran. 'So's not to disturb you.'

'But you should, Gloria!' Jeremy exclaimed, peering inquisitively over her shoulder into the horsebox. 'It looks so pretty, and so exciting – almost like a piece of performance art! Have you converted it inside? Can I see?'

'Course I've converted it,' Fran scoffed, but she was more than pleased with his reaction. 'Do you think I sleep on straw?' Going in, she switched on a couple of table lights so her home could be viewed at its best and cosiest. 'There y'are – home sweet home.'

Jeremy was practically speechless with admiration, and wanted to see how everything worked. As he marvelled at the ingenuity of storage space, at the shower (unaware that he was paying for its use), at the way the table swung into the wall when it wasn't needed and the chairs folded away, Fran saw his face transform into that of the enthusiastic, sweet-natured young boy he had once undoubtedly been. It was all she could do to prevent herself reaching out and tousling his head. 'Tek it back now, what you said about Mrs Holdaway?' she teased him.

'Absolutely,' Jeremy confirmed. 'She really must be the most extraordinary person. Quite an individual.'

'She is,' Fran agreed with fervour. 'You'd like her if you met her.'

She watched his return to the Big House with a little pang of longing, and when she was alone she started a journal to write out some of the feelings which were demanding her attention. As she began to fill the page with reports of the present, she found that she had to describe the events which had led up to this day. Scribbling like mad, her thoughts coming faster than her hand could jot them down, she marvelled at her own story. Her life had become stranger than fiction.

Thirty-One

Sure enough, and true to his word, Jeremy returned the favour of cooking dinner for Fran a few evenings later. He was a more than adequate cook, and professed to having enjoyed himself tremendously in the kitchen during its preparation. He'd made a creamy fish pie with monkfish and scallops and prawns, coloured with saffron and flavoured with garlic. They laughed at keeping the vampires at bay, and shared a relaxed evening together (or at least, as relaxed as Fran could ever feel when she was having to remember to speak as Gloria), listening to some of his CDs. After that, he was invited in return to a barbecue at Casa Nova which he loved, saying it reminded him of his camping days with the Scouts.

Clearly Jeremy was a man who enjoyed company, but, as he confided to Gloria, it was a tricky time at work, in the early stages of his new job, to make friends with his colleagues. Everybody was all too aware that he was a new broom and feared he might sweep them away, so the tendency was to toady to him, rather than reveal their real selves. 'It's important that I see how it's been running before I go in and shake things up,' he told her. 'So at the moment I prefer to keep my distance socially – as hard as that is for me – till I've made my assessment. After that, I hope they'll see that I'm not a threat, but a help, and start to relax around me a bit more.'

Fran was only too grateful of the arrangement, and sympathised. 'Must be lonely at the top,' she said, with barely a trace of irony. 'So have you been brought in as a troubleshooter, like, or will you be stopping on?'

Jeremy considered this. 'I hope I'll be staying on for some years to come. I really like what I see so far of the company and I'm sure I can improve things, and I have to say I'm enjoying living out of London even more than I expected.'

London continued to call him at weekends, however – or rather, Nikki did – and Fran found that she had the house to herself from Friday night through to Sunday. Naturally she took advantage of this. Her shower in the horsebox was all very miraculous, but it was as nothing compared to her gorgeous bathroom in the Big House. And as long as she'd left no trace of herself by the time Jeremy had returned, she didn't see the harm. She continued to sleep in Casa Nova – she didn't know how she would talk her way out of being found in Daddy Bear's bed if he were ever to return home unexpectedly early – but apart from that, while he was away, she was still mistress of her own house. It was an arrangement which she found very satisfactory, particularly when it came to doing her laundry. And as a small thank-you – even though Jeremy didn't know why he was being spoilt in this way – she always left out a pie or a cake she had baked for him, awaiting his return. Before long, she came to view her weekend ownership of her house as the norm, and Jeremy, if he suspected it, certainly didn't object.

An easy, affectionate familiarity began to develop between them as the weeks rolled by and they visited each other for dinner, turn and turn about, and by the time that Fran spoke to Allie on the phone, they had entertained each other five or six times.

'Would he ever shag Gloria Mop though?' asked her friend, cutting to the pith as per.

'I dunno,' said Fran, who had been thinking the same thing

for some time. 'Doubtful I reckon. I know he really likes me –
her – but I think it's in a kind of brotherly way. I've been
wondering if it isn't time for Gloria to get herself a more
revealing outfit – display the goods a bit more prominently.'

'A pinny with a plunging neckline?' Allie chortled. 'A fan
dance with feather dusters?'

A humourless laugh was Fran's reply.

It was, however, arranged during that phone call that Allie and
Trevor would visit her the next weekend, and that they would
stay in the Big House on the Saturday night – the naughtiness
of her proposal, of course, instantly appealing to Allie's sense of
anarchy. And Trevor, apparently, liked the countryside, and was
looking forward to them all going out for a good long walk. In
preparation, Allie had even bought herself a pair of hiking boots.

'Do they make those in slingbacks?' Fran marvelled. 'It's
nothing short of a miracle, this change in you, Kate,' she
continued, adding wickedly, 'And how *is* Petruchio?'

It was Allie's turn to laugh humourlessly, but nothing could
disguise the affection in her voice (and absolute lack of shrewish-
ness) when she spoke of Trevor, and when they arrived that
Saturday morning it was clear to see that she had never been
happier in her life. Indeed, her good mood lasted for at least the
first mile and a half of their walk along footpaths, until she
started to complain bitterly about her shoes. 'These legs weren't
designed for walking on the flat,' she whined, 'or if they were,
they've forgotten how. It feels as if two inches has been ampu-
tated off my heels.' Her good mood returned, however, at the
first pub stop, and when she learnt that there were two more to
be had on this circular walk she felt that, thus anaesthetised at
intervals, she might just stay the course.

Naturally Fran was eager to show off Archie's and her handiwork at Sam's cottage, which was now almost completed, and
she had plotted their route accordingly, to take that in. Trevor

was duly impressed, particularly when she handed round the photographs she had taken before their transformation procedure had started. The kitchen, gutted and completely rebuilt, now looked as if it were twice the size, and an upstairs bedroom had been partitioned to provide a small, but perfectly formed, en suite shower room and loo. The disastrous living room wallpaper had been replaced by soft neutral tones, and the whole place had been cleared of the evidence of Sam's collector's instincts.

'What has happened to all the dollies and teddy bears?' asked Allie, peering at the colour photograph of Sam's bedroom before its make-over and comparing it to the sparseness now in evidence. 'Don't tell me she's visited them on Margo?'

'No, I rather think that Margo has replaced them in Sam's affections now,' Fran smiled. 'They've been donated to a charity shop, along with the china animals.'

'You've got a real talent for this,' Trevor complimented her, as they concluded their inspection. 'And you've enjoyed it?'

'Absolutely,' said Fran with enthusiasm. 'And it's been great working with Archie again – we make a good team. Good for him too, I think – he regrets having retired. Don't know what either of us will do after we've finished,' she said sadly, turning the key in the lock as they left. 'We should be done by the end of next week.'

'Have you thought any more about your writing articles?' Allie asked her. 'Made any contacts at any of the local rags?'

'No,' said Fran gloomily. The thought of possible rejection had driven that course of action further from her mind. 'But I've started keeping a journal,' she added, trying to sound positive. 'Just to get into the discipline of writing every day, practising my craft. I don't know about supporting myself like that though.'

'It was good enough for Samuel Pepys,' Allie reminded her. 'But then again, am I in it? Is it libellous? If you haven't made me beautiful, sexy, and with a rapier-like wit, I shall sue.'

Fran regarded her friend with an enigmatic smile. 'I write as I find,' she said. 'So what do you think?'

They had all been invited that evening to dine with Margo and Sam, and at seven thirty they had to do the usual trick, when visiting that establishment, of squeezing themselves through the front door while keeping Cecil and Cecilia Sheep firmly on the outside.

'Mm, lamb chops,' Allie threatened them, licking her lips as she pushed the door shut in their inquisitive faces.

'I heard that,' said Alice snootily, who had recently turned vegetarian, and who was swanning down the staircase at that moment, 'and I don't think it is very funny.'

She flounced off ahead of them into the living room, leaving Allie to make a face at her back and to whisper to Fran, 'Hell hath no fury like an adolescent girl full of hormones.'

'Except perhaps a middle-aged woman who is emptying of them?' Fran queried, but Allie riposted that she had simply no way of knowing if that were the case, and that further- more it would be decades before she would find out, before flouncing off in Alice's wake in an unconscious, but accurate, impersonation.

After dinner Sam expressed her surprise that Allie and Trevor were staying so late, given that they had to drive back to London that night. She was predictably appalled when she learnt they were the uninvited guests of her client.

'Jeremy's cool about it,' Fran protested, 'or at least he would be if he knew. He always tells me to help myself to the facilities at the weekends when he's away. He knows I do my washing there, and as a return favour, I also do his – it suits us both. And I often work longer than I'm paid for.'

'Heavens, you sound like a wife,' remarked Allie.

'But without the fringe benefits,' Fran reminded her with regret.

'But still,' said Sam crossly, 'it's an invasion of his space. And his girlfriend would go hairless if she knew.'

'I don't think we'll be seeing much of Nasty Nikki for some time,' Fran countered, and entertained them all with the story of her rival's bid to become the Housemate From Hell – a bid which looked as if it might be successful, since she was still in the running and the shortlist of would-be contestants grew daily ever shorter. 'If she does get on the show, I shall be relying on you all to keep her voted in,' she instructed them. 'At the moment, Mr Sinclair seems unaware of Gloria's charms – apart, that is, from her winning ways with housework, and her company as a friend. It might take me a while to persuade him to see her in a different light.'

'Trade in your overall for a French maid's outfit,' Allie suggested. 'It's never failed with me.'

Trevor smiled happily – no more confirmation was needed than this – and, seeing Sam gathering up the dirty dishes, elected to give her a hand on the condition that neither of them would have to don short skirts and suspenders.

'He's so nice,' Margo complimented Allie when both their lovers had disappeared into the kitchen.

'He is,' Fran agreed. 'But I still don't understand what's come over *you* in the niceness stakes. In all the years I've known you, it's not exactly a quality you have prioritised in your choice of men.'

'Niceness is not his only quality,' Allie returned smugly. 'Let's just say he tickles my fancy.'

'Although, God knows, that's been tickled before,' said Fran, at which, instead of her customary dirty laugh, Allie grew unexpectedly serious.

'Actually, *you* are probably responsible for my reordering of priorities,' she told Fran. 'When you left Q&A, it made me think about my own quality of life. I've been obsessed with work and only work for years, the men who flitted through my life were more of a divertissement than a raison d'être. And whereas that suited me fine when I was younger, the weekends had started to seem longer, and coming home in the evenings to an empty flat less attractive. I suddenly found my life had a hollow ring to it. Now I'm even learning to cook,' she bragged, 'other than in the microwave.' She leant forward, as if to impart a risqué secret. 'There are even some evenings when we do no more than go to bed to sleep,' she confided. 'It's rather comforting, I've found.'

Margo agreed that this was indeed true in her recent experience too, and Fran looked at them both enviously before remarking that perhaps she had been too precipitate in chucking out all of Sam's old teddies – she ought to have kept at least one for her own cuddles at bedtime.

Later, when they had returned home and were sitting in the living room of the Big House having a nightcap before Fran set off down the garden path to Casa Nova, Trevor asked her how committed she still was to a career as a writer, and if she wouldn't be interested in restoring property for a living instead. Fran tried to control her features, but it was like being slapped in the face. Trevor was too sensitive not to have anticipated her dismayed reaction, but as her unpaid financial adviser and the lover of her best and oldest friend he felt it was incumbent on him to provide some guidance in managing her affairs. He had been talking to Sam about the profit she hoped to make on her cottage, he continued, now that it had been renovated, and had been suitably impressed. She planned to buy another house once she'd successfully sold this one, and although that might take some time, there would be more work for Archie and Fran. She'd even offered to advertise them to her clients at the estate agency in the meantime, to keep them gainfully employed until she could hire them again.

'It certainly hasn't hurt your bank balance,' he reminded her. 'A few more jobs like that and you'd be in the clear.'

'I suppose I could do it pro tem,' Fran admitted reluctantly. 'But it's never been what I've seen myself becoming. It's been my hobby. It's how I've amused myself, and how I managed to afford buying the house, let's face it. I could never have paid somebody else to do all that work.' She gazed into the distance, looking rather defeated, trying to imagine herself as a professional house fixer. 'I've always thought of myself as an ideas person,' she concluded sadly. 'It seems like failure to give up on that.'

Trevor stretched and yawned and announced his departure for bed, cannily leaving it with her. 'Think about it,' he advised. 'But bear in mind, to mere mortals like myself, who have no visual talent or practical skills in home-making to speak of, you *are* an ideas person. To me that's a gift which shouldn't be underrated. And if you can make a living at it, so much the better.'

Fran watched her friends the lovebirds ascend the stairs to their cosy nest, and set off down the garden for Casa Nova. She was too depressed to write in her journal. She lay awake for some time, staring into the darkness, feeling that her life had gone horribly wrong since she had set out on her career path fifteen years before. Dolefully, she pictured herself at an old school reunion, walking into the midst of her childhood friends, all of whom would have achieved their goals: Margaret Beasley would be running a company now, she thought; Sarah Brightling would be a doctor; Lindsay Steed, she already knew, was a working journalist. There they all were, in their designer suits, fulfilled in their work, flashing round photos of their young families and their handsome husbands. As she imagined it, when it came to her turn to show off, they all stared at Fran in her paint-splattered overalls. 'Decorator,' she mumbled, shamefaced. 'Divorced twice. No kids . . . But I've started keeping a journal,' she called after them weakly.

At that moment, lying bleakly alone in her convertible bed in a horsebox at thirty-five years of age, kept out of her home through her own stupidity and profligacy, in love with a man who was spoken for, she felt that she couldn't possibly have cocked up her life more if she'd tried.

Poor Fran. Little did she know.

Thirty-Two

That Gypsy Brenda had foreseen that Fran must weather a storm before her luck turned, merely proved the clairvoyant had less than no future in the Met Office. Indeed, as things turned out on that fateful Sunday, a hurricane warning would have been a touch on the mild side.

Naturally Allie was late to rise, and when she did finally consent to join Trevor and Fran downstairs for breakfast she seemed tetchy and out of sorts. She arrived at table still dressed (or to be more accurate, still practically naked) in her black nightie and negligée, and when she saw the scrambled eggs Fran had prepared, her hand flew to her mouth and she fled to the loo.

'Too much to drink last night,' Trevor confided to Fran, unsurprised, as she followed in Allie's wake, and he helped himself to more black pudding. 'She was out like a light before her head touched the pillow.'

'Are you okay in there?' Fran enquired of the cloakroom door. 'Can I get you anything?'

'Bleurggghhh!' was Allie's favoured reply of the moment, but when she finally emerged she was sufficiently recovered to launch an attack.

'What was that dreadful wine Sam and Margo served last night?' she demanded, taking her seat at table but turning a determinedly blind eye to the food. 'Do they make it themselves in their cowshed?'

'It was a perfectly nice Australian Chardonnay as I remember,' Fran said gently, pouring coffee as quietly as she could, 'but I think it's meant to be enjoyed in small glassfuls rather than in pints. How's your head?'

Allie pushed the proffered cup away and went to the kitchen in search of water. 'Which one?' she growled on her return, and sat down heavily, scowling.

'Still got her sense of irony, then,' Fran reassured Trevor. 'So what do we feel like doing today, boys and girls? I guess the pub's out. Another country walk, perhaps?'

'Actually,' said Trevor, finally laying down his knife and fork and patting his tummy appreciatively, 'I've already made plans. Sam and Margo are coming over later, and we're all going to look at Sam's cottage again.'

Fran was immediately on the defensive. 'Why, what's wrong with it?' she demanded. 'Isn't she happy with how things are going? What did she tell you? We've consulted her every step of the way!'

'She loves it,' Trevor assured her, patting her hand, and with a smile that spoke of secret surprises he continued, 'Almost as much as me.'

Allie's eyes flickered dangerously, her posture changing in an instant from that of a dying invalid to one of attack. A velociraptor would have seemed sluggish by comparison, Fran mused in that moment, not to mention more compassionate. 'What the hell are you saying, Trevor?' Allie challenged him in a chillingly measured tone. 'Are you suggesting that *Sam* is in love with *you*? What the hell were you two up to out there in the kitchen last night?'

Trevor laughed easily, delighted, it seemed, by Allie's misapprehension. 'No no,' he returned indulgently. 'Try *this* end of the stick, my heart's desire: Sam loves the *cottage* almost as much as *I* do.' He sat back, grinning at them expectantly, but both his heart's desire and her best friend were completely stumped for a response.

'And?' Allie challenged him impatiently, when it became clear that no further elucidation would be coming her way. 'Spit it out, Trevor, for God's sake – you know how I hate charades.'

'Sounds like . . . ?' offered Fran, in an attempt to lighten the mood.

'Sounds like I'm going to buy it from her,' Trevor told her with glee, his secret out at last, and turning to Allie, concluded, 'For you, my love.'

Despite her astonishment, Allie's idea of graciousness and gratitude were quick to be expressed. 'What the *fuck* for?!' she demanded. 'If you think I'm moving to the country, you must be mad!'

'For fun?' said Trevor doubtfully, a little less sure of his ground, his smile now a pale ghost of its former self. 'For weekends and holidays, a rural retreat – and so you can see more of Fran?'

'That's fantastic, Trevor!' Fran enthused on Allie's behalf, her eyes appealing to her friend for support. 'I *love* that, that's great!'

Seeing them both looking at her expectantly for her approval, Allie pouted a small protest before riposting, 'What's for you to love, Frances? It's *my* present.'

'From both of us,' said Trevor generously, relieved now that things seemed to be going his way. 'Fran's done all the hard work, and I'm merely paying for the privilege. Besides, it's a damn good investment. The prices here are astonishingly low compared to London. More profitable than poker in the gambling stakes,' he joked, at his own expense.

'The way *you* play it, certainly,' rejoined Allie, but her tone grew fonder as she turned to Fran to explain. 'He glows like a beacon if he has anything approximating a good hand. Even if he only has a pair of twos he can still illuminate the whole of Regent Street at Christmas.'

Fran grinned at them, happier than she'd been in ages. Having Allie as a weekend neighbour would make all the difference to her present lonely rural life, she felt, and she could have kissed

Trevor for his kindness if she hadn't feared the instant return of the velociraptor's jaws.

'Well,' said Allie, recovered now it seemed from her attack of biliousness and looking almost human again, 'I'd better shower and change if I am to survey my new property portfolio.' She squeezed Trevor's shoulders affectionately as she passed behind his chair and whispered something in his ear which made it glow a violent pink, proving her earlier point about his luminescent qualities.

'You are so lovely,' Fran told him when they were safely alone, and she chanced a quick peck on his cheek. 'Thank you.'

Trevor grinned. 'If I'd known earlier the effect that buying a cottage had on women, I'd have bought up an entire estate by now,' he quipped. 'All of them designed and improved by you, of course, you clever woman.'

Fran felt herself glow with the praise. 'Not forgetting Archie,' she said magnanimously. 'In fact, I'll call him, get him to meet us at the cottage so he can join in the celebrations,' she added, making for Jeremy's phone. 'When are Sam and Margo due?' she checked as she dialled Archie's number, but the sound of a car suddenly speeding in to the front drive seemed to answer that question for her.

'Gosh, they're early,' said Trevor, glancing at his watch, and 'Don't worry, I'll get it,' were his famous last words as, opening the door, he got it by the shovelful from Nikki.

It is a little known medical fact that human blood can actually freeze stone-cold in the veins, despite a clement ambient temperature, if a shock of sufficient magnitude is delivered with no warning. The symptoms, as experienced by Fran when she saw Nikki and Jeremy walk in unexpectedly to reclaim their territory – *their* phone in her hand, *her* breakfast dishes on their table, her naked friend upstairs in their shower, her friend's lover rudely bowled out of the way by the second female velociraptor

sighting of the day – were to remain slack-jawed and silent as
Archie Scaysbrook's voice demanded 'Hullo? Hullo?' in her ear,
her heart to stop beating, and for her to endure a sneak preview
of the kind of instant perspiration attack she wouldn't actually
experience in all its glory for another twenty years.

Perhaps the appalled shared silence between the incomers and
the outlaws lasted an hour or more, perhaps it was over in a
second: in her mummified state, Fran was an unreliable witness.
Certainly it was Nikki who found her tongue first, storming
round the room, screaming blue murder and appealing to
Jeremy about the cheek of the '*cleaning* lady, for Christ's sake!'
who had usurped their space, while Fran murmured 'Aaargh,
aargh,' down the receiver in a small stricken tone, to an increas-
ingly mystified Archie. Never a tall man, Trevor appeared to
shrink to a tenth of his size in an astonishing display of natural
camouflage, astutely staying mute as he judged the lie of the
land, until finally Jeremy took control.

'Gloria?' he asked in a frighteningly controlled voice, his face
white with anger. 'What on earth is going on here?'

Fran put down the phone and whimpered.

'*Now* will you believe me?!' Nikki demanded of him shrilly,
circling Fran like a hungry shark. 'Is this taking the piss or what?'
Her eye suddenly lighted on Trevor, despite his diminutive
disguise. 'She uses this place for her *fancy men* as soon as your
back's turned! She probably told that hairless four-eyed *midget*
over there that this house is hers! Well I've got news for you,
Baldy – Jeremy pays through the nose to rent it, and your
pathetic girlfriend is the *char!*'

Despite being in the wrong Trevor bridled and stuck out his
chest, quickly resuming his full height of five foot six inches in
stockinged feet. 'I fully accept that we shouldn't be here,' he
protested to Jeremy, 'and for that I apologise unreservedly. But
really, I don't think that insults are called for.'

'Quite,' said Jeremy tersely, and turning back to address

Fran enquired again, 'Gloria – an explanation, if you please.'

'Chuck her out, Jez, complain to the agency!' Nikki screamed, in her element in a crisis, and to emphasise her point she grabbed a plate from the table and hurled it against the wall, missing Fran's head by inches. 'Have you been at it in our bed as well as eating at our table?!' she screeched.

But at that moment her attention was galvanised – as indeed was everybody's – by a polite cough from the stairs followed by Allie's regal (and, to Fran's huge relief, fully dressed) descent.

'Mr Sinclair, I presume,' she said graciously, as one who had gone before her had claimed the acquaintance of Dr Livingstone in straits no more dire than this, and she elegantly proffered her hand.

'And you are . . . ?' Jeremy queried, completely bouleversed, his hand now held captive in Allie's.

'I am Fran Holdaway,' she said severely. 'Your landlady – come to check up on my tenant.'

'I—' spluttered Jeremy, the tables turned, suddenly blushing and wrong-footed. 'Mrs Holdaway! How do you do. I've heard so much about you.'

'All of it good, I hope, Gloria?' Allie asked of Fran, who had been ready, open-mouthed, to attempt some kind of introduction but who was now completely out of her depth and lost for words.

'Is that *it*, Jez?' Nikki demanded, furious to be out of the spotlight. 'Is that all you're going to say – "how do you do"? What about trespass? What about calling the bloody police?! I don't give a *monkey's* if she's your landlady – she isn't allowed in except by prior arrangement! And what was she doing upstairs?'

Not one to be sidetracked while she had the advantage, Allie gestured to the pieces of broken plate sprayed around the room. 'I see what you mean, Gloria, about the appallingly badly behaved juvenile delinquent who has been moved in without my knowledge,' she said darkly, flicking a withering glance at Nikki before bringing her full attention back to Jeremy. 'Really, Mr Sinclair, did you not read the clause in your contract about no pets and no children, or did you just think you could get away with moving your daughter in behind my back?'

Jeremy glared furiously at Fran, but his reply, already choked by indignation and embarrassment in equal measure, was cut short by a merry burst of knocking on the front door.

'Ah,' said Allie seamlessly, going to the door (for one who hated charades she would have been a natural at Cluedo), 'that will be Miss Talbot, the estate agent, and her senior partner Mrs Ford-Roberts. You may complain to them, if you like, young lady – or perhaps it will be *I* who'll be doing the complaining. Come in!' she instructed the party at the door, and unable to resist as a puzzled Margo, Sam and little Jocelyn all trooped into the crowded room she crowed, 'And how charming – you've brought a playmate for Mr Sinclair's daughter! Why don't you take her upstairs, dear,' she said kindly to Nikki, 'while we grown-ups talk boring business?'

An expletive entirely unsuitable for Jocelyn's young ears preceded another plate being hurled with force at the wall, followed swiftly by Nikki's storming exit up the stairs, and for a halcyon moment, the rest was silence.

'Well,' began Jeremy, outnumbered by Fran's friends and suddenly a stranger in his own home, 'if you'll excuse me, I'll just—'

'Yes, do, by all means,' Allie granted him as he slunk towards the stairs in Nikki's wake. 'They're such a problem at that age, aren't they?'

It was all Allie could do to muffle her delighted guffaw as they waited there in silence for Jeremy to safely disappear, and when he had, she clutched her chest and laughed until the tears ran down her face. 'I should be an actress,' she gasped, accepting Trevor's handkerchief. 'I am too utterly brilliant to be true!

Revenge, Fran, I've got you your revenge! Did you *see* the look on the little minx's face?'

Sam had the stricken look on her own face to deal with at that moment, and as a consequence was beyond humour of any kind, despite (or perhaps because of) Allie cracking up even more when she saw her terrified expression. 'I knew it, I *knew* it!' she asserted vehemently. 'What did I *say* about Allie and Trevor sleeping here? Is Jeremy furious? Will he cancel the contract? He could, you know, with this kind of provocation, and be perfectly within his rights!'

'Oh do calm down,' Allie instructed her, 'I've got everything under perfect control. He thinks *he's* in the wrong at this precise moment – she broke two of my best plates!'

'*Your* plates?' Margo queried, slipping a supportive arm round Sam's shoulders.

'Ah, yes,' said Allie, quickly recovering her wits. 'Now listen carefully, this is important. *I* am Fran Holdaway – and *that* is Gloria Mop. Margo, you're Sam's boss. I don't think we decided who Trev was, did we sweetness?'

'Nikki decided for us – I'm the bald four-eyed idiot midget,' Trevor supplied equably. 'You'd be surprised. There's always call for one – I'm never short of work.'

If Sam and Margo were confused, young Jocelyn was quick to spot the naked Emperor in their midst. 'No you're not, *she's* Fran – you're Allie,' she corrected her. 'And Mummy isn't Sam's boss, she's her specially best best friend.'

'But you'll accept that I'm the bald four-eyed idiot midget, I take it?' Trevor asked her with a twinkle in his eyes.

Upstairs there was the sound of banging and crashing and harsh words being screamed, punctuated by fierce shushing and strict tones.

'Oh dear, Daddy's *very* cross with his little girl for being so rude to the guests,' said Allie, still up for the joke, but she had undoubtedly lost her audience, for all eyes were now on Fran who was finally attempting to speak.

'I have *completely* buggered everything up,' she said hollowly, looking lower than any of them had ever seen her, even in her alcoholic suicidal days.

'But I have retrieved the situation, never fear,' Allie couldn't resist bragging.

'*You?*' Fran exploded, enraged. 'You've just made everything ten times worse – pointing the finger at me as your informer, insulting Nikki, practically calling Jeremy a cradle-snatcher to his face!'

Allie shrugged insouciantly. 'If the cap fits,' she sniffed.

'It isn't funny!' Fran insisted furiously. 'He'll *hate* me now, and he'll be right to. I've betrayed his trust. I've made a fool of him. I can't live here in the field any longer – he wouldn't wear it, and why should he? What am I going to do? Where will I go?'

'Does that mean I shall *never* get my sleepover with you in the horsebox?' asked Jocelyn, cut to the quick. 'I came along specially to remind you.'

'Oh Jocelyn, darling, now is simply not the time,' Margo murmured. 'Fran – if the worst comes to the worst you can park the horsebox in *our* field. You'll just have to be careful of Ralph.'

'There you are, you see,' said Allie, nothing daunted. 'A new love interest for you straight away!'

Those in the know turned to stare at her in disbelief. 'What?' demanded Allie, aware that for some reason she had regained her audience's attention but was now losing its goodwill. 'I'm terribly sorry; is Ralph one of your children, Margo?'

'Ralph is a bad-tempered donkey,' Sam supplied flatly.

'Oh, well, heavens, *I* live with an idiot four-eyed dwarf,' Allie countered, quickly recovering quickly her aplomb, 'and do you hear me complaining? I think not.'

★

Upstairs in Fran's old bedroom, Nikki and Jeremy were packing suitcases and trading insults.

'Jesus, Jez, you are such a *doormat* – you just let everybody walk all over you,' Nikki complained as she flung clothes out of her wardrobe and drawers in roughly the direction of her cases.

'Yes,' Jeremy returned shortly, eyeing her meaningfully; unable to bear the chaos of her packing style, he caught the clothes as they came his way and folded them into neat piles. 'I've been thinking that myself recently.'

Alerted by his tone, and quick as always to see herself as the only topic of conversation, Nikki stopped what she was doing and turned to confront him, a wooden coat hanger grasped threateningly in her hand. 'And what is that supposed to mean?' she demanded.

Jeremy straightened from his labours and returned her malevolent stare in equal measure. 'I think it's good that you've been accepted on *Housemate* and that we'll be apart for a couple of months. It will give us some much-needed time apart to think things over.'

Nikki stuck out her chin, her eyes aggressively narrowed. 'Like what?' she growled.

'Our compatibility for one,' Jeremy supplied crisply, dropping her gaze, and he returned to the business of packing. He had had a bad enough weekend with Nikki even before they had arrived home and found themselves caught up in the bizarre brouhaha downstairs. More and more, recently, she had been behaving like a spoilt brat, but since the call had come through from the producers the day before, telling her she was going to be on television, her egocentricity had known no bounds. As deeply embarrassed as he had been by Fran Holdaway's barbed comments about Nikki's age (had she *really* mistaken her for his daughter, or had Gloria neglected to include sardonicism in the list of her employer's qualities when she'd described her to him?), privately he had been making unflattering comparisons himself, during the last twenty-four hours, between Nikki's behaviour and that of an overwrought three-year-old.

'Yeah, well,' Nikki spat now, as she applied herself again with Olympic zeal to her new hobby of clothes throwing, 'if you mean me not being able to stand men who are wimps, you're dead right.'

If Jeremy had thought that his dander was already up, it astonished him now with its headily sharp ascent. He stopped dead in his tracks, the importance of orderly packing now forgotten, and strode over to the bedside phone.

'How long do you think you'll need to finish your packing?' he asked her as he jabbed the number of the local cab firm into the keypad and ordered a taxi to the station. 'Ten minutes? Five?'

'Oh, so what? Now you're not even going to drive me there yourself?' Nikki whined accusingly. 'What a gentleman. Nice one, Jeremy. Thanks a lot.'

'*If* you were a lady,' said her surrogate father stiffly, 'I might take that criticism seriously. But as it is . . .'

'God, you are a boring old fart sometimes,' Nikki marvelled spitefully, her pretty face contorted with rage as she surveyed her former lover. 'Tell you what, Jez, why don't you just piss off downstairs and join the rest of the party from *Saga*? They've probably started playing bingo by now – you could be missing out on the chance to win a lace doily!'

'I'll tell you what I can't *stand*!' Jeremy began hotly, his eyes blazing, his temper stretched to its very limits by her rudeness.

'What?!' screamed Nikki into the pause that he'd left while he bit his lip and tried to regain his composure. '*What* can't you stand? Me going out clubbing late? I know that already!' She pushed an imaginary shirtsleeve further up her arm in a cruel impersonation of Jeremy and examined an imaginary watch. '"Going out *now*, darling, at *midnight*? I've got an early start tomorrow, it's actually time for my bed." Or what? My new tattoo? Me being popular? My friends thinking you're a dork? What?!'

'I dislike trading insults intensely,' he said, with as much dignity as he could muster. 'It helps nobody, and renders effective communication impossible. Perhaps we can talk about this at some later stage, when we're both feeling calmer.'

Nikki stamped her feet in frustration. 'Jeremy, we're having a *row* for God's sake! That's what *normal* people do when they're pissed off with each other! Spit the frigging dictionary out of your mouth and get stuck in, you spineless—'

Never a man of violence, Jeremy astonished them both with the speed at which he crossed the room to seize Nikki roughly by the shoulders and shake her. 'What I can't stand,' he hissed, holding her at arm's length the better to eyeball her, 'is your rudeness, your lack of grace, your *aggressiveness*!'

'Look who's talking!' Nikki crowed, delighted at last to have a sparring partner worthy of her weight. 'You're hurting my arm, you bastard, get off me!'

Appalled by his lack of self-control, Jeremy released her and took a step backwards, but continued to pin her with his angry gaze. 'What your "friends" think of me or what time you come home from nightclubs is completely beside the point and irrelevant to me. I have always been perfectly happy for you to "do your own thing", as you call it, and I have never – not until now, at least – felt the differences in our personalities to be a problem. On the contrary, in fact. But frankly I have begun to find your recent behaviour both embarrassing and boorish. There are a lot of things I can put up with,' he continued coldly, 'but public displays of infantile temper tantrums isn't one of them. Nor, while we're on the subject, do I enjoy hearing you scream at the cleaning lady as if she were a member of a leprous third class and beneath your contempt! Your attack on her just now was one of the most obscene cases of snobbishness it has ever been my misfortune to witness. I shall be downstairs if you need help carrying your cases. Your taxi will be here in five minutes.'

Glaring at him venomously as he crossed the room away from her, Nikki grabbed the filthiest ammunition at her disposal. 'Oh, now I get it! You've been having some pervy thing going with the bloody peasant charwoman while I've been down in London! Well be my guest, Jez,' she drawled sarcastically, 'if rubber gloves and Harpic turn you on, have her! She's more your age anyway than me!'

Turning briefly in the doorway, all passion spent, Jeremy heaved a heartfelt sigh and regarded her with incredulity. 'For your information—' he began, but then shrugged in a gesture of hopelessness. 'No. I give up, words fail me. Enjoy your time as a *Housemate From Hell*, Nikki. Gloria was right – you're a natural.'

Safely outside on the landing, Jeremy closed the door on this Hadean woman and heard the flung coat hanger crash against the wood just behind his head. He only hoped that the party downstairs hadn't heard it too, or for that matter the row which had preceded it. How on earth was he going to face them now? And what were they doing here anyway? What had brought Fran Holdaway all the way from her Highland retreat to check up on him, and why had she arranged to meet the estate agent here? Were they about to try to terminate his contract, and if so what were his rights? Although he had just hotly defended Gloria, he had been truly shocked to learn that it had been she who had alerted her employer to Nikki's presence in the rented house, and moreover lied about her age. Was it possible that Gloria could betray him like that and, if so, why?

Not for the first time, Jeremy wished fervently that Nikki looked her twenty-six years – in some lights she still only looked eighteen (and in all lights, she still behaved as if she were). More and more recently, he had been wondering what the hell he been thinking of that night of the party when he'd met her. Of course it had been immensely flattering that Nikki had been interested enough to pursue him, but what had ever possessed him to try to make a meaningful relationship out of what should clearly never have been more than a one-night stand?

He shook himself. Standing here, inelegantly trapped on the upstairs landing, caught between the screaming harridan in his bedroom and the aggrieved owner of the house downstairs, now was definitely not the time to be reviewing the wisdom of his earlier choices. He tiptoed over to the top of the stairs to listen, hoping against hope that the party in the living room might have tactfully withdrawn in his absence. No such luck. He could hear them talking together in urgent whispers – no doubt reviewing their options. He was fairly certain that Mrs Holdaway couldn't just sling him out, despite Nikki's display of violence with her fixtures and fittings, but he imagined she would certainly be within her rights to choose not to renew his contract, and what a terrible shame that would be, when he loved the house so well and was so happy here.

Squaring his shoulders, he started his descent, determined to beg if needs be. On the plus side, he comforted himself, they should be mollified when the taxi arrived and they saw Nikki moving out with her stuff. He was furious that she'd put him in this position, but breathing deeply he reminded himself that he must strive for calm. What if the estate agents gossiped – or Gloria, for that matter – and news of this incident got back to people at work? How then would he persuade his new workforce that he was the man to lead them onward to success?

No sooner had his foot hit the level ground of the living room and six pairs of eyes turned in his direction (Gloria's looking stricken, he just had time to note), than the sound of a car door slamming in the outside drive immediately preceded a ring on the front doorbell.

'That will be the minicab to take Nikki to the station,' he asserted with as much dignity as he could muster, and without breaking his stride he ran the gauntlet of their curious stares and crossed the room to open the door.

'She'll be with you in a moment,' he told the middle-aged woman outside, but realising his mistake at once he broke off and asked instead, 'I'm sorry – can I help you?'

'I should jolly well hope so!' came the surprised reply. 'Who are you, and what are you doing here?'

Feeling his mastery of the situation slipping ever further from his control, Jeremy was forced to explain his presence in his own home to a total stranger for the second time in half an hour. 'I'm the tenant,' he answered shortly, 'Jeremy Sinclair. And you?'

'The *tenant*? My God, it's worse than I thought!' the woman squeaked in reply, and bunching herself up like a terrier she pushed her way determinedly past him, crying, 'Where is she – where's my poor little lamb?'

Turning to watch this diminutive intruder take his living room by storm, Jeremy saw Gloria's face pale, her panic-stricken eyes darting everywhere as if she were looking for escape.

'Darling!' said the woman, and launched herself into Gloria's appalled embrace. 'It's all right now. Mummy's here to make everything better.'

Thirty-Three

Now that Rachel was in their midst, it was an entirely pointless exercise for Allie to continue to insist that she was the real Fran Holdaway, but continue to insist it she did, despite Rachel's indignant denials.

'Mummy, you're going to have to go in to a home if you keep this up,' Allie threatened her for Jeremy's benefit, and catching his eye, she tapped her head and mouthed, 'Her brain's going. Very sad.'

The confusion which Rachel's appearance had brought to the proceedings was made not one whit easier by the real minicab driver arriving only seconds later, and Nikki's descent of the stairs being preceded by her hurled suitcases, one of which almost knocked dear little Jocelyn clean off her feet. As glad as he was to see her go, as he helped to carry the cases outside, Jeremy had to fight down an urge to join her in the cab rather than return to the mayhem in his living room.

'Good luck with the programme, then,' he managed to say stiffly, politely closing the car door for Nikki. Her answer was one finger stuck in the air through the window, which remained there until she was quite out of sight. Standing there, alone in the drive, Jeremy looked with longing at his own car, but even had he given in to his craven impulse for flight, it wouldn't have been possible to leave. His Jaguar was jammed in by several others, making the driveway look more like a car park than the entrance to a rural dwelling.

When he returned inside, his normally quiet abode had turned into the Tower of Babel, with everybody gesticulating and shouting at once, and nobody listening to anybody. He had just time to make out Fran Holdaway grappling with Gloria's mother and screaming 'Look! Just *pretend* that I'm your daughter, you stupid woman!' and to hear that woman protest, 'Never! I would *never* allow a daughter of mine to dress in such décolletage!' before Gloria herself, wild-eyed and frantic, picked up a pile of plates and smashed them on the floor.

'Will you all *shut up!*' she cried into the shocked ensuing silence, but everybody already had except Rachel.

'*I* bought you that as a wedding present,' she complained in an aggrieved voice, as she picked up a shard of broken crockery.

'Yes you did,' said Gloria viciously, wresting it from her grasp, 'and I've always hated it. Now sit down, Mother, and be quiet.' She gazed around at the assembled company and gestured for them to follow suit. 'And you, Jeremy,' she instructed him, but in a rather more placatory tone, as they all jostled for seats. 'You'd better sit down too. You're going to need to.'

Now that she had their undivided attention, Gloria appeared to falter for a moment, unsure where to start. 'Okay,' she began at last, addressing Jeremy as if he were the only one there. 'I am not Gloria Mop,' and pointing at Allie, she continued, 'and she is not Fran Holdaway.'

'What did I tell you?' Rachel appealed to the room at large. 'You see? A mother knows these things.'

Jeremy's perception of the world did a giddy flip, and he grasped the arms of his chair to steady himself. Not Gloria Mop, after all this time he had known her? 'Then who are you?' he asked simply, when at last he found his voice.

'I am the real Fran Holdaway,' said the ex-Mrs Mop.

'Not for much longer!' Rachel cried. 'That's why I'm here – Roger heard Paul telling someone at the golf club that he was getting a divorce, so he could remarry Helen! Why didn't you tell me, your own mother? I didn't even know you were having problems!'

Jeremy closed his eyes for a moment, his mind reeling, trying to grapple with these new characters. Who the hell was Roger when he was at home, and why was Paul remarrying Helen such an issue? Surely that was no skin off Gloria's nose – or Fran, as he'd have to learn to call her – for wasn't she a single widow, her husband having been cut down by a combine harvester? But perhaps that too had been a lie. There was too much information coming his way at once, or more likely, not half enough.

'I didn't tell you, Mother, because I knew you'd behave like this,' Fran told her through clenched teeth. 'This is *my* drama, mine! – not a crisis for you to make a meal of.'

Rachel opened her mouth to issue the aggrieved reply, 'Well, if you'd prefer your mother not to care what happens to you—' but her whining was cut short by a murderous look from Fran.

Sam meanwhile was squirming in her seat, struggling in vain to keep the lid on her own desire to clear matters up for the tenant until, unable to contain herself a moment longer, she suddenly blurted, 'I never agreed to any of it, Mr Sinclair, I just need you to know that! I told her at the time that it was highly improper, and possibly illegal, but by then it was a fait accompli!'

'Well thank you, Judas,' drawled the woman with the décolletage, formerly known as Fran. 'But haven't you forgotten the kiss on the cheek?'

Sam's own cheeks reddened, her wide eyes threatening to spill over with tears, and to Jeremy's astonishment the woman sitting next to her, who was supposed to be her boss, enveloped her in her arms and kissed her forehead. As keen as he was himself on good labour relations, her hands-on style of management surprised him.

'Perhaps I might explain,' she offered now, Sam still held in her comforting embrace, 'being less emotionally involved than some.' She gestured towards Fran, who was now pacing the room in frustration. 'Fran's husband left her for his ex-wife – a terrible blow, and quite unexpected – and since she had just walked out of her job, the timing couldn't have been worse—'

Margo broke off, startled as they all were by the sound of glass being smashed from the direction of the kitchen, and a moment later Archie Scaysbrook arrived in the room at a run, wild-eyed, his hair on end, a hammer held aloft in his hand. He stopped dead in his tracks at the sight of the assembled company, looking more gormless than Fran had ever seen him.

'I one-four-seven-oned,' he floundered, lowering the hammer, and in his embarrassment his hand flew up to his head in a vain attempt to flatten his unruly bush of hair. 'Just got out the shower when you phoned me, so I dint have time to mek messen look respectable. I thought you was up to yer old tricks,' he continued, by way of explaining to Fran his unorthodox mode of entry. 'Killing yourself and that.'

'Well thank you, Archie, for your contribution to this edition of "Fran Holdaway – This Is Your Life",' Fran said drily, deceptively calm.

Watching her carefully, this stranger whom he had thought he had got to know quite well over the previous few months, Jeremy found it hard now to judge her mood. Certainly she had the feverish look of hysteria, her eyes overbright, her complexion flushed, but whether she was about to burst into raucous laughter or floods of tears he had absolutely no idea.

In fact, if little Jocelyn hadn't taken the opportunity of getting all the facts straight for herself, in this brief lull in the hubbub while everybody struggled to assimilate Archie's sudden armed entrance, it is just possible that Fran might have seen the funny side of her predicament. As it was, however, tugging at her mother's sleeve in an attempt to get Margo's attention away from comforting her special best best friend, Jocelyn pointed at Jeremy and asked, in a loud childish whisper, 'Is that the one Fran wants for her new boyfriend, Mummy?'

After that, things spiralled out of control very quickly indeed. All eyes swung to Jeremy, and then back to Fran, with various people rallying to help or to hinder (a cry of 'Gag that child!' from Allie and, 'Don't tell me you're going to try marriage *again!*' being Rachel's contribution). Uttering a cry of absolute despair Fran fled towards the kitchen door, where her flight was arrested by Archie, barring her way with his outstretched arms, the hammer still held in his hand.

'You're not going nowhere,' he said firmly. 'Least not in this state, not till you've calmed down.'

A small dance ensued between them, a feint to the left from Fran quickly countered by a quickstep in the same direction from Archie, until, desperate as a caged animal, Fran suddenly threw herself to the floor and lunged between his legs to make her escape, catching his knee with her head. As she scrambled to her feet behind him, her hair now as wild as his own, Fran caught a glance of Archie's brief, unsuccessful attempt to regain his balance. His arms flailing like a windmill in a tempest, his legs buckling beneath him, he lost his grasp on the hammer, which flew through the air (missing Jeremy's head by a heart-stopping whisker), before smashing through the living-room window.

Fran, recovering herself sufficiently to issue a yelp of maniacal laughter, looked around them with feverish eyes. 'And to think,' she asserted shrilly, 'that only the other day I was thinking my life had become stranger than fiction! Now it's turned into Grand Guignol!'

The doorbell rang and everybody froze.

'Can't be anyone important,' Fran shrugged, with a brittle, hysterical gaiety. 'Everybody I know is already here!'

'Except Paul and Helen,' offered Rachel, all innocence.

Fran gasped under the weight of the descending last straw, as it landed on her already breaking back. 'Shit a brick!' she groaned, 'Enough already, enough!' and in that instant she shot behind the safety of the kitchen door, locking it quickly after her.

The doorbell rang again, and Jeremy finally got up heavily to answer it. He still had less than no idea who this Paul and Helen were, but seeing the effect their names had had on an already beleaguered Fran/Gloria, and in this heady atmosphere of heightened emotions, he was fully prepared to deliver a bloody nose to both of them on her behalf.

In the event, it was only old Mrs Bonner doing her rounds with the parish mag, but by the time her identity had been established it was too late to offer this comfort to Fran. Because by then she had fled from Little Langton with all her possessions, including the kitchen sink.

Thirty-Four

When she ran blindly down the garden path, away from the farce her life had become, Fran's only thought was to take sanctuary in Casa Nova, to lock the door and close the curtains and to hide under the bedcovers for as long as possible, preferably for several days. But once she was secure in her bolthole she realised that it still offered her scant protection here, being so close to the house, and that it would be only a matter of minutes before everybody came rushing down the garden to torment her again.

She was an utter, utter failure, she castigated herself, as she sank heavily onto her bed and stared dully at the walls. Her life was in ruins yet again. Here she was, having been given a miraculous second chance after she'd messed up the last time, and already she'd blown it. For, as she had demanded of Allie earlier, how *could* she stay here, now that Jeremy knew how she'd deceived him? Just sitting here thinking about the events of the last half-hour, she felt her cheeks grow hot with shame, let alone if she ever had to face him again. Not only did he now know that she had made a fool of him by lying about her true identity, but thanks to Rachel he also knew that her husband had left her for his previous wife, and, thanks to Margo, that she'd walked out of her job, and worse, thanks to Jocelyn, that she fancied him – not forgetting a huge vote of thanks to Archie that she had once sunk so low that she had tried to do herself in. She laughed hollowly. Jeremy must be wishing as fervently as she was at this moment that at least she'd been successful at that.

So what was she to do, where was she to go? She could, she
supposed, take Margo up on her offer to park the horsebox in
her field, or even ask Allie and Trevor if she could camp out
in their new cottage for a while, but neither prospect brought her
comfort, both being still too close to Jeremy. What if she were
to run into him in the supermarket, or see him in the pub? No,
she told herself, she needed to be far, far away, to put herself out
of sight, to crawl under a stone and stay there, if needs be, for
the rest of her miserable life. So great were her crimes – against
herself, more than anyone, if she were honest – that she needed
the expiation of a harsh and cruel punishment. Sackcloth and
ashes, solitary confinement, dry bread and water – even these
were too cushy, she felt. Transportation would be nearer the
mark, perhaps, to be taken in chains to the other side of the world
and dumped there, far away from family and friends. But alas,
those rat-infested prison ships no longer sailed to the Antipodes,
and how could she, Impecunious Fran, ever afford her own
airfare to Australia?

If she had been a religious woman she would have fallen to
her knees at that moment and given praise to God. For it was
then, when she was at her absolute nadir, that her eye finally
lighted on the solution to all her problems. The key that would
open the door to her atonement was right there in front of her,
staring her in the face. It was also the key that could turn Casa
Nova into a means of escape.

She was in the cabin, behind the wheel, and revving the engine
of the massive old horsebox before she could entertain another
thought – thus sadly adding to the mess she left in her wake. As
she slammed it into gear and drove like a hell-cat across the
bumpy field, the electricity cables and water pipes which had
connected her to Jeremy's bounty strained and then broke,
fusing all the lights behind her in the Big House, and causing a
leak which would keep Archie busy for the rest of the day.

As she careened around corners in her first-ever lesson of

Teach Yourself To Drive A Terrifyingly Huge Vehicle While Running Away From Your Life, never had the streets of Little Langton seemed so mean, nor its inhabitants more like lemmings. Indeed, old Mrs Bonner's waning faith in the Lord was restored (she had sold only two copies of the parish magazine, and those to herself and her neighbour) when she found herself to be still mercifully alive after the One Horsebox of the Apocalypse had raced past her. The fact that she was also on her knees, having dived for safety behind a bus shelter, seemed highly appropriate in her later retelling of the tale, and as the members of the Mothers' Union agreed, it was indeed an ill wind . . .

The wind which blew against the high sides of the speeding Casa Nova, however, showed signs of doing nobody any good, particularly when Fran made a mistake at the Misterton roundabout and found herself on the motorway slip road, now committed to travelling north. Fleeing cars honked angrily around her, dodging out of her way, as she joined them in the inappropriately named slow lane, swaying dangerously from side to side. Inside the cabin, a terrified Fran was in complete agreement that her speed was well over the giddy limit, and she had begun to slow down of her own volition even before the engine gave its warning cough and, spluttering, started to die. Wrenching the wheel desperately, she at least made it to the hard shoulder before her less-than-mobile home ground to a shuddering stop. She didn't need to be a mechanic to know that when the petrol gauge had fainted all the way to the left, she had reached the end of the road.

In fact, after she'd pulled herself together, located the empty jerrycan under her seat and had trudged for half an hour with traffic whizzing past her and the wind whistling round her ears, she started to doubt that this road had an end at all, let alone a service station within walking distance. Would she never be free of this evil curse which dogged her so determinedly? she asked herself bitterly, when at last she saw a sign telling her that salvation was still two miles away. But even then she wouldn't admit to herself the truth of the well-worn aphorism that you can try to run from trouble, but it will follow wherever you go.

By the time she had bought her gallon of petrol, walked back with it to the horsebox and returned to the service station on four wheels instead of two legs, she was frozen, exhausted and starving, so after filling up Casa Nova (and being appalled at her capacity to guzzle diesel fuel), she repaired inside to feed herself. Now that her escape had been at least temporarily arrested, and she was over the panic which had made her drive, willy-nilly, away from everyone she had once held so dear, she had no idea what she should do next. But standing in line at the burger concession she was cheered as always by the prospect of comfort food, and after carrying away her swagbag of The Big One! and fries she resettled herself in Casa Nova's cabin to chew things over.

Fifteen minutes later, her stomach full but her head still empty, she chucked the take away carton onto the passenger seat and, sighing, turned on the engine. She had questions but no answers, a means of transport but nowhere to go. Since fate had decreed that she was travelling north, she decided arbitrarily to continue in that direction until the motorway ended or she fell off the edge of the world.

But as she rejoined the traffic, this time a little more confidently, fate intervened again to show her the way. She had been following the same juggernaut for mile after mile before she saw the writing on the wall – or rather, before she read the advertising copy on the juggernaut's tailboard. The sign said *The Highlands – Home of Scotch Whisky*, and now, she decided giddily, it would be her home too. How could she have forgotten the story of her own making? Mrs Holdaway lived on the shores of a Scottish loch, communing with Nature and thinking Great Thoughts. Good enough for the fictitious Mrs Holdaway, and more than good enough for the real one. Extraordinary Fran was back in the driving seat.

Meanwhile, back at the Big House, when everybody had stopped running round like headless chickens and a large patch of yellowed grass had been discovered where the horsebox should have been, patching up the fused and leaking utilities kept some of them busy while the others were free to address the puzzle: 'Where the hell has she gone now?' After several hours they were no closer to an answer, but at least the electricity was back on and they could have a cup of tea.

By the time they were all reassembled in his living room, the broken crockery swept up and a semblance of order restored, Jeremy had at last been apprised of the whole of Fran's story in minute detail – not only the circumstances which had led up to his own entrance in her drama, but, courtesy of Rachel (who of course was delighted to be back at the centre of attention), the agony of her birth and the three-day labour her mother had had to endure to get her out, her tardiness in toilet training, her troublesome childhood illnesses . . .

'Do you think she might do anything silly?' Jeremy asked Archie finally, impatiently cutting Rachel off mid-flow in her reminiscences of 'The Adolescent Years', and Archie nodded glumly.

'Could be,' he said, glaring at her mother himself. 'She's had a lot to put up with.'

'Should we call the police?'

'And say what?' Allie demanded. 'That our friend, a grown woman, has taken herself off for a drive? She could be gone for a week before they took an interest.'

'Actually,' Sam said suddenly, and shot out of her chair, 'she could be sitting in our field even now – we should go and see!'

'Or be round at my house, talking things over with Hilda!' offered Archie, momentarily cheered.

'Or at our new cottage,' said Trevor. 'She's still got a key.'

The party quickly broke up, all members swapping phone numbers, and promising to keep the others informed of developments. With everybody else swarming towards the door, eager to do something, Rachel was at a loss for a moment as to what her own important role would be, but Jeremy, longing to be rid of her, swiftly suggested that Fran could be phoning her at home even now, desperate for her mother's advice. However improbable the others found that idea to be, they were polite enough not to say so, and Rachel seized on it with alacrity.

Alone at last, Jeremy poured himself a whisky and sank back into his armchair to ponder the day's extraordinary events. He'd chucked his girlfriend (good riddance), he'd made the startling discovery that Gloria Mop had been his imaginary friend, and within moments of at last meeting the real Fran Holdaway she had disappeared again into thin air. Sifting through the information about this dual persona which had recently come his way, he felt like a detective, assembling the profile of a character he'd never fully known. As her friend Archie had said, she'd certainly had a lot to put up with: she'd had the most terrible run of bad luck. But what inventiveness she'd shown in trying to surmount it – what bravura! Despite how she'd turned his own life upside-down that day, he kept finding himself grinning at her cheek.

Hours later, long after he'd answered the phone several times and been told in each instance that Fran had not been found, he was sipping his fourth whisky and still wrestling with the one piece of information he'd gleaned that day which he now found astonished him the most. Was it a case of mistaken identity, or a question of 'out of the mouths of babes' that had prompted young Jocelyn to point his way when she'd been checking where Fran's heart lay? And if it was the latter . . . ?

The unanswered query swirled around his aching head until,

exhausted, he climbed the stairs to put an end to this action-packed day. But as he drew the curtains in the bedroom and saw no string of coloured lights where Casa Nova should have been, he found to his further surprise that his heart ached even more than his head.

Thirty-Five

Had they known it, Fran and Jeremy were laying down their sleepy heads at about the same time, but whereas in the comfort of the Big House all Jeremy had to do was to snuggle down under the Egyptian cotton and reach out lazily to turn off his bedside light, in the back of Casa Nova Fran had to blindly crunch her way over several road casualties, locate the candles, and then, in their flickering light, deal with the devastation before her.

If Archie had known when he had refurbished the horsebox that it was intended to be a mobile home, he would have built in various features to hold things securely in place when it was on the road. As it was, and since Fran had left at such speed with nary a thought to batten down any hatches, her prized table lamps had bitten the dust, drawers and cupboards had been flung open and had disgorged their contents, and dripping from the now-defrosted fridge was the yellow goo of uncooked scrambled eggs.

She had driven for hours and hours, her exact destination still unknown to her, and finally acknowledging her tiredness somewhere north of Carlisle but still south of Glasgow, she had pulled in to a truck stop to rest for the night. Or so she'd thought. Returning now from the twenty-four-hour café with her bacon butty and cup of tea, she was forced to sweep the bed of broken debris before she could even sit down to wail. Once she had done so, and after she had foregone her tea in favour of a large slug of gin, she decided that it wasn't worth tidying up until she reached her final destination, wherever that might be, and she pulled the duvet over her head and lost consciousness immediately.

The next morning, resolutely ignoring the mess, she purchased a road map and set off again in search of the Highlands. At the back of her mind had been the thought that she would drive to some pretty lochside location, choose the nicest caravan site, and negotiate a cut-rate winter deal with a canny Scot, who would be delighted and surprised to have a source of income out of season. It almost goes without saying that she had no such luck. Driving round in circles, albeit through some stunning scenery, she followed the fool's gold of happy camper signs to no avail. Every track she took ended in a padlocked gate or a closed reception centre, boarded up till the spring. Up here in the frozen north, when the season was over, it was *over*.

Finally, fearing that she would be spending another night in a lay-by without running water or electricity, she stopped for a late pub lunch in a picturesque village whose name was profligate with consonants but parsimonious with vowels. Over a half-pint and a ploughman's she quizzed the landlady in the deserted bar, and by the time she left the comfort of its roaring fire, phone calls had been made and she had a verbal contract and directions to Flora McAllister's farm.

Two hours later, having taken every high road and low road in a ten-mile radius, she finally bumped Casa Nova up an unlikely looking stony lane in the gathering dark, hoping to God that she'd got it right this time – she didn't know how the hell she would manage to turn the horsebox round if the track didn't lead to somewhere wider. She felt absolutely drained, her shoulders aching from peering anxiously over the steering wheel, her buttocks having lost all feeling from sitting so long on such dodgy suspension. Two barking dogs announced her arrival *somewhere* where life must exist, their eyes reflecting her headlights like Baskerville hounds, and as she turned the next blind bend she was relieved without measure to see the back of a large house, and a figure coming out of it.

'Mrs Holdaway?' the woman enquired doubtfully, eyeing the horsebox with frank astonishment.

'Yes, hi – sorry I'm late,' she'd said. 'I got lost.'

'Aye – I see you took the scenic route,' said old Mrs McAllister phlegmatically, and rather sibilantly, since her dentures had long since outgrown her. 'There's a perfectly nice road here to the front, saves about twelve miles of hard driving round the loch.'

Not having the energy to leap down from her cab to nut her, Fran smiled politely and asked to be told where to park. Back half a mile down the trail she'd already blazed, apparently, she'd find a clearly marked field for 'caravans' (more rolling of her eyes at Fran's unlikely looking domicile) with electric and water supplies.

'You're no one o' these new agey travellers are you?' Mrs McAllister asked her doubtfully as she'd been about to take her leave, unable to slip Fran and her strange means of conveyance into a convenient pigeonhole in her mind.

'No, no,' Fran assured her, wishing she would come with her in the dark. 'Just taking a break from routine.'

'You can choose whichever berth you want,' Flora McAllister called back as she disappeared into the warmth of the house. 'Most folk come in the summer. You'll be on your own there. You know that, don't you?'

Bouncing into the field and peering through the gloom of the cold, cloudy, moonless night, Fran suddenly knew it from the pit of her stomach to the marrow of her bones. Alone. Completely and utterly alone in the wilds of nowhere, with her living quarters strewn with wreckage and coated in raw egg. What the bloody hell had she done?

The next morning, driven by her rumbling tummy to rise early and scavenge round her galley floor for anything edible at all, she slowly started to put things back to rights, and in so doing thought of Archie. He'd be heartbroken now, she thought guiltily, if he could see this mess she'd made of his handiwork, and once the floodgates of her bad conscience were opened, she became filled with remorse at what she'd done to him by coming away. They still had a good week's work to do on Sam's cottage, and that would have been with the two of them at it. Now he was left on his own he would have twice the amount of work to do – and would he cope with the design decisions? Fran still hadn't made a final choice as to the exact shade of lemon that she wanted for the kitchen, nor had she recently chased the glazier for the coloured glass panels she'd ordered for the bathroom splashbacks. Had she even told Archie that she'd already measured up and paid for them? Last she could remember, they'd been discussing white glazed tiles.

When Casa McNova had been restored to something like her former glory, Fran made a shopping list and flung on her coat. It was still well before dawn – if dawn ever came in the winter this far north – but stepping outside and feeling the pleasant crispness in the air, she decided in a foolhardy rush of holiday spirit that she would walk to the village, buy some provisions and phone Archie from the pub. If she made good time, and if the pub opened early, she could catch him at breakfast before he left home. She left with a lightness in her step and the sense of adventure blossoming in her heart.

An hour and a half later, lying dazed and wet in a boggy ditch into which she had fallen, in a mistaken attempt at a shortcut off the road, she felt the first flakes of snow landing on her frozen cheeks. A strange sense of surrealism and dislocation filled her, and for a moment she toyed with the idea of just curling up into a ball in search of the Big Sleep, like a lost Arctic explorer finally giving up the ghost. But on opening her eyes she met the curious gaze of a strangely elongated head peering down at her from the banks of the ditch, and with a scream of terror she scrambled to

her feet in time to see a sheep fleeing for safety, now more frightened than her.

Arriving finally at the pub, whose downstairs windows were
still in darkness, her wet clothes clinging to her frozen skin, Fran
hammered on the door until the surprised landlady, still in her
rollers, climbed down the stairs to see who it was who so badly
needed a drink at this time of day.

'You again?' she asked in surprise, but not altogether un-
kindly, and drew Fran inside to sit by the radiator while she
rebuilt the fire. 'I don't open till lunch in the off-season,' she told
her, busying herself with wood and coal, 'there's normally no call
with the folk around here.'

'I'm sorry to trouble you,' Fran said at once, her teeth still
chattering, and she made to get up. 'I should go.'

'You'll go nowhere in that state,' her hostess told her firmly,
looking her over critically in the harsh overhead light. 'You'd
better take off those wet clothes and wear some of mine while
they dry.' She scurried away to return with a Fair Isle twinset
and a sensible box-pleat skirt.

'There now,' she said, pinning its capacious waistband into
place with a kilt pin, 'you just sit tight and I'll bring us some
breakfast. You'll like porridge?' she checked, as she made for the
upstairs flat with Fran's clothes.

'Lovely,' Fran lied, hoping the stories weren't true about the
Scots serving their national dish with salt in place of her
Sassenach preference for golden syrup and cream. 'Actually,'
she dared to continue, 'I know it sounds ungrateful to ask you
for more, but could I possibly borrow your phone to make a
long-distance call? Naturally I'll pay.'

'Aye, help yourself,' her benefactor granted generously.
'There's one just behind the bar.'

Dialling Archie's number, Fran caught sight of herself in the
mirrored glass behind the optics. In her present garb, all she
needed was a corgi or two wrapped round her ankles to be a dead

ringer for her majesty the Queen – although in her case she was
rather less than majestic, she decided, as she turned her back
resolutely on the mirror and heard the familiar, motherly voice
of Hilda Scaysbrook answering her phone.

'Hilda,' she said, fighting down the tears of relief which threatened to engulf her. 'It's Fran. Could I speak to Archie?'

Feeling relief himself that she'd finally called, and fighting
down his own fatherly impulse to tear her off a strip for giving
him so much worry, Archie listened patiently while she instructed him on the proper way to suck eggs.

'Ar,' he said finally, 'I were going the glazier's anyroad this
morning. It were me who measured up them panels, if you've
forgot. As fer the kitchen paint, I seen your scribbles on the colour
chart and I reckon "Lemon Meringue Pie"'s the closest match to
the units. Now where the bleddy hell are you, and when are you
getting back? There's people here worried sick about you.'

'I'm – in Scotland,' was the most Fran would divulge. 'And I
don't know when I'll be back. Maybe in the spring. I'm really,
really sorry to walk out on you, Archie, before we've finished the
job, but I just had to come away – get some head space, think
things over. Decide what I want to do if I ever grow up,' she
concluded, attempting a weak joke at her own expense.

'There's nowt you need to decide on that score,' Archie told
her sternly. 'You're an interior decorator, same as me. We've got
contracts back to back from Sam, if we want them.'

'You take them, Archie – you don't really need me.' She felt
her lip tremble as she said it.

'Course I need you!' Archie answered desperately. 'You're the
ideas man – I just do what I'm towd!'

'Got to go now – my money's running out,' Fran said,
pretending she was in a call box. 'You'll manage. 'Bye Archie,
and good luck with it all!' She hung up quickly, before she went
and spoiled it all by saying something stupid like 'I love you.'

★

Back in Leicestershire, the connection to his friend and partner having been terminated, apparently for ever, Archie replaced the receiver with a worried air and sat down heavily.

'Where is she?' Hilda demanded.

'In a call box, in bleddy Scockland!' Archie told her, his eyes moist. 'Says she ent coming back and I'm to carry on without her.'

Wordlessly, Hilda handed him her hanky and went off to get him a strong, sweet cup of tea, but when she returned she saw that a dogged look of triumph had replaced the tears in his eyes.

'What are you up to?' she demanded.

'Ssh! I'm one-four-seven-one-ing,' he said, taking down dictation from the mechanical lady's voice on the phone. 'Now at least I've got a number for her.'

'Thought you said it were a call box?' Hilda reminded him practically, reluctant though she was to burst this brief bubble of his happiness. 'She's most likely left it be now, and it could be ringing for ever with nobody to answer it, in the middle of nowhere, up in Scockland.'

'Oh ar,' he said, and replaced the receiver with a hangdog air of defeat. He took a revivifying quaff of his tea and, bracing his shoulders, picked up the phone again. 'Well I'll just bleddy well keep ringing it,' he said stubbornly. 'All times of the day and night, until some bugger passes by and picks it up! How will I know where she is, else?'

'Before you do that, you'd better ring the rest of them, tell them she's safe,' said Hilda, handing him a collection of their cards.

'Ar, all right,' Archie conceded, holding them at arm's length to squint at them without his reading glasses. 'But I'm only ringing Sam and that lot, not that bleddy Rachel,' he continued loyally. 'If I'd had her fer a mother, I'd have been tempted to bugger off messen!'

★

When Margaret reappeared with breakfast, Fran, sniffing and drying her eyes, discovered it was Liberty Hall here where porridge was concerned. She could have anything on it she liked, but personally Margaret was going to have her family's old stand-by for times of stress – a dram of scotch stirred in to it: Porridge Royale – voilà!

Like most pub landladies, Margaret was a keen observer of the human condition in all its forms, and she was a very good listener. Before she knew it, Fran had relieved herself of the better part of her life story and when the phone rang, as Fran knew it would, she begged her not to answer it.

'It'll be Archie at it again with his bloody one-four-seven-one-ing,' she told her. 'Trying to track me down.'

'You've no been having a very good time of it, have you, honey?' Margaret said sympathetically over the sound of the ringing phone. 'But it sounds like you've got some very good friends who love you.'

Fran's eyes watered again, and she nodded. 'I know. I just needed some—'

'Head space,' nodded Margaret, and she patted her arm. 'Well, you can get that here any time, pet, and welcome.' Mercifully the phone stopped ringing, and Margaret grinned, enjoying the story. 'Now, let's get back to the love interest. Tell me some more about the handsome fella, the one who's living in your house.'

'Jeremy,' Fran supplied, her face softening. 'He's lovely – a really nice man – and I've been awful to him.'

'Dodgy taste in girlfriends though,' Margaret offered. 'I shall watch out for that Nikki on the telly – she sounds like a real piece of work.' She eyed Fran carefully. 'You're in love with him, aren't you?'

Fran felt herself blush. 'Is it that obvious?' she asked, admitting it to herself at last, as much as to her new friend. 'Well, who wouldn't be? You would be if you met him. He's charming, he's funny – he's got beautiful hands – he's intelligent, kind . . . But you see,' she continued, her smile disappearing as she took out her whip to self-flagellate again, 'I even failed at that. I should have stood my ground, made a play for him when Nikki was in London all that time. But I didn't have the guts. I'm just a miserable coward.'

'If there was one thing I'd call you it wouldn't be that,' Margaret said firmly, and poured another wee dram into both their coffees. The phone rang again. 'Doesn't give up, does he, your friend Archie?'

'No,' Fran said anxiously. 'Listen, Margaret, if he rings again when I'm gone, don't tell him you know me, will you? Promise?'

'I promise,' Margaret reassured her. 'But that's only because I know you'll pull through this, and when you do you'll go back to those friends of yours of your own volition. Good friends don't grow on trees.'

Fran nodded, although she didn't share Margaret's confidence about the pulling-through bit. 'He could even come up here; I wouldn't put that past him. He'll find out your address, and he'll drive up and nose around. If you see him – wiry man, in his sixties, always wears a checked cap – I think it's welded to his head . . .'

Fran's face was softening again as she described Archie, Margaret was glad to see. Her own life had not been without cataclysmic event, and she had reason to know the value of friendship. 'If he comes in my bar, I won't say a thing,' she promised, clearing up their empty plates. 'But you keep coming, sweetheart. I love hearing people's stories, me!' she told her, eyes bright. 'And I know everybody's here already. That's why I love the tourist season. In winter time, like now, you're like a ray of summer sun to me!'

Fran was moved and grateful. She felt that she hadn't lit up anybody's life much recently. On the contrary, she was more used to thinking of herself as a dark cloud.

Thirty-Six

Her earlier fantasies of this retreat to a simpler way of life, Fran slowly started to realise during those first few days, had been like watching a romantic film – a carefully chosen montage of moving images seen through a rose-tinted lens – which homed in on the nice bits and cut out the dross and grind of daily living. In reality even shopping for food here was a huge chore, as was visiting her new friend Margaret, since she either had to walk for miles to the village in freezing weather or she had the business of disconnecting Casa McNova from the facilities she was moored to so she could drive there.

She had travelled hundreds of miles, given up the luxury of the more clement southern winter weather of the East Midlands (and the use of her own washing machine) and all for this: being parked in a field rather like her own at home. It was true she had swapped her view of the hedge for a magnificent view of a loch, but never, ever, had she felt such a profound feeling of loneliness. There was no work with Archie during the day to give herself the satisfaction of having achieved something – in fact, on the contrary, there was only her feeling of guilt at abandoning him – and there was no one to talk that over with in the evenings. She had tried several times to engage old Flora McAllister in conversation, but she it seemed was a woman of few words, and those she uttered were usually gloomy predictions about worse weather to come.

It wasn't as if Fran didn't make a valiant attempt to live out her fantasy of becoming a best-selling writer. Most mornings she forced herself to get something down on a page whether she wanted to or not. And it wasn't that she was completely without talent. It was just that everything she wrote, even her poetry, came out sounding like advertising copy for direct mail shots. She had so far failed to find her own voice, or worse, perhaps, her own voice had only ever wanted to bang on about financial products. Most days it required a great effort of will to stop herself climbing up into the cab and driving herself back home, tail between her legs, but her pride wouldn't let her. She had staked everything on this, and if it wasn't the answer, she wasn't about to let everybody else know that yet.

The downside of this foolhardy adventure, she thought glumly one day as she dragged herself through the gloom for yet another bracing walk, was the amount of quality time it gave her to think. There was absolutely nothing here to distract her from the inside of her own head, and it came as quite a shock to realise just how much energy she was used to expending in order to avoid that. Trapped in the detritus of her own mind without anybody to bounce her ideas off, she felt invisible and stupid, frozen into inaction, and terrifyingly, horribly alone.

Standing on the shore, buffeted by the cold wind, she gazed out over the huge grey expanse of the loch and the empty hills beyond and felt a sudden wave of panic overwhelm her. This had all been a terrible mistake. The more she thought about it, the more she was forced to acknowledge how much she actually *loved* doing up houses with Archie, and that it was merely her own snobbishness which had led her to think she'd been settling for second best. She shivered, drawing her coat around her. The solution to her problems wasn't out here, in this great sweeping landscape, where all she saw by comparison was her own puny insignificance and solitariness. It was back home, in a small sheltered field in Leicestershire, accepting as her lot that which had already been given to her.

But remembering the circumstances under which she had felt

forced to flee that field she also recalled, with a burning sense of shame, the great injury she'd done Jeremy by her odious deceit, and she knew in her bones that there was no going back. No, she told herself, shivering, the only going back for her was to return to the comparative warmth of Casa Nova. She turned into the freezing headwind to trudge back there now, eyes disconsolately cast down at her feet, remembering the halcyon summer mornings when Jeremy had greeted her in her garden with mugs of coffee, and the evenings they had spent together, cooking for each other in her kitchen.

Was it too late to call him to apologise, she asked herself suddenly, to beg that she might be allowed to return to her former billet in the field? She could offer, as a penance, to do his cleaning and gardening for nothing, and naturally she wouldn't expect his friendship any more. She let the idea float in her imagination. She didn't think she had the guts to speak to him on the phone, but perhaps she could write him a letter? She started to frame the words of apology in her head as she walked, trying to find the right balance between snivelling abjection and a dignified request for undeserved clemency, and she was practically back at her own door before she lifted her eyes again and saw him there, sitting on the steps.

'Surprise,' he said, smiling, and it certainly was. He just managed to catch her before she fell in a faint at his feet.

When she came round a few minutes later she found she was examining the pattern on her carpet at close quarters, propped up by Jeremy, her head down between her legs.

'Ngaah!' she said, her eloquent words of apology now beyond her.

He helped her sit up, then laid her down on the bed, tucking the duvet around her. 'Will you be okay there while I make you a cup of tea?' he asked her with concern in his voice.

'Ngg,' she replied, blinking her eyes slowly, trying to make sense of any of this. Had her fantasy life become so comforting and seductive that she had now retreated to it permanently? But apparently not, for if it were a fantasy of her devising, she would be doing the apologising, not him.

'I'm sorry I took you by surprise like that,' he was saying, opening cupboards in the tiny kitchen. 'But I couldn't call ahead because of you not being on the phone, so when I got here and found you weren't in, I thought I'd just sit and wait for a while. Are you feeling any better?' he asked her, rejoining her to sit on the bed and peering at her anxiously. 'The kettle's on – shouldn't be long.'

'Why . . . ?' she attempted thickly, her dry lips sticking to her teeth. She felt clammy and cold, but even in extremis, she wished she had a mirror and comb. 'How . . . ?'

'Well, the "how" bit is easy,' Jeremy smiled, looking a trifle embarrassed. 'Your old friend Archie, and his redoubtable methods of detection. He did his usual one-four-seven-one and called the pub.'

'I knew it, I knew he'd do that!' Fran protested, struggling to sit up. She was disappointed in her friend the landlady. 'But Margaret gave me her word she wouldn't give me away.'

'Nor did she,' Jeremy hastened to add. 'At least, not knowingly. After a few times of getting "No comment" from her, Archie handed things over to Hilda. She called her one morning, pretending to be from the brewery, and checking the pub's postal address. Made up some convoluted story about all their records having been lost in a fire.'

'And Margaret loves stories,' said Fran, seeing how the wily Hilda had found Margaret's Achilles heel.

'So, once we knew that, I came up.' The boiling kettle drew Jeremy back to the kitchen, and over the bustle of the tea-making he called back, 'I might say I almost had to arm-wrestle Archie for the privilege. But Hilda threw her weight in behind me, so here I am. Margaret still stuck to her guns at first, though, insisted she didn't know who you were,' he continued, returning to hand her the tea. 'At least, not until I'd explained to her exactly why I was here, and why I needed to find you so urgently.'

Fran felt an icy coldness grip her heart. 'Why? What's happened?' she demanded tensely. 'Is everybody all right? How's Archie?'

Jeremy smiled elliptically. 'Everybody's fine, and sends you their love.'

Fran was lost. 'Then why did you need to find me?' she asked him. 'Something about the house?'

'In a way,' said Jeremy, glad to be given a lead, and bravely he continued, 'It was empty without you.'

Now she was even more confused. 'Sorry?'

Jeremy sat on the bed beside her, his legs suddenly feeling less than reliable to hold him up, under the circumstances. He cleared his throat, searching for the right words. 'When you saw Nikki leave the house on Sunday, it was for ever,' he explained.

'She finished with you? Because of me always getting up her nose?' Fran asked guiltily.

Jeremy was quick to set her straight. 'Other way round, I finished with Nikki,' he said, and looked Fran meaningfully in the eyes. 'I've been doing some hard thinking. I've been an idiot, Glor— Fran,' he broke off, grinning. 'But then, I have had good reason to be confused, haven't I?'

Fran dropped her eyes, full of shame. 'I'm really sorry about that, Jeremy. It started as a silly joke – I hadn't meant to do it really. But when you arrived unexpectedly, "Gloria Mop" was out of my mouth before I had chance to think, so I was stuck with her.'

'Yes, tricky one that,' Jeremy conceded. 'Because now, of course, I'm not sure who I'm in love with.'

Now Fran was even more confused. 'Nikki or . . . ?'

'Gloria or Fran,' Jeremy finally admitted, dropping his own gaze in his embarrassment. 'Or both. There I was, enjoying your company more than anybody else's, and after you'd gone I realised how much I missed you. And loved you.'

'Missed me? Loved *me*?' Fran asked, astounded.

Jeremy nodded and smiled. 'Both of you. All of you,' he said simply, and slowly bent forward to kiss her.

In her stupefaction, after returning his kiss, Fran didn't know whether to laugh or cry or spill her tea, so she did all three at once. And some hours later, after she had made several other incoherent noises of surprise and delight, lying with her head on Jeremy's chest, wrapped in a tangle of bedclothes, she started to weep all over again.

'Why are you crying, Glor— Fran?' he corrected himself. 'Aren't you happy?'

She nodded dumbly, hot tears scalding her cheeks. 'I'm crying *because* I'm happy. Because my curse has been lifted. Because I never dreamt in a million years . . .' She broke off, her tears easing also, and propped herself up on one arm to gaze down at him, one ironic eyebrow raised. 'We're going to have to address this confusion you have about my identity, though,' she joshed him naughtily. 'Ent we, me duck?'

It turned out that Jeremy had taken time off work for his quest to find her, which was just as well, since neither of them felt much inclined to leave the cosy confines of the passion wagon called Casa Nova – except, that is, to visit Margaret in her pub to repay their debt of gratitude by telling her the end of their story. Needless to say she was over the moon, and that night drinks were on the house.

It also transpired that Jeremy had flown up as far as Glasgow, then hired a car, so they travelled back together on the long journey home, singing songs and feeding each other chocolate, taking turns to drive the great horsebox back to where she belonged.

At first, thinking they shouldn't rush things on their return, they decided that Fran would continue to live in the field, and that she would visit Jeremy in the Big House only at weekends. But as Allie said, and Sam agreed, when they were both let in on their secret – who wants to be sensible when you are *hot* to trot? So as it was Fran was back in her old bedroom, enjoying her power shower (among other things) in the week, and on weekends she and Jeremy holidayed in Casa Nova, for the sake of auld lang syne.

To celebrate her return to Little Langton and their partnership, Archie had a sign painted which bore the legend *Scaysbrook and Holdaway, Interior Transformations – No Jobs Too Big*. He was very proud of his choice of the word 'transformations', which he'd found in Hilda's crossword 'theo-saurus', and Fran didn't have the heart to spell out for him what their acronym would be.

And, for those of you who, like Margaret, love to hear other people's stories, I can reveal that Margo divorced Nigel painlessly, and continued to live happily ever after with Sam, the children and their livestock. Paul was surprised to get his own summons of divorce, having thought that Fran would fight him, but she and Jeremy were determined to have a spring wedding, keen as they were to start a family at once, leaving Paul free to repeat his miserable history with Helen all over again. Allie and Trevor took up weekend residence at Sam's old cottage, and once the symptoms of Allie's continued hangover had been correctly diagnosed as morning sickness, she surprised everybody (no more than herself) by becoming a natural at motherhood. Though she was at first astonished at her capacity still to conceive at her age (and she alone knew what that truly was), she was happy to ascribe it to Trevor's magnificent potency, and, not unnaturally, Trevor was delighted to agree. And, as Gloria Mop had prophesied, the nation did decide that Nikki was indeed The Housemate From Hell.

As for Gypsy Brenda, unaware that, for once, one of her

predictions had proved so uncannily true, she retired early to Bournemouth, finally hanging up the crystal ball which she used to find so draining.

But her legend lives on in Little Langton even to this day. For great gains had surely come, though disguised as great loss. And Fran Sinclair had weathered the storm.